KRALL

KRALL

SHELLEY CASS

*For those who see the threat that can arise from division,
and who seek to heal the world.*

Print ISBN-9781764180153
Ebook ISBN-9781764180146

Eirian Isle
Miridoon Cave
Margate Isle
Jenra
Midroone Pass
Cursed Valley
Northern Province
Western Sector Eastern Region
Southern Domain
Wastelands
Krall
Prison
Lixrax
Takal
Border Lands
Trune Territory
Sylthanryn City
Willow
Bwintam
Scorched Land
Wrilapek
Wanru
Giltrup
Gangroah
The Jewel
Awyalkna
The Great Forest

Locations and pronunciation guide

Sylthanryn: (Sil-than-rin). The Great Forest. Where the Lady, or the Mother of Nature, and the Elves and Nymphs live.

Awyalkna: (A for apple-why-elk-nah). A mortal Kingdom under the reign of King Glaidin (G-laid-in) and Queen Aglaia (Ag-lay-ah).

The Awyalknian Palace is also known as the 'Awyalknian Jewel', and is protected by the internal Gwentorock (G-when-toe-rock) and external Gwynrock (G-win-rock) walls. The lands beyond the city are green and flourishing, with many self-contained villages.

Bwintam (B-win-tam) village was a key provider of Awyalkna's fresh produce, before it was razed by Krall. Gangroah (Gang-row-ah) and Giltrup (Guilt-rup) are examples of smaller villages, while Wanru (W-an-roo, an isolated, hilly place) and Wrilapek (W-rill-ah-peck, a horse rearing place) are larger and more greatly populated.

Krall: (Crawl). A mortal Kingdom ruled by the immortal Sorcerer Darziates (D-are-zee-eights), who is the heir of the first Sorcerer to have lived; Deimos (Day-moss). Darziates is assisted by the psychotic Warlord Angra Mainyu (An-gra Main-you) and the Witch Agrona (Ag-groan-ah), and is responsible for the genocide of all of the *Larnaeradee* Fairies (La-nair-ah-dee), the Unicorns and Sprites.

Nature dies around Darziates' unnatural power, so he pumps his magic into Krall's earth to force a type of growth and food production. However this has corrupted Krall's seasons, which involve intense heat or extreme wet and cold. Sorcery has reduced the land to barren plains of wastelands or desert.

Jenra: (Jen-rah). A Kingdom circled by, and built into the mountains by the sea. The mountain Kingdom is isolated from the rest of the world, and was once known as *Karanoyar* (Karen-oi-ah), the original home of the Unicorns. It has lush valleys, but the peaks of the mountains are now infested with Griffin eyries, and King Durna's (Der-nah) brother – Warlord Aeron (Air-on) must work tirelessly to contain the infestation.

Lixrax: (Lix-rrr-axe). A desert nation, with people who have been tempered by the harsh environment. They are skilled survivors, and are a united family because of their surrounds. Their Emperor, Razek (Rah-zeck) regards all of the tribes and Takal residents of Lixrax as his children.

The Other Realm: a separate plain of malicious spirit beings. When King Deimos wanted to unite the world under one kingship, he used a piece of his soul to bargain with the demons of the Other Realm, who gave him powers to help him in his quest.

He became so powerful that the *Larnaeradee* Sylranaeryn (Sil-ran-air-in) and her Unicorn Kinrilowyn (Kin-ril-owen) had to fatally deplete their combined magic to defeat him as he faced the Army for the World.

Though he was overthrown by the first Army for the World, he made the first of the experimental Evexus beasts. The Evexus (E-vex-us) are creatures possessed by the spirits of the Other Realm.

Margate Isle: home of the Giants.

Eirian Isle: home of the Dargons (D-are-gone-s) and the Dwarves and Gnomes. A cliffy place of soaring heights and deep, tunnelling caves, perfect for creatures of flight as well as rock loving peoples.

1

One

The Sorcerer

The blazing desert heat – a whirling, physical force by day, had receded with the last brutal hours of light. The sand was cool under the darkness now, and it swirled like glistening pinpricks in the wind that shifted over the desert plains.

There was only the sand, with no trees or human dwellings to break the wasteland's endless skyline.

The Sorcerer was so completely still as he looked out at it, that his darkly robed body could have been overlooked in a visible sense, and almost seemed void of life in the moonlight. Yet terrible energy rolled off him in waves; his senses so keenly focused that he was aware of things the wild looking Warlord beside him would never even guess at. He could see and feel more in this realm, and the next, than any mortal would ever know.

Beyond the ragged panting coming from Warlord Angra Mainyu, the Sorcerer could hear continuous cascades of pouring sand disturbed by the stirring of the wind. He could sense the infected Dragons trapped far in the distance – their earth shaking movements almost visibly disrupting the atmosphere. He was aware of the smooth rubbing of slippery scales as much smaller reptiles dashed about and burrowed down securely. He could even taste the raw minerals deep beneath the surface of the desert plane.

But right now he was especially listening for a small group of Krall castle guards as they ran uselessly away. These guards had somehow developed feelings of disobedience and had foolishly sought to betray their all-knowing Sorcerer King.

There ... yes, there they were. They were tripping pointlessly through the wastelands. He could hear their frenzied footfalls, thudding and sinking and flicking up sand.

'Can ... can I have one?' Angra Mainyu exhaled heavily, stooping forward.

The heat radiated from the sweetly insane Warlord as if he were a dog boiling for the chase. A globule of saliva swung from his bearded chin as it often did.

'This kind of hunting would only get you lost in the desert. This kind of hunting is just for me,' Darziates told the Warlord.

'But they're *my* soldiers!' Angra gurgled. 'Their disgusting hope over rumours of the *Larnaeradee* ... and a new Army for the World ... could spread! I need to make examples – I need to punish. To tear! To riiiip.'

'I've let you maim many soldiers, Angra.'

'This is different. These ones were going to be just like the traitorous Krall soldiers already marching with the Awyalknian princes,' Angra glowered now. 'And they run like cowards.'

'Rest assured, they won't find safety in the desert,' the Sorcerer stated quietly. 'But I'm keeping *you* safe for our very special purpose.'

The Warlord sighed. 'So you can keep using my beautiful, demented soul,' he slavered sulkily.

'All those fragmented pieces inside of you,' Darziates agreed. 'Nobody else has a broken soul quite like yours. You must keep safe for just a little while longer.'

Darziates began to stretch his mind so that Angra felt the building of poisonous magic around his master, and the hulking Warlord started to yammer to himself. But the Sorcerer King refocused his attention on the panicked breathing of the fleeing guards.

The air around Darziates shifted, becoming heavier, and a nearby sand bank shuddered and collapsed with the pressure of the thickening atmosphere.

Then Angra yowled, the red light of insanity showing in his eyes as Darziates at last swept into action – surging across leagues in moments, and leaving his Warlord alone in the dark to listen for the faint, distant screams of one guard after another as they were hunted down and punished.

2

Two

D^{alin}

I reached out a hand and felt for the wall in the darkness.

Cool, damp rock met my fingers. It was smooth under my palm, as if the rock had been shaped by running water instead of flowing magic.

I couldn't see my hand, though my face was now inches from it, because the light of the golden horn had faded as Aeron had taken it to scout ahead.

Torches would eat up our air, so now the whole army huddled blind within the mountain, uncertainly feeling for places to rest in the eternal night. The tunnel was filled with whispered, echoing curses and soft shuffling.

'Come on Raiden,' Thorin's husky voice was accompanied by some scraping sounds as he sat beside me. 'Might as well sleep.'

I turned to sink down the wall, closed my eyes tightly and leaned my head back against the rock. The cold immediately began to ebb through my clothes and skin, radiating from the mountain's heart and into my prickling body.

'I'm bloating up with all these deep breaths, and pinching my hands isn't working now that they're numb.' I heard Noal mutter as he lowered himself down in the dark as well.

'Don't fill up on too much air,' Tane joked wearily. 'It's got to go somewhere, and we're all stuck in this sealed tunnel with you.'

'I'll just try not panicking in this claustrophobic hell, then, shall I?' Noal huffed a bit defeatedly, and I shuffled closer to him so that he could lean on me.

'If you could,' Tane answered. 'But you're right. The golden heat of Jenra seems so long ago.'

On our final day in Jenra I had walked with Kiana's firm hand held in mine. We had stepped through wide grassy fields and seas of bobbing yellow flowers, like drops of sunshine fallen to the earth.

Kiana and I had let the swaying petals kiss our fingertips, and when we had stopped to rest, laying side by side peacefully, the flowers had seemed to shelter us with a ceiling of yellow.

The memory of it brought a growing ember of warmth to my heart and my hands began to unfurl from the stiff, cold claws that I had curled up in my lap. I could almost pretend that she was here, and that our surrounds were not so oppressive.

'Raiden?' a rough voice broke into my thoughts, and I blinked and became aware of the sounds of the tunnel once more.

I peered through the dim light now filling the entire passage, realising that Aeron and the Unicorn's golden horn had returned, and that Thale was offering me his hand.

'Time to be back on the march,' he told me.

'Has it really only been three days?' I grimaced, even more unwilling to return to the endless monotony of our trek after my hazy, dreamlike memories of the One *Larnaeradee.*

'Warlord Aeron could be completely making up his measurements of time,' Thorin shrugged ahead of me. 'We'd never know.'

'Even the earthquake of magic that it took for Durna to open this tunnel seems like a distant memory,' Wolf commented from behind us. 'Feels like we were just always in here.'

As we moved off again I remembered how, just before we had gone into the tunnel, Kiana had embraced first Noal and then me while the sounds of the thousands of Jenrans gathered to farewell us had faded into the background.

We had been speechless ourselves, all keenly aware of the loss we were faced with at the breaking of the Three. And then, too quickly, I'd been left to watch as she'd walked away.

I'd put my hand over the lingering warmth of where her fingers had been over my heart, and had looked after her as she'd strode through the crowd, ready to begin her own lonesome journey across the ocean.

It had felt like a piece of me had been carved out to fly away with her while we had marched in the opposite direction, to be swallowed by the tunnel's darkness.

'At any rate I wouldn't criticise a Warlord's measurements while in a tunnel that amplifies every sound,' Tane teased. Though he had to raise his voice over the resumed noises of the march.

'At least we aren't climbing our way back *over* the mountains on the outside,' Ferron said, trying hard to be positive.

'Yes, but when we were above ground we had Kiana's help,' Cadell sighed.

'Kiana could have made even this tunnel seem bearable,' I agreed. Missing her all the more.

3

Three

N^{oal}

'Perhaps Darziates has tricked us all into walking into the Other Realm unawares, and we'll keep marching into eternity.' Phrixus scuffed along the trail with a maudlin expression.

'Aeron says we will soon find ourselves outside with the rest of the world again,' Dalin replied.

'But Warlord Aeron would have been tricked right along with the rest of us,' Purdor mused.

'My lungs ache for clear air,' Thorin grimaced. 'It feels as if my skin must be paler and my eyes more bulbous after perpetually straining through the dim light.'

'You do look sallow, and your eyes are quite bulby,' Tane told Thorin sympathetically.

'Perhaps you should go down the lines to the healer wagons. Maeve always spoke highly of Lady Amarantha's healing ability,' I told Thorin, feeling a pang at the thought of Maeve. 'She used to volunteer her help with the head healer.'

'That would mean retracing my steps,' Thorin answered. 'I'm not wasting any more steps in this tunnel than I have to. And definitely not so the lead healer can tell me I have bug-eyes.'

'I'll be glad to be out doing something again, to be a part of the action,' Dalin reflected, shrugging his pack up higher on his shoulders.

'That's the spirit Raiden,' Nikon grunted.

'Yes lads. Chin up. A spot of marching to battle does wonders,' Tane agreed.

'I think the cool damp of the passage is decreasing a little, so perhaps we really are getting closer to the surface,' Phobos reflected.

'Ahh, to be free of this oppressive darkness,' Tane waved his hands about wistfully.

Wolf shook his head, refusing to be excited. 'What if that horn's run out of magic and we get trapped inside the mountain?' he asked, shuddering.

'I'll comfort you,' Tane promised.

Yet in hardly any more time at all, Aeron's voice was booming along the tunnel, calling for a halt.

'WE'VE REACHED THE END! KING DURNA WILL OPEN THE WAY!' his great voice thundered, and a churning knot of tension in my stomach began to unravel. I hungered for the outside world as though I were a starving man craving a morsel of food.

'Finally,' I heard Vulcan utter as we peered forward and registered that the darkness ahead was now made up of mountain wall rather than ongoing emptiness.

Clumsy butterflies danced in my stomach as Durna raised the horn, and we covered our eyes in expectation, remembering how bright the flash had been when the horn had first opened the way.

'We are the ancestors of the last Karanoyar dwellers, and the children of Jenra,' Durna called. 'Open the way to let us through!'

And then came the moment of dizziness, the mind boggling gushing of power that stormed like wild gales from the horn.

My hair and clothes were plucked at and loose pebbles in the tunnel whipped crazily through the air. I could vaguely hear the distant wagon horses screaming over the ear splitting rush, and the ground shook so that many of us stumbled forward.

I was almost staggering as the oxygen was ripped from my mouth and lungs before, abruptly, the magical vortex dropped away. The entire army was left raggedly cheering and gasping as we blinked at where a giant stretch of the wall had disappeared to let the sunlight stream in.

It was as though we were peering through a gateway into the forbidden garden of the Gods, and it took extreme control of will for the army to exit in an orderly way, rather than in a surging stampede.

When it was my turn to step out and stand at the base of the mountain my eyes watered and I was grinning so much that my face hurt.

'I feel like dancing,' Tane sighed dreamily, stretching his arms out to embrace a Sylthanryn tree trunk as though he'd never seen such beauty before.

'Your woman at home would be jealous of the way you're holding that tree,' Nikon smirked.

'*You're* just jealous,' Tane returned with a serene smile while, one by one, each ordered row of Jenran soldiers left the mountain tunnel to stand beyond Jenran soil for the first time in their lives, staring about themselves in similar wonder.

For a moment I frowned as I caught sight of one volunteer healer, who was crying with relief while a hooded maiden at her side made shushing sounds.

'Does that look like ... Kerrin?' I asked Vulcan, who was beside me. 'Maeve's friend?' I tried to point out the weeping girl, and strained to catch a glimpse of the hooded maiden, but the pair had melted into the crowd, which was quickly regrouping under Warlord Aeron's watchful eye.

Vulcan regarded me sympathetically. 'You're seeing things, my friend.'

'Am I seeing things too?' Tane asked then, peering past his well-loved tree. 'Because I could swear that looks like an Elf.'

My focus shifted immediately and a cry of surprise came from the crowd nearest us as one blur, and then another burst from the trees.

'That does look like *two* Elves,' I replied, and a wide smile spread across my face.

4

Four

*K*iana

There had been no jagged rocks to rest on for days and I could no longer remember how enjoyable I'd first found flying to be.

Despite my magic, every breath raked through my lungs, every inch of my skin felt bruised and each flashing raindrop was like a hornet's sting.

The oppressive grey skies hurled salt filled, gale force winds that stung my eyes and tore at my wings. And like parchment, I felt my wings would soon tear away. Perhaps the bones in my spine and shoulders would be warped forever.

Below stretched a world of surging waves, and I had learned the hard way that losing consciousness led to a fast plummet into rough waters, a fight to lift my weight back out, and a water logged food pack.

Days passed into nights. And a storm rolled in. But even as I was dashed about in the craziness, flipping and tossing helplessly, I knew I could not close my burning eyes.

Sleep would mean to drown.

Sleep would mean to die.

Oh dear! Oh dear! Wake! You must wake!

I gasped. Just yards from smashing into the broiling waves again. I cried out with the effort of catching myself.

Careful! Careful now!

A wayra seabird was flapping purple and silver wings urgently at my side, chittering and plucking at my damp sleeves – compelling me out of my stupor.

Forcing every ounce of energy into a painful stroke of my wings, I drove my way upward and let the wayra guide me away from the water. But I did not expect the sudden change when she led me to a wind pocket and at once the air seemed to run under my wings, lifting me up.

I half sobbed at the unexpected reprieve, my shoulder muscles spasming with relief.

Drift. Learn from me.

I tiredly noticed that the wayra wasn't struggling, instead simply holding her wings out firmly – gliding along with the sweep of the current.

No fighting the air. Float. Hold wings as I do.

I forced my agonised, stiff wings into that same position, finally groaning as I felt them instinctively lock into place so that the wind itself now carried me.

Drift and sleep. I watch, the wayra soothed.

'Thank you,' I choked. 'Thank you so much.'

And each time I slipped into and then away from aware-ness, I felt the wayra by my side, guiding me into air pockets that relieved the pain in my back.

It was not until the storm had long passed that the wayra's song woke me more forcefully, and I saw the massive reflection of the moon in the ocean – along with an expan-sive, shadowy shape in the water. A shape so large that I thought I was hallucinating.

You are close to Margate Isle!

'Yes,' I husked. 'Although I fear my wings won't give me a proper landing.'

The wayra began crooning worriedly. *Oh dear. Down slow. Drop slow.*

'I'll try,' I grimaced.

But as soon as we left the calm of our last air pocket to descend we both felt the overwhelming tug of the wind, and soon the island was rushing up to meet us.

I vaguely heard the wayra crying in warning as I overshot the gleaming sand, and plunged into the tropical trees. I was lashed by exotic ferns and branches until, finally, I ploughed into the ground amongst an explosion of leaves and flowers.

Alive? Alive? Please, alive?

Wheezing and gasping, I rolled onto my back as the wayra landed, crying beside my ear.

Insects hummed and the waves splashed distantly behind me. The humid air pressed in warmly.

'As the last remaining survivor of my kin,' I moaned. 'As the Summoner of the magical races. As the first outsider to set foot on Margate Isle ... I have made a very unimpressive entry.'

The world surged and tilted before my eyes and I felt I would surely slide away from the land. And as though the ocean had come for me at last, waves of blackness rushed in again.

5

Five

A *hanu*

Ahanu had been cheerfully marching along, rattling the Isle trees, bustling through exuberant flowers and cracking the rocks below.

But he was suddenly brought to a stop, mid-step, by the shrill, disgruntled cheeping of a tiny seabird.

Ahanu, whose head was as high as the towering treetops, laughed as he peered down and saw the little seabird flapping crossly around his raised leg.

He moved his foot, crushing a patch of shrubbery somewhere else instead, and stooped down from his great height to see what had caused the alarm.

He felt terrible when he realised he had narrowly missed squelching another small winged being into some ferns. And as he registered what the little thing amongst the ferns was, his eyes widened.

'The Gods sent you to protect this creature's life from my big feet,' Ahanu told the wayra.

Then, with the wayra bird eyeing him suspiciously, Ahanu carefully picked the winged female up, trying very hard not to break her.

And he set off for the beach again.

6

Six

*K*iana

My fingers sought the hilt of my dagger before I allowed
my eyes to open. Then I froze, having opened them to a ceiling view of the ocean.

I was in a room filled with glowing blue light which emanated from the somehow transparent roof. The ceiling appeared to look out at endless water, bright schools of fish,
and exotic coloured coral.

'Calm, little one,' a relaxed, pleasant voice tore my focus
from the watery ceiling.

The biggest being I'd ever seen was sitting with his extremely long legs stretched across a woven rug on the
pearlescent floor. Rivers of black hair fell down his back
in hundreds of tight braids that were woven and banded
into one at the base of his neck. He wore only a pair of
fitted brown trousers that covered to just below the knees –

golden almond skin so similar to Dalin's otherwise left bare across his massive chest and arms. And, amazingly, I saw that luminescent blue art covered most of his body.

The lines and swirls were a part of his skin and, faintly, even as he breathed, each blue marking glimmered. The designs wound up his chest, around his biceps, past his wrists and calves, probably dancing up his spine and shoulders, and even running up his neck, over one cheek and around an eye, ending somewhere beyond his hairline. The side of his head was shaved, and the designs laced along his scalp.

He raised his huge hand reassuringly and said again, 'calm little friend, you are safe. I am Ahanu.'

I registered that a fine webbing joined all of his digits.

'Well met,' I answered in a guarded voice. 'How are you already speaking *Aolen*?'

The sociable smile spread further across his face.

'You were murmuring in your sleep and I eventually began to understand,' he told me delightedly. 'The Elders said that they could sense some big things about your tiny self – something about how you must be the almighty Summoner. And I agree that you really are very good, being able to teach me a new language so quickly.' He rapped on his head. 'Normally I'm not one for retaining very much. One thing drives out another and life remains one great big surprise.'

'Oh?' I replied carefully, puzzling over how another group was apparently aware of a small part of the second prophecy.

'For instance,' Ahanu went on brightly. 'When I arrived home just last week I was surprised to find my clan gathered here to congratulate me on my five hundred and seventh year. They have done the same thing for five hundred and seven years in a row, yet I am always very astonished.' He shrugged cheerfully, crossing his long legs comfortably. 'But that's the fun of it. Something else is always in my head because I'm still young and free hearted, doing my part to enliven our bubble of a city.'

My eyes flickered up to where the invisible ceiling seemed to be holding out the entire ocean. 'We really are under water?'

'Yes,' he affirmed amiably. 'With the fishes.' His face lit up as a school of little pink fish flitted by as if to prove his point. 'The bubble is all a layer of magic,' he added conversationally. 'A film of enchantment that holds the water out and keeps our oxygen flowing. The *Larnaeradee* made it for us.'

I finally sat up properly. 'Why do you live on the sea bed when you could build on the coast?'

He splayed his webbed fingers. 'Because we are a water people. We are built for swimming. And the island above doesn't have enough room. Under here our city can sprawl forever, we can swim when we want, and we don't have to be soggy full time.'

I nodded, less wary.

'You know you truly must be 'the Summoner' the Elders mentioned. For someone so puny, your aura really fills the room in a way you'd expect a 'Summoner's' aura should.'

'I prefer to be called Kiana,' I informed him, peering more sharply at my surrounds. 'And, swollen aura or not, I must seem less than impressive on this bed.' I grimaced. 'It's too high for me to even climb down.'

I stood, flexing my wings and stiff limbs. My right wing had a raw purple mark in its very centre, but I was fortunate that whatever had done it had not punctured the wing entirely.

'Worse,' Ahanu replied. 'This is not a bed at all.' There was smothered laughter in his voice. 'You are in a newborn cub's cot. With the sides lowered for dignity of course.'

I sighed. 'Oh how grand I am. The last of the *Larnaeradee* seeks refuge from her perilous quest ... in a baby's crib.' I walked to the edge of the bed. 'Which infant has been robbed of a sleeping space?'

'No fear, my most recent cub has not yet arrived to fill it,' Ahanu replied easily, watching a giant sea creature of some sort flapping by over our heads. 'The twin cubs, Aysel and Dai, no longer need it, though they are only five years in this world. The younglings each finished with the cot years ago – little Johari, at fourteen years in this world and Einion, who has existed twenty two years. And my lovely eternal partner, Eolande, who has been joined with me for only one hundred years would never mind lending our cot to a 'Summoner'.'

'I am grateful,' I answered, listening for the sounds of a young Giant family.

'My mother Ayita, and Eolande's brother Toru also live here,' Ahanu went on. 'Because Eolande and I have such a small clan, they keep us company.'

'Considering you have lived five hundred and seven years, you do have a very young family,' I acknowledged.

'Oh, I have around thirty siblings myself, living with their own clans. But Eolande and I have only just settled down – she waited to let her fertility start so that we were truly ready for Einion because we are ourselves still so young and fun and lively. We have many years to build our own clan up.'

I gestured to the cot. 'How many months pregnant is Eolande at the moment?'

'She's nearly at the two year mark,' Ahanu answered flippantly. 'So not long to go now.'

I sucked in my breath. 'I see. And where is your clan now?'

Ahanu shrugged with easy going charm. 'Eolande is probably off to see some friend or other with Ayita. Toru is most likely on the training grounds.'

'And your younglings and cubs?'

'Johari loves being a sun dweller. She is probably wandering the island above. And Einion is much like me. The water runs strong in his veins, so he has probably taken the cubs off to swim,' Ahanu explained. 'At such free hearted ages there's no point in stifling their games, though younglings are always surrounded in Giants wanting to share a lesson.'

'And what do you usually do with your days?'

Ahanu stretched luxuriously. 'Swim, explore, make fun for the younglings ...'

I laughed. 'No, I meant what is your work?'

'Oh, I help the Elders,' he replied as though this were unimportant. 'Record their meetings, carry their messages, sometimes give my intelligent opinions. That kind of thing.

But now I've been appointed as your guide because, out of everyone, the magic chose me to be the one to find you.'

'Ahanu, that is perfect,' I told him. 'Could you take me to the Elders?'

He cocked his head to the side. 'Why? The Elders are already convinced we should join your cause.'

I gaped at him for a moment.

'The whole Giant tribe of Margate Isle is convinced,' he continued lightly. 'As soon as I carried you into our city we all knew what a Fairy – the traditional Summoners of all races – would be here for and what we must do. You are our sign that the time is right. And we know that we have more hope of joining in your war against Darziates than facing one of our own eventually anyway.'

I let out a big breath, at a loss after having crossed the ocean, and having been fuelled by the intent to fight to persuade the magical races to join our quest.

'At the moment the Elders are probably having long winded conversations about how much time it will take to swim the ocean, and how many Giants will want to come. We avoid internal feuds, because they could end up lasting for centuries, but this is a cause worth stirring the blood for. We've known the Sorcerer would be a threat to us one day.'

'I can hardly believe I have gained the allegiance of an entire nation in my sleep,' I answered. 'I think I should at least meet those I have enlisted.'

I took hold of the light cot sheet and used it to slide down to the smooth floor.

'Ahh yes, I'd better show you off to the others. You look as restless as a teeny youngling.' Ahanu remarked happily, and I noted that I was barely the length of his forearm before he stood and stretched himself out to his massive height, leaving me to crane my neck to gaze all the way up at him.

'It's time I show you more than a cub's cot,' he said, and held his hand out to me, keen to leave.

7

Seven

D^{alin}

Two figures blurred to a stop beside Noal and I, their towering forms, midnight features, and the sheer force of their magic giving the entire army pause behind us.

'Frey! Vidar!' I greeted them with joy as the Elves both swept into graceful bows towards Noal and I, and then toward where Durna and Aeron watched on.

Immediately the Jenran King and Warlord broke from their reverie, managing to mirror the respectful gesture, and venturing bravely closer.

'Welcome to Sylthanryn, our neighbours of the mountains,' Frey addressed the Jenrans. 'And welcome back to the Raiden, Noal and Krall soldiers.'

I turned to Durna and his officials, who were still as transfixed as the rest of the army.

'King Durna, I would like to introduce Vidar; warrior of Sylthanryn, and Frey; Elvish Commander and member of the Lady of the forest's council.'

'Well met, friends,' Durna uttered.

'It is an honour to be conversing with a King of Jenra for the first time,' Vidar smiled. 'The gift of *Aolen* bestowed by the One has made this world a better place already.'

'Yes,' Durna agreed. 'If we are given the chance, we should never let the language fade as our ancestors did.'

'Gods let it be,' Frey answered seriously. 'The Lady has begun writing a guide to *Aolen*, laced with her own magic so that the tongue can be passed on for generations. Though for now,' he turned to me. 'We have come to greet and speak with you only briefly, to relay word of movements abroad.'

'What news do you have?' I asked, and Vidar put a hand on my shoulder, nearly weighing me down.

'Main word has come from Asha, who did as you bade – spreading a message of hope to Awyalkna,' Vidar reported. 'Asha has leant her aid to both Queen Aglaia and King Glaidin against attacks of Dragons and Rucksha – or Ogres, sent by the Sorcerer. Rest assured that Awyalkna's defences have remained strong against each test.'

I winced grimly. 'You have made me gladder than ever to be on the move for the quest once again.'

'The forest dwellers are also as determined as ever,' Frey said. 'We will be ready when it is time to march and we will cover ground faster than ever to be by your side when you face Darziates at last.'

Vidar smiled, but there was little humour in it. 'The Sorcerer does not realise our numbers. He underestimates our energy. But we are not the dwindled race he thinks we have become. We are awake. And we are waiting.'

'And we are grateful, my friends,' I answered, noticing how awed the army remained in the presence of these two magnificent beings.

'Hey, aren't those your mares?' Wolf's asked in his gravelly voice then.

The Elves' faces lightened and I laughed in surprise as Ila and Amala now calmly meandered from the trees to a patch of thicker grass to graze.

'They wished to be reunited with you,' Vidar explained. 'They miss the One, and feel that you need them, as they helped you to survive most of the quest before you reached the forest.'

'I miss Kiana too, Amala,' I whispered in greeting as I approached the bay and she placed her nose in my hands.

'Ila, you look majestic!' Noal exclaimed at the Elvish finery she had been saddled in, and then he chuckled as he caught sight of another friend. 'And yes, greetings to you as well.'

The Lady's Granx was splayed lazily across Ila's forehead, catching a ride and waving regally.

'They are magnificent creatures,' King Durna stated in admiration. 'My own gelding is a sturdy charger, but most of our other horses are work or carthorses.'

'Thank you,' I told the Elves, aware that it would have cost them to have travelled close to the Cursed Valley to come in wait of us. 'Seeing you for even just a short moment has bolstered my spirits, and the spirits of all of us.'

Frey gave his wisp of a smile. 'It is a shame that we must part so soon and that you must march on.'

Vidar clasped my arm and then Noal's, letting his sparks of energy flow invigoratingly into us. 'March hard knowing that the hope and pride of the forest are speeding you along. Hurry to King Glaidin's side and give Awyalkna your strength. Soon you will be reunited with Kiana. Soon we shall join you.'

Frey turned from our private farewell to address the whole company again, raising his usually low voice. 'Be well, mighty friends. We shall meet again.'

There were bouts of cheers and shouts of agreement that echoed along the ranks.

'Be well, and we shall meet again,' Durna agreed reverentially in farewell, and though we all watched after the Elves a little wistfully as they blurred with their incredible speed back into the forest, the army was galvanised and alert.

We marched for leagues throughout the rest of the day, only setting up a winding camp along our path between the forest and the mountains when the light began to fail.

8

Eight

*K*iana

Apparently it was more of an indignity for me to jog along beside a Giant than to be carried like a 'cub'. So Ahanu had smugly tucked me into the crook of his arm.

'When your wing heals you'll easily keep up,' Ahanu was saying. 'You don't want everyone you meet to have to bend down to greet you.'

'Being nursed like an infant is hardly dignified,' I began to crossly argue, before we exited his house and I gaped at Margate Isle's city beneath the ocean.

I saw that the 'bubble' sheltered the entire city like one gigantic, transparent dome. Above us the ocean yawned, and through the dome I could make out all kinds of unimaginable marine life.

I could also make out, much more astonishingly, the massive forms of Giants swimming over their city – steering easily and joyously through schools of fish and twirling like acrobats through the water. The tattooed patterns covering their bodies were glowing brilliantly blue, illuminating their skin.

'We were born for the water, and our designs light up, like a song from our souls as we swim,' Ahanu explained.

It appeared that Ahanu didn't live in the city centre, but on its outskirts. And it seemed that living against the bubble's filmy sides was more desirable than living in the heart of the city. Each dwelling seemed to be built with a leaning, sprawling design to cling to or at least make contact with the bubble's walls.

'The *Larnaeradee* helped to make this city?'

'I've no idea how,' Ahanu admitted. 'The ancients wanted it, imagined it and it happened.'

'I obviously haven't reached that level of mastery yet, or something like an easy flight here wouldn't have tired me so,' I remarked.

'The ocean offers an abundance of energy, but perhaps you are still learning to channel the power around you,' Ahanu offered. 'You do already have gifts that will come in handy though,' he went on. 'While we're on our tour you can just introduce yourself to everyone and then they'll learn *Aolen*. It'll spread around the Isle from there.'

'Why don't we gather the Giants together so I can pass the gift on all at once?' I asked, but Ahanu shook his head with a grin.

'You'd never fit everyone in one place. Any announcements we have are spread simply from one Giant in conversation with another.'

He was heading towards another massive, sloping dwelling. 'Now, just say the usual things, 'well met, I'm the almighty Summoner, and then we can move on.' He had already covered a great distance in moments. 'We'll start easy,' he said. 'I'll introduce you to Eolande, Ayita and the neighbours first.'

He didn't knock, instead bursting through the slanted door to at once be met with four voices of welcome.

'Ahanu, meari lek,' a deep woman's voice greeted.

I peered around his arm and there were further exclamations of welcome.

They were all stunning. Each of them with flowing black hair and richly tanned skin, and each of them with different blue patterns across their bodies.

'Well met friends, I am Kiana.'

Without any pause, but with complete confidence, the female who sat with her hands resting on her unbelievably swollen stomach, and who could only be Eolande, smiled and replied: 'well met Kiana. For someone so tiny you've caused a lot of excitement.'

'That's my life partner,' Ahanu told me proudly, and she winked an eye that glowed with blue light.

'Well met, Summoner. I am Ayita. What would you like for supper?' the oldest Giant of the group asked in perfect *Aolen* then.

'Something small for this little bean of a thing,' Ahanu cut in, and she frowned but nodded in thought.

'Giants are very easy to get along with,' I remarked as we next headed toward a Giant sitting in the sand outside his hut, mending an expansive fishing net.

'We're very relaxed,' Ahanu replied contentedly, and the Giant with the net nodded as we passed.

'Well met friend!' I called to him.

'This is Kiana,' Ahanu added.

'Well met,' the Giant answered easily in *Aolen* before returning to his task.

Ahanu continued on to a group of younger Giants sitting in a circle on the sand.

'Younglings, meet the Fairy who has come to call our great tribe to savage conflict,' Ahanu introduced me as if this were all positive.

They lolled about and showered me with praise and support in response.

'Very relaxed,' I reaffirmed as Ahanu and I left to repeat the process.

Whether working in a group, bartering for goods, or resting by themselves, each Giant I met seemed to be taking their time with tasks that were a pleasure rather than a chore.

'Does anyone rush around here?' I asked curiously as we passed the most languid marketplace I'd ever seen. We were moving further into the city, and apart from larger, more overwhelming crowds and noise, the bustle was just as friendly and as carefree as before. Giants leaned or lounged or loped easily along together.

Ahanu shrugged and I laughed as I was lifted quickly up and down in his arms. 'There's not much of a rush when you've got all the time in the world.'

At last we came to a very large training ground, which was a vast, cleared pearlescent circle.

'One thing we appreciate is physical challenge to help us burn energy and pass time,' Ahanu called over the sound of wood thwacking against wood, which echoed from the centre of the crowd as two Giants battled skilfully with their staffs.

'The taller Giant is almost an artist in his movements,' I called back as I watched the two in the middle. Despite his powerful movements, the warrior Giant appeared strangely calm – almost contemplative.

'That's Eolande's brother,' Ahanu told me. 'My spirit is as free as his spirit is introspective. He loves peacefulness.' He sucked in a breath. 'HEY TORU!' Ahanu hollered, and Toru's opponent appeared faintly relieved when Toru halted.

Composed, Toru lowered his staff, and I noted that he was even bigger than Ahanu when he approached, his presence breathtaking as he halted and thumped his staff into the sand.

He looked to be the most silent and brooding Giant on all of Margate Isle, and after he nodded to Ahanu in salutation, he turned to me.

The designs on his body left very little free skin and they ran between his brows, along his nose, and circled around his glowing eyes like a war mask.

I was captivated as, slowly, he raised his hand with his palm toward me. Instinctively I reached mine out and pressed it against his.

My whole body could have been crushed by that impressive hand, but as soon as we touched Toru closed his eyes, as if listening.

Ahanu nodded to me and I closed mine too, breathing deeply, and instinctively relaxing my grip on the magic, letting it softly surround his hand and mine.

I gasped in surprise as I heard a sudden rushing of water in my mind, and then suddenly I could feel Toru's thoughts. He was welcoming me. I saw flashes of memories of immeasurable years. Swimming through the waves. Weapons clanging together. The peace of the island above.

Smiling, I opened my eyes to find that Toru was glowing brilliantly – every line across his skin shining as our magic entwined.

Well met, his mind communicated in *Aolen*, before he was lowering his hand as I let the magic soften and dissolve.

'Well met,' I answered reverently in the Giant tongue, amazed at all I had learned from him.

Toru nodded deeply and took up his staff again, returning to his now even more admiring and apprehensive opponent.

Ahanu released a big gust of breath. 'Well that was a very rare display of honour and connection. I don't think it has ever been done with a non-Giant.'

I broke from my reverie. 'What hasn't?'

'To bind power and share knowledge like that is to make a lifelong pledge of friendship and loyalty. A bond of great trust. It is very like the power that is used for linking life partners, cubs and parents, or clans to leaders. Look at your forearm, and Toru's.'

I followed his gaze, and was delighted to see a still faintly glowing, swirling design encircling my skin. It was exquisite – delicately winding about my forearm like a band, as though it had been meant to be there. The complete opposite to the branding I had been given in enmity by Agrona.

'Toru has no life partner, and though he is silent and withdrawn, he watches and understands and connects deeply. He is well respected, and is a quiet mentor to many of us,' Ahanu said. 'But such a link with someone who is not of our kind is quite impressive. And it's making me ready to move on again,' he winced, carrying me off once more. 'The force of the magic is making my essence itch.'

By the time we were heading back to Ahanu's dwelling for Ayita's dinner I had met many Giants, though I hardly felt like the day of collecting allies for the quest had been work at all.

I then quickly felt like a tiny member of Ahanu's chaotic clan as they conducted a loud family dinner, and Aysel and Dai confided happily that they were glad to give up their future cub sibling's cot for me – seeing as I was the mysterious Summoner and yet was so embarrassingly tiny.

The youngling Johari patted my shoulder heavily, promising that my magic at least made me seem big. She took one of the smallest of the many tropical flowers braided through her hair and tucked it behind my ear.

And I realised that I felt at home among the Giants, in spite of how very different we were.

9

Nine

Kiana

Everything sounded muted from within the bubble that Ahanu had guided me to form for myself.

He was pulling me along through the water while I made more experimental, filmy bubbles stretch between my fingertips, all the while enjoying the dry, oxygenated ride.

'The Elders had to help me form a bubble when I first found you,' Ahanu explained when he pulled me up to the beach so that I could let my sphere burst. 'You're making it look simple.'

'It's heartening that I can at least do one impressive trick,' I replied.

'Well here's a useful trick I can do,' Ahanu joked, crossing the sand and easily reaching up to the top of one of the trees. 'Snack?' he offered amicably, plucking a couple of hard, round fruits free of a branch and cracking them open effort-lessly.

'You are a skilled provider indeed,' I smiled, accepting the swollen melon-like offering and following him into the cool foliage.

We drank the juice and scooped out the fruit inside as we explored, and while the one fruit was enough to fill me, Ahanu stomached ten.

'Johari used to be so small that she could wear these flow-ers like bonnets,' Ahanu told me wistfully. But the vibrant flowers he'd gestured to were each so large that I could have seated myself in one of their petals comfortably.

'She still comes up here often, to sing along with the songs in the rainforest,' he went on, directing me to notice the music of the oversized waterfalls, and of the chattering birds in the impossibly lofty trees.

'Not many others seem to leave the city,' I commented, running my fingertips over a twirling vine.

'Most Giants find all the peace they need from the ocean,' Ahanu agreed, washing his hands in a stream and then tak-ing one step to cross the rushing channel of water. 'Many only come up if they want to see how rough things are dur-ing the cyclone seasons.'

I jumped from one rock to another to get to the other side of the stream while he waited.

'Though, the Elders are really the only ones who can stay up here without being overwhelmed during tropical storms,' Ahanu continued.

He pushed his way through a patch of bulging, bright orange flowers, sending a cloud of hand sized, iridescent butterflies fluttering away.

'I'm enjoying our tour, but I still want to meet those Elders,' I told him. 'Are they somewhere nearby?'

'Ahhhh,' Ahanu paused, as if he'd just remembered something of great interest. '*That's* what we were meant to be doing.'

I followed as he turned to climb an upward slope, breaking from the trees and stopping just before he trod on three Giants, who were sitting cross legged upon the sand in a circle.

Startled by the sight and magic of the Giants, I halted at once, wide-eyed and breathless.

'You can feel their combined power,' Ahanu explained cheerily, as if they weren't right beside us. 'See how the designs in those big, leathery wrinkles are permanently alight? Their magic is ancient.'

One of the tanned Elders fixed her glowing eyes on him. 'Ahanu,' she commented dryly, entirely magnificent as her long, wispy hair floated about like silvery white web. 'You made it.'

'Though making it *on time* would also have been appreciated,' the other wisened female of the three added sourly. 'We've heard you wandering around all morning.'

Ahanu grinned at them. 'You've got nothing else scheduled,' he scolded their impatience. 'Don't be rude in front of our guest.'

Then he turned to me, completely carefree.

'Kiana, these are the Elders we're meant to be meeting.'

I composed myself. 'I don't remember you mentioning a meeting.'

'Oh.' He frowned. 'Anyway, here we are.'

Then he unceremoniously made room for himself to sit cross legged with the Elders, squashing his way into their circle before sweeping me down into a collapsed sitting position beside him.

The male of the three Elders rolled his glowing eyes. 'Typical, disorganised Ahanu,' he said, and his withering voice crackled like old parchment. 'But at least he eventually brought the Fairy.'

When the Elders all turned their marvellous eyes upon me I suddenly felt smaller than an ant. Each of their skin designs were identical. Swirling wave-like pictures covered almost every inch of them, and they emanated with overwhelming power.

'Well met Summoner. It brings great joy to us that we should see a *Larnaeradee* again in such dark times,' the first Elder woman said. 'We always knew war would find us. But with your miraculous appearance, we will follow your Summons and have the courage to face Darziates with all of the races united, before he seeks each of us out alone.'

I sat up straighter, returning their gaze. 'I appreciate how quickly you have joined the quest,' I answered. 'And I'm fortunate to have so easily inspired you.'

'We had always hoped that the stories of old might be true,' the Elder male replied. 'That the Summoners would rise again to unite the races if ever the world was faced with another threat.'

'Yet we had not dared to really believe there might be truth to those tales until we first learned of you,' the Elder female nearest me spoke then. 'And that was only when you sent a faint echo of power to us across the seas, when you found your earthstone.'

Ahanu folded his arms, mightily unimpressed. 'You never told me that!' he said in an accusatory tone.

'You would have quickly forgotten anyway,' the male Giant told him. Then he returned his calm gaze to me. 'Take heart. Though we are a slow moving race, your appearance will spur us on. It will not take long for the Giants of each clan to select which members will leave to fight.'

The second, aged female inclined her head. 'Those who will go shall be ready to set off once you have spoken to the Eirian Isle dwellers. Then our Giants will show you that they can swim quickly across great distances in order to reach the mortal lands.'

I felt my shoulders drop a little as I remembered the horror of my flight again. 'It is a very great distance to swim without rest,' I answered gravely.

'It will take time,' the male Elder agreed. 'But that is what a Giant is built for. We can eat, breathe and sleep underwater. Even our weaponry has been made to cope with our lifestyle.'

I shook my head in amazement. 'The thought of having an entire army hidden by the water until the very last moment is a welcome one.'

'And,' Ahanu interjected brightly, 'from there it won't take us long to march across the mortal lands.'

'Yes. But before all of that, you — our dear, scattered Ahanu, will accompany the Summoner to Eirian,' the first female Elder said, resting her wrinkled hands upon her knees and fixing him with an evaluating look. 'You shall need to keep whatever wits you have about you.'

'Of course I will be the great guardian!' Ahanu cried proudly. 'Because out of every Giant I'm the one who found the Summoner.'

'Such fortune,' the male Elder told me dryly.

'Don't worry,' Ahanu beamed. 'I'm a whole lot of fun to have with you on a long journey. You'll see.'

Ten

D^{alin}

'The stories never mention how much walking and halting is involved in war,' Phrixus grumbled, wiping at his sweaty brow.

'Or the tent pitching,' Ferron agreed.

'Or the welts you get from heavy bag straps,' Nikon asserted.

'Oh, I'm sure I've heard a war ballad or two about chafing and blisters,' Tane remarked.

'I can picture the first stanza about our great quest already,' Thorin nodded. 'It would start off along the lines of: 'the whole thing was painstakingly slow.''

'The camp food isn't so bad,' Noal commented charitably, leading Ila around a ditch in the path while the Granx perched on his head, hugging his scalp like a hair piece.

'Yes, an insert about eating on the track could be quite inspirational,' Tane gushed. 'We could create an epic marching song to get everyone in the spirit!'

'If you do, I'll start marching in the opposite direction,' Vulcan threatened from behind him.

'Tane's just trying to brighten your day Vulcan,' Thorin enthused. 'Don't you feel brighter after a good singalong?'

'Not with the kinds of vocals you two have to offer,' Phobos cut in, crinkling his nose with distaste.

'Don't pull that face, Phobos,' I grimaced. 'It reminds me of Wilmont.'

'Yes!' Noal laughed. 'That man could achieve some incredibly sour looks.'

'Wilmont ...' Cadell pondered the name curiously. 'Have you mentioned him before?'

'He was our tutor and chaperone in the palace,' I explained. 'He seemed even more intent on ruining my life than my enemies in Krall ever were.'

'Perhaps he *is* another enemy from Krall,' Vulcan asserted. 'Could be a spy of Darziates.'

I waved my hand at him. 'Not all villains come from your homeland. This one is just a nuisance.'

'No matter either way,' Vulcan shrugged, taking a bear-like swig of water that drained his pouch down to a shrivelled pulp. 'Nuisances don't live long if they interfere with royals.'

'Yes, did you two lock him up and throw away the key?' Aiolos asked from where he, Gideon and Lydon were listening.

'It's not quite like that in Awyalkna,' Noal shrugged.

'No, in Awyalkna someone's word against another's isn't enough,' I explained. 'Evidence is needed for any form of punishment.'

'Even if it were the heirs to the throne making the accusations?' Purdor asked in surprise. 'If Darziates or any general so much as blinks in your direction you could be locked up and forgotten about in Krall. If you're lucky.'

I sighed. 'I did protest about his constant power over our lives, but it was assumed I simply resented his authority. Which, of course, I did.'

'So,' Noal grinned, 'old, ringlety Wilmont really had the worst job in the palace, watching us two.'

'Actually that role probably made him terribly appealing to Darziates. I'm sticking to the villain theory,' Thale remarked.

'Well, I'm just glad I haven't seen that old crank for nearly two years,' I answered.

'He won't trouble you if you ever meet again,' Wolf reassured me. 'Now that you're a world saving Raiden.'

'I'm not sure even that would impress him,' I laughed. 'He'd just be less than thrilled to see me.'

Thorin threw an arm about my shoulders. 'Well, we somehow learned to like you, so take comfort in that.'

'Even Kiana struggled to like you at first,' Noal snickered. 'But that changed.'

'Thank the Gods,' I grinned, though it felt as if my heart bruised a little at the thought of her. 'Perhaps soon she'll come back.'

11

Eleven

*K*iana

Ahanu and I sat next to a bonfire of my magic on the sand, watching the moonlight in the lapping waves.

I was stroking the purple and silver form of the sleeping wayra bird, who had come to me after my meeting with the Elders.

'Ahanu,' I asked thoughtfully. 'What were the names of the Elders?'

'Ohhhh ...' he stretched lazily. 'I don't know.'

I stared. 'They are your people's ancient leaders, and you personally work for them.'

'Mmm. Well I was never formally introduced,' he yawned. 'And even the Elders don't know.'

'The Elders don't know their own names?'

'Nope,' he answered matter-of-factly. 'They have simply been the Elders for all of Giant time. They came to be not long after the Lady came to be, and they began our race and they embody our entire population and power.'

I shook my head in amazement. 'What an incredible lifespan.'

'It's probably why I got the job of helping the Elders,' Ahanu reflected. 'Because after a long life it takes a very intellectual, witty, amusing Giant to keep Elders occupied. Organisational skills are not so important.'

I rubbed my bruised wing thoughtfully. I'd been practising on it after our meeting, using Ahanu as a launching pad and listening to the wayra crooning advice. She had helped me to learn new, helpful techniques and I had experimented with manipulating the air to create my own air pockets.

'You're likely right,' I deliberated. 'After so many years it would take a lot to amuse me, too.'

Ahanu grinned. 'I remember the day I was chosen, over two hundred years ago, when I was a livelier and more free spirited youth. They practically begged me to take the job.'

'And you're neither lively nor overly free spirited now?' I asked sceptically, ignoring his doubtful embellishments of the story.

'I've matured under the burden of duty,' he shrugged, entirely unburdened.

'Do you truly remember events from so long ago?' I asked while he rolled onto his back lethargically.

'Oh, I know many things slip my mind,' Ahanu scratched his head. 'My thoughts are always roaming, and details like celebrating my day of birth and getting home in time for dinner can wander from my memory. But I remember my cubhood with perfect clarity. And I remember every moment of my binding day with Eolande,' he chuckled. 'She was disappointed that the skin design that appeared on the both of us when we united wasn't shaped like water droplets. She says it's too wriggly.'

He held up his arm, where two lines of waves decorated from his shoulder to his wrist, spiralling loosely around his whole limb. I'd noticed the same design on Eolande's arm and on each of his cubs.

I gazed down at the gentle line of delicate waves encircling my own forearm, symbolising the connection I now shared with the silent Toru.

'A Giant's markings appear when a Giant loves or is devoted to something. A life partner, the ways of a warrior, the ocean, our cubs; they are symbols of things that are part of us,' Ahanu explained. 'To share a marking with someone is the ultimate link that shows you are one with them,' Ahanu said. 'And you are *the* One,' he joked delightedly – loving the title from the second prophecy I'd told the Elders about earlier. 'The One who is One with everything purely natural. Like that rock, and that little crustacean by your foot.'

'One with everything natural?' I repeated, moving the small sand creature away carefully.

'Of course! You are able to let nature's magic into your very veins, and you breathe it in with every breath,' Ahanu affirmed. 'To use your magic you just have to let it flow about, within and then beyond you. You need to use it like you use your actions – without thought, an impulse, like lifting a finger.'

I frowned. Perhaps I had not developed further yet because I'd been too focused on meticulous control while I channelled the energy around me. Being too picky over what I wanted and not letting it just happen.

'You remember how I was telling you about going bubble free to swim home and surprise the cubs?' Ahanu interrupted my thoughts.

'You never said anything about that.'

'Oh. Well I must've just been thinking it.'

I shook my head in exasperation. 'What would you have said if you were thinking out loud then?'

'Well, I would have said, let's swim in through the bubble roof in the cub's room and surprise them.'

I laughed as even the wayra opened one eye to stare at him in disbelief.

'Shouldn't I just travel by miniature bubble again so that I don't drown?'

'Well, I admit it is a fair swim from here to reach where I live,' Ahanu pondered. 'You would get tired if you were alone. But it's more fun to swim, and I can easily propel you there if you hold tight around my neck.'

'And the problem of me not being able to hold my breath all the way down to the seabed?' I queried.

He waved a hand in dismissal. 'You can make another bubble if it gets too much, but at my speed it will only take a short time. And even with a smaller link to Giant power than the one Toru gave you, you would be able to last a while without air in the water.'

I processed his words. Not only could I speak the Giant language – I could also hold my breath for long enough to make it to the ocean floor.

Toru truly had blessed me with a priceless gift.

'Alright,' I smiled in anticipation, standing while the wayra lifted off, peeping out a tune of good night.

'You'll love it!' Ahanu bounced up from the sand and swept me along in a rush.

In moments the fire was extinguished and I was being plunged with a cold shock through the waves, my eyes wide as Ahanu – glowing in front of me – made us dive to incredible depths.

My lungs endured so well as Toru's glowing gift sparkled through the dimly lit water at my wrist, that I hardly remembered I should even want to breathe.

We passed colossal creatures and I could hear them singing eerie and beautiful melodies like underwater lullabies. They swam beside us, using flippers and tails to propel themselves as their songs rolled through the water in complex ripples.

I saw that coral forests swayed below us, teeming with tiny coloured fish, and we flitted amongst them until eventually I felt a little niggling need to draw new air into my body.

Ahanu drew me close to the massive bubble city, glimmering brightly like another world, and together we found the entrance to the cub's room – swimming forward through the film and into a world of air and clear sound once more.

I was dry and far from breathless as I landed on the cubs' cots while they squealed in delight, and I laughed as they bounced around me.

'That was incredible,' I smiled at Ahanu.

'Surprise,' Ahanu told Aisel and Dai.

12

Twelve

A*grudek*

Agrudek was in pain. Constant, gnawing pain.

It was his body reacting to the foul presence of Darziates. Always so near, always accessible, through the burning little scryer scorching against his chest.

And the guilt that Agrudek felt for being the Sorcerer's spy made him wretched with a sick feeling that swelled like an emotional tumour within his body at all times. For Agrudek knew that he would be the one to cause the downfall of the Three, and that he would be the cause of many deaths for this army of hope. He would be the one to lead Darziates and the Witch to destroy them, because he had no choice but to obey the Sorcerer's compulsion, pleasing Darziates just enough to perhaps save his loved ones.

Poisonous images of his family still polluted his mind, not relenting since Darziates had first whispered his way into Agrudek's head in the forest. And the small inventor would truly do anything to be with them. Even give up his other hand. Even give up information on the only Three powerful enough to get rid of the worst King to have ever lived.

Trying to carefully limit that information was about the only thing Agrudek was willing or able to risk doing to protect the Three, as, thankfully, the Sorcerer had so far been content with whatever random mental images Agrudek offered.

Darziates was most satisfied by visions of the army's positioning on their trail – and also with images of Kiana from Agrudek's past memories. The Sorcerer had not questioned him on the forest dwellers or as to whether or not Kiana was actually with the march, and it was simple enough for Agrudek to be kept in the dark about any of the recent plans or news of the army, for nobody much liked to be near him.

People tended to avoid his worsening ticks, his increasingly deranged muttering, and his haunted, bloodshot gaze.

He knew he especially appeared just a bit too hungry whenever he paused to lurk and watch the princes as they laughed cheerfully with the lucky, untroubled warriors of Krall.

Unlike him, they did not have to worry that their master might plague them at any moment. The Sorcerer wasn't sending them cruel reminders of why they must be loyal, and he wasn't forcing their minds open to be trawled through without a care for the damage.

'Here,' a familiar blonde maiden eyed him coolly when he started uneasily at her approach, breaking from his intent focus on the princes and warriors. She offered him a ladle of water, but kept her distance.

When Agrudek returned the ladle he moved away from her stony stare, for he was sure she was one of Prince Noal's closest admirers from Jenra, and he hated that her unconscious distrust was justified.

Agrudek rubbed nervously at the rounded stump of his small wrist and shuddered into his brown hood. He saw a flash of bloodied button noses, darling braids shaved off, rosy cheeks turned to sunken hollows.

Yes. He was willing to do anything he could to get them back.

Anything at all.

13

Thirteen

*K*iana

Ayita woke me as she had each day of my stay in her home, her pretty face smiling. Yet as I remembered that this morning was to be different from the others, I felt a slight pang of sadness.

'Are you rested for your journey, Summoner?' she asked.

'Very rested.' I tried not to sound downcast.

'Your wing looks ready for the trip,' she commented comfortingly, lifting me down from the cot. 'But you'll have my papa and your wayra friend to keep an eye on you if you tire.'

Somehow, after even a short stay, Ahanu's clan were just as hesitant to say goodbye as I was, but much too quickly I found myself leaving their ocean realm.

Soon even the golden sands and swaying trees were fading from sight, before once again the world seemed to be just a vast expanse of blue sky and rolling waters.

'Thankfully this time my wings are strong and I feel free rather than trapped in the air,' I told the wayra as she glided next to me.

Good island practice. Eased you back into the sky, she sang with approval, stretching her own purple and silver wings.

'Dear One! The outside world has welcomed you back with open arms!' Ahanu called to me, surfacing below us easily to glide along on his back. He made it appear effortless to ride both under and over the waves. 'It's as if the weather is apologising for your stormy entry to Margate Isle!'

'I can only hope it is a positive omen for what is ahead,' I answered, dipping down toward him and landing on his glowing chest.

'Think of the things you have already done as the Summoner,' Ahanu told me. 'Toru's gift is a symbol of friendship with the Giants. You hardly need good omens from the Gods.'

'You're right,' I mused, feeling every motion of the waves. 'What I mostly need is to stop trying to stifle my magic. I know I must allow it to flow through me as freely as my own blood does.'

'Do not worry so much little One,' Ahanu replied, sending a splash my way. 'Nature's magic is your inheritance. When you have in every way become ready, it will happen. It will be instinctual.'

'I do hope that is the case,' I remarked. 'There's a great deal of trouble ahead if it's not.'

14

Fourteen

The Sorcerer

'Engrark.'

Darziates observed the puny man's haggard face in the scryer as the inventor huddled close to his pendant, cupping it in his one hand to keep the light of the globe secret.

'M-m-my Lor-d-d.'

There were worse tremors than ever before in Agrudek's voice, his brain getting more scrambled with every intrusion.

'What news?'

Agrudek licked his lips fearfully. 'W-we have … have t-t-travelled well, S-sire.'

Darziates sent his consciousness forward with a surge of hot magic that travelled through their connection to pick through Agrudek's mind.

The Sorcerer saw images from memories that suggested the Jenran army was strong, but inexperienced in the world. And they had been met by only two Elves from the forest when they'd left the mountains.

The Lady herself hadn't even made an appearance.

'Exactly how far have the 'Three' led the Jenrans, Agrudek?' the Sorcerer probed, forcing his way further into the inventor's cringing mind, sifting through information as if Agrudek's brain was nothing more than a chest full of scrolls.

He flicked through images of passing trees, until he was drawn to a stop by a memory of the dark haired beauty, Kiana, which had been embedded especially firmly in the inventor's mind.

The vision of her was so stark that Darziates could hardly make out any details in the background behind her. And, truly, he did not care to. His attention was caught as he examined her face keenly, wishing to meet her for himself. To possess her.

'... My L-liege ...' Agrudek's voice whimpered as he felt the Sorcerer brooding over the Fairy. 'The Three h-h-h-have led the army very far through the d-d-dense tree-pass between the mountains and th-the forest ...'

And because Darziates didn't question his power over his scared little servant, he did not now delve deeper as he listened to the inventor.

Instead, he assumed that the One he wanted most was with the rest of the Jenran army.

'Your mind tells me that the time for an Evexus attack draws near,' Darziates resolved at last.

'Ye-yes. In a c-c-couple of days ...' Agrudek shut his eyes in distress. '... I'm sure th-then th-the army will have reached a part of the trail where the E-e-evexus and W-witch will be able to survive, even if be weakened by, the Lady's m-magic.' The little man shivered. 'I can feel your effect g-g-growing in the atmosphere here the further that w-we travel.'

'Good. Then in a couple of days you can sit back and watch the beasts that you helped me to create as they tear through the Jenrans and bring me my One.' Darziates scraped his presence away from the inventor's mind, knowing that too much more of this and the raggedy man would be completely useless.

'Engrark,' he uttered – ending the conversation.

Immediately he reached his mind out to the edge of the borderlands of Krall and the forest. He kept reaching until he felt the dark, oily glimmer that was Agrona's mind.

The Witch was soaring over the dry land in her raven form, and he felt her crow with delight at the sudden, intimate contact from her beloved master.

Then he pumped her mind with images of what he wanted her to do, ignoring her predictably heartbroken, furious squawks as she saw her instructions and his unveiled desire for the One *Larnaeradee*.

He withdrew from her mind, leaving her only with the glorious vision of the Fairy that he had pilfered from Agrudek's memories.

15

Fifteen

R*azek*

The Emperor of Lixrax started with dread as the Sorcerer of Krall materialised in front of him.

Darziates and his throne of steel had both suddenly appeared opposite Razek's own gold throne in the spectacular Takal – thankfully late enough into the night that Razek sat almost alone, fretfully thinking in his emptied hall. The guards at the hall entrance, dressed lightly in their shrouds and trousers, let out gasps as they saw Darziates appear as if from the waves of a heat-born mirage. But when the guards made to rush to their Emperor's side, Razek quickly recovered and held up a hand to stop them.

Warily his guards dropped back, their dark eyes glittering with loathing for the Sorcerer who had enslaved the children of Lixrax in his war.

'Razek,' Darziates began. 'Your desert forces must soon commence the march to Krall.'

Razek's mouth was a hard, grim line under his oiled beard and tattooed cheeks. 'They are readying themselves, Crishnarx,' the Emperor replied acidly.

'I am pleased,' Darziates answered coolly. 'When Agrona completes her current assignment she will escort your forces across the wastelands.'

Even in the heat of his halls Razek shivered at any mention of the hag. 'The Desert Storm needs no escort across the sandy planes,' the Emperor spat. 'Our forces are at home in this terrain.'

'Be grateful Razek,' the Sorcerer cautioned the Emperor. 'You have deadlines to meet. And with Agrona's help your march will be shortened and less life will be wasted in the crossing.'

'We are not cattle in need of transportation. We will use our own strength.' Razek tried to keep his hands from shaking by gripping his gold armrests tightly.

'You had best hope your strength does not fail then,' the Sorcerer replied softly at last. 'Or it won't just be the Witch who is sent to compel you.'

Darziates' expression did not change, and yet the arctic cold in his eyes suddenly seemed to strip all of the heat from the desert Emperor's flesh and an inexplicable image was driven like a shard of ice into Razek's mind.

An image of what could only be the Awyalknian Jewel, besieged by Trune raiders, Griffins and fire breathing beasts that rained fury down from the sky.

It was implied that the Takal could be besieged just as the Awyalknian Jewel had been, or was soon to be.

Then Razek was blinking his vision clear, and he found that the Sorcerer had disappeared.

Those last words, and the threat in them, still somehow seemed to linger behind.

16

Sixteen

Noal

'Something's got to be amiss,' Dalin croaked tiredly, smoothing his ruffled hair while we both hurried after a Jenran page boy.

We had been woken by the young messenger long before camp was due to be broken.

'Let's hold onto hope that the magic of the forest is still protecting us from Darziates,' I grimaced, straightening my rumpled shirt.

But as we drew nearer to King Durna's tent we saw the nervous expressions of those already gathered.

'I don't think you'll get to hold onto that hope for too much longer,' Dalin sighed as we joined the muttering crowd.

I patted the wriggling Granx distractedly as she surfaced from my pocket while Durna and Aeron delivered their briefing.

'A strange beast was sighted amongst the trees by a scouting party last night,' the Warlord announced grimly, and a gnawing pit of fear opened in my stomach. 'By all accounts it was very like the Evexus creatures that the Three were dogged by on their quest to Jenra.'

'We had presumed the Lady's magic would protect even this part of the forest as it extended into Krall,' Durna continued. 'But we can no longer presume safety from Sorcery here.'

There was no question left in my mind when the leader of the party from the night before stepped forward to describe the encounter.

'We first heard a snapping sound from movement deeper in the trees,' the wiry man recalled, and sweat beaded across his forehead despite the briskness of the dawn. 'Then we felt the cold,' he went on. 'It was ... unnatural. So we were wary as we made our way through the trees. And though I'm not usually afraid of searching out danger, my thoughts became confused and fearful.' He grimaced. 'Before I had even seen the beast my heart was racing, and when my eyes picked it from the shadows I was frozen by the foulness that seemed to spread from it. But it was in no way bothered by me, and simply melted into the trees. As if it had seen and learned enough.'

'You did well,' Dalin spoke then, all traces of sleep gone from him. 'Now we can be ready for when the Evexus stop watching,' he said resolutely.

'If these creatures are unnatural invaders from the Other Realm, and only the purest of magic can truly hurt them, what could we do against attack?' one of the gathered Jenran leaders asked, her face ashen.

'While we cannot hope to be unscathed by all-out battle with them, we can develop methods to defend against the Evexus – and to prevent them from overrunning us,' Dalin answered, glancing over the camp where fires were being stamped out and tents were being folded up.

'Is there no way to do more than defend and cower from these things?' another councillor asked.

Dalin rubbed the scar along his jaw. 'It will likely be that we have little choice but to engage with them when they force violence upon us, but seeking them out when they hide is useless without magic. Instead we could focus on trying to trap them during an attack to contain the harm they do. Doing that might give us an opportunity to see if there actually might be any kind of damage we can do to them.'

'Perhaps we could use the golden Unicorn horn as a weapon?' I asked when Dalin had finished, and Durna considered the idea thoughtfully.

But Aeron shook his head. 'A non-magical wielder of the horn could not achieve the pure power needed to kill the Evexus. While the horn would surely grievously wound an Evexus, just as in our King's hands it can open the mountain, the beast would live – and so the wielder would most certainly not.'

Maeve's idol, Lady Amarantha, was present as the lead healer of Jenra, and she agreed with Aeron calmly. 'Displaying such magical strength would make our army seem more of a threat. The horn should only be used if there is someone willing to give their life and to wield the horn far from the rest of the army. Perhaps only the combined magic of the One *Larnaeradee* with that of the Unicorn horn would be enough to really hurt the Evexus,' Amarantha finished.

'If we ever get to dire need, as one of the Three I would be willing to take the risk of trying.' Dalin said at last, and I felt a pang of both pride and worry. 'I've been fortunate in having both the Lady and Kiana channel their magic through me, and I know it has made me stronger than before.'

'You would not go alone if you ever had to try,' I told him as we returned to our Krall soldiers.

'Thank you brother,' he answered. Then he nodded toward our comrades. 'It appears that word has already spread.'

Many of the Krall warriors were wearing rather than carrying their intimidating spiked armour.

'Are you lot in the mood for looking shiny again?' I asked as we neared them.

Thale shrugged. 'Half of us will be on guard duty at all times from now on. No more cruising off the Jenrans and forgoing night watches.'

'And the treasures you guard are ...?' Dalin asked with a small smile.

'Our two precious princelings,' Thorin answered with a widening grin.

'Take comfort, Raiden,' Tane declared. 'I sparkle in the sunlight, I rattle while I march, and I find it damn hard to sit comfortably or to go to the toilet. Your enemies shall indeed fear me.'

'So, was it definitely the Evexus?' Ferron asked.

'Big. Oozing fear and ice ...' Dalin sighed. 'It's definitely them.'

'We'll march well today, then,' Phobos predicted. 'Everyone will be keen to make a roaring hike away from where the Evexus have been spotted.'

17

Seventeen

D*ren*

Dren had been twelve when he had first decided that his loyalty to the princes of Awyalkna would be unshakeable. And it was the same burning sense of loyalty that had led both himself and his archer comrades out into Krall's borderlands to find Prince Dalin and Noal now.

After his father's death Dren had become the provider for his struggling family, and with his bow he had fought to keep them alive. But one day when he had been angrily scuffing his boots along outside the palace Gwentorock Walls – having caught nothing but a small bird that would hardly feed his baby sister, he had stopped at the sight of a tree that grew over the great wall.

The tree bore the brightest, shiniest apples that he'd ever seen, and Dren had fitted an arrow to his bow in an instant, positioning himself on an angle that would keep his prizes from being launched to land out of reach on the other side of the wall. Then he had shot six homemade arrows in quick succession, accurately skewering six apples neatly through their middles, and sending them in an arc to be pinned harmlessly against a wooden house opposite him.

Elated, he had dashed to pluck the arrows free, only to hear the word 'halt!' yelled in fury.

He had felt his entire world shake as he'd turned to find himself being circled by soldiers who bore the insignia of royal guards.

'What is the meaning of loosing arrows at the palace?' the closest soldier had demanded.

'Arrest him!' another had growled as the colour had drained from Dren's face.

Then two new voices had cried out: 'wait!'

Two noble boys, who must have been lounging in the boughs of the very tree he'd fired upon on the other side of the wall, now stood holding the trunk to lean over the stone ledge.

Amazingly the surrounding soldiers had stopped their advance to stand to attention for the boys, who had both appeared younger than even Dren was.

'I do not think apples are worth arresting someone over,' one of the boys had said then.

'I don't even like apples,' the other, fairer haired boy had affirmed. 'The archer can have them.'

'But, Your Highnesses,' a soldier had started to argue. 'He fired upon the palace. He fired in your vicinity. He must be punished.'

Dren had quailed before at the thought of prison, but he'd almost swooned at the thought of having fired anywhere near royalty.

'No,' the first prince had negated calmly, despite his youth. 'Look at that aim. I think taking him to the training masters or even Conall would be better.'

'Prince Dalin, I'm not sure ...' one of the soldiers had started again uncertainly.

'You're right. Conall is too busy, Sumantra is the better choice. We can't let such talent slip away.'

The other prince, Noal, had pointed at the apples. 'Let him collect those, though. He needs them.'

The soldiers had appeared helpless in the face of the princes' commands. Even princes who barely came up to their navels had to be obeyed.

'My father will be glad to hear his men supporting new talent,' Prince Dalin had remarked warmly.

Then there had come a whining voice from the other side of the wall.

'Wilmont calls,' Prince Noal had declared with a roll of his eyes. And with an air of reluctance both of the boys had turned to slide back down out of sight.

Soon after, Dren had collected his six juice coated arrows and six delicious apples before being led to a future with regular pay that had provided for his family from then on.

Now, sweating beneath the heat of Krall's unnatural sun, Dren was on the trail of the princes to support them as best he could in a time of their own need.

'Gods, the forest is massive,' one of his companions, Ander, complained – his gaze fixed on Sylthanryn's border trees at the edge of Krall.

'Gods, it's *too* massive,' another of the archers – Dwyn – winced. 'We're never going to find them.'

The dew on the grass in the forest glittered like settled magic, and fresh mist poured outward like steam around the ancient roots. Opposite the cool forest shade, Dren's archers and their mares puffed with the intensity of the hot Krall morning.

The archers had followed the edge of the trees until they had been led into the Krall borderlands, all the while searching for a trail that the princes might use to lead the Jenrans into Krall.

'It will be a relief to find the most likely path, just to get into the forest's shelter,' Rai, who was the youngest of the group, said.

'It will only be a short reprieve when we find them,' Dren reminded Rai. 'Then we'll be back out to journey across the borderlands to King Glaidin.'

'It's fortunate we are a steadfast bunch,' Dwyn's brother, Glyn remarked.

'First we survived Sumantra's farewell glares,' Ander said. 'Then we crossed Awyalkna in record time.'

'Don't forget how bravely we entered the poisonous atmosphere of Krall,' Dwyn added.

'Bravely, or stupidly?' Ander mused. 'Only fools would choose to cross a distinct line of green grass where Awyalkna ends, freely entering the scorched plane beyond that.'

'Bravely and stupidly, we pushed ever onward!' Glyn waved a finger in the air.

'Yes, a truly hardy bunch of archers the likes never before seen,' Dren congratulated them.

'There was also that time we faced off with a Dragon in the city,' Rai recalled.

'So many times, so many heroics,' Dren agreed, eyeing the glimmering trees on his left and then the barren wasteland on his right.

'The Gods should look down on us with great favour right now as we complete our greatest task yet ... and as we work on our sun spots,' Glyn remarked, wiping at his damp brow.

'Do the maps suggest the Gods have appreciated us enough,' Dwyn paused, readjusting and taking shelter under his cloak. 'To make it so that we are at least close to a more likely trail into the forest?'

'Well, we can pretty much discount the next few we're going to find, going by these maps,' Ander replied as he squinted down at his parchments.

Rai nodded from where he rode beside Ander. He had a handful of maps spread out on his own saddle pommel. 'They appear to be mere game trails. Overridden by trees and unworkable for an army. But they could take any of the other dozen paths marked out through the forest to get into Krall.'

'I can guess that two trails in particular would have more appeal to the princes and the Jenran army, though,' Ander added. 'One would be more appealing because it is clearer, bigger, and closer to a great stream running through the forest. But it is the obvious choice if Darziates is watching them. The other path is a likely candidate because it winds along a road in between the cover of the forest and at the base of the Jenran mountains.'

'Getting to the path would have been hard going through the mountains,' Rai speculated. 'So the army might still be weeks away from even reaching the forest. But that particular trail finishes quite far into the borderlands, close to where King Glaidin should pass.'

Dren took a swig of water from his flask. 'We'll check the small trails and make sure they really are too irrational for an army to attempt before we discount them. They're on our course anyway.'

But, as expected, as the days passed and they reached each trail – they dismounted, inspected and discounted all but the path between the base of the mountains and the forest.

'We'd better hope their logic is like ours,' Ander said tiredly as at last they followed their way along the final track – finding nothing as further days passed.

Dren stretched his cramped muscles, creaking in his saddle. The colours of sunset were flickering between the leaves above.

'We could wander for months without purpose if we've guessed wrong,' Rai agreed cheerfully. 'But I don't mind. Our time on this trail has been a real break after the wasteland.'

'Some sign that we're not toiling deeper into the forest for nothing would still be great,' Glyn drawled back from where he and Dwyn were meandering along ahead of the group on foot.

Then suddenly Dwyn threw his arm out to stop his brother.

'What is it?' Dren asked, quickly reining in beside Ander and Rai.

'I thought I heard ...' Dwyn glanced down the darkening path, tension rising in his shoulders.

And then they all heard it.

'A shout of alarm,' Ander affirmed.

'I think we have our sign,' Dren said, reaching for his bow.

18

Eighteen

D^{alin}

It had started at dusk with the unmistakeable screech of a raven. There had been the feeling that hidden watchers were peering from the trees, and cold air had seemed to pour from the darkening forest like invisible fog.

Then we had heard rough, grating voices speaking from hidden positions in the treetops. The Evexus – communicating.

There had barely been a moment for the army to form a rough circle around the camp, which stretched along the trail.

Then the raven had shrieked again and the five Evexus had been on the move.

'What the frarshk?' Thale uttered as our nearest Evexus began inspecting and easily tossing men away from itself.

It was sifting through the crowds as if in search of somebody, and we all ducked as a Jenran was sent hurtling over our heads.

'Encircle it!' I yelled out. 'Together we can pin it down or drive it back!'

Another man who had charged independently got thrown into a wagon.

'Swordsmen!' I called. 'Quick slicing attacks! Don't give it a chance to heal or leap away.'

The Evexus lowered itself into a half crouch, its glowing eyes fixing on my face.

'Raidensgra,' it hissed between needle sharp teeth, its slitted nostrils flaring.

'That's right,' I told it, and then looked to the ready group of men. 'Now attack!'

At once three Jenran swordsmen rushed out from different directions of our circle, hacking at three separate places on the beast's body. Before it could lash out at them they had disappeared back into the crowd and another four were charging.

'Pikemen!' I ordered, and they were fast in stepping up, making quick stabs at the flailing beast's arms.

'Swords!'

Fifteen or so men rushed in, chopping and forcing its legs to begin to buckle.

'Tane,' I growled. 'Get ropes.'

He grabbed Gideon and Roth before sprinting away – ducking under a screaming cart horse as it was sent flying by one of the other Evexus in the camp.

I kept up the call for swords and pikes until Tane and the others dashed back with bundles of heavy siege ropes.

Our Evexus was hissing and spinning after each darting enemy while Tane distributed the ropes and the pikemen leapt in to pin the Evexus through its shoulders, legs and core, forcing it back on its haunches.

'ROPES!'

Noal charged with his rope, looping an end quickly and securely around the beast's neck while Thorin burst forward to do the same from the other side.

Vulcan added his strength to Thorin's and Wolf added his to Noal's, all heaving from opposite ends until strangled choking sounds came from our beast.

'If it frees its arms it'll tear through the ropes like cotton,' I commented to Thale.

He nodded. 'I'll be at your side.'

Sucking in deep breaths, we both charged from our side of the circle and managed to catch the swinging arms, looping more rope around its freezing wrists and retreating as Ferron and Aiolos quickly moved in to try to catch the beast's legs.

Ferron retreated but Aiolos was caught by a kick that brought him to the ground, and his cry was cut off by the Evexus' foot as it stomped down on his chest – leaving only fifteen free Krall men in the world.

I heard cries of anguish as Rendor, Gideon, Roth and Lydon launched at the beast with their sabres, making the beast howl. Thorin, Noal and the other rope holders were dragged a few steps and I grunted as the rope burned my palms.

Then, unexpectedly, five perfectly aimed arrows plunged into the joints of our Evexus – making it pause with a jolt and wail.

'What in the Gods' names ...' I panted, before, inexplicably, I heard Awyalknian voices.

It was like going home for the first time in years and I craned to see five expert archers galloping into the camp, arrows raining from their bows.

'More Awyalknians I've already come to like!' Phrixus crowed in wonder, while Nikor and Cadell helped me to yank my rope back so that the Evexus was pulled flat by the pressure.

'We've got it trapped!' I heard a Jenran gasp. But then, as if in response, one of the other rogue Evexus suddenly sprang into our midst.

It inspected us, its gaze lingering on Noal and I, before it turned and slapped our captive, screaming Evexus across its face.

Our Evexus stopped wailing at once, chastened, and then its comrade swept its talons through the ropes so that all of us holding them toppled to the ground.

Our now freed Evexus straightened almost contritely, plucked the arrows from its flesh and stepped on any Jenran not quick enough to retreat.

They both loped off to bombard the pikemen around the healer wagons at the heart of the army – simply wading through and swatting Jenrans out of the way.

I swore, scrambling to my feet and pulling my sword free as the beasts reached into a cart and began pulling out and inspecting only the brunette women.

'Frarshk ...' Thorin cursed. 'They're after Kiana.'

'Defend the healers!' I roared as one young lady was dragged up and a talon flicked her hood back to reveal red, curly hair. Then she was tossed away.

'Repeat circle tactics!' I yelled, and the Jenrans and Krall warriors branched off into groups to surround the two Evexus.

The beasts kept rifling through the wooden wagons, dropping one emptied, shredded cart and dragging another closer while screams came from inside.

'Thorin!' I panted as we surrounded the Evexus. 'We'll all distract them. You get up there,' I nodded to the split open roof of the cart. The door had been barricaded by the terrified women. 'Get them out!'

Thorin gestured to Nikon, Vulcan and Tane. They stood back to await their chance for a run up while the Evexus remained unconcerned, continuing to claw chunks of the wooden roof away.

'Ready!' I called to the men in my circle and the circle beside ours.

Thorin and his team were set to sprint.

'Swords go!' I yelled.

Immediately Noal, Thale, Phrixus and Wolf darted forward with the Jenran swordsmen on their heels. Thale wedged his sword under our beast's armpit and I saw the beast recoil, dropping the cart back down so that a burst of screams came from its occupants.

Thorin and his team were already scrabbling up the cart's wall to the hole in its roof, but on the ground I saw Phobos and Thale being bashed in opposite directions, and Wolf being flicked out of the way.

I ran forward to hack at the beast's arm as Noal joined me, skewering it through the wrist.

'CHARGE!' I roared to the Jenrans to spur them on, only to be flung backward myself and to see Noal's legs suddenly flying up past my face.

He came crashing down on the other side of the cart and Thorin dropped to his hands and knees, peering over the side worriedly to check my brother was still alive.

'He's just dazed!' Thorin yelled, and I was relieved to see that his team had taken the opportunity to begin lowering woman after woman from the roof of the cart to be caught by Purdor and Lydon below.

But, catching sight of the women dashing away, our beast ferociously launched for the cart again, yanking it into the air so that Vulcan toppled and the others dangled precariously.

'There are still two healers in there!' Purdor called out, and then we all winced when Tane lost his grip and landed painfully below the cart.

Noal had recovered, and quickly darted forward with Lydon to drag the fallen soldiers out of harm's way while Thorin and Nikon still grimly hung from wood shards jutting from the cart roof.

I could hear the two healers rattling around inside the broken cart and the Evexus reached in past Thorin and Nikon, pulling one of the maidens out. She screamed and struggled in the beast's grip as Noal and I ran forward with a group of Jenrans, desperately stabbing at the Evexus' spiked legs.

Nikon made a heroic effort to swing from the airborne cart, landing heavily on the Evexus' shoulder and grimly wrapping a bear-like grip around its throat.

Gurgling in irritation, the Evexus made a squeezing motion and the girl's wailing was cut off, a claw sliding into her middle before she was dropped.

The beast clawed around to try to dislodge Nikon while Thorin swung his legs to get into the cart to save the last girl.

'Noal!' I gasped, from where we were both still hacking at the Evexus' thighs. 'Catch the girl. Get her to safety!'

He nodded and sprinted to stand under the cart just as Thorin managed to swing himself into the entrance. A moment later the girl inside was boosted into view as she struggled to climb out.

Nikon thumped to the ground beside me, dislodged at last and sporting a massive dent in his chest plate, but he rushed to cut at the Evexus' legs with me, wheezing painfully.

'It's alright, I've got you,' I heard Noal's encouraging voice before the hooded girl dropped into his arms and he whisked her to a safe distance. She clung to him gratefully for a moment, before I heard Nikon's grunt of surprise.

The Evexus had kicked him backward and now dropped the cart, with Thorin cursing loudly inside, while I leapt out of the way.

The Evexus reached for the girl clinging to Noal, but lightning-fast Noal threw back her hood and the beast stopped at the sight of her blonde hair.

Then I held my breath as the Evexus finally turned away.

'Norlarxere!' it cried, and suddenly all of the Evexus stopped to look towards the tree tops.

The whole army cringed and ducked when there came Agrona's infuriated screech.

And then the Evexus were gone – melting into the darkness and leaving destruction and a bewildered army behind.

It was a moment before I noticed that Noal was still staring at the healer woman.

'Maeve?' he whispered in shock.

And she buried herself in his arms, tears wetting her cheeks.

19

Nineteen

*K*iana

The wayra and I swooped down to Ahanu when the jagged outline of the Eirian cliffs at last came into view.

'Ahanu,' I perched on the Giant's glowing stomach with a frown. 'Why are the skies empty when a whole flock of Dragons are supposed to live in this area?' I asked. 'I'd heard Dragons fly.'

Ahanu chuckled. 'Of course they fly, but not during hibernation,' he explained. 'They like to be unaware by the time the weather changes.'

'They're hibernating?' I groaned in disbelief. 'You never told me that.'

He shrugged as he swam. 'Thought I'd mentioned it.'

I gritted my teeth in exasperation. 'If they are completely unaware, what am I meant to do to get them to join the quest?'

'Well, you'll have to wake them. Convince them to skip their nap,' Ahanu answered matter-of-factly. 'And convince them to help us get the Dwarves and Gnomes on side,' he added. 'Without the influence of the Dragons, they might take a year to decide.'

I flew in an annoyed zigzag over his head. 'All this is great to know now that I have no time to think.'

Ahanu grinned. 'I'm here to help.'

Then he quickly resubmerged and didn't resurface until we reached a pebble beach at the foot of the cliffs.

'They live at the cliff peaks,' Ahanu announced, beaching himself languidly. 'And the Dwarf kingdom is below, in underground caves.'

'Mmph,' I deigned to respond. 'Let's move then.'

Ahanu began to pick his way up the cliff wall as if it were as simple as scaling a tree. 'The only time the Dragons go below the level of their eyries is for hunting fish in the sea below,' he remarked.

'They live off fish?' I asked curiously, getting over my annoyance despite myself. 'They aren't afraid of the water putting out their internal flame?'

Ahanu continued to pull himself upward with complete ease. 'Their fire is more for keeping their bodies warm in the air and water, or obviously for attack if needed. But,' he swung himself up another absurd distance. 'They really only resort to fire skirmishes when the challenge to leadership arises.'

'What happens then?' I questioned.

'They compete by strength of mind and body through a series of secret tests. The physical tests are enough to cause tidal waves all the way back at Margate, and enough to make these cliffs shake. I don't know about the secret mental tests. But all this only happens every two hundred years or so, when an old leader calls for challengers to replace her.'

'Her?'

Ahanu dangled from the alarming height for a moment as his feet wriggled into a crevice for a foothold. 'Oh yes, all Dragon leaders, fighters and officials are female. They really only keep the male Dragons to watch over hatchlings and to breed.'

The wayra made a nervous peeping sound and I peered upward. I could now vaguely make out dark, gaping cave entrances high above us, and something glittering from one cave mouth caught my eye. I couldn't decide on what it was.

'But fortunately for us,' Ahanu continued conversationally. 'The current Empress, Scandra, is in her prime.'

'Splendid,' I muttered as we drew near to the gaping cave arches above. 'Nothing to worry about.'

The wayra flew a little closer as we both saw how the massive rocky entrance mouths had been worn smooth after sliding movements from generations of powerful, scaly bodies. We could also now see that the glittery thing hanging from the largest entrance was in fact the end of a golden, spiny tail.

Scales as tough as boulders but as beautiful as polished discs lined the tail, and the mind boggled at the thought of the size of the creature attached to it.

'Here we are,' Ahanu beamed, taking a grip on the tail and using it to swing himself up into the cave.

The wayra nearly fell out of the air and I watched in agonised disbelief – waiting for a deafening roar of pain from beyond the shadows. Surely being used as a Giant's swing was nothing to scoff at, but to my utter relief the tail didn't even twitch.

'Their hibernation sure is deep,' Ahanu commented, dusting his hands with loud, echoing clapping noises while he peered about the eyrie speculatively. 'Come on One,' he waved casually over his shoulder, gesturing for me to waltz carelessly after him into the Dragon den.

Instead I turned to the wayra.

'There's no point in him getting the both of us roasted,' I whispered. 'It's time for you to be back in the open air.'

The Dragons were the mythical leaders of the skies, and I knew she was content to leave them in mystery.

'You've taught me how to handle long distances,' I reassured her. 'So if Ahanu blunders I'm sure I can get away.'

She made a frustrated noise, her eyes on the Giant as he moved further into the dim cavern beyond.

'Thank you for saving and teaching me my friend,' I told her, and she crooned gently, then circled me in a rush, tearing around me in farewell.

I waved as she broke away to fly back towards Margate, her purple and silvery colours disappearing among the clouds before I shifted my attention back to Ahanu's crunching footsteps.

I floated after him, cautiously entering what I found to be a colossal, high ceilinged cave – filled to the brim with humungous, sleeping forms.

Each golden creature was the length of four Giants. There were echoes of dreaming growls, and the sounds of spikes and claws shifting against the ground.

'Well,' Ahanu declared in his alarmingly unrestrained baritones. 'Time to wake them up.'

I gritted my teeth and slapped his arm, and he gave me an appraising look.

'I'd prefer to have them roused on my terms, not because of a lumbering Giant!' I hissed into his ear.

'Oh,' Ahanu chuckled jovially. 'No fear, they'll only wake when you stop reining in your magic. They won't bother for anything else, because they're pretty safe with their golden, scaly armour.'

He slapped at a nearby taloned leg to prove his point.

'Your size isn't enough to alarm them?' I asked sceptically.

Ahanu shrugged. 'Perhaps if there were lots of Giants and a heavy Giant scent, they would wake. But even then they would just torch us and roll over.'

'Well,' I grimaced. 'Which is Scandra?'

Ahanu scanned the room. Then he pointed out a magnificent, sleeping form in the distance.

Beyond the many sleeping bodies in the space between us, I hadn't at first noticed the upward dip of rock at the end of the cave. It was like a dais or a perch-like throne. But now I could hardly take my gaze from the sparkling form resting regally upon it – bigger than all the others even while half hidden as she curled around and behind the dais.

I followed Ahanu towards the Empress as he picked his way through the Dragons without any particular care, and soon I could properly see the exquisite beauty of her sharp, powerful features.

There were glinting spines on all of her joints, across her broad snout, and down her lustrous body to the tip of her monstrous tail.

'Go on,' Ahanu encouraged. 'Give them something worth waking for. Make them want to meet you.'

I nodded, contemplating what magical yet unthreatening deed I might do to seize their attention, and at last I remembered how the Lady had shared and communicated with me, when words would hardly suffice.

Then, stroking my tourmaline earthstone, I closed my eyes and began to form a stream of pictures in my mind. I focused on stringing together feelings and smells and sounds that I could remember. A vivid message for the golden beings in the room.

I concentrated on the wild, natural energy about the cavern. I pictured myself slowly drawing the power of the atmosphere in, making it part of myself to be channelled. And as I did I began to feel a warm prickling in my fingers, my nose, my ear tips, my wings.

Drawing a deep breath, I pictured opening all of my being to the magic. Every organ and every pore.

And I gasped with ecstasy as a sudden wave crashed through me. The atmosphere rippled and a piercing light shone from Toru's design on my wrist, while Ahanu was almost completely lost in a blue flare of brilliant illumination to my side.

Then Scandra's eyes opened.

Hundreds of brilliant, golden eyes opened.

But all traces of apprehension had left me, and I bowed to Scandra while my magic spread outward to roll over her scales in awesome torrents.

I saw her golden irises shrink and expand, and the cave was rumbling about us as I sent out my collection of melded memories.

All ending with the words 'I am the Summoner'.

20

Twenty

Noal

'I'm so sorry,' Maeve sobbed into my shoulder. 'I didn't want to worry or distract you,' Maeve said. 'But I had to enlist with Amarantha. I couldn't let you disappear when I'd only just found you.'

I held her tighter.

'Kerrin was afraid but she wanted to help too. And now she's ...'

I recalled that there had been two healers left in the cart. One had been impaled by an Evexus talon before being discarded.

I stroked Maeve's neck, and glanced towards Kerrin's body, now recognising her face, which even in the moonlight seemed faintly blue from the Evexus' chill.

Beyond Kerrin's body there were countless other dead, and I saw Lady Amarantha in the distance kneeling beside one of the wounded Jenrans who would soon be joining them.

'I have never been more horrified or glad to see you,' I told Maeve softly. 'But you are where you are needed, by me. And by your people.'

I felt her straighten to gaze up at me, and there was gratitude in her eyes as she nodded. 'I volunteered with Amarantha for many years, and have already learned much more as an apprentice healer on our travels so far.' Her face hardened. 'And I have much to offer right now.' She sniffed and pressed her hand to my neck with a frown. 'I could start by helping you. You're bleeding.'

I shook my head. There was a gash of some sort at the nape of my neck. 'I'm blessed compared to others. You're needed more elsewhere.'

Our eyes both shifted towards the limping, scratched, bruised, dented, and in some cases broken men of Krall stirring around us. I caught sight of a young Jenran page boy heading our way, and saw that he was missing some teeth and part of an ear.

'Yes,' Maeve agreed, pressing herself to me for a moment, and then stepping back as the page neared.

The boy made an effort to speak clearly through a bloody mouth. 'King Durna requests that, after visiting the healers, all leaders and council members meet in his tent. It will be raised soon.'

'I suggest you see the healers, too,' I told the boy with concern, and the page nodded.

Maeve and I shared one more look before she turned towards Kerrin's body. Then Maeve quickly drew her friend's hood up like a shroud, and left to join a growing gathering of recovered healers.

I turned my attention to my own comrades, seeing Thorin and Tane helping the Jenrans to upend a wagon. Nearer to me Wolf was stirring from where he was flopped dizzily on the ground, and most of the other battered and bloodied Krall warriors were rousing themselves.

I saw Lydon, Roth, Gideon and Rendor moving with ashen faces toward where we had last seen Aiolos. Vulcan and Thale were staggering off to help gather the contents of another cart that had been spilt.

'Thale?' I caught up to the Krall leader, knowing I still had some time before Dalin and I were required. 'I am going to find a place to bury Kerrin.'

Thale nodded, his gaze flickering back to the now covered Jenran maid. And then his eyes shifted to where the bodies of Jenran soldiers were already being collected and lined along a clear part of the path ahead.

'Would you bring Aiolos to be buried in his own place too?' I asked.

Moved, Thale took a deep breath. 'It would be an honour well deserved for Aiolos to be buried by his comrades and the true princes we now serve,' he answered gruffly.

'I saw a small clearing just past the trees,' Nikon grunted from near us, wincing as Purdor managed to help him pry his severely dented chest plate off.

'I can still find it in the dark,' he added, moving his right arm about and holding his bruised ribs.

I nodded, and returned to lift Kerrin's form, trying not to think about the terrible chill that seemed to radiate from her.

And soon we were assembled, our sombre group each taking turns to dig the two graves and to collect rocks to create safe covers for them.

Ferron took the time to mark a stone with the Krall sign of resistance, a rune of fire, for Aiolos' grave, and after asking one of the Jenran healers what the sign of a celebrated healer was, he carved the rune of a 'healing hand' into a rock for Kerrin.

We were all still quiet and glassy eyed when our group was assigned a healer shelter later.

I had no energy to be surprised or dismayed at the Elf-like healing I received, as the healer set about stitching the wound at the nape of my neck, neatly pulling my split skin back together. Instead I numbly patted the Granx, seated anxiously on my knee.

She had continuously tried to prick her way out of my pocket during the fighting, but I had pushed her back safely each time, only allowing her out now when all was quiet.

Dalin was also at my side, watching grimly as Wolf and Phobos were attended to across from me – Wolf having his head bound, and Phobos having his dislocated shoulder manoeuvred back into position.

'Aiolos would be proud,' Lydon broke his silence as my healer tied the final knot against the skin at the bottom of my neck.

'He tasted freedom, and died a warrior's death in a fight he actually believed in.'

Phrixus leaned forward and clasped Lydon's arm while in the middle of having an abrasion across his own cheek and forehead scrubbed. 'It is the best any of us can hope for.'

Thorin poked his head around the tent door, not missing a beat as Phobos' shoulder crunched back into place. 'I've had word that King Durna is ready,' he told us.

And Thorin, Tane and Cadell, who were slightly less battered and bruised than the rest, rose to accompany Dalin and I to meet the serious crowd at Durna's tent.

Despite my exhaustion, I was again fascinated to see the five Awyalknian archers with Aeron, already using *Aolen* that they must have unconsciously picked up from the Jenrans.

'It seems this was a search rather than full scale attack,' Durna began as we joined them. And then we all made our disheartening reports on how hopeless our defences had been against even a simple search.

'It is a relief to have at least one positive and improbable event to discuss,' King Durna concluded at last, and all eyes turned admiringly to the archers.

'King Durna,' Dalin stood forward to quickly vouch for them. 'I want to inform you that Awyalkna is privileged to have highly skilled and renowned archery teams. And it seems we have somehow gained the help of one such team,'

Dalin turned to the archers. 'Though I have not formally met you,' Dalin said to their leader, 'I am relieved to see you. Your team are an invaluable asset.'

There was a murmur of interest at that, and King Durna managed a slight smile. 'We welcome you,' he said. 'We have left many of our best archers in Jenra to defend the people from Griffin attacks while the army is away. Perhaps you could observe and advise some of our general archers.'

The lead Awyalknian archer bowed to Durna, Dalin and I. 'Your Majesties, I am Dren. My team and I wish to have found you under better circumstances. Though we were surprised to have found you so soon at all. You must have covered mighty distances to be as far along the trail as you are — when we expected you to still be crossing the mountains.'

Durna did not mention the golden Unicorn horn's help, and Dren continued speaking.

'We have in fact travelled from the Awyalknian palace with the sole intention of aiding our princes and their allies. Queen Aglaia herself sent me in search of her sons, once the palace was fortified against more Dragon attacks.'

I saw faces blanch at the mention of Dragons, but Dalin nodded gratefully, and Thorin and the other Krall warriors clasped the arms of our new archer comrades respectfully when the meeting was done.

Despite everything, I felt somewhat heartened as we left the King's tent together. Until I noticed a small, wretched figure in a brown, monk-like robe watching us.

Agrudek — shivering and wearing a haunted, stricken expression.

I shook my head and moved on.

21

Twenty One

The Witch

Her claws bit deeply into her perch on, scarring the clean bark as her beady raven eyes viewed the Jenran army.

The Evexus were crouched nimbly in the surrounding trees, balancing like acrobats from a warped travelling circus.

She and the Evexus now knew that the Fairy was not with the army. And the Witch was becoming convinced that Kiana would have only left the princes ... to instead seek out Agrona's own Sorcerer.

The Fairy had to be planning to poison Agrona's master further with the inexplicable, lustful weakness that had crept over him ever since Kiana's magic had been revealed. He might be blinded enough to give up their war. Or to give up his Witch entirely.

The devious One was after Darziates and he needed to be saved.

To do that, Agrona required information. She had to know where to hunt for the Fairy.

She would need one of the Fairy's beloved princes.

22

Twenty Two

N*oal*

We rode near to Maeve's healer cart as the army limped back out on the march, and as the archers and Krall soldiers began forging a strong friendship.

'The Raiden and Noal are hard to guard,' Phrixus was cautioning the archer called Glyn.

'Noal carries a deadly Granx in his pocket,' Tane supplied as an example, and the archer named Ander shot a sideways glance at me.

'Do both princes always make such poor choices?' he asked.

'The Granx wouldn't harm a fly,' I defended her as she wriggled against my chest.

'Actually, I'm pretty sure a spider's diet consists almost entirely of flies,' Tane informed me.

'Yet in spite of their oddities, we free men of Krall have pledged an oath of allegiance to the princes and Kiana,' Wolf told the archers, shrugging.

'And it appears that you take your oath quite seriously,' Dren remarked, eyeing the bandages around Wolf's head. 'We will take our duty just as seriously.'

A grizzly smile spread under Thale's beard. 'Then we shall heartily enjoy fighting beside five more men of Awyalkna.'

'All the more to protect us weaklings,' Dalin agreed. 'Seeing as us two princelings are just delicate flowers.'

'Exactly,' Tane nodded, his curls bouncing. Then he uncorked his flask threateningly. 'In fact, you look droopy right now! Care for some watering?'

I laughed, and stretched in the saddle as the morning drew on and they talked. I felt the Granx mimic my movement from within my pocket, stretching her long legs luxuriously against my chest and I grinned, patting my tunic pocket gently.

It had become a little cool, but the sun was still high and our spirits were up. So we were all taken completely by surprise at the sudden reappearance of the five Evexus.

They raked their way through the army lines like arrow heads, running straight for Dalin and I.

'Frarshk!' I heard Thorin cry before Tane was thrown out of the way, Phrixus was hurled into a tree, Ferron went down cold, and the nicks that their curved blades had made in the beasts' skins were already sealing back up.

The Evexus bowled through Phobos, Cadell and Wolf. Purdor and Vulcan were forced to leap out of the way of viciously slicing claws.

Awyalknian arrows were fired and Jenrans rushed forward with nets and ropes as the nearest beasts skidded towards Dalin, their snatching talons meeting his and my own fending swords.

A spiked fist pounded towards Dalin and I pulled him out of the way.

There was a blur of human bodies, jabbing blades, and writhing, chilled arms before a startling knock to the wound at the back of my neck sent me sprawling to my knees with stars in my eyes.

Then a breathtakingly tight hold wrapped about my waist and bursts of cold lanced through my body.

Ice spread from my core and made even my blood ache so that it felt as though my veins would shatter.

I wheezed as I was ripped upwards to be held at the Evexus' great height.

I vaguely noticed Dren and Glyn firing arrows into the beast, but it didn't seem to be troubled.

I heard the screams of a woman, along with the shouts of Dalin and the men below as they rushed desperately at the Evexus. But I was half unconscious already and I felt my body jerk while the beast pounced, launching us both up into the trees.

Branches and leaves blurred by as the Evexus travelled at lightning speed, and then my mind shut down completely.

23

Twenty Three

K*iana*

There was uproar as the last of my projected memories died away. The cave echoed with massive bodies shifting and deafening voices all mingling in confusion. Bursts of flame even erupted from a group of smaller Dragons, all shouting fearfully.

But the din was immediately cut off when a mighty roar nearly blew me out of the air and Scandra cast a piercing glare about herself.

The silence was sudden and total, and Scandra turned her great, jewelled head back to me.

I didn't waver.

'I am the last *Larnaeradee* and Summoner,' I announced, lacing my *Aolen* with magic and sending it around the cavern. 'I have come to ask for the Dragons to ally with all other races against the one true threat to the world as it enters the tenth age. The threat of Darziates.'

I saw Scandra's sharp pupils widen and narrow.

Then, in a low, surprisingly human voice that issued around the tensely suspended cavern, she asked: 'You wish us to trust you? To join you?'

Scandra's golden lips drew back in a curling sneer.

'The Witch Agrona has powers such as yours. Powers to shape minds and to ensnare. We have already lost too many of our kin to her, a flying intruder of the outside world – just like you.'

There were furious growls that rattled the rocky walls, and Scandra's scales almost seemed to glow with the dangerous fire that was surely building inside of her, but I only rose higher; emboldened.

'I speak to you in the ancient and unifying tongue of the *Larnaeradee*. Sharing knowledge and trust in allowing you to understand *Aolen*, as only a *Larnaeradee* Summoner can. I show pure magic, and friendship. Do not be blinded by suspicion. Open yourself to be able to feel the truth. Purity knows purity. We should feel this in each other.'

'I feel that your cause is not our cause. You are unwelcome here, trespassers.'

A hint of steel crept into my own voice and posture.

'I came to Eirian to find a race that I had heard to be the fiercest of all,' I said. 'A race that I had hoped would be willing to face a threat to us all. Yet if you wish it, I will leave you to cower, in wait of death.'

The temperature in the cavern was rising and plumes of heat danced in the air – the strain radiating from the Dragons becoming increasingly obvious.

I realised that my own magic was swirling agitatedly around me, as if my passion had taken on a tangible life of its own.

'Leave, stranger,' Scandra breathed. 'And quickly. Or you will find yourself tested against my strength.'

My heart leapt as I remembered Ahanu's words about the Dragons and their secret challenges.

'Test me,' I answered. 'I will prove myself, the purity of my magic, and my cause.'

'A test!' hundreds of strange, deep voices growled around the cavern, hissing and snarling.

'You *want* a test?' Scandra snarled. Grey smoke wisped from her nostrils as they flared in preparation.

My eyes did not leave hers. 'I am ready, and I am unafraid.'

She had been so poised and so unmoveable that though I had expected her sudden violence, it was still one of the most terrifying things I had ever seen.

There was a quick flash of massive teeth and, with a bellowing roar that made the entire cliff shake, she released a plume of red hot flames.

Immediately the silvery light that had been swirling about me solidified as I raised my arms in defence. I was instantly encased in an orb so bright that the flames paled in comparison, pouring around me harmlessly like water running around a stone.

The heat and sound of the roaring fire was intense while I remained untouched, and I also heard Ahanu laughing incredulously below. It appeared that I had unconsciously sent a protective shield of glowing silver to cover the jubilant Giant too.

At last, Scandra's furious onslaught was over, and the fire erupting from her jaws – which had almost turned her golden scales lava red, eased away.

I allowed my pure magic to fade to a thin protective veil, shimmering just within sight while Scandra's eyes fixed on me, evaluating.

Ahanu crowed in delight. 'You know none could have survived such pure magic, without purity of equal or greater strength to withstand it!'

'The Summoner?' Scandra's withering voice took on a softer, more thoughtful tone as she recalled the memories and prophecies I had sent out.

'I do not wish to ensnare or even lead your kind. No one race or leader can take charge of our cause – as all races must unify and co-operate. Our quest needs your help and in turn our quest is the best hope you've got. If we fall, so shall you all.'

There was a moment of suspenseful silence as my words hung in the air and Scandra regarded me closely.

'Calm the storm in your eyes,' she at last replied, smoke tendrils slowly playing about her teeth and nostrils.

Then she began to rise.

The rocky dais she had rested on crumbled at the edges and groaned as she rose to her full, glorious height and towered over us magnificently.

'My kin, you must prematurely stretch your wings. Venture out, soak in the last of the warm sun, and feast. For it seems that the Summoner and I may have some things to discuss.'

One after another, massive bodies rose and golden wings with glimmering scales along bony joints were stretched.

'One,' Scandra said. 'Let us talk.'

24

Twenty Four

D^{*alin*}

A blow across my forehead and explosive visions of red made me think my skull had been crushed inwards. My brain was pounding and I felt a moment of blind panic as screams rang in my ears.

When my sight returned and slowly matched back up with those surrounding sounds I tried to stand, but my knees crunched back into the dirt as my head swirled dizzily and my stomach lurched.

There were Jenran and Krall boots stepping everywhere, kicking up dirt. Flashing sabres and pike blades, and fists at my eye level.

And then I saw Noal's legs flying past my face as he was torn away from the fight. I heard the intake of breath that was all he had time for.

I pitched myself up unsteadily, reeling as Dren's arrows whistled near my ears.

Men surrounded me in case I was to be taken too, and they bravely swamped the Evexus holding Noal. But, with a lurch, the Evexus sprang away and Noal was gone.

I cried out at the same time that a woman's voice cried out with a tearing sound of grief.

'No – Maeve!' I whirled blearily as I saw her somehow sprint through the crowd and launch herself fiercely at one of the Evexus.

The ghoulish figure was un-concerned and it caught her effortlessly, snatching her thoughtlessly from the air even as she sprang. And in a heartbeat she had been swept away too, screaming into the trees.

The stillness and disbelief that gripped the army was overwhelming compared to the struggle and onslaught that had just taken place, and the eyes of every soldier felt as if they were fixed on me. The one remaining quester in their midst.

'Noal ...' I gasped as Thorin came closer to grip my arms before I sagged.

The burning wetness above my eyebrows, beneath my hair line, told me that something was wrong where I'd been dealt a blow. But all at once the gravity of my loss, and the stunning agony of my forehead compounded, and I lost awareness.

It was not until some time later that I woke with a throbbing headache and a sickening taste in my mouth – opening my eyes to find a tent roof above me, rippling with a breeze, and Thorin, Thale and Vulcan by my side.

I could hear the archers talking outside and registered that night had descended.

Thorin lifted his water flask in offering, but I was already struggling to sit up.

'Take it slow,' Thale admonished. 'Healers said your skull could have caved in if you'd been hit any harder. We're lucky you're still coherent.'

'You have a dent in your head,' Vulcan added.

I grunted, swinging my legs over the side of the cot and gripping its edges until the dirt floor stopped spinning and I could slip forward to stand.

'Thanks friend,' I muttered as Vulcan steadied me, but then I made my own way out of the tent.

'Raiden!' I heard Ander exclaim in surprise as I passed the archers and crossed to where I could see Aeron, Durna and a couple of council members still talking in the King's tent.

'Highness, Warlord, members,' I announced myself as coherently as I could.

'Raiden,' King Durna greeted me carefully in return.

My head was excruciatingly heavy and sluggish, but I looked directly at the King.

'When the march resumes tomorrow, I will lead one of two groups of Krall men and any willing Jenrans to search for my brother and the healer Maeve.'

'It is acceptable,' Durna agreed. 'We know the maps and will continue on our trail.'

'I am not abandoning my duties here,' I assured them. 'And I swear that I am not wavering in my quest. But I must try.'

'If it were my brother, I would search for him for as long as I could,' Durna assured me. 'Noal could escape or be found. There may be time.'

Aeron was grim and doubtful. 'You must be extremely cautious,' he said. 'The Three are important to the prophecies, and it is dangerous to risk the only member we have left with us.'

I nodded slightly, making my head fill with explosive regret, and then turned to stumble back to Vulcan, Thale and Thorin.

Thorin subtly put a hand at my elbow to keep me upright while we moved to join the rest of the warriors and archers.

'Raiden,' I heard Thale say as I staggered my way over to lean against a tree trunk by the trail. 'We will be by your side in this search.'

And I saw that, despite their own grief and doubt, all of my friends were determined to support me.

I slid down the trunk of the tree, staring and clenching my hands to stop them from shaking.

Phrixus and Ferron quietly reassured different Jenran soldiers that I was alright when they approached to ask, and Thorin, Tane and Thale stood around me to stop anyone from getting too close.

I squeezed my eyes shut until they burned with the tightness and I could hear the blood rushing in my ears. The broken, bruised skin across my forehead stretched and throbbed. And I prayed to the Gods for a miracle.

25

Twenty Five

K*iana*

Glittering reflections of light sparkled like stars upon the rocky walls as Scandra unfurled her incredible wingspan. The golden talons scratching into her dais were each proportionate in size to one of my legs.

'I wish to know more of you,' Scandra told me appraisingly. 'Perhaps if we reach deep and see far, we will find that you and I are the same in nature.'

I considered her for a moment, and then I nodded, at last allowing myself to relax slightly.

As Scandra began to descend I was struck by how almost feline her movements were. Her feet were weighty, but she lithely coiled her way downward, her tail sweeping elegantly behind.

'I am Empress,' Scandra reflected in her deep voice. 'So it is obvious that in my nature I am conniving. I am mean.

Clever. Brutal. Strong. And I am loving and compassionate. I feel that you may be similar.'

I wryly reflected on how she had been willing to obliterate me and how I had been willing to test her. Both of us completely committed to our cause.

'I am honoured that you see a likeness between us,' I replied tactfully as she moved to a place where Ahanu and I could sit on high rocks at her eye level.

'Yes. I see it,' Scandra remarked. 'Because seeing the truth and reaching a deep understanding is something that female Dargons, and particularly the Dargon Empress, are skilled at.'

'Dargon?' I questioned her with a frown.

'Mortal records are imperfect, and other long lived races do not use the correct terminology,' she said scathingly in answer. 'Our true name is Dargon. In our tongue that name means foresight and truth, while 'Dragon' means violence. A title only fit for those stolen and warped by the Sorcerer.'

She drew closer so that she filled my vision and I was ensconced in a scent of incense-like smoke and ash. Her eyes held mine, her pupils like golden flames, and I felt suddenly that I could become lost in them.

'If you look deeply into a she-Dargon's eyes, and if we focus solely on you, you will see everything there is to know about yourself. It is a dangerous and wondrous thing. Some cannot handle it.'

'The Elders never mentioned that,' Ahanu chimed in. 'Unless it slipped my mind.'

'It is our final, and greatest test before an Empress transfers power,' Scandra went on, as if Ahanu was not there. 'If the Dargon candidate stares into the eyes of the current Empress, and is found to be lacking, they do not just lose the chance of leading. They lose themselves to the shock of that truth.'

I shivered. 'I am humbled that you share this with me. And I fear that I would not handle such insight,' I confessed. 'I am still learning about myself.'

Scandra's voice was like velvet when she replied. 'You are wise to be cautious. Your memories did suggest that you have been on a profound journey, even beyond your physical travels.'

I nodded. 'I have progressed inwardly, as much as I have on my travels across the lands and seas.'

'And now,' Scandra's warm, musky breath heated my arms and cheeks. 'The last *Larnaeradee* wants for the worldly part of her journey to become ours.'

'Yes. I want you to trust me, and to see that your survival depends on joining my journey.'

'It is much to ask,' Scandra stated flatly. 'Very much indeed.'

I shrugged. 'It would be just as much if you asked the rest of the world to fight on your behalf, if you were to contribute nothing.'

There was a rush of smoke as the Empress of the Dargons released a deafening snort of dark mirth.

I couldn't help but quirk a slight smile in response.

'Well, I have heard your scoldings. And I understand your wise reservations on the matter, but will you take a leap of faith to convince me?' Scandra questioned. 'Will you look into my eyes so I can see you and your journey in full? It will be like your own kind of test, though I will not push you beyond what truths you are able to share.'

'So a test of trust rather than ability this time,' I surmised. 'I must trust myself to you.'

I had allowed Toru and the Lady to see me through a magical connection, but Dargon sight seemed to offer something riskier – stripping away all guards. It was hard not to be mesmerised by Scandra's gaze without her even trying to draw me in.

'It is only fair that you put your faith in me. For I have known you for but a moment, and may have to leave for war with you before another day passes,' Scandra reminded me – the golden scales along her snout inches from my nose now.

'However I swear I will not look into your spirit for your truth, but rather into your mind to come to my own conclusions. I will protect you.'

I took a breath.

'Trust.' I uttered and lifted my hands up to rest on her nose – looking into those penetrating eyes and at once feeling drawn in.

Something within me, something different to my physical body, was pulling toward Scandra and I felt her presence in return reach back, gently nudging me away from getting too near to the vastness of her own mind. I let her turn me towards my own internal self. And I became aware of a vision of colours – all spiralling into a representation of who I was.

Scandra's presence seemed to cradle my own as we watched my childhood and then my terrible losses together. She held me as we both felt ourselves racked by grief, before the girl I had been became hard and guarded to survive it.

It was the first time I had seen it all as though through the eyes of another, with objectivity. It was also the first time that I felt glad for the vulnerable girl, instead of disgusted by her – knowing that one day she would break free of the suffering and trials to become something more.

And through it all, as though Scandra was not so much bigger than I, and as though we had known and loved each other for years, our spirits stayed close. It felt as if I stood hand in hand with an intimate friend.

She saw my failures and triumphs – individual puzzle pieces joining to create a greater whole. I was not embarrassed as she watched my most vicious moments on the hunt, or as she saw my tenderness towards my princes. And I felt Scandra's own joy as we both revelled in the moment when I first found my magic in the forest.

I was laid bare before her, and I was thankful. Because I was also laid bare before myself. And when we began to fall deeper than surface memories I felt Scandra pulling away to allow the comforting and normal boundaries of my mind to return.

When my vision cleared again, I saw my sharpened features and wild eyes reflected in Scandra's until my hands slowly came down to rest in my lap.

'You have honoured me,' Scandra spoke at last.

'The honour would be to someday explore my own spirit further, and to pass the real test,' I answered, feeling like it had been some time since I had last used my vocal chords.

Scandra bowed her head, making a musical humming sound in her throat. 'Through your trust I have been moved. And I have seen that I have hardened my heart to other pain in this world. I have become absorbed by the Dargon's own plight and their safety, discounting threats to any other race. However I must admit that the Sorcerer has proven we are already his targets, and I must see that any threat is one against us all.'

Grey wisps of smoke coiled in thin tendrils around us as she spoke.

'This is a hard choice to make, as apart from the hundred stolen from us, plucked from the air by Darziates, only four hundred and twenty-five other Dargons are left. Twenty four of which are children.'

Her gaze shifted momentarily to the cavern mouth, drinking in the glorious sight of the golden Dargons gracefully navigating the air outside, each of them glimmering like riches of the Gods under the sun.

'And yet, Summoner,' she went on. 'I will pledge two hundred of the female warrior Dargons to you. Aside from that, the rest of our flock will stay here to keep our race alive.'

My heart was thumping. 'I am grateful to have your sisters join our quest,' I said, feeling the gravity of her words.

'Though, perhaps just one hundred and fifty Dargons would be enough to journey to Krall.'

'Why only one hundred and fifty to go to Krall?' Her sharp tongue whisked about her even sharper teeth.

'Fifty could come to the Awyalknian Jewel with me,' I answered. 'Darziates has been using your imprisoned kin to assault the palace, and if the Sorcerer ever orders more than an assault, I don't believe the Awyalknians will survive.'

'They won't,' Scandra agreed. 'They will need aid.'

I peered closely at Scandra's ornate face. 'So, we are allies?' I asked, and a massive bout of air swelled out of her, blowing my hair about as she sighed.

'We are allies.'

The spines along her head were like a regal crown shining in the warm light.

'It is time for my kind to journey back out into the wide open skies. And whether it brings evil or good fortune upon our dwindling race, we will fight at your side. By tooth, claw and flame.'

26

Twenty Six

Noal

A hard floor was grinding into my cheekbone and the tight, hot throbbing at the back of my neck told me that some stitches had burst.

I squinted up at where orange sunlight filtered like strips of fire down through a barred window. And with an effort I manoeuvred my cuffed hands out from under myself and slowly sat up.

My mouth was dry and my body was covered in a sheen of sweat from what could only be Krall's unnatural heat, yet when I gingerly lifted my shirt I saw lingering bruises of cold from the Evexus.

I was lucky that icy marks were all I had for now, and I let the shirt fall back down, rubbing a shaking hand over my eyes until I became aware of a sound beyond my own cell.

Straining to listen, I realised that I was hearing the faint sobs of another prisoner and I made the effort to stand. With shackled hands out for balance, I shambled to the heavy door, which had a second barred window for the jailor to see into the cell.

I wrapped my hands around the bars, peering into the dim prison hallway.

'Hello there,' I called softly, and the crying stopped.

I heard quick footsteps and two small, unshackled hands came out of the darkness to grip the bars in the door across from mine. Then a round, pale face framed with golden hair peered out at me and my heart sank.

'Are you hurt Noal?' Maeve asked me worriedly.

Where before there had been nausea, now pure dread dropped like a weighted stone to the base of my gut.

Had Agrona's spying shown her my attachment to Maeve? Had the Witch purposefully snatched her?

'How are you here?' I choked out. 'Are *you* hurt?'

Her face was smudged with dirt and tears. 'No, I'm fine. I just got in the way of an Evexus and it took me along without thinking.' Her voice wavered.

'Gods,' I husked. 'We are in quite a spot of bother, aren't we?'

'Yes,' she agreed shakily. 'I've checked. They make their prison doors very well.'

I felt at my pocket and was glad that at least the Granx had fallen out or escaped.

'I wish I could comfort you,' I told her dismally. 'Or even better, I wish that you were miles away with the army. Actually, back in the mountains.'

'I would not wish for you to be here alone,' she told me sadly. But before I could reply we both stopped short, recoiling as the sound of voices came from beyond the dim corridor of cells.

I could make out a fearful male voice that probably belonged to a village jailor, and a second silken female voice that was the stuff of nightmares.

'Maeve,' I whispered. 'Pretend to be in a faint. Do not draw attention, or seem valuable or threatening. No matter what you hear, do not make a sound. They cannot know that I care for you or you for me.'

She forced her wide eyes to my face, away from the heavy door at the end of the passage.

'Promise me,' I said deliberately, and I could see the dread for us both in her eyes. 'Please?'

Tears made trails down her cheeks, but she nodded.

'Go,' I told her. 'I am determined that not a single useful word will pass my lips while the Witch is here. But I will try to talk to you when Agrona leaves.'

And even as the door at the end of the corridor opened, I watched Maeve disappear before I quickly slumped down against the wall.

Footsteps drew near, as though grim fate approached, and my breath came rapidly; my body tensing when keys rattled at my door. But despite a vile worm of fear twisting within me, I did not look away from the Witch when the door opened.

She was of course devastatingly, breathtakingly, inhumanly beautiful. Raven hair poured down her pale shoulders – darker even than the blackness of her garb. But her eyes were soulless, and her painted lips smiled with malice.

'Well met once again, young princeling.'

She let her words drop like poison, and it took me a dazed moment to process that she spoke in crude Awyalknian. She knew nothing yet of *Aolen*, if such a foul one could learn it.

'Please, be my guest. Have a seat.'

I gasped as I suddenly lurched upward and forward, pulled by a fist of magic, to land in a high backed chair that had flashed into existence in the middle of my cell. My shackled wrists were now fastened to the long arms of the chair.

'Where are your manners?' she purred. 'Not a word of greeting, though we have not met in so long?'

My chest was heaving while the sweat of panic trickled down my brow – my mind still catching up with my body's surprise journey.

Breathe. Just breathe.

'I did not miss you.' I forced out some Awyalknian for the first time in months, squinting up as her black lips curled.

She took a step toward me, and my skin crawled as she drew her face close. She reached out to cup my cheek and I cringed at the darkness of her touch.

'You may not have,' she said. 'But I value your company nevertheless.'

Her breath brushed against my lips and she leaned in as if she might kiss me. Her dark hair brushed against my skin and even that left a stinging sensation.

'I need you to tell me where the One is,' she said. 'The One that I have always really been after.'

I swallowed. She wished simply to find and destroy the last *Larnaeradee*.

For a sickening moment I wondered if it was because Darziates and Agrona had somehow found out that Kiana was fulfilling the second, secret prophecy and Summoning the magical races. Afterall, how did she even know the title – 'One' – to begin with?

'I have no idea where the One is,' I said stiffly. 'We had a falling out. She flew away.'

Agrona let her fingers lightly lift my chin, tracing shock-waves of agony there.

'Protect *yourself*. Don't protect her,' Agrona advised. 'Tell me where the One has gone.'

I paused. 'I've forgotten. May I leave now?'

My stomach was scrunching with inner regret, knowing that petulant remarks were going to have a price. But perhaps if I enraged Agrona she might end things quickly.

The thin corners of her dark lips rose, and my heart fluttered. I tried to sit still and straight backed.

'You could save yourself damage,' she warned. 'But it's all the same to me. As long as I get the Fairy.'

My heart was racing so much that I felt like I was going to throw it up. I felt like every pulse point in my body was going to explode.

'So ...' I swallowed. 'I guess I'm going to get damaged.'

'It was your choice.'

And in a red flash a large green bottle appeared in Agrona's bony hands.

I gulped, feeling as though I was choking on my vocal chords.

'We'll start easy,' she told me, showing me the bottle and its swishing green liquid. 'While impermanent, one sip of this every few hours will ensure that any slight discomfort you feel will be amplified. It is very effective. Especially when *my* magic is causing the discomfort, and the last thing you want is for it to last longer.'

She put her long fingers across my forehead and pushed my head back. I felt the burst stitches prickle at the crinkles in my neck, but I refused to open my mouth to cry out against the wrongness of her touch.

'Now open up,' she crooned. 'Or I will make you.'

I kept my jaw locked tight – even as I felt her fingers press harder into my skull, and as my vision suddenly filled with red sand.

I blinked frantically, but red, burning grains blinded me, scratching under my eyelids. Then the heat surged in my ears and they were filling up; thick sand granules pouring into each ear canal. My nostrils became blocked, the sand piling through the passages and into my throat. My wrists strained at their binds, scrabbling to get to my throat and eyes as I gagged on the dry grit, choking on my tongue and fighting to draw air in.

And instantly my hearing and sight cleared, the sand disappeared, and the Witch forced the green liquid past my lips to bubble down my throat.

I immediately grew still, winded. Stunned.

'Ahh. There,' the Witch uttered. 'You feel it already.'

I remained frozen. For I had somehow become acutely aware of the pressure on my lungs to simply breathe. My eyelids felt weighted. Each root of my hair and every eyelash felt too heavy a burden to bear. The back of my neck felt like fire.

'It hurts all over, doesn't it?' Agrona purred while I gaped. 'Even using your muscles to sit up must be intolerable, for you are feeling every bit of your mortality.'

And then she pulled a glistening knife from the air behind her head.

With quick precision she made a shallow slit across my collar bone and I screamed and writhed with torment. My head and torso arched backward, driving into the high backed chair with a pain that seemed to lance through every particle of my being.

It seemed as if the steel, already having vanished back to nothingness, was still carving into my flesh. Slashing and digging deeper with a thousand strokes, gouging out rivets and chunks of me, down to the bone.

When I realised I could smell my own charred flesh I craned to look down at the single thin slice, and found that the wound steamed as though acid burned beneath the raw surface.

'The liquid absorbs rapidly into your veins and into every layer of skin,' Agrona explained while I watched only a small flow of blood spilling onto my shirt. It felt as if gallons were gushing out.

'It will seem like knives are sawing through your bones for quite some time. Unless you utter the words that might warrant some relief.'

'I don't –' I tried not to retch. 'Feel up to talking.'

Her black eyes glittered. 'A shame.'

She rested her fingers gently over mine, and now her menacing touch was enough to make me cry out.

'I want you to imagine me doing this to your sword hand next,' she said in a silky voice. Her grip around my digits tightened, and she used her other hand to select just my captive little finger. 'What use would you be if you couldn't fight?'

Then she made a quick wrenching movement and the cracking sound and massive explosion of hurt sent me roaring and jerking as if a blacksmith's hammer was mashing my finger into an anvil. I felt the poison heating up inside me, rushing to the area of pain, making it worse and worse. Filling me with a swelling, boiling, radiating horror.

'Settle ... settle,' she whispered, her face close. 'That was just a sprain. Won't you end your torture and tell me where the One is?'

Even as I spasmed uncontrollably, I was still dimly aware that if I talked to Agrona, Maeve and I would still never be free. My heart wrenched at the thought of what Maeve was hearing.

'Ever ... heard that joke?' I gasped. 'Pull my finger? Do it again and I might just have a surprise for you.'

This time a real cloud of anger crossed the Witch's face. I could almost see the red magic stirring in her eyes – the same red magic that had cut off my air and sight before. And, with a snarl, she took an iron grip around my other three fingers. Then with the power of ten men in her bony hand, she dislocated each of them.

I jolted in fits with every click out of place. But this time I smiled through the blinding agony. Because, at the same moment that she'd twisted, I'd thrown up everywhere. And I was proudly aware that I had spattered most of it on her.

'Surprise,' I muttered weakly.

She made a wrathful slice with her hand through the air and the contents of my stomach disappeared from her dress and the cell floor. Then she aimed a clobbering blow into the side of my head, making my eyes roll back.

I hoped for oblivion but her hand gripped my face again and I had the awful, skull scraping sense of her rotten magic pulling me away from unconsciousness. And when she was sure that I was watching her pale, mask-like face, she put her hand over my ruined fingers and squeezed.

I felt as if I'd stopped existing for a few moments while the pain washed by in waves of awful suffering. But a part of my retreated mind could still hear my voice yelling and rasping without control.

'Perhaps your heart cannot withstand so much,' I heard her voice as if we were under water. Her awful hand loosened my shirt and pressed against my chest. 'Such a young, smooth chest,' she crooned. 'But that youthful heart is stuttering.'

'Don't hold back,' I groaned. 'Do what you like. I'll never tell you a thing.'

'Oh, how you hurt me,' she said sinisterly. 'Right here.'

She shoved her hand against my sternum, shocking me with a bolt of crimson lightning.

'I am very upset,' she sneered, and hurled her fist into my chest repeatedly, pelting more red magic into me with each shove.

My whole body bounced with the force of the charges. Lightning was dancing through my lungs and rebounding off my ribs while my heart was shuddering and stuttering for life. My eyes were wide and my mouth gaped as I helplessly felt it palpitate and pause.

And then when I was on the edge of nothingness I felt the chair disappear, felt myself clatter to the floor, and felt the chains reappear between my shackles.

It was all just more amplified pain.

'Sleep, if you must,' I heard her, and I felt her stoop close and grip my head. 'But you'll dream on my terms.'

27

Twenty Seven

It was early as Aglaia walked to Wilmont's office, and Friendly muffled a yawn when he thought she wasn't looking. She was tired herself after having spent hours with General Sumantra, supervising a reconstruction and repair group as it finished clearing rubble from the last Dragon attack.

Since the Nymph Asha's help, the last few surprise attacks had not been as bad and the Dragons that came had kept their distance from key areas and what they sensed were traps with Nymph magic on them.

But no amount of good fortune made visiting Wilmont seem more appealing, and Aglaia twisted her golden ring around her finger darkly. Frowning as she got to Wilmont's closed office door, she nodded to the steward there, who readied to knock.

Completely unaware in his office, Wilmont – who had consciously never overworked himself in his life, was greedily consuming a sugared, cream filled bun that he had demanded from a serving girl.

He'd been insulted that it was assumed he would go along with all of the other nobles and follow the same rationing system as every peasant and servant in the palace. He hadn't clawed and manipulated and lied his way up to such a comfortable position just to spy on his country's leaders and make the lives of their brats miserable. He felt entitled to the comforts that came with status too.

The serving girl, who was now cleaning his office, was also furtively and hungrily glancing at the delicious bun. And he was just taking another big, obvious bite when the knock sounded at his office door.

'Enter,' he said imperiously, with his mouth full, chewing slowly as the door opened and the steward announced the intruder.

'Her Majesty, Queen Aglaia.'

Wilmont choked on a sticky raisin and hurriedly scoffed the rest of the bun down, hiding the sugary plate in his desk drawer and quickly flicking a creamy crumb from his ringlets as he stood.

He was wiping his mouth with a frilled handkerchief when the Queen and her lapdog guard entered.

'Majesty,' Wilmont simpered with a bow. 'Surely you did not have to come all the way to my lowly office to see me yourself ...' he had some raisin stuck in his throat and coughed delicately into his frills. 'As your faithful servant I would gladly have come whenever you bade me.'

He knew she had come for a list of food and weaponry stocks that he was required to write up as part of his extra wartime duties, and he could have taken the initiative to go to her himself. But he really hadn't been bothered to make the expedition.

'Are your lists finished, Wilmont?' she asked. The parchments in her hands suggested she had already collected other reports on reconstruction efforts and numbers of wounded from various officials who were just as dedicated as herself.

'Of course, of course, Your Majesty,' he answered, glad that he had earlier signed the official papers that his page boy had written up for him. 'I have gone over them meticulously.'

He fished around in his desk again, careful not to brush the documents through the sugar and cream smeared plate.

'I thank you then,' she replied tersely as he handed them to her and bowed over her hand.

And he maintained his smile until both the Queen and her glowering 'Friendly' had gone off on their business again.

Then he toyed with a red sphere hanging from a golden chain around his ruffle covered neck.

He leaned comfortably back in his chair, daintily resting his crossed, frilly ankles on the desk.

He knew that in the next few weeks big things would be happening in Awyalkna City, and that no number of thoughtful lists would help the Queen.

And he ... well, he was a valued confidante of the Sorcerer of Krall. He was privileged. So in a few weeks Wilmont would give word of where in the palace the Queen was, and he would find himself an excuse to be inspecting the safer lower levels of the palace.

He would be in no danger when the time for Aglaia and Awyalkna's fall came.

28

Twenty Eight

*T*he Granx

The Granx had been quite disgruntled when she'd been so inconsiderately woken by her Noal boy and the noisy pumping of his heart beside her lovely head.

Granx had stretched her luxurious legs lazily, accustomed to the blissful life of a warm pocket, before the black black hairs all over her pretty body had stiffened.

Awake! Her fangs had tingled with deadly deadly lethal poison when she'd sensed what had made her Noal boy's heart race like wriggly food before the wriggles stop.

She'd known at once, things were coming that were evil evil evil!

She had tried to poke her many eyes out of her Noal boy's pocket, but the jostling and shouting had begun and she'd almost been squashed as one of the evil evil evil things had snatched her Noal boy up.

Wiry hairs on end, she had felt Noal boy's body go cool and she had thrashed and wriggled.

Then, so brave so strong so clever, after much bouncing, she had come free from her Noal boy's pocket.

But worse than broken webs and swatting hands — she had come too far free!

Her legs had splayed in panic as she'd dropped right away from her Noal boy, falling to the ground right when the evil evil evil thing made one last big jump from the trees to land in the dusty rotten dirty borderlands.

With rows of gorgeous beady sad eyes, the Granx had watched after Noal boy for a moment.

Then, so loyal so heroic, she had scuttled out and onto the hot dirt.

She would follow.

She would get her Noal boy back.

29

✷

Twenty Nine

N*oal*

'Noal, wake up.'

Dalin was shaking me, and I sat up with a start.

'Easy brother,' he said. 'You were just dreaming.'

I was lying in a clearing under the forest canopy. Thousands of emerald leaves swished in a dance above and the air felt so clear, so clean.

In fact everything seemed distractingly vivid. Every colour of every flower and leaf was impossibly bright, as if Dalin and I were in a painting and it had just been freshly daubed.

'What is this?' I asked in wonder, squinting against the light's glare. 'How am I here with you?'

'You came back to us,' Dalin smiled. Something in his voice sounded forced.

'Maeve?' I asked, sitting up a little.

'The girl?' Dalin frowned.

I focused on him completely this time. 'I wouldn't have left her prisoner there. I wouldn't have left anyone suffering in the Witch's captivity.'

'You are noble, brother.' Dalin's hand felt cold on my shoulder. 'But you had to ... and that's why you have convinced me to go back to help you save her.'

'You are prepared to risk the quest?' I asked him in disbelief.

'For you,' he answered. 'But we will need Kiana.'

'How could we possibly get Kiana's help?' I protested.

'She would do anything to help you, you know she would.' Dalin seemed oddly serene and removed. And I noticed that there were no sounds of an army camped nearby, and no birds calling or little animals foraging in the undergrowth.

Everything was overly green and the sunlight was too golden. Too dream-like.

'Of course I know she would, but she can't right now,' I said, feeling a flare of sad disappointment.

'She can't be that far away,' Dalin insisted. 'She would come back if we knew exactly where to find her and could let her know we needed her.'

I stood abruptly and Dalin stood too.

'Where are you going brother?' he asked. 'We cannot go without Kiana. Only her pure magic would be strong enough for us to face Agrona. Where do you think she would be?'

He stepped towards me, but I stepped away. All of Dalin's natural warmth seemed non-existent in this blank person before me.

'Where are Ila and Amala? Or the Granx?' I asked. They would have come with us if we had truly left the army to search for Maeve.

'Ila and Amala ...' Dalin's face creased faintly.

'Surely you have not forgotten our two lovers?' I questioned him with a sinking feeling.

'Certainly not,' he responded easily. A smile touched his lips but did not reach his green eyes. 'Who could forget such beautiful maidens? But they cannot help. Only Kiana can.'

'Oh, my brother,' I said wistfully. 'If only this were real. If only you were not just one of Agrona's pale imitations. I long to be back by your side.'

A cloud of fury passed across Dalin's face and suddenly his body erupted into black and crimson smoke that spread to fill the clearing like midnight fog. The leaves and grass withered and blew away in flakes of ash.

Before my eyes the noxious fog touched the beautiful trees like a poisonous disease and they shifted and became deformed, grey and twisted. Their bark bubbled and blistered, and oily black sap oozed from their branches in globules like sticky blood. They seemed to lean over me and their roots began to struggle to be free of the dirt. The sky beyond their naked, skeletal branches now filled with violently rolling clouds as if the world was ending.

Where Dalin had been standing, the spiralling tendrils of fog were joining back together to form the solidifying shape of a towering, grey cloaked ghoul, stepping out from the haze.

The trees were groaning, ripping their roots up from the dirt to slither towards me, and the ghoul lifted its arms and began to sweep forward too.

Snake-like roots wrapped themselves tightly around my ankles so that I fell backward. They latched onto my waist and snaked up my spine, wrapping around my throat. I coughed and gasped as they tried to pull me down into what was now a writhing mass of roots and vines, all strangling and consuming me as I desperately clawed for my sword.

Slashing wildly, I saw the roots recoil and spurt black oil that landed in hot clotted blobs on my legs. But my gaze was drawn back to the ghoul, which was leaning down toward me and I looked up at its cowled, hidden face in horror as the trees above it swayed.

I struggled, wheezing at the pressure of a root on my oesophagus, and I drove my sword into as many snake-like roots as I could, each of them bursting as if I'd sliced my way through giant arteries. But then I realised that the black oil was rising and that it was too thick and sticky. I could barely move at all.

The ghoul reached for me, and it took hold of my throat to drag me upward so that my feet kicked in the air and my eyes popped. Gasping and struggling, I lifted my sword again to plunge the shining blade into the creature's stomach.

I was dropped into the oily sludge once more while the ghoul doubled over and then began to shrink quickly into the folds of its cloak.

I gasped when the massive cloak fell away from the slight figure within, revealing a beautiful woman standing up to her knees in black oil, with my sword through her middle.

Honey coloured hair flowed down her shoulders and a warm face gazed sadly at me, her hands hovering helplessly over the hilt of my sword as I cried out in anguish and forced my way toward her again, catching her swaying body as she sank down.

'Mother,' I gasped as we landed back in the oil that congealed in her hair and soiled her dress while I tried to hold her above it all.

But the oil began to spread from her wound now, seeping out from where the sword was buried, and it rolled down her face in gluggy, dark tears.

'I am so sorry,' I whispered in anguish, holding her tightly while the lapping slick rose to my elbows and nearly engulfed her.

'We are in the spirit world ... and you have wounded my soul for all eternity,' my mother said, gripping my arms. 'Only pure magic can heal me.'

My own clear tear drops fell to land on her cheek, mingling with her oily tears.

'You must end this agony for me,' my mother begged. 'Do you wish me to suffer forever?'

'No, never would I wish this!' I cried.

She gripped my arms more tightly. 'You must call for your Fairy. Only pure magic can save me.'

'I cannot,' I rasped over a choking lump in my throat.

'You refuse?' my mother's grip tightened further. 'You do not understand my suffering. The suffering of everyone who has been hurt by darkness, and who could be saved with Fairy magic.'

Suddenly she started to draw my arms down, dragging my face closer to the rising oil and I looked at her in shock.

'I will show you. I will make you save me.' Her teeth were stained black, and she allowed herself to sink downward, pulling me with her.

'Mother!' I cried out as her honey coloured hair disappeared into the oil and her face began to be swallowed up.

'You will see. You need to bring Kiana,' she said. 'Come with me to the realm of the dead.'

Her staring eyes and lips were slowly engulfed, and the tip of her nose disappeared, with only her vice-like hands remaining, pulling my arms after her.

The blackness sucked thickly at my chest as her hands finally disappeared, and I yelled and struggled frantically as my face was drawn closer and my neck was pulled into the liquid.

It reached my chin and I sucked in a huge breath, squeezing my eyes shut before I felt the thick oil seep into my ears and close in over the back of my head.

Everything was muted until we dropped free, coughing and landing in a gluggy puddle.

When I dug the blackness from my eyes, nose and mouth, gasping for air, I saw my mother taking sloppy, oil dripping steps across a dark cavern-like room, drawing my sword from her middle.

I looked more closely at the walls behind her, and lurched backward as I realised that they were not made of rock or clay but were instead made up of decomposing, yet feebly animated bodies. Hands, heads, legs and feet were discernible, and many eyes seemed to be watching me.

I turned back to my mother in horror, but the beauty had evaporated from her face.

Her skin and lips were yellowed and puffy and a couple of her fingers had rotted away.

'You see?' her voice was bitter. 'We have not moved on. Agrona and Darziates' darkness has ruined the natural order. We are trapped.'

I gasped as I felt something cold grip my ankle. A hand had reached out from the floor.

'We need Kiana's pure magic to be freed and healed. It is constant pain. Constant torture.'

I felt as though a tear had been made in my heart.

'No,' I said grimly. 'Kiana will not be coming.' I took a breath. 'My mother was so pure in life, that no amount of evil spreading in the world above would have kept her spirit from being guided onward by the God of Death to its final rest.'

She gasped, and abruptly my mother seemed to become nothing more than an empty puppet. Her rotting body dropped to the floor, and the walls and floor of corpses all began to crumble until I found that I was now looking at the stars through the barred window of my cell.

I heard a vicious voice spitting curses and retreating.

With extreme effort, I turned my head from where I was splayed on the floor and saw the orange light of a burning torch fading beyond the barred window in my door.

My teeth chattered and my body jerked with spasms of shock and sickness, but as I heard the end door slam shut with a final spiteful curse, I felt a flicker of triumph.

Even my subconscious had refused to betray the quest.

30

Thirty

N*oal*

An involuntary jerk made me gasp awake again, and I knew I had come back to reality now – because it felt like I was dying.

It was just becoming light through the bars of my window and I was scrunched up in a ball, cradling my aching, mutilated hand.

'Maeve …' I croaked weakly. But I barely heard my own voice and I had to force myself to try harder. 'Maeve?'

'Noal?' I heard her torn voice reply. 'Noal, what state are you in?'

'I'm … fine,' I managed. 'Haven't said … a thing she wants.'

'I wish you could make it stop,' she sobbed.

My eyes were too dry for tears. 'It's not so bad.'

I carefully levered my head so that I could see my injured fingers. They curved strangely like gnarled claws, sticking out at stiff, odd angles. The nails had already turned purple and my entire hand was blue with bruising and pooled blood. 'There's a … sweet girl in the cell across from mine.'

There was a tearful sniff from Maeve's cell.

'And defying Agrona is … satisfying,' I said with a steadier voice. 'The Witch is obsessed with Kiana.' I frowned. 'She hasn't asked –' I drew a halting breath, 'about any other plans we have.'

'I wonder how she and the Evexus even knew which path we were on and when the time was right to attack us,' Maeve said miserably. 'They shouldn't have expected us so early.'

For a moment I was truly distracted. 'You're right,' I grimaced, remembering Dren's bewilderment at our army's speed through the mountains. It could only have been luck on Agrona's side, or some kind of betrayal, that had allowed us to be found so early.

'Noal,' Maeve drew my focus back. 'I have to tell you,' she drew a big breath. 'That I –'

Hinges scraped and I heard the prison door slam. I somehow both heard and felt the Witch sweep down the corridor before my own door clanged open.

'Awake?' the derision stretched across her gaunt face.

'S'pose so. Unless you are … my nightmare again.'

I flopped through the air like a rag doll, back into my shackled state in the reappearing chair. My mind swam and my bones protested as if I'd aged quickly, but for a moment I clamped my mouth shut again as the green bottle materialised in Agrona's hands.

Then the red sand was back, making my traitorous mouth reflexively gag, and she again easily forced the green acid down my protesting throat.

'Do you have my answer?' she hissed.

'Can't ... recall the question,' I groaned.

Her fist pounded into my chest, and another red blast accompanied it. Then four more blasts in quick succession.

As though lightning had struck me, my body convulsed in the chair. Smoke rose from my chest and the poison amplified the pain of even my throat as my howls scraped their way free.

Her hands gripped my face, locking it into place, and I felt her power seeping into me like a disease.

'My magic is clogging your lungs. Filling your brain like dust. Eroding the lining of your gut,' she stated. 'Just end it. Tell me if the Fairy is trying to get to Darziates.'

Agrona slapped me as my eyes trailed away from her.

'Is she getting close to him?'

Like a maniac, with my head lolling, I laughed loudly in relief, my voice breaking.

'Oh yes, she's after him,' I smiled with actual happiness. 'She's somewhere in Krall right now ... Biding her time.'

Agrona's hands tightened like a muzzle around my face again, willing me to talk. Her black, glittering eyes were wide and mad.

'That's all Kiana wants,' I coughed and chuckled. 'She just wants to face Darziates.'

I was almost shocked when Agrona reeled away from me in revulsion. I hadn't been ready for it and my head fell forward with its own weight.

I hadn't predicted that it would seem so outrageous that the most powerful being on our side of the quest would be trying to get to Darziates. It only made sense that Kiana might try to kill him and prevent the war at all. Yet Agrona was seething, her hands balled up into fists, and she came at me in a rage – forcing round after round of red magic into me.

Crimson fog began to cloud the room, spilling out of my nose and mouth. So much magic couldn't fit into my body all at once and I gagged on the burning mist churning inside and overflowing back up through my airways. Drowning.

'Where is she?!' Agrona screamed between punches. 'How close? Tell me!'

She waited for my response as I choked up some more red smoke, but I just shook my dangling head with a grim, taunting smile as more smoke swirled out from between my teeth.

She screeched and bashed my head backward into the chair, grasping handfuls of my shirt.

Her fists became a glowing red colour as she streamed something like lava into my body. I felt my chest scorching and red smoke spouted from my lips, nostrils, tear ducts and ears to swirl angrily about us in a roiling twister.

But even as I felt myself suffocating, I knew I was torturing Agrona just as much as she was torturing me.

'She's ... so ... close ... to ... him ...' I garbled, and tried to form more words between the onslaught, but my brain seemed too shaken to form anything of sense.

This time when she stopped and pushed me back a trail of blood drizzled down from my chin to my pant leg. I was frying inside.

'Speak!' she shouted.

'By now,' I managed weakly. 'Kiana must be near the castle ... just trying to find a ... way in.' I felt my cheeks quirk upward with a drowsy smirk while another string of blood dribbled down to my chest.

Agrona shrieked in response and whirled. With a gesture my cell door was open and so was Maeve's, and abruptly Maeve was hurtling across to where Agrona stood, stopping with a jolt and a terrified scream, face to face with the Witch.

Maeve's eyes were wide as they darted to me, slumped and quivering in my chair, and then to Agrona.

'Why ... bring ... anyone else ... into this?' I groaned through gritted teeth, tilting my head up and back against the chair so I could see. 'She is a healer ... she knows nothing of our plans.'

'Because when I'm done with you, I'll be rid of you both and hunt down the Fairy.' The green bottle was back in Agrona's hands.

'It hardly seems fair, to kill us both, when I have given you so much,' I pleaded weakly.

But Agrona simply forced my head back and let me writhe and suffocate on her magic again before the screams forced my mouth open for more of the poisonous liquid.

I heard Maeve crying out as she hung in the air, but I was too overwhelmed to think.

'All's fair in love and war,' Agrona hissed, and then she began pounding my chest with red magic – again and again and again.

I passed out three times, but she brought me back. And each time she gave me a chance to change what I'd told her before she relaunched her torture regime.

Finally, Agrona crushed my mashed fingers as a last test – a couple of my fingernails dropping off with the pressure, and then she seemed certain enough that I had said all I knew.

She gave me an appraising look as I was left dangling forward in the chair, my sweat soaked hair dripping before my face.

'Alright,' Agrona said quietly. 'So she's in Krall.'

I moaned in exhaustion, unable to even pride myself on the lie. Unable to move without pain as I breathed raggedly, gasping on red smoke.

Agrona's hand made a sweeping gesture and I was suddenly back on the floor, my shackles linked together again. Maeve was released from where she had been frozen mid-air, and with a cry she fell to the ground before rapidly crawling across to me, protecting me with her own body.

I knew Maeve had no idea what Agrona or I had been saying in Awyalknian, but she could tell that things were coming to a close.

'You do not know this spare that was brought along?' Agrona eyed Maeve, seeing a peasant girl grovelling over me in the dust.

'She is ...' I forced myself to pant in agony. 'A loyal servant ... of the quest.'

'Mindless,' Agrona mused. 'And she gets to die with you for it.'

Hate made my eyes burn as the Witch raised both of her thin arms, and a swirling storm of red magic at once began to rage in the air above her head, making her an incredible and awful sight.

Maeve tightly closed her eyes and put her arms around me.

But my own eyes went wide with shock and recognition as, at that moment, I spotted something crawling up Agrona's dress.

It was fast and moved on many legs, and its fangs were wet with poison.

Agrona was leaning back, ready to throw her mass of swirling energy down upon us, and she hadn't noticed the fist-sized Granx crawling along her stomach to stop on her shoulder.

Maeve felt me gasp in wonder, and glanced up in time to see the Granx sinking deadly fangs into the Witch's shoulder, right where the Witch had once branded Kiana.

Agrona felt the painful sting and actually stumbled to one side while the red incinerating magic above her head evaporated and she stared down at what had afflicted her.

Her face was already draining of colour before she saw the fatal little spider waving defiant legs.

Agrona shrieked, filling her hand with magic once more and blasting the Granx away with a sizzle.

I cried out as the small spider whirled away, but the Granx was dead before she had landed in the dust beside me, her legs curled up beneath her.

'Gods,' I heard Maeve whisper, looking at the little spider that had saved us.

And the poison of the Granx – the most fatal of all poisons for mortals – was now in Agrona's immortal body, where, rather than killing her, it was transforming her.

Agrona reeled backwards, clutching at her face and shoulder. She crashed into the wall behind, but hardly seemed to notice through her own blinding pain.

I had managed to sit up, and with sobs of terror, Maeve tried to help drag me away to the cell door. But our eyes were fixed on the screaming, flailing Witch, who was now scrambling in the dust.

Agrona's face and neck distorted and blistered. Her shoulder swelled and hunched with a bulging hump of poison. The rest of her pale skin began to sink in and melt as every inch of the flesh that had been close to the bite bubbled and scarred like burns before our eyes.

Maeve supported me while Agrona rolled in a horrific panic to face her escaping victims.

'Stop!' she screeched, one eye half melted closed.

The skin on her cheeks was stretching and sizzling like cooking meat and she reached out with a withering hand in terror.

I ignored the Witch's hand and gently picked up the already cold Granx, putting her carefully in my pocket. Then I let Maeve help me to stand.

With hard eyes, I gazed at the now cowering Witch.

'All's fair in love and war,' I rasped, and then Maeve was half helping, half dragging me away.

31

Thirty One

K*iana*

Scandra and I made our plans and her kindred hunted across an ocean that reflected a sunset of oranges and pinks.

Ahanu sat nearby, noisily playing with a pack of scrabbling baby Dargons that were each nearly as big as he was. The Dargons seemed to perceive him as my oversized pet. A lumbering, amusing stranger.

Scandra seemed to disregard him rather than viewing the Giant as a threat. But I was certain that neither Ahanu nor myself needed to fear our new allies – and Scandra had reassured me herself that I would have no trouble from her followers as it seemed certain that I could knock a Dargon from the air if needed.

'I am glad you will come to help me persuade the Dwarves,' I told her. 'After Ahanu's descriptions, I do not know if I would have the patience to diplomatically listen to their debates as the world faces the end. Your presence may inspire them.'

'It is normally below my dignity to leave my eyrie to fly down to them,' Scandra remarked wryly. 'Especially because they hardly have room in their tunnels to receive me properly.'

Before I could respond there was a commotion at a smaller cave entrance that made us turn, but the source of the noise seemed too small amongst a gathering crowd of returned Dargons to be seen.

'What now?' the words curled from Scandra's lips as the crowd of Dargons began to snarl and roar.

The booming, echoing sounds shook the cavern and Ahanu easily caught a falling rock loosed from the ceiling before it crushed his head. Others rained down and glanced off Scandra's scales unnoticed.

'Enough!' Scandra growled, and at once there was stillness in the cavern. 'Noise maker, come forward.'

The crowd obediently parted and then, coming towards us, was a very embarrassed baby Dargon. His mouth had been tethered closed by a vine so that he could be ridden like a flying horse, and sitting between his shoulder blades like a regal King was the tiniest brown and green man I had ever seen.

Scandra's eyes narrowed, but not at the crafty little being who had obviously captured the fledgling. Instead her scorn was for the young Dargon himself, for allowing himself to be captured, and the Dargon lowered his head in shame.

Meanwhile the tiny smirking man was unruffled. He would have been able to sit in my two hands comfortably, and was abnormally round and hefty for his size. Like a lumpy, unnaturally large potato.

He puffed out his chest rather regally and obstinately for his diminutive size.

'I am Gnome Spud,' he announced grandly. Then he raised an accusing finger and jabbed it in my direction. 'And you, I'm guessing are the pandemonium raiser who caused me to be called away from my garden burrow!'

I tilted my head, regarding him. 'Pandemonium does sometimes happen around me. But I'm unsure what I may have done to disturb you.'

The Gnome crossed his toy-sized arms; a grubby, frowning ball. His hair stood out like potato roots, and he was littler than one of Scandra's smallest scales.

'Earlier today, as the Dwarves and Gnomes went innocently about their lives, there was a surge of some unknown power so great that every magical stone in the mountain lit up,' the Gnome declared. 'So brilliantly bright that the entire population was stopped dead in our tracks to see a vision of some woman on a quest as a Summoner!' he gave me a surly look. 'Needless to say we know that all of the *Larnaeradee* are dead and so the woman declaring herself to be the Summoner – you –must be a Witchy imposter! Then after only hours of deliberation the Dwarf King and his government proposed to send someone to find out if the Dargons were alive ... and if Agrona had gone away. So,' he stated, eyeing me. 'Watch out.'

'They sent just you? And after hours of discussion? I'm glad we didn't really need help,' Scandra said flatly. She flexed her talons experimentally.

'You lit up a mountain!' Ahanu congratulated me.

But I leaned closer to the cross little Gnome. 'Now that you're here and have seen the Dargons and I at peace, do you truly believe me to be the Witch?'

The Gnome sniffed and wiped at his turned up nose roughly, stubborn and suspicious. 'You got the pale good looks and the flowy dark hair. And I can definitely feel magic about you.'

'But do you feel foulness in my magic?' I asked. 'Not even Agrona could disguise that about herself.'

He scrunched his dirty features with a furrow of uncertainty, but he persisted. 'Why have you come then? And how? None have come since the dark times began.'

'I flew,' I said simply, and I let my wings shine into visibility at my back while the tourmaline stone shone at my throat. 'Because I am the Summoner. I am the One, or Kiana, the last of the *Larnaeradee*. And I have come to unite the magical races against those who have caused the dark times.'

'The vision was the truth?' he demanded. 'There was a second prophecy? The Three?'

'The vision was the truth,' I confirmed, and I saw the shift in his face. However he quickly tried to regain a semblance of tough impartiality.

'You had better come down to the tunnels with me then so the government can hear of this.'

'What a bright idea,' Scandra muttered with a puff of annoyed smoke.

'You'll have to keep up,' Spud announced, at last dismounting from his bashful captive. 'King Herb is just going to love this,' he chortled to himself, using shockingly strong fingers to easily snap the thick bonds holding the baby Dargon. 'A Fairy, a Giant and the Queen of all flying lizards are coming to visit. It sounds like a joke.'

Then he imperiously waddled past us and lowered himself over the rocky lip of the cave entrance. He at once began a speedy, expert descent, using his stout hands to dig into the rock face – literally digging in.

'Come, then,' Scandra invited me wryly. 'Let us put fear into the little people to prevent years of prattling. Bring your Giant so that my sisters can have a rest from that infernal racket,' she added, glaring at Ahanu as she stretched out her powerful legs.

Ahanu sheepishly shooed the crowd of young Dargons that still hung around him and who had earlier been squealing in high pitched voices, thrashing around him loudly in a game.

Scandra shook her massive, glimmering body as she prepared to fly out, her wings unable to fully spread even in the gaping cavern entrance.

'Why did Spud capture a Dargon to get up here if he's such a good climber?' I asked the Empress.

'Lazy exhibitionist,' she replied archly before launching magnificently into the air and swooping down the cliffs.

The air resounded with the sound of her wing strokes and Ahanu caught me as I was dragged forward in the enormous suction of air left in her wake. Then he provided me with a more accurate explanation. 'It's more like big versus little race rivalry. The insult was intentional.'

I laughed as he let me fly from his arms and he lowered himself over the edge too.

32

Thirty Two

The Witch

Her screams were terrifying even to herself, but they just kept coming.

Her body was tearing up. Her flesh, her veins, her blood – everything burning and melting and ripping.

Her mind was blank to all but the agony, and the one name that meant everything to her.

Darziates.

Agrona screamed her master's name over and over like a mantra, with such magical force that it must have been ricocheting through the Other Realm.

He had to have felt her calls, and yet he hadn't pulled her through the Other Realm to himself. Instead the screams echoed around her as day became night and she thrashed and shrivelled in torment. All while knowing that the Fairy was trying to get to the Sorcerer – while he wouldn't answer his own Witch's cries.

The pain of it all was too much and she clawed wretchedly at her bubbling face as chunks of her black hair fell out. She scrabbled in the dust, not looking at the pink, shiny skin covering her arms, or the blisters and bleeding craters on her melted chest.

She sobbed, alone, into the dark because the jailor had fled, her prisoners had escaped, everyone in the village was hiding, and even the Evexus were off hunting.

It was not until her immortal body had begun to force her oozing wounds to heal in scarred, blurred welts that at last she felt herself being dragged away.

She was buffeted and stung by the Other Realm and by Darziates' own magic until at last she materialised at her master's feet in his private throne room.

The torches burning in the chamber radiated heat that was almost unbearable on her scorched body, but she cried out gratefully, pawing at the Sorcerer's ankles.

'Master,' she whimpered. 'Master heal me! My beauty!'

And Darziates fixed his icy blue-grey stare on the deformed wreck at his boots for a moment, before he pulled his foot out of her clawing, hopeful grasp and slid her away with the toe of his shoe.

'Master ...' she was almost hyperventilating.

'You have been useless,' Darziates stated. 'You could hardly serve me before, or protect your own self as it turns out. And now you are reduced further.'

'No!' Agrona choked. 'I captured one of the princes ...' she reached a marred hand out to him, her fingers like claws. 'I was able to get information!'

'I know. I can see it all in your mind.'

'I discovered that the Fairy is coming for you!'

'It's fortunate, seeing as you couldn't bring her to me in all this time.'

Then he – the passive, immovable Sorcerer – unconsciously rubbed at his chest, as if there was a stirring there that had never been there before.

Agrona felt her world collapsing. Despite her burns, cold liquid trickled through her veins.

Beyond all doubt the ensnaring enchantment of the Fairy had warped her beloved King and the physical and mental agony was all consuming.

'Why didn't you bring me here sooner?' she keened broken heartedly then. 'You must have heard me.'

Darziates' eyes were regarding something beyond her. 'I heard you. But I ignored you.'

'We were in a meeting.'

Agrona flinched as she heard a second, sniggering voice and she rolled to see Angra Mainyu, sitting comfortably in a chair on the other side of her.

'Not so pretty now, Witch,' the Warlord grinned through his grizzled, filthy beard.

The humiliation gave Agrona enough strength to be vicious and she reached out to send a red blast at him. But, like her body, the magic was weak, and Angra took it in the belly with a psychotic laugh.

'Enough of that,' the putrid Warlord cackled. 'You need to be careful now. You're damaged goods.'

'It is most merciful to simply cast her out,' she heard her master comment then, and before she could turn, she was screaming again as she lurched back through the Other Realm to reappear in the wastelands.

There, helpless, she curled up into a ball in the sand, holding her scarred head in her hands and keening to herself in petrified anguish.

33

Thirty Three

N^{oal}

We stumbled and ran blindly away from the prison and Agrona's awful cries.

Nobody in the tiny Krall village made a move to stop us, even as we stole a bony mule that had been tethered to a broken fence. Instead they were all ducking for cover as they heard what they thought was the Witch's rage.

Somehow Maeve got me up onto the mule with her, and she threaded herself into the circle of my shackled hands so that I was supported against her back. Then we pushed the miserable animal to trot us away from the hovel-like dwellings and on towards the distant green blur that could only be the forest on the edge of the border lands.

Finally the mule was stumbling as the heat of the day intensified and Maeve and I slid down from its back.

'I think he's dehydrated,' Maeve commented despondently as we let the sagging animal turn back to its home, which was now a distant speck through the hot atmosphere.

'*He's* dehydrated?' I puffed as Maeve and I plunged onward, her arms supporting me.

'At least he saved us some time,' Maeve tried to sound positive as the sight of the great distance between us and the dark shape of Sylthanryn wavered in the radiating sun.

'I used to ...' I sighed. 'Relish our walks together.'

It was only with great will power that I didn't collapse with every step as we hurried on. My shackles made it hard to balance and weighed my throbbing hand down, but worse, I knew that my breathing was loud and rasping and my body felt as though hot crimson bunches of magic were still circulating inside.

Every movement was agony until at last Maeve and I were hobbling, and when there was a moment that her grip on me slipped, I helplessly toppled and landed on my crumpled hand.

Maeve was crying quietly as she turned me over in the dust, but I could barely see her in the haze of my vision as I gasped and everything blurred.

'Don't cry,' I half whispered, half croaked, reaching up towards her sobs with my good hand. I only realised I'd missed her face when she put her hand in mine, but kept crying.

I was certain that on horseback the border of the forest would have been half a day's ride. But at my rate, we wouldn't get there even if we shambled on through the night.

I was dizzy and every muscle was screaming, but I forced myself upright and felt Maeve try to steady me into a standing position.

'What would I do without you?' I murmured into her golden hair before we lurched on through the most scorching part of the day with Maeve taking most of my weight.

We progressed slowly, and we both realised that I was becoming delirious as I began to mutter in Awyalknian to Dalin and Kiana, until in moments of clarity I heard what I was doing and abruptly stopped.

I could tell Maeve was frightened for me, but without water we were both struggling. At one point she ripped her skirts to make us both shrouds to protect our necks and faces, but they eased little else, and finally, when the afternoon was growing late and while the forest was still hours of slow steps away, my legs buckled again and we both went down.

'Noal, open your eyes,' I heard her plead, and after great effort my eyes forced themselves open to focus on her beautiful face as she crouched over me.

'My angel,' I whispered and went to stroke the dirty tears from her cheeks. But I saw that my hand was a broken claw and I lowered it again. 'If you stay with me we will both be out in this desert for days.'

'I won't leave you,' she choked. 'There is no shelter, and you can't protect yourself.'

'If you don't go,' I told her gently. 'Neither of us will survive. But if you do, you will be safe with the army, and perhaps you will find Dalin in time to save me too.' I sighed weakly. 'The Evexus are nowhere in sight. Nobody is wandering these parts. If you pace yourself you will be safe, and will reach the forest.'

She let out a heartbreaking groan, putting her hands to her eyes as she realised our best chance was for her to leave, and I resignedly dragged myself backward to rest against a hard, dust coated boulder.

She gently wrapped her arms around me.

'I will be waiting for you Maeve,' I told her as she kissed my cheeks and lips.

'And I will come back as soon as I can,' she replied with only a small tremor in her voice.

I exhaled as she turned and I watched her fade out of my sight, running away into the blackness closing in on my vision.

34

Thirty Four

We spiralled around to where a hole gaped in the far side of the cliffs. And there we were met by a line of Dwarves in startling, glittering armour who were blocking our way to a gleaming entrance gate.

Unlike Spud, the Dwarves were bulky, waist high boulders rather than fist sized rocks. Their heads were bald and their green beards were stiffly pointed.

Scandra swooped at the Dwarf guards, landing in the large tunnel before the gate, while Spud dropped from the tunnel roof to its floor with a solid thump, and Ahanu shuffled down more noisily after him.

'Come on, if it was Agrona you'd all be dead by now,' Spud waved his hands at the wall of shining armoured guards as if to brush them away. 'As it is, there's a Dargon here, and your mighty fists won't do much against her fire either.'

'Yes, stand apart, stand apart,' a fussy voice called, and the guards separated to allow their leader through – a Dwarf who was almost identical to all the rest. The only difference was that there was a ridiculously large crown planted like an over-sized, jewelled egg on his head, and he was also flanked by about twenty silver bearded, wizened Dwarves.

'What did you discover Spud?' he frowned, holding the giant egg jewel on his head to keep it still.

'They're so little,' Ahanu whispered out of the corner of his mouth. 'The cubs would love them.'

'She really is the Summoner, like we saw in that vision,' Spud unceremoniously called out to the Dwarf King. 'She's called the One.'

Spud turned to me and gestured to the group behind him. 'Kiana, that's my brother Herb. And – yes I know he's a Dwarf and I'm a Gnome.'

'*King* Herb,' Spud's brother corrected him waspishly, only just catching the heavy crown as it slipped over an eye. 'So we're expected to go on some quest for the world?' he blustered. 'We'll have to discuss this very thoroughly indeed.'

At once the governmental Dwarves around him began muttering into their beards in agreement.

'Spud, take them to a place where they can wait the days in comfort,' King Herb ordered, already turning to leave in a cluster of debating officials.

'You will not keep me waiting long, Dwarf,' Scandra told the King icily. 'And I highly doubt I am going to be comfortable anywhere in these damn worm holes you call a kingdom.'

'Just avoiding concussion is going to be hard,' Ahanu winced, already rubbing where he'd bumped his head. And Scandra deigned to agree with him.

Spud turned, rubbing his tough little hands together. 'Right. Let's find a place to stash you lot for the big wait.'

35

Thirty Five

D*alin*

In frustration I turned Amala to follow the retreating search, heading back to see what progress the army had made without us while moving slowly as a whole.

Another day since Noal had been taken was turning into dusk, and any last hopes I'd had were turning to ash, until I heard Thorin's shout.

I had been in a search party with the archers near where our trail left the forest, but Thorin had been in a different party further out from where the army planned to leave Sylthanryn.

Amala and I wheeled around to face the direction of the shouts as Thorin charged around the border of the forest towards us, galloping at breakneck speed on a horse loaned to him by the Jenrans.

There was a golden haired woman on the saddle in front of him, and I felt a flare of relief as Thorin reined in amongst a cloud of Krall's kicked up dust.

'Raiden,' Maeve rasped, clutching Thorin's water flask in her hands.

'Tane and I found Maeve staggering through the border lands,' Thorin puffed while the rest of his search group; Tane, Wolf, Phrixus and Cadell – all riding borrowed Jenran horses, now caught up.

'We need to hurry,' Maeve croaked urgently. 'Noal and I escaped but he was too weak to make it back here. I left him a day ago in the desert and have run all this way for help.'

'Bring Aeron and Durna the news, and send for a healer,' Dren was instructing Rai, and in moments the young archer had charged away on his mare.

'You ran all that way?' I grimaced at Maeve's sunburned skin and tattered garments; all testament to a hard journey.

'Agrona tortured Noal with magic,' Maeve's exhausted voice cracked. 'But the Granx saved us! The Granx's bite has grievously weakened the Witch and we've not heard from the Evexus since.'

There was a silence so thick that for a moment the air around me felt stuffy.

'The Witch has been reduced?' Wolf gasped at last while the others made sounds of shocked jubilation.

Then, almost impossibly quickly, Rai was charging out on a fresh horse with Lady Amarantha in the saddle behind him, gripping her healer bag.

'We have to go,' Maeve said pleadingly. 'I am sure I can guide us.'

I nodded, and in moments our group was galloping through Krall's late afternoon heat, with Maeve crying out and urging us on while our horses thundered together and the hard ground melted away.

With each of Amala's juddering footfalls my own fragile head pounded, but I ignored it – determinedly praying that we would find Noal alive.

Please, alive.

'There!' Maeve called at last, and we steered toward where she pointed, slowing our advance.

She slid from the saddle as if she'd been riding all her life, landing before Thorin's mount had properly pulled up. Then she ran to a crumpled, almost unnoticeable figure and in a rush I was off Amala and pelting across to them, falling to my knees beside Maeve.

'Noal,' she said desperately, her hands fluttering in distress around his heavily bruised and blistered face. 'Please, it's time to wake up.'

For a moment I couldn't see a flicker of life about him, but then the faintest smile played on his lips.

'Did you sleep well?' Maeve asked with a tearful, small smile of her own and for a moment he struggled to simply form words.

'Not at all,' he rasped, opening his eyes with an enormous effort. 'I missed you.'

Amarantha had joined us and now leaned across Noal to lightly examine his hand, but she was unprepared for the alarming, hoarse cry that rose from his throat.

Suddenly his eyes rolled back again and Maeve moaned while his body spasmed.

'The poison!' she wailed. 'Agrona poured it into him, and now he finds that everything is an agony.'

Amarantha was grim. 'Agrona is creative. We must revive him and learn of the poison for me to treat it.'

I panicked, leaning over Noal and grasping his ruined shirt, which was covered in scorch marks.

'Noal!' I said desperately. 'You have slept enough. Come back!'

He looked as if he were dead.

'Noal!' I growled. 'Say something!'

His lips moved ever so slightly and I leaned in closer.

'Be ... quieter,' he managed.

'You smart-alec!' I crowed triumphantly.

'Yes.'

'Noal,' Lady Amarantha broke in, lifting a bottle of clear liquid from her pack. 'I'm going to need you to drink something.'

That got a weak frown instead. 'Again?'

'This will rehydrate you,' she promised.

There was a puff of air that suggested a sigh, but he allowed her to slowly drizzle the fluid into his mouth. He gallantly made the effort to swallow it and his face cleared a little.

Dren moved forward as Amarantha tended Noal, the archer's eyes on a couple of glinting instruments in the healer's pack. He borrowed the delicate tools, and with infinite care he picked at the shackles around Noal's wrists until they opened. Thorin had also begun leading an effort to make a simple stretcher to tie between the horses.

'Now, Noal,' Amarantha said. 'I can see some of the things ailing you, but some I need you to tell me about.'

He nodded faintly.

'Your fingers,' she prompted. 'Most have been dislocated or sprained by a device.'

Noal winced. 'By Agrona's own hand. She had quite ... a mighty grip.'

Amarantha's lips pursed in an effort to conceal her disgust while I sat back on my haunches.

'And what of the poison? Do you know what it was?' Amarantha asked, feeling Noal's forehead, peering into his eyes.

'Don't know,' he said. 'It was green. Burned like acid. Made any source of pain greater.' He drew a breath. 'Even blinking felt worse than any agony I had ever thought possible.' His battered form was wracked with a shudder before he added: 'though she said ... was not permanent. She needed some life in me.'

Amarantha did not appear reassured. 'I've never heard of a poison made solely to heighten pain.'

'I haven't heard of such a concoction in Krall either,' Thorin informed her sombrely, having finished the stretcher. 'It has to be a Witch specialty.'

Noal grimaced. 'I think it will pass.' He was starting to struggle again now, but he was too tired to be upset. 'Because she had to keep forcing new doses into me.'

'And she beat you with something? A cudgel or weapon of some kind to cause the pain?' Amarantha asked, her hands lifting the top of his burnt shirt to reveal dents and enormous purple coloured bruises.

'It wasn't a weapon,' Maeve answered for Noal. 'Agrona sent magic blasts into him from her fists.'

'I see,' Amarantha commented. Then she stood briskly. 'Maeve,' she said then. 'Assist your friends in securing Noal on the stretcher as you've been taught. We need to get him to camp and into care.'

Maeve nodded and the men behind her began fussing over Noal.

'What are you thinking?' I asked Amarantha quickly as she stood back.

She frowned. 'I cannot predict how well the prince will recover because Agrona did not use ordinary means to cause his injures. We can't know what to expect or exactly what is going on internally. The only certainty I have,' she went on as I grew increasingly nauseated. 'Is that each of his fingers will need to be put back into place and then set.'

With Amarantha's words in my head, it was a long ride back as Noal was carried between Dren's and Rai's horses.

This time Maeve rode with me, directly behind Noal, so that we could both see him, now semi-conscious ahead of us while Amarantha and Thorin rode close beside him.

'Somehow we have beaten all odds,' Maeve told me tiredly, as if sensing that I was fighting off despair. 'We have found our way back to you. It has to be for a reason.'

36

Thirty Six

The Witch

At first all she knew was pain, emptiness and panic.

There was the recurring image of the Sorcerer's hand touching his chest. As if he was feeling something. Feeling something for someone. Someone who was not her. For he had abandoned her.

The days passed around her huddled, unmoving form and Agrona could only bend her will toward blinking and breathing.

Her skin shrivelled further in the blistering heat of the desert to become like dried leather, but her immortal body needed no real sustenance and instead her brain turned all of its energy to one thought.

Survival.

Survival, so that she could destroy the threat of Kiana.

Before the end of the tenth age

37

Thirty Seven

D*alin*

Many Jenrans had gathered to wait for our return, and they parted like a guard of honour as Noal was brought down the trail to the nearest healer marquee, where even the other patients inside remained respectfully silent when we entered.

'Careful lads,' Noal breathed in a wispy voice as his litter was set on a healer bench. 'Precious cargo.'

Thorin and Thale stayed, and the rest of our warriors crowded around the tent entrance quietly while Amarantha, Maeve and two other healers entered.

One healer selected some herbs while Amarantha consulted a book that had illustrations of hands. All of the bones of those hands were properly aligned.

'This is going to hurt,' Noal husked, and my eyes flickered to his own mangled hand cradled over his chest. 'She pumped more of that poison and magic into me than I could fit. It's still roiling inside.'

I pushed the sweaty golden hair from his forehead. 'Yes. It'll hurt until it's over. But you will live.'

'And we will be by your side,' Thale rumbled.

'It's time to sit him up,' Amarantha told us, her face grim with concentration.

'Joy,' Noal sighed, but obligingly gave me his good arm, letting Thorin and I manoeuvre him into an upright position.

'First I'm going to put pressure on different parts of your torso,' Amarantha warned. 'If you feel even a flutter of pain out of the ordinary, tell me.'

'That won't be a problem,' Noal assured her as she loosened the tie of his shirt and started to dig her hands unmercifully into his back and chest, pushing along bones and muscles.

He gritted his teeth against the sharp aches of her hands over his chest, which was littered with burnt looking bruises. But, thank the Gods, there were no outbursts or cries of intolerable discomfort.

'That's good, isn't it?' Thorin asked hopefully, still supporting Noal's drooping frame.

Amarantha didn't glance up as she answered, instead examining the colouring of the fingertips on Noal's good hand. 'It means I haven't found invisible damage within. It doesn't mean it's not there.'

'Reassuring,' Noal uttered softly as Amarantha put her ear to his chest, listening carefully as he breathed.

'Well,' Amarantha straightened at last. 'It doesn't sound like the magic has shredded your lungs.'

I heard Maeve let out a breath of relief.

'First we will mend those stitches at the back of your neck,' Amarantha said, while one of the other healers approached with a readied needle and wetted cloth.

Noal lowered his head to my shoulder in resignation so that Amarantha could reach, and she rubbed the wetted cloth over the torn skin at the back of his neck to get rid of the dried blood and dust caked there.

His good fist clenched my shirt and his head buried even further into me as the prick of Amarantha's needle then began its journey to first un-pick the damaged stitches, and then to replace them. And I remembered how just days earlier he had easily endured the same procedure without a qualm.

He did not relax when Amarantha finished her stitches, as he knew what would be coming next.

I felt myself wincing as Amarantha gave the attendants her equipment and then held out her hand. 'Noal,' she said. 'I need those fingers.'

Noal groaned but raised his mangled, purple hand while I hugged him a little tighter.

Amarantha examined his hand closely and Noal shuddered as she felt each of his fingers and examined the way they were twisted.

'This one is sprained. It's very swollen, but not out of place,' Amarantha muttered to the other healers and Maeve, who nodded tensely with understanding. 'Agrona has bent it so that the ligaments inside were stretched beyond their capability,' Amarantha went on. 'Thankfully it hasn't stiffened up, but it will need to be splinted for a while before we start manipulating it with gentle exercises.'

She moved then to the other puffy, oddly-angled fingers and thumb. 'These are more severe. The joints have been disconnected and pulled out of alignment to give maximum pain. They have to be put back if normal movement is ever to return.'

Noal's breath was warm against my shoulder as he drew air in to calm himself.

Amarantha's face was almost blank with focus. 'Are you ready princeling?' she asked.

'Wait ...' Noal husked. 'Thale, my pocket...'

Thale quickly reached for the pouch of scorched material at Noal's chest and, with surprise, gently pulled out the body of the Granx. She looked like she was sleeping.

'She saved us,' Maeve said in understanding. 'She was the only one strong enough to stop the Witch.'

'Bury her?' Noal asked Thale.

'Of course,' Thale replied simply. 'She was no ordinary spider.' He cradled the Granx in his palm and, satisfied, Noal readjusted his grip on my tunic and nodded.

Then Amarantha's lips pursed into a grim line, and with all of her strength, and as quickly as possible, she crunched the first finger back into line.

Noal jolted as Thorin I held him, before his body became rigid. But my eyes grew wide as something beneath Noal's damaged flesh heated up.

His knuckles bubbled beneath the surface of the skin, as if acid was stirring in his blood, and his flesh started to steam and smoke.

'The poison,' Maeve whispered, and as the strange magic beneath his skin took hold, awful cries wracked free of Noal like demons scraping their way out of the Other Realm.

He arched into me in torment as the poison burned within him. But he held his hand as still as he could while Amarantha worked.

Finally the fire beneath Noal's flesh became such that Amarantha's own fingers were getting burnt as she worked on each of his and she had to stop to get a cloth to protect her grip.

I held my brother in support until Amarantha had finished and Noal hung limply at my side, only Thorin and I keeping him upright.

I knew I was as pale and anxious looking as Thale and Thorin, and I could see the wide eyes of the other patients and gathered Krall men while sweat rolled off Noal's face and he panted against me.

'Lay him down, carefully,' Amarantha said, and even as we lowered him his eyes were closing.

The attendant who had provided the needle earlier now began cleaning the arm and newly wrenched fingers on Noal's bad hand. She had to dab at the pits where a few of Noal's fingernails had detached.

Another attendant began sponging at the dented, burnt bruises across Noal's torso. But he was already so deeply unconscious that he didn't even flinch.

'Lady Amarantha, I can't thank you enough,' I croaked.

'Nor I,' Maeve agreed fervently. 'You have saved me from losing everything.'

Amarantha brushed our thanks away. 'I didn't particularly want to lose a member of the Three,' she said. 'Now Maeve, I'm ordering you to your own rest. You need it.' She handed Maeve a water flask.

'Go,' I reassured Maeve gently. 'He won't wake for a while, and I'll stay up. After all,' I smiled, 'I'm not the one who ran across the desert to save him.'

A smile touched her face and she nodded, finally convincing herself to walk away after a final glance at Noal.

38

Thirty Eight

K*iana*

'This is Grub, Jumble, Pip and Bounce,' Spud was pointing out more potato featured people over the noise of mass merrymaking.

There were swarms of Gnomes everywhere, beating drums, playing pipes and dancing crazily around us in a welcome party that had lasted five days.

I tried to appear pleased to keep meeting everybody. Because, while the governmental Dwarves had held endless debates, rebuttals and reasoned discussions about the quest each day, the Gnomes had done their best to fill our nights more positively.

'We haven't even discussed potential numbers or hypothetical travel arrangements yet,' Scandra glowered darkly from beside me. 'So much for my fearsome presence.'

I cringed at the thought of the boring King Herb, and how there always seemed to be another critical issue that absolutely had to be examined.

'It's not so bad,' Ahanu chuckled from where he was teeming with clusters of little potato people. 'They gave us the biggest, nicest, most open cavern here.'

He was juggling dozens of Gnomes so high in the air that they nearly brushed the dazzling, gem encrusted ceiling as they roared with laughter.

Ahanu was right that we were not uncared for. On our first night's stay Spud and his hordes of Gnomes had ploughed their fists into the solid rock floor of our room, and had somehow manipulated it all to change. Like soft clay being modelled by an invisible artist's hands, the rock had flowed and rolled into a basin-like bed for Scandra and had formed comfortable nooks for Ahanu and I.

But Scandra's lip now curled disdainfully at our accommodation and, like the Empress, every night I somehow found less inspiration to celebrate.

'I have enjoyed seeing how each race lives,' I told Ahanu. 'But I ache to be on my way.'

'Oh, come Kiana! Join your voice with ours!' Spud begged. But I shook my head this time, sitting back with Scandra's coiled tail keeping me warm.

'The One is not joyous,' Scandra told him. 'Shoo.'

But even as he poked a tiny green tongue out at her, I could tell that despite her annoyance she was developing a soft spot for the Gnome and his kind.

She was particularly accepting of the multitudes of little Gnome men and women who sat adoringly beside her, polishing her golden scales and treating her like a God. And while the Dwarves were less rowdy, she tolerated them for the fact that they openly admired her glittering form as well.

In fact the Dwarves seemed attracted to all things that shone, and to combat sight problems that they had developed from rarely venturing outside, the Dwarves had even invented strange eye glasses with thick gem lenses that wrapped around their bare heads, protecting their eyes and making them look like giant insects.

In contrast to the devilish Gnomes, only handfuls of the Dwarves sat in clumps around the room with us. Their pointed green beards made them easy to spot, even if their behaviour was placid. And it was the Dwarves who had indirectly added to the festive noise of the cavern, as they had been the ones to create more pipes and drums when the Gnomes came to them with random materials, begging for instruments to be made.

The resulting creations were always astounding, given what types of scrap the Dwarves had been given to begin with.

'We – are – so – different,' I heard a Gnome tell Ahanu as she was juggled up into the air and caught again at intervals. 'But – I – like – you. Giants – have – free – spirits – like – Gnomes.'

'Thank you friend,' Ahanu told the tiny female.

'Wecouldkeephim,' another Gnome rushed to get all of his words out, before he was tossed back up toward the glowing, multi-coloured roof crystals.

'Just when he'd finished convincing me he wasn't your pet,' Scandra muttered to me. 'These little rocks with legs want to adopt him.'

'I would never fit in the burrows you've delved outside,' Ahanu said brightly. 'And my life partner would miss me eventually.'

'Whaaaat?'

The whole stack of Gnomes dropped down and clutched at his hands.

'This is a design that signifies my lifelong bond,' Ahanu told them, showing them the faintly glowing mark on his skin.

'You stay with someone *forever*?' a Gnome protested in disbelief. 'You're not so free after all.'

'Eolande is the only one I would want to spend forever with,' Ahanu tried to tell them.

'Such a bond is an unnatural, impossible, almost fool hardy sacrifice in Gnome customs,' Spud explained, pulling himself up to sit on Ahanu's knee while the other Gnomes regarded the Giant pityingly. 'Why else would my Queenly Dwarf mother have had no qualms about both Dwarf and Gnome mates?'

'And that's why we've got such an energetic Gnome War-lord in Spud, and such a wind-bag of a political King in Herb,' a lady Gnome giggled.

Spud rubbed at his round nose. 'Oh, the Dwarves may deliberate too much and make it seem that the Gnomes are the workers around here. But, look around you. Look at the perfect crystals lighting the walkways, look at the gleaming walls, the armour and jewels they can fashion.' Spud shook his head. 'When the Dwarves are stirred to passion, they are the almighty race that your folk would know from stories. They are powerful and fierce. They can work rock and earth like no other. With so much more detail than us Gnomes could ever be bothered to achieve. When they reach passions like that ... the Gnomes are simply swept along with them or left behind.'

I cocked my head to the side, evaluating his words. 'I do wish they could be stirred to such passion about the quest,' I remarked. 'Their very lives and way of life depend on it.'

Spud lounged back on Ahanu's knee. 'They'll get there. Look more closely,' he said, nodding at the walls.

Crystals and treasures had been mined carefully from the walls so that they were visible. Some of them glittered with a life of their own. They were the dim light source of the whole tunnel city.

'Every treasure used to light this city like the stars light a clear night,' Spud went on. 'They were left in the walls to continue to bring light and to live for a reason. We feel and nurture the life of the rock, and it glows and grows for us.'

I realised that over half of the treasures in the room were dim or not glowing at all.

'But since Darziates has strengthened, the natural energy and purity of the magic of the rock has been dying. Most of our crystals and gems are dead. Soon we will weaken and live in darkness. My people will do what they can to protect this part of nature, but we have been living in dread and growing fear for so long as each light has gone out, that it may take a while to break that fear.'

'So you think the Gnomes and Dwarves are likely to join the quest?' I questioned Spud thoughtfully.

'Yes. Eventually,' he shrugged, licking his palm and slicking down his sprout-like hair. 'When they remember why they should. And I'll be ready for it.'

39

Thirty Nine

D alin

Thorin and I had kept vigil by Noal's bed into the night without him stirring, so we both jumped when he suddenly woke to sit bolt upright at dawn.

His face screwed up with the pain of the abrupt jolt, but then he turned to us, wide awake.

'You both alright?' Noal asked sarcastically, finding us wide-eyed and clutching our chests.

'Just go back to sleep and don't do that again,' Thorin admonished him.

'Can't go back to sleep,' Noal retorted, carefully manoeuvring his legs so he could climb off the bed.

I put a hand out and unceremoniously shoved his legs back under the covers. 'And why not?' I asked.

'Firstly,' Noal puffed. 'I have critical information. Secondly,' he said, 'I need to empty my bladder.'

Thorin crossed his arms. 'The 'firstly' part can wait.'

But Noal, as pale, crumpled and feverish as he was, had a stubborn gleam in his eyes. 'No. It can't.'

I sighed.

'Tane,' I called softly, trying not to wake the other patients.

Tane's curl covered head poked around the tent door almost instantly.

'Can you please ask King Durna and his council for a meeting before camp is broken?'

Then I helped Noal across to a screen that concealed the wooden pail privy, and Thorin left to fetch clean clothes from Noal's pack.

'What a devoted brother I am,' I teased as I helped Noal to change, and I tried not to wince at the shocking array of burns, all still seeming to radiate with palpable heat from his torso.

'You don't really mind,' Noal replied, leaning heavily on me.

'No. I don't really mind.'

He grimaced for a moment and put a hand to his chest, pausing. Then he saw my worry and smiled in reassurance. 'It just feels tight. Let's go.'

I wasn't reassured, but helped him to Durna's tent, slinging his arm over my shoulders for support while Tane, Thorin and Ferron flanked us.

'Noal,' King Durna said as I lowered my brother into a seat. 'We could have waited, you don't have to address the council immediately. Nobody expects such strength after what you have gone through.'

'Nobody would expect to still be alive after what you have gone through,' one of the generals added.

Noal shook his head. 'There are things I must tell you. By now you must know of Agrona's weakening. But I also learned that our suspicions were correct. The Witch really is fixated solely on locating Kiana. She never pushed to know anything else.'

Aeron winced. 'Has the Witch discovered that Kiana is trying to unite the other races?'

'No,' Noal answered, trying to keep his voice clearly projected. 'Agrona has no idea that Kiana is no longer even in the lands of mortal men.'

He paled and paused for a moment. 'The Witch is intent on killing the last *Larnaeradee*. Probably because she's our one hope against the Sorcerer. Yet while the Witch is now reduced anyway, I can tell you that she has been convinced that Kiana is in fact hiding in Krall, plotting to get to Darziates to avert the whole war.'

I raised my eyebrows and exhaled with relief and admiration.

'You have protected the quest under the worst of conditions,' Durna replied sombrely and with respect.

'I also came to a grim realisation,' Noal ploughed on. 'That perhaps someone else in our midst has not done the same in protecting the quest.'

The group became still, listening attentively.

'Maeve and I discussed how odd it was that the attacks had started so soon after our exit from the mountains. Really,' he flinched and caught his breath. 'They shouldn't have expected us to appear on any path until now. I began to consider ...' another wince. 'That we may have suffered a betrayal.'

'Be careful to accuse,' one of the lady members cautioned. 'It's a serious insult if inaccurate.'

'Yes,' Noal agreed with a pinched expression. 'And it is personally devastating when this individual has travelled with and been saved by us. But it's easy to do ... when this person has betrayed me before.'

The tent was silent and strained. I felt a heavy knot form in my stomach.

'I'm accusing Agrudek,' Noal stated grimly and firmly. 'Because he has had reason to betray us before, and has the same reason still. Therefore I ask the council to search and question the inventor.'

Durna nodded to two of his guards standing with Thorin, Ferron and Tane at the entrance. And when the guards returned with the squirming, terrified inventor held between them, it was clear that Noal had been right.

'Oh *frarshk*,' I hissed under my breath, seething.

'Sorry!' Agrudek was crying. 'I'm s-s-s-sorry!'

The two men dropped him in the middle of the circle and he huddled there, his eyes darting to the door.

'What exactly are you apologising for?' Durna asked coldly.

'Sssoso very sorry!' Agrudek wailed. 'I h-had to do it … had to … Darziates has my,' he swallowed and gulped. 'My family!'

'What exactly have you done?' Aeron glowered.

'Just … just talked …'

My fists were clenching. 'There are hundreds dead or wounded, hundreds of other families changed forever, because you gave an early slip of information to the enemy.'

Agrudek gulped and quickly scrabbled to his haunches. 'I … I … h-h-had to!'

And in a blink Agrudek was up and darting for the door, surprising his Jenran guards and ducking between the chairs of two officials in a rush. But Thorin's reflexes were lightning fast as he pounced forward to catch the struggling, shouting man in his unforgiving arms.

Thorin dumped Agrudek back in the middle of us, and it was as Agrudek landed that I noticed a flash of red from within the folds of his robe.

I gasped and leant forward, seizing the chain about his neck and ripping it free. He yelped while I heard the Krall men exclaim in horror. But Noal was quiet.

Twice this man had nearly cost Noal his life when Noal had only ever pitied and supported him.

'What is it?' Aeron asked in consternation.

I held it up over Agrudek's head to show everyone. 'It's smaller than what I've seen before, but it must be a scryer globe. An invention of Darziates' that allows him to contact his minions.'

Durna was like stone. 'Prepare for an execution.'

'I didn't t-t-tell about the t-tunnel! Or Miridoon c-caves. Or about the One g-go-going!' the inventor cried.

'Please,' Noal spoke again. 'King Durna, not death. He is an example of what it is to be a helpless slave. He didn't do this without compulsion, and I feel somehow that he should not be ended by us.'

Agrudek turned to grovel and thank Noal, but the fatal look from both of us was enough to send him cowering back at Thorin's feet.

Noal glared down at the inventor, holding his chest as if it cost him to speak. 'Do not expect that this is anything but compassion to one lower and more wretched than I.' He rasped on a cough for a moment, his shoulders shuddering. 'Perhaps it is even the prophecy that is forcing me to do it. The very prophecy you shared so easily with the Sorcerer.'

With one normal and one mangled hand Noal pulled at his collar and showed Agrudek a patch of blistered, bruised skin, which almost looked like it was radiating red with heat now. His chest was heaving and glistening with sweat, his breath heavy.

'This is where the Witch sent red fire through me. My mind was plagued by her ghouls, and my soul was toyed with. And yet you are the one who has truly hurt me. You are the one who has betrayed our trust, and you have cost us many lives by putting your wishes above the safety of all others.'

Agrudek whimpered and covered his eyes with his stump.

'Lock him up, then,' Durna growled. 'In a small cart with only basic provisions. Isolated from everyone.'

Agrudek was mewling pathetically as he was hauled away, and everyone sat in shock for a moment, until Noal stirred once more.

'That's all I had to say,' he told us as he stood with an effort, and I quickly rose to support him again.

King Durna nodded in understanding, fighting to maintain a level voice. 'I thank you, Noal. Your bravery, and your return to us is a comfort.'

He nodded once more before we stepped back out into a stirring camp that would soon be broken.

'Dalin?' Noal asked faintly as we walked away.

'Yes?'

'I think you should call Amarantha.'

I glanced at him quickly and found that his face was pale with exertion while he was trying valiantly to look well for the smiling soldiers that we passed.

'What's wrong?' Thorin asked worriedly as he, Tane and Ferron walked closely behind us.

'My chest,' Noal grunted. Sweat was beading on his forehead. 'It's killing me.'

Thorin and I shared a glance.

'Please get me back to the tent ...' Noal gritted out. 'I don't need everyone to see.'

Thorin quickly slung Noal's bad arm over his shoulder to help me, and we both picked up the pace.

'Purdor!' Thorin hissed at the warrior as we passed. 'Find the head healer!'

Purdor took one look at our faces and dropped the bucket of water he'd been carrying to hurtle off through the carts and tents.

'Please hurry,' Noal gasped. 'I suddenly ... can't breathe.'

We half carried, half supported him to his healer tent, rushing to lift him to sit on the bench, and he stooped over – clutching at his chest with his face crumpled while he dragged each breath with an effort.

Amarantha burst back into the tent, followed closely by Purdor and the Krall warriors.

'Gods!' I caught Noal as he suddenly slumped completely forward.

The rasping had stopped.

Amarantha rushed forward and pushed Noal back to lie down flat. His head lolled to the side, eyes closed.

'Come,' Amarantha ordered curtly, and the two other healers of that marquee, who had been taken by surprise over the rush, quickly crossed to her side.

Thorin and I stumbled out of the way as Amarantha tore open the fresh shirt that Noal was wearing to reveal his chest.

'Frarshk ...' I hissed as I saw that all of the scorch marks were now definitely glowing and even faintly steaming as they radiated heat.

One of the wide-eyed healers put a hand to the glowing marks and yelped, but Amarantha ignored the danger and splayed her hands over Noal's heart.

Her skin started to smoke too. But she grimly began pounding into his chest.

She pressed down savagely once, twice, a third time –
continuing at the pace that a heart should thump to.

The rhythm that Noal's heart had stopped following.

'Breathe!' she hissed at the second healer, who quickly
scurried to take a grip on Noal's face. She shakily opened his
mouth and pressed her lips to his. Giving him her own life
breath.

I had never seen such methods – this way to give breath
to someone who had lost it, and I was terrified as the healer's
fingers pinched Noal's nose to keep the life she was offering
him inside. I saw his chest rise and fall until the young healer
stopped and Amarantha began pushing into Noal's chest
again. This time more desperately.

I could smell her hands burning, and could hear her
telling Noal to wake. And then suddenly Noal's body arched
up against the bench, and he was screaming as searing red
light shot with a spinning stream of storming smoke from
his open mouth.

The smoke kept coming, whirring around the tent in a
growing tornado that threw Amarantha and the other healers backward and blasted Thorin and I from our feet.

I was sent tumbling back to land between the cots of the
other terrified patients, who were clinging to their rocking
bed frames to keep from being thrown by the surge of red
air too.

Amarantha tried to rise, but she was sent scraping along
the dirt floor until she caught hold of the marquee's middle
support beam, covering her eyes with her free hand as torrents of whirling dust surrounded her.

Nikon had caught Thorin as he'd gone flying towards the door, and the whole shaking, red-lit tent was billowing on its frame so much that I heard fear filled cries and horses whinnying outside.

We huddled against the unnatural, surging red wind and the sound of Noal's screams while the smoke whipped in a vortex around us, plucking at our clothes and stealing our breath.

Until suddenly, all at once, the red smoke seemed to deplete. We all dropped forward, and Noal's body slumped on the bench.

Stunned, we all panted as the burn marks across Noal's chest quickly became less angry and the remnants of the red magic in the tent dropped away like dust settling down to rest.

Then Amarantha and I both picked ourselves up, hurrying to Noal's side in time to hear him suck in a gigantic gulp of air, his eyes opening wide with a fast fading red glow.

He was tense for a moment. And then he relaxed.

'Ouch,' he rasped in a half moan.

'Ouch,' I agreed incredulously.

Amarantha half laughed and half sobbed herself, and though her hands were burnt she leant over and hugged his weak frame.

'It seems you have expelled Agrona's magic,' she told him. 'What a strong warrior you are.'

He managed a shaky grin. 'What a brave healer.'

'Oh Gods, Noal!' Thorin collapsed out of Nikon's arms, sitting feebly on the grass outside the door.

'I feel much better,' Noal coughed at the gaping men. 'Now that that's all out of me.'

I took his good hand in my own, falling gratefully into the chair I'd occupied the night before. The other patients appeared rattled to the point of being traumatised.

'Dalin?' Noal said with a hoarse voice.

'Yes?'

'Three things,' he coughed again.

'Yes?'

'Firstly,' he began. 'There's no need for Maeve to hear of this.'

I nodded, though the maid, or healer, had proven herself to be resilient.

'And secondly?' I prompted.

'That dent in your forehead is gruesome.'

I rolled my eyes. 'Lastly?'

His expression became very sincere. 'Can we get something to eat?'

'Oh, thank the Gods. Of course,' I told him with a sense of growing relief. 'Any fancy camp food you like.'

40

Forty

Kiana

'What are you thinking about dear One, you've hardly said a word,' Ahanu commented as he ducked his way back into the dreaded government hall.

'I didn't sleep until late,' I replied, my eyes passing over the many crystals decorating the cavernous hall. 'I kept thinking about today's meeting.'

'If the Dwarvish armour didn't shine so brightly, you could probably catch up on sleep during the proceedings,' Ahanu grinned, referring to the silvery, glowing armour that was so light in make that many Dwarves wore it daily.

'I don't think you'd miss much,' he added, and I nodded distractedly, playing with my earthstone as I took my designated seat.

Ahanu sprawled out on the floor next to the front half of Scandra's body, which was now taking up the entire entrance of the circular, forum styled hall.

'Like Spud said, the Gnomes and Dwarves have the potential to be powerful allies,' I whispered up to Scandra when the speeches began at the front dais again. 'They can shape mountains and move rocks with only their hands for tools.'

'Sure they could. But they are too caught up with politics and plans,' Scandra drawled back. 'They need something to shake them into action.'

'Yes,' I agreed. 'They do.'

'... Therefore I call on Minister Jessip to outline the risks of heat stroke in Krall ...' a wrinkly Dwarf sat down and another one stood up, clearing his throat.

Before Minister Jessip could begin, I let my wings unfold with a big rush of magic to bring me into the air and draw everyone's eyes.

'Please excuse me King Herb and members of the government,' I interrupted. 'But I feel the time for debate is over, and that the time for choosing is here.'

The Dwarves in the hall fell silent, craning back to blink at me through crystal spectacles in bewilderment.

'Thank the Gods,' I heard Scandra mutter.

'Honoured Summoner, One *Larnaeradee*,' King Herb blubbered as the flustered Minister Jessip sat back down in a huff. 'While we welcome anything you care to suggest –'

'I hope you do,' I said gravely. 'For I have much now to suggest.'

I hadn't meant it, but the pent up, restless passion I'd been feeling within was now starting to manifest, vibrating in the air.

'I am moved to speak because I must soon leave here with or without your allegiance. As you have discussed at length, Darziates is at his strongest and the Three have travelled far and wide to complete the prophecy – gaining the support of the forest dwellers, the mortal races, the Giants of Margate Isle, and the Dargons of Eirian Isle.

'Now representatives of every free race left alive but yours and Lixrax's has pledged to join the Army for the World. And though you would be mighty and creative allies – able to work rock and earth – I cannot linger here to wait for your aid.

'The choice is your own, and you are free to make it. But be warned, if we all fail without your help, the Dwarves and Gnomes will hold the last front against the wrath of the Sorcerer alone.'

I rose higher into the air, letting my magic spill outward, spreading through the hall to touch the walls – and as my power touched each dying or dead jewel in the rocky hall, their rainbow lights returned with new vigour.

There were gasps of wonder as my touch renewed the entire hall's glory with dramatically dancing, multi-coloured sparkles that reflected off Dwarvish armour and made flaring patterns in the air.

'With all of this in mind I ask you to consider how the world has much beauty to be saved. And I ask you now to declare if you will take part in saving it.'

While a hall full of large green and brown eyes stared at me and at the stunning lights cast by the crystals in the walls, I willed my magic to absorb into each shimmering jewel and to stay there so that at least this one room could be rejuvenated and nurtured against Darziates' influence.

At last a Dwarvish voice was raised to break the mass reverie. 'The Dwarves are no cowards ...'

And a surge of voices quickly joined with protests against cowardice.

'We must fight for our own future!'

'We could tip the balance!'

Suddenly Scandra was getting to her feet, and an enormous growl that made my flesh prickle brought silence again, and all attention fell to her – and the bustling swarm of Gnomes that she had allowed to climb over her, now spilling in hordes into the hall.

Spud was the only one left precariously standing at the top of her head and I watched expectantly as he cleared his throat.

'I don't know about you and your Dwarves, Herb, but the Gnomes and I are going. We decided as much when we met the One and after we'd heard her Summons was real.'

Scandra actually appeared smug now, no longer bothering to hold up pretences of scorn for the Gnomes while the hall began to fill with outcries as the Dwarves in turn rounded on their leader.

'They're going to leave us behind?'

'She'll leave here without us ...'

Herb waved his arms for quiet, his egg crown slipping slightly.

'Brother!' Herb exclaimed, pushing his egg so that it tilted precariously in the other direction. 'Even if we do agree, we cannot leave in haste in any case.' He crossed his arms. 'We haven't even discussed what we need to take.'

'Brother,' Spud echoed, and a wave of bald heads swivelled back toward him. 'I have foreseen this problem, and as leader of the armies and the only member of royalty that will be attending the war, I have taken it upon myself to do all of the planning for you. In fact it was an easy matter to go through our stores to sort out rations while you've all been locked up squawking in here. And I didn't have to do much calculating in the way of making armour, seeing as every Dwarf and Gnome of age has made and owns some. I've also already had a peek at the maps and know that the Dargons are capable of flying over the sea at roughly the same pace as the Giants, so we can all hitch a ride in baskets carried by the Dargons, and so can our provisions.' He grinned brightly. 'Therefore, hence with and all that ... we can leave tomorrow.'

'The Dargons will definitely accept this charge,' Scandra put in, not at all insulted by the idea of becoming the transportation if only it would end all the quibbling.

'Where do these baskets come from? Who will do the sorting of the rations? This will all take more than today and tonight!' Herb protested.

But Spud waved a hand of dismissal. 'There's already been six days' worth of time. And I've had countless volunteer

Gnomes making baskets that are now finished and strong enough to withstand a hundred Dargon crashes and that are big enough to hold a number of heavy Dwarves,' Spud shrugged. 'Once that was finished I had the Gnomes start dividing and packing provisions and that should be finished by this afternoon.'

Scandra refrained from contesting the crashing remark while Herb was quiet for a long moment.

'We still need to plan numbers properly,' Herb pouted glibly, though the hapless King didn't truly seem bothered by his brother's assumptions. Spud had possibly just saved him from a very sudden turn toward public disfavour.

Spud held up a tiny finger. 'All done. One hundred and fifty Dargons will be flying. Fifty can carry baskets of provisions and will also be strong enough to carry forty Gnomes in those baskets too. The rest of the Dargons will be able to carry twenty Gnomes and twenty Dwarves per basket. That means six thousand soldiers can be accounted for if that many want to come. So again, we're pretty much ready.'

'The Dargons have already eaten enough to carry us through a period of hibernation, which means we are ready as well,' Scandra attested smugly.

'And the Giants will also likely be prepared and impatient to go by now,' Ahanu joined in.

'Well then. All settled,' Spud surmised with satisfaction. 'Now all we need to do is get a good night rest, strap on our armour, and set off for our adventure in the morning.'

At Spud's declaration there was an explosion of cheers from the crowd of spectators.

'Wait!' the King called over the excited exclamations from his now thoroughly impassioned government. 'I must at least officially announce it!'

He cast about at the unusually enlivened crowd.

'So ...' he blustered. 'The army will join then.'

41

Forty One

The Sorcerer

It was the first time that Darziates had seen the return of Agrona's raven form, drifting mournfully over Krall. But he ignored it. The black bird was just a deformed blot in the sky and the Witch herself no longer needed to be kept as a last resort for a mate.

Not now that there was the last *Larnaeradee*. A female as powerful as himself.

Thanks to his own culling efforts, the Fairy had the inherited magic and blood of all her ancestors combined, and only the extra power flowing into him from the Other Realm meant that he should be strong enough to control her. His one.

A challenge that he had become oddly fixated on with the passing of time.

He desired mastery of her and to keep her for his own, an almost equal companion as he swept across the globe on his crusade. And despite the fact that he had only ever seen her through the envious mind of Agrona, the fearful eyes of Agrudek, and once through the scryer she'd been holding; for the first time in the Sorcerer's long life he was beginning to feel the hesitant ebbing of actual anticipation, and perhaps even *yearning*, deep within the cold confines of his chest.

He had to take her into his possession and to force her to understand his quest. Then, together, they could achieve the salvation of not only this world, but the universe and every realm in between.

'Do you want me to shoot at it?' Angra's voice growled from where he stood behind Darziates, gazing out from a high tower balcony.

'Focus on more important things,' the Sorcerer replied while the black speck of Agrona began drifting dolefully away.

Angra clambered heavily out to join his master, scanning the view below. Troops in rows now extended as far as the eye could see, crowding like ants outside the gates.

'Millions of worthless little men gathering,' Angra wiped his mouth with the back of his hand. 'It'll take a week just to set camp. I've got plenty of time to do other tasks for you.'

'You can keep an eye on our guests,' Darziates replied, and Angra's small, manic eyes flickered across the horizon to where Razek's enslaved forces were camped like a foreboding cloud on the wasteland border to the other side of the castle.

'You let them camp in the sandy heat. They're comfortable. There's no challenge there,' Angra huffed sullenly. 'They won't need to move at all until the Awyalknians and Jenrans get here.'

'That won't be too long.'

The Sorcerer had sent two Evexus back to herd the Jenrans along, and three to herd the Awyalknians.

'You're sending more Dragons to Awyalkna too, aren't you?' Angra sulked.

'Fifteen Dragons. Along with a horde of Griffins.' More of the winged vermin had been migrating to Krall each day.

'And all of the Trune raiders in existence,' Angra pouted. 'But not me.'

'There are only two hundred Trunes in existence. But that should be more than enough to wipe out the leaders in the Awyalknian palace.'

'A bunch of wild, vagrant bandits who serve nobody loyally,' Angra bunched his fists. 'If I was there ...'

Darziates reached an invisible hand of magic into the Warlord's seething, unhinged mind, purposefully stirring up Angra's level of tension while the twisted mortal was oblivious to the obtrusive visit. The more agitated the Warlord became, the more valuably splintered his soul grew.

'If you were there, you wouldn't be here when I need you.'

The Warlord hunched. 'For my precious soul again. And to help with the army.'

'Exactly.'

'But when you used five pieces of my soul last time, I hardly felt it,' Angra complained like an exasperated child. 'I wasn't really doing anything anywhere near as helpful as cutting throats or scaring your enemies.'

'Soon I'll need more than five pieces,' Darziates replied. 'Though in many ways you'll feel less and less each time.'

'Alright,' Angra intoned dully. 'I guess I'll just go and shake up the men down there then.'

'Nobody inspires them quite like you,' Darziates agreed.

The Sorcerer's magic swept the Warlord up and sped him over the balcony and city sectors – depositing him beyond the walls. From the moment his boots touched down the Warlord was roaring at the startled men for faster, better, harder work. He rushed at and beat at any nervous soldiers, scaring them into action. And even from the distance Darziates could see further fracture lines growing in the Warlord's soul – which was exactly what the Sorcerer needed.

Satisfied with proceedings at the front of the castle, the Sorcerer turned and reached his mind out to Razek's. The mortal Emperor's mind was strong enough to feel and recoil from the contact, but nothing too interesting was happening there.

Returning fully to himself, Darziates wished fleetingly that he could search out the *Larnaeradee* just as easily. But her mind was protected and, as yet, he had not felt her presence or magic near him.

He forced his hand down from where it had flickered, ready to rise to press once again against the odd recurring ache in his chest.

If she would only come as Agrona had warned ...

In the distance, the wavering dot that was Agrona let out a miserable screech as Darziates turned away from the balcony, as if she knew exactly what he was thinking.

42

Forty Two

*K*iana

King Herb, surrounded by his government, had long been delivering a great speech while the whole Dargon army sat impatiently along the clifftop above, ready and waiting to leave.

Baskets were already loaded onto their stomachs and most Dargons had stopped bothering to look fearsome and impressive, and were instead sharpening their talons against the rock lip while muttering to each other. Similarly, a large number of elderly Dwarves who had come out to farewell us were nodding into their beards – females and males alike – their eyes closed behind their gem spectacles. And many little roly-poly potato children had given up listening – instead wandering off to cackle up and down the pebble beach in the distance.

Scandra's eyes had grown blank, and I was myself struggling to focus on the rambling King, even though I was the one standing beside him being publicly presented with a special parting gift of silvery Dwarf armour.

My initial excitement over the gift had faded, however, because Herb had been holding the armoured dress and matching boots – explaining that the ensemble would stop arrows, bend knives, protect against all weapons – for nearly an hour.

When he finally passed them over my own sincere thanks were in return as heartfelt but as short as possible, before I quickly flew to my place on Scandra's back.

'I know that armour is priceless,' Scandra muttered to me while the remaining Dwarves, Gnomes and King Herb all cheered madly. 'But that was torture.'

The rows of female warrior Dargons shook themselves awake as they heard the change of pace down below. Spud in turn climbed up to sit himself comfortably at the very top of Scandra's head, where she had amazingly deigned to have a small harness attached to a pointed horn there.

When he was in place, Scandra let forth a ground shaking, roaring jet of flames to call her warriors to action and the Dargons above roared with answering flames of their own.

I felt the powerful muscles beneath Scandra's sleek scales ripple and quake, and then she spread her magnificent wings wide and launched into the air.

Her Dargon warriors in turn stretched their wings in a monumental vision of sparkling light, and they swept from the clifftop like a shower of gold – while the yells and tumbling sounds of the Dwarves in their baskets were also clearly audible at the motion.

Cheers rose up from below as the sky filled with Dargons, but they faded as we left the island behind with the powerful wings of the Dargons carrying us swiftly to Margate, where Ahanu had returned after the Dwarf council to warn the Giants of our coming.

As we swooped over Margate Isle Scandra once again issued her mighty roar in a call to arms that sent ripples over the ocean surface. And in response, countless Giants began to appear under the surface of the ocean, soundlessly joining us and sparkling in the water as they followed our flight.

'The Gods will be seeing a spectacular dance across the world,' Spud commented as he lounged against the spike he was tethered to quite comfortably. 'Everything's coming along nicely.'

'I'm not sure everyone agrees that it's going 'nicely,'' Scandra replied, and I again heard the groans of many basket bound Dwarves, amongst the cackles of many Gnomes.

'The Dwarves are more used to the underground,' Spud agreed. 'I imagine they're huddled down like gibbering balls in their baskets. But they'll have a scenic flight for a couple of weeks. A healthy trek through the mortal lands for a few more weeks. And a life changing battle against the Sorcerer after that.'

'It sounds as if you've got it all sorted out,' Scandra remarked, her voice vibrating sarcastically.

'Of course,' Spud shrugged. 'It all feels easy after a life-time spent trying to make sure Herb does more than talk about running the kingdom.'

I sighed. 'I'm certain it won't be easy. But it is definitely time I went home.'

43

Forty Three

G*laidin*

The sun was still hours from rising, yet the Awyalknians were already marching to avoid the vicious heat of a Krall afternoon.

It was a small mercy to stop when temperatures blistered most, but marching through the obviously corrupted environment at any time felt similar to trying to run through deep water. The people of Krall themselves seemed withered by prolonged exposure, and the sight of them saddened rather than threatened the passing army.

'We are fortunate,' Warlord Conall commented quietly, speaking to Asha as she floated above his dusty head. 'I heard that one of our men sampled a limp vegetable from a dry field. But it tasted less appealing than our stale supplies from Awyalkna.'

'I would believe it,' Asha replied. 'The yield eked out of this land would hardly nourish the farmers who struggle to tend it.'

Whenever the army had drawn near, the skeletal, tough skinned farmers of the desolate border lands had mostly fled to their hovels. Or, at best, had paused in their back breaking labour, leaning on their tools to grimly watch the army pass.

'We're also fortunate that they have offered us no resistance,' Conall went on. 'I would not have liked to treat such creatures harshly.'

'Yes, very fortu –' almost as if the word she'd been about to parrot had been a curse, Asha unexpectedly felt a pang of foreboding.

'Asha?' Conall asked, alarmed by her change.

'We will not be feeling fortunate for long,' she gasped. Then she stopped abruptly to call out a warning sound to the whole army.

'What is it?' Glaidin asked, quickly nudging his horse closer to Conall.

But before she could explain, there was a terrible rushing noise of colossal, beating wings.

The sound grew, accompanied by a vortex of swirling air and dust. And all at once the entire army was ducking under a sky that had suddenly become filled with giant, scaly beasts – each beating grey wings that spanned for yards to keep themselves airborne.

Smaller, noisier, feather covered creatures flew with the swarm of reptilian beings, and they yowled with foul voices and clicking beaks, adding to the thunderous sound of the horde passing by.

The army huddled anxiously under the deafening clamber but the winged creatures did not pause, and when the incredible procession had passed, many pale, shaken faces turned to Asha.

'They were Dragons and Griffins,' Asha told the King. 'Off to plague your Queen.'

'Gods,' Glaidin uttered in horror. 'The Sorcerer means to ruin the palace and Aglaia at last.'

'I am sorry, Glaidin,' Asha told him quickly. 'But they were not the only threat that made me call the alarm. We have other worries of our own.'

Glaidin gaped at her. 'What other worries?'

She looked as if she wanted to be ill as she answered him, speaking in a low voice. 'The Evexus who hunted Kiana and your princes are coming,' she said. 'It can only be them. I have not felt such evil since the Other Realm spirits came with Darziates to massacre my race.'

Glaidin's eyes widened and hoarse whispers of fear began to spread through the crowds. He heard Asha's Nymph comrades shouting orders as his own mortal generals rounded men into better formation.

'Are we ready for this?' Conall asked Asha.

Out of the morning's darkness her immortal eyes could only just begin to see the low running figures stalking across the sand towards the army. They were like silent wolves, but their bodies were long, sharp, and filled with a nameless evil.

She shook her head. 'Not now, or ever.'

44

Forty Four

Kiana

The night sky was clear, and only the sounds of strong wings swooping expertly through the air disturbed the silence.

I sat by Spud, watching the beauty of the passing sky and feeling warmed by the radiating heat from Scandra's scales.

'You know,' Spud said. 'You could wear that armour in the salty ocean water and it would never even need to be cleaned for rust.'

I followed his gaze to where, in the darkness, I could see the glinting shine of the silver ore dress of armour even as it was tucked carefully away in my pack. I reached over and pulled it out to inspect it more closely and found that the cool, slippery material was so light that it felt almost like liquid silk.

'How is that so?' I asked. 'I have never heard of any armour, no matter how delicate and mysterious, ever being unaffected by the elements.'

The little Gnome wriggled out of his harness, stepped along Scandra's spine and nestled under my elbow, making himself at home.

'The ore is not something we've mined or invented. It's just something we shape,' he explained.

I stroked its satiny texture with a curious frown. 'Where does it come from?'

'It comes from the strongest hides in all the world,' the Gnome grinned, lightly leaning over to touch Scandra's scales.

My eyebrows raised and my eyes darted from the faintly glowing, feather-light garment in my hands, to the powerful, indestructible scales beneath us.

'Dargon scales?' I questioned in wonder.

'A great gift,' Spud agreed. 'And scarce. Usually you have to inherit a full suit of scales as an heirloom because fallen Dargon scales rarely land anywhere but in the sea or in their own eyrie. But some brave Gnomes sneak into their lair and search. Or lucky Gnomes find them on the beach. They turn silver when they are loosed from the heat of the Dargons, but continue to glitter with strength and magic. Then we take them to the Dwarves.'

I remembered the Dwarves who had made instruments out of any material that the Gnomes had presented them with and nodded thoughtfully.

'Gnomes can shape these scales with our tough hands and magic, but we don't have the masterful artistry of the Dwarves to create such beauty with these priceless things,' Spud went on. Then he took a handful of the delicate looking armour and showed me how impossible it was to tear. 'And you can rest assured that, even though I can break rocks with these hands, I could never damage this strong garment, and neither can most weapons.'

'Your people have honoured me,' I answered. 'If Sylranaeryn had worn such a thing, no arrow could have hurt her.'

'Ah, but then Kinrilowyn would not have made his mighty charge against Deimos and all would have been lost earlier than now,' Spud replied wisely. Then his pudgy green and brown cheeks grew rounder as he grinned. 'Besides, it wasn't just my people who took part in making you this armour. The greatest of all Dargons also had a role.'

I shook my head in realisation. 'Scandra,' I said, gazing down at the magnificent Empress who was effortlessly gliding through the night air.

'Scandra donated her own golden scales, to keep the One safe,' Spud nodded. 'Can't beat a personal gift like that.'

'You're right,' I agreed, lying down across the Dargon Empress' back with Spud in my arms and the stars passing above. 'This quest has given me many great gifts,' I told him. 'And I am beginning to feel that I am at home anywhere in the world, and will never again be an observer from the shadows.'

There was a snort. 'Not in a garment that glows that bright, anyway.'

I closed my eyes. 'You're right again, of course.'

45

Forty Five

D^alin

'Boy oh boy, it's great to be home,' Tane moaned, his curls sticking to his forehead.

We were back in Krall, and the heat was unbearable – every breath was just sucking in more hot air, and water was now a precious thing to be saved.

'I sure missed this,' Ferron scowled.

The Krall men had been keeping up a sour commentary since leaving the forest.

'I can't say *I* missed it,' Noal commented ruefully. He was still worn from his ordeal despite having slept almost constantly for days.

'Oh but this time you'll experience something other than a jail cell,' Tane reassured him. 'You see, we've made it back right in time for the cycle change.'

'Now that's always delightful,' Wolf intoned.

'From desert heat and blistering sunburn, to mud, floods and unbearable cold in just one week,' Thorin added, as if he were trying to sell Krall at a market.

'Our beloved leader's almighty power has really made all the difference to Krall.' Even Thale seemed happy to keep up the complaints.

'But not everything about coming home can be terrible?' Rai, the youngest of Dren's archers asked hopefully.

'Surely you have friends and family you long to see?' Dwyn the archer also questioned.

I saw Tane's face grow serious and he looked to the ground as he thought of his young wife and son.

'Aye,' Nikon said gruffly. 'For those of us who have loved ones left at home, it would be nice to see them. If we weren't joined in a war against them.'

'Oh,' Rai's shoulders slumped. 'Right.'

'I'm pretty sure we wouldn't fit straight back in with our comrades either,' Vulcan mused. 'Now that we are their sworn enemies.'

'When the war is over, if the right side has won, you'll fit back in,' Noal said. 'Because your people will be confused and in need of help to understand the great changes to their land, and to themselves. You all remember how it was when Darziates no longer controlled you.'

Phobos grimaced. 'Disorienting.'

'Of course,' Thale sighed. 'It's just difficult to think of any time after the war. We've got to get past killing our people; soldiers we have trained with and farmers who have been coerced to fight, before we can focus on how much it will have helped them.'

'And we have to get through this blasted cesspit of a desert before all that too,' Phrixus muttered.

'Well at least we're doing an efficient job at that,' I said, satisfied by how quickly we'd been slicing across the desert after having left the forest path to march at a severe angle across the dry lands.

Amazingly, our progress had been such that we had already come upon recent tracks from the Awyalknian forces, still visible in the dust. But I tried not to think of the other sights we had also found, of wiry, starved looking Krall villagers who ran from us.

'Now, because you have been such enthused tour guides so far,' I heard Dren say to Tane and Thorin. 'Can you tell me exactly what kind of bird that is?'

And we followed his gaze toward the horizon, squinting to make out a cluster of winged creatures that appeared to be circling over something ahead.

'Nothing like that normally lives in Krall,' Thale frowned, becoming more sober at once.

'They're definitely not native birds at that size,' Nikon rumbled, shielding his eyes with a hand.

As a number of Jenrans spotted the now swooping creatures, animated voices were raised while everyone began to make their own assumptions.

'They have a much larger wingspan than any bird I've ever seen,' Dren commented. 'They could carry off big prey.'

'And those are some nasty talons,' Ander grunted, while Glyn and Dwyn reached for their bows simultaneously and Rai had already nocked an arrow.

'Gods,' Noal breathed. 'If Darziates has sent Griffins that aren't after us, then...'

'They're after the Awyalknians,' Wolf finished.

'And if they are hovering and diving slowly like that?' I asked sickly.

'Then they have found an easy dinner that isn't fleeing,' I turned as Warlord Aeron steered his horse up to where we rode.

Feeling dread, there was nothing we could do but continue on, trailing the Awyalknian army and drawing closer to the hovering shapes. And our sense of foreboding only worsened as the tracks that we were following began to tell a very frenzied tale.

There were signs of hurried fleeing, of fighting, and finally we came upon our first soldiers of the Awyalknian army, whose dusty, scavenger picked remains must have been abandoned in a rush.

'They don't even look human anymore,' Rai breathed, staring at the piles of meat-stripped, beak scratched bones that had been left by the Griffins.

Their Awyalknian uniforms still blew about in scraps around the remains.

'I am saddened that this is how you are first reunited with your kin after your great journey,' Aeron told Noal and I in a low tone. 'But I am certain that it wasn't the Griffins who first killed these men,' he said. 'The way that the Griffins were simply hanging in the air tells me that they have been following along and making a dinner of the destruction left behind from something else.'

And his words were proven true when we later found a whole flock of reeking Griffins just settling onto a fresh scattering of dead Awyalknians.

'G-reat,' one of the creatures hissed. 'An interrupted dinner.' It ripped an arm from the body it had been gnawing at and flapped off above our heads.

The other winged creatures lazily lifted into the air and flew out of reach when Dren's archers and a bunch of Jenrans let loose a round of arrows.

Yet the fallen Awyalknians who had been left un-pillaged were still too torn and broken to be recognisable anyway – with only their injuries left to tell their tale.

'They died in the desert heat, and yet are covered in slashes that have turned their skin blue,' Phobos remarked unhappily, peering at the icy, vein-like bruises that flowered from the gouges on each body.

'They don't stand much chance if they're facing both Griffins and the Evexus,' I heard one Jenran mutter to the soldier nearest him. They were both squinting further ahead, toward the desert we would be covering to get to the Awyalknians, and toward where many Griffin specks dotted the horizon.

'They will be on the run. We'll have to catch up,' Aeron stated beside me.

'Let's move,' I answered grimly, and Aeron nodded his agreement.

46

Forty Six

*K*iana

The steady, unbroken pace had taken no toll as yet on the immortals, who either didn't technically need to sleep until their next hibernation, or who could both sleep and swim at the same time.

The Dargons had also found ways of passing their loads around as well, much to the horror and discomfort of the Dwarves, and the squealing, adventurous delight of the Gnomes.

And somehow I now hardly seemed to tire from flying either. Instead I spent the days happily alternating between swimming with the Giants and flying with the Dargons, while also making rounds to each basket to reassure the Dwarves of our progress.

During those basket visits I always encountered Gnomes who happily snoozed or played games or talked, while the

Dwarves slumped nauseously or huddled dejectedly, praying for the ride to end.

'You're getting restless,' Spud observed as we launched away from another basket.

I glanced down at where many of the basket free Dargons were skimming above the water surface, basking in the fascinated attention of the darting and diving Giants who came to talk to them.

'We've been in the air for a while,' I agreed, holding his heavy little body as I flew us down to balance on the back of a Dargon who was propelling herself over the water.

Giants surfaced when they saw me, laughing and hitching onto my Dargon's horns so that they could be dragged along in the surf too.

'In fact,' I said, setting Spud down on the Dargon's snout so he could hold onto a horn. 'It's time for a swim.'

The blue pattern lacing around my forearm was already alight with my link to Toru.

'Say hello to big old Ahanu for me,' Spud waved as I dove into the cold water, where at once the contrast of the clear, sharp world above compared to the dim, slowed underwater world gave an energising shock to my body.

Then I let out a stream of bubbles as I was swept up into a game between Ahanu and three of his friends, who had seen me coming.

I was somersaulted through the water like a toy before Ahanu tossed me upwards for air.

'Nice to see you dear One,' Ahanu called gaily as he joined me at the water's surface.

'I missed you,' I spluttered.

'And I'm so glad!' Ahanu laughed, before he grasped my ankle to dunk me back under.

He wove around me like a lit up dolphin and the blue light surrounding the scores of swimming Giants was enough to illuminate the deep. But I was glad when I felt a new hand take me around the waist – gentler than the other playful Giants, and I saw that Toru, as well as Ahanu's oldest 'youngling' Einion had found us, slowing Ahanu's frenzied pace.

When I began struggling to keep up with the enormous strokes made by the Giants, even with my wings to help propel me, Ahanu and Toru each took one of my hands to let me cruise between them.

I was content to pick up on watery, bubble filled conversations being conducted by many of the Giants as they swam around us, and did not need air for a long time while I was close to Toru. It was only when he sensed that the sun was setting that he floated up to the surface with me, and waved as I used his shoulder to push off into the air once more.

I was almost sad to leave him, but I was glad to settle on Scandra's warm scales while I dried.

'Have fun?' Spud asked lazily, appearing even browner after cooking in the sun for the afternoon.

'She certainly looked like a dignified leader of the magical races as she flitted around like a fish,' Scandra snorted.

'Oh shush,' Spud chuckled. 'You and I have both been watching your sister Dargons playing chasey with the Giants instead of hunting for fish themselves.'

I just grinned. 'For a war march, this has been a rather enjoyable day,' I told them, wringing my hair out.

'Yes. Well,' Scandra commented. 'We are a very strange army going to a very deadly battle indeed.'

47

Forty Seven

G*laidin*

Nightmares chased them though they had not slept for days.

Any efforts that they'd made to stop and fight had been useless. Soldiers had been torn down one by one or had been sent flying in handfuls.

Even when the Nymphs had drained their fire in attempts to slow the pursuit, the three Evexus had simply maintained their dogged herding of the army – taking their time to heal the magical burns.

While Glaidin's soldiers staggered and shambled on through the burning heat of the day, the Evexus loped along easily. Then they bit at the heels of stumbling stragglers throughout the endlessness of the night.

So the Awyalknians moved ever onward. They could not stop running unless they consented to death. And it seemed certain that the fiends would make the whole army run all the way into the arms of the Sorcerer – or that they would be diminished to nothing in the process.

Glaidin himself had accepted that it was hardly likely he would make it to the castle of Krall with his own life, let alone with an army still behind him, and when the King at last heard desperate yells coming in strangled fits from his tortured army – despite the fact that they had long since given up yelling in fear, he was sure that the end had come.

Hopelessly he peered upward to find Asha's fatigued form, expecting to see horror on her face over some final attack or monstrosity. Yet instead he found her far above him clapping her hands for joy.

'Stop! Stop!' Asha cried above the army, while Conall and many dazed soldiers paused in confusion.

The yelling and shouting from the men of the back ranks was growing louder, and as the soldiers in front of and around Glaidin began to turn and squint back through the settling dust of their stampede they began to yell too.

'That isn't the sound of dread,' Conall husked, craning to see over the swaying crowd.

Then in incredulous wonder, Glaidin realised that it was hoarse cheering.

'Have they all been driven mad?' he rasped.

He managed to pull himself up onto his wheezing stallion, trying to gain enough height to see.

And then his jaw dropped, inspiring Conall to suffer his own stallion – bleeding from the nose and frothing at the mouth as the creature was – to bear his weight as well.

'It's not possible ...' Conall croaked a moment later. 'Not possible ...'

48

Forty Eight

D^{alin}

'It's getting chilly,' Dwyn commented in surprise, glancing at the still brightly burning sun.

'I'm feeling it too, despite our pace,' Noal frowned.

The army had kept up a faster march since the trails of death and carnage had started to clog our path.

'The cycle change is coming,' Phrixus suggested.

'Forget about it,' Thale added dismissively. 'What's a chill in the middle of a sun blazed desert when it's Darziates' territory?'

'A normal occurrence,' Cadell answered dryly.

'A quaint national feature,' Tane added.

'Annoying,' Thorin remarked flatly.

'Perhaps it *is* that we're approaching Darziates,' Nikon said gruffly. 'Because that familiar feeling of constant fear is back in my stomach.'

'I thought you never felt fear,' Rai told Nikon honestly. 'You don't seem to.'

'Perhaps Nikon just ate something that doesn't agree with him,' Wolf speculated.

'Like, half of the Jenran rations,' Thorin added with a straight face, rapping his knuckles with a drumming sound on Nikon's armoured middle. An area which still sank inward slightly, despite the warrior's best efforts to fix the pummelling the Evexus had given the metal.

'I feel no shame in admitting to a seed of unease in my own gut,' Vulcan frowned, looming over Tane and Thorin. 'Though following a trail of corpses likely makes us all uneasy.'

'That's true. But it still feels wrong to be cold in the middle of a desert,' Dwyn repeated.

'Stop complaining and wrap your cloak around yourself,' Ander answered with disinterest.

'He needs his cloak where it is. On his head to protect his milky complexion,' Dwyn's brother, Glyn, replied airily.

'Perhaps Phobos will lend you his cloak. His head doesn't need the protection,' Thorin mused.

'That thick white skull of his reflects any light that hits it,' Tane agreed.

'Shut up,' was Phobos' only, yet still very convincing reply.

And then a shout of alarm rose from the sentries and two Evexus bounded out through the desert haze.

They angled their bodies closely to the ground, taking on lethal speed and releasing resounding hunting cries before they stampeded into our forces.

There was a moment where shouts were loosed, where weapons were clutched and where soldiers scrambled. But the lithe Evexus swept through our ranks as though diving into water, while we were all left spinning to try to keep our eyes on them.

'There's no purpose to their attacks,' Thorin cried while the Evexus clawed and pounced in quick blurs.

They were slashing at whoever was within reach before disappearing and then re-appearing to begin again in the next spot.

'This is a cull!'

We hardly registered the shadowy blur whirling towards our own group, and the creature manifested as if from nowhere. Tane managed to push Thorin and Vulcan out of the way, before meeting the Evexus with a raised sabre.

The beast lashed quickly at Tane and felt the bite of his blade in return before the fiend leapt away again.

Then in another moment both of the attacking Evexus had gone, disappearing into the swirling dust, and their whirlwind attack was over.

Cries and groans were left in their wake, but our group stirred when Thorin and Vulcan struggled up from where Tane had thrown them.

'Gods, Tane but for the strength of your arm, I would be gone,' Thorin uttered gratefully.

'And I have never been more thankful to be thrown face first into the dust,' Vulcan brushed himself off.

Tane did not reply as he turned, but Thorin swore and bounded to catch his friend as Tane sank down.

Thale ran for the healers while we all surged forward in dread, seeing the punctures in Tane's armour.

'Frarshk, that hurt,' Tane gasped while the colour drained from his face.

'Watch out,' Thale cried urgently as he dashed back and drew Maeve through the crowd, whisking her along so fast that she was being half carried.

'Get his armour off,' she commanded, slicing decisively through our numb shock as Thale put her down so she could crouch over Tane.

Thorin obediently held his friend still against the jostling while Thale and Wolf expertly slid the chest plate and spiked coverings away, and Noal winced sickly beside me as we saw the holes of the Evexus' claws through Tane's gashed flesh.

Maeve grimly ripped bloody cloth away from where the skin was rent open and I felt my insides recoil while everyone else fell quiet.

The wounds bit too deeply into his stomach and chest, as well as chopping into his hip bone.

'Wolf, Dalin and Thale,' Maeve gestured to us briskly. 'Put pressure here, here and here.' She showed us how to hold the skin together to try to slow the blood, though there was no hope on her face.

Tane was breathing rapidly and laboriously, and my hands slipped with his blood as I struggled to pinch and press the gaping skin together. But he calmly looked at each of the faces about him.

At Maeve's gesture Ferron and Purdor helped Thorin to sit Tane up, only to then find that the hole made in his hip had gone through to end at the base of his spine.

Maeve pursed her lips, her eyes meeting Noal's for a moment.

'Let him go,' she said softly. 'There is too much here. Let him rest now.'

'No!' Thale and Thorin both refused together, keeping a tight hold on Tane's wounds. 'Call for Amarantha!'

Wolf tried desperately to clutch the hole in Tane's hip and spine closed, but the crimson flow refused to be stanched, seeping thickly between his fingers.

'Stop,' a steady voice said then. 'Please stop.' Tane waved us away. 'I know what has come for me.'

Maeve gently nudged our hands away. 'It is hurting him more to be pressed unnecessarily.'

Thorin's face was tortured as he saw us pull back and Noal let out a choking sob.

'Always wondered what my end would look like,' Tane gave a slight grin.

He managed to clasp a hand over Thorin's shoulder.

'Apart from wanting it to be on a battlefield, with dead enemies around me ...' Tane continued. 'I'd always hoped I would otherwise be surrounded in the faces of my kin.' Tane gazed again at each of us, fixing his still bright eyes last on Noal, myself, and finally Thorin.

'Thank you brother,' Thorin croaked as he clutched at Tane's hand on his shoulder.

'Walk easy in the afterlife,' Nikon grunted gruffly. 'And wait for us when you get there.'

'Not at the pace you lot blunder along. Aiolos and I would be waiting an eternity.' Tane sighed affectionately. 'Big oafs.'

Vulcan knelt in the dirt wetted by Tane's blood. 'We will carry word of your glory to your wife. To all of Krall. And I will live knowing that the Gods have graced my steps, giving me such a saviour as you.'

'You'll be fighting alongside us on the battlefield,' Phobos promised, his face drawn with sorrow.

'You die a warrior, Tane,' Thale stated solemnly. 'Fighting for the greatest cause we've ever known.'

'I die a happy soldier, then,' Tane replied, his voice just a wisp. 'A very happy soldier. Yet ...'

Tane seemed to be sinking into himself, but his eyes focused on Thorin and understanding dawned on Thorin's face.

'Oh Tane ...' Thorin's voice cracked. 'I swear you will not be forgotten as a husband or father. I will care for them. Mil and Locke will never be left wanting.'

'You'll need to be there to hear my child's first words. To guide my son's steps. To keep my wife from facing these things alone.'

'I will fight to be there,' Thorin promised. 'They will not be alone.'

My heart seemed to fall down into the empty cavity of my stomach while Tane nodded. His whole form relaxed and the faint trace of his familiar smile spread further across his colourless lips.

And we all huddled quietly as the hand on Thorin's shoulder became slack.

49

Forty Nine

*K*iana

'I smell danger on the wind,' Scandra's voice woke me early in the morning.

I was instantly alert and climbed across her scales to sit beside the bleary eyed Spud.

'Is it Witch magic?' he grimaced, trying to shield his face from the glorious sunrise.

'No,' I answered with a frown. 'The air feels dense. There is some kind of sizzling tension in the atmosphere, and I'm tingling all over. But,' I hesitated. 'I don't feel anything unnatural.'

'What other danger could there possibly be?' Spud asked. 'If it's not unnatural then it's not an approaching raven and we should be fine.'

'This danger is greater than any power Agrona could ever have against us,' Scandra rumbled.

'Ey? How's that?' Spud sat up now. 'You feel a Sorcerer floating upwind or something?'

'The power I feel brewing is not from a Sorcerer's darkness either,' Scandra drawled. 'But a threat from nature itself.'

'Oh,' Spud said, his shoulders slumping. '*That* wild beast. With Sorcery spreading and stirring her up she's hard to predict. Calm one moment, in a bad mood the next. Pure and lovely, but damned aggressive.'

'You're right in some ways. Lady Nature is sick, rather than vicious,' I told them. 'And the sky is red. Always the sign of bad weather.'

'Not just bad weather,' Scandra warned. 'I can taste the electricity growing up here, just as you are feeling it. This is going to be a storm that even the strongest of Dargon wings will have to do battle with.'

And, as the day progressed and the sky became an angry, grey roof that pressed down low, I could feel a sense of foreboding. Within and about myself I registered an incomprehensible and limitless power building while rumblings began to roll like distant war drums amongst the bunching clouds that loomed ahead.

'It's like there's static coming off you,' Spud told me at one point, letting go after he'd taken hold of my hand with both of his to keep himself from blowing around in his harness. He had to hold the spine that his harness was tethered to instead, when normally his strong grip allowed him to freely run amuck up and down Scandra's back.

'I'm sorry,' I raised my voice over the rushing air. 'I can feel the energy of the coming storm sparking around me.' I rolled my shoulders restlessly – my muscles beginning to feel as though they were overflowing with the power that was surging into me from all around. 'I feel ... on edge.'

Moisture from the air was beading on Scandra's scales and I wiped at my damp skin as we navigated through increasingly threatening cloud clusters.

It was an effort to relax my clenched jaw, but my stomach churned and I bunched my fists with tension as if the storm was growing inside me while the thunder sounded from closer by.

'This is the first time you are so open and attuned to nature,' Scandra called back to me when I groaned and held myself at the same time as a fork of lightning scarred the sky. 'Since you have let your magic run more freely, it seems almost to have its own emotions.'

'Yes.' I held my breath at the overwhelming sensations that were beginning to flood my being. 'And it is *furious*,' I managed to reply at last, feeling as though my blood and skin were both crackling. 'Furious, and in love with being so wrathful. And yearning to be let loose.'

'You draw your magic from this ferocious part of nature just as you draw it from the aspects of nature that bring gentle waters, rejuvenated life and warming sunlight. But you must not let its hostile side dominate you,' Scandra cautioned me.

I sucked in a breath and closed my eyes as a clap of thunder made me feel almost splintered in half with energy. I was churning and roiling inside.

'I'm just so new to this,' I replied through grinding teeth – suddenly controlling an impulse to fly into a rage, as if *I* were the approaching storm now.

'Girlie,' Spud said, taking the risk to crawl up and lean on my crossed legs. 'You've got the wildest look in your eyes. Like there's lightning in there.'

'I'd believe it,' I agreed with severe effort.

'Up here you are in the heart of the storm's energy,' Scandra called again. 'Perhaps in the ocean with Toru you could dive below the waves and be buffered from it all ...'

'No, I cannot,' I growled with effort. 'If anything happens to the Dargons, or to the poor Gnomes and Dwarves in the baskets. I can help.'

'It is going to be tough up here,' Scandra affirmed, but she seemed satisfied by my answer. 'Yet this is part of who you are. You are as tempestuous as nature, and must learn to deal with it without losing all other aspects of who you are as well.'

'Yes,' I gasped back, feeling almost unable to contain myself as thunder boomed over us again. 'This is one battle I will not lose.'

50

Fifty

D^{alin}

One moment Tane had been animated with mirth, and then so suddenly we had lost our laughing hero. His blood was drying in the dirt while the scorching sun of the accursed land he had wanted to save beat down unforgivingly.

When I led the way to King Durna the Krall warriors and archers fell in behind me. Durna and Aeron shared a glance when they saw us, nervous of what was coming.

'Raiden,' Durna greeted me.

'I've come to beg you, as a friend and ally, for your help and trust yet again,' I stated.

Durna replied without hesitation. 'Of course.'

'What is it Raiden?' Aeron asked, and I did not waver.

'The Evexus have so far been able to wreak havoc unchallenged. But it is time that we show them that we are not completely at their mercy,' I said determinedly. 'I wish to teach the enemy that they cannot always simply sweep their way through our forces, killing and maiming us with no answering challenge. They must be taught to fear. So,' I steeled myself with a breath. 'I beg for the golden Unicorn horn of your people to help me do it.'

The colour drained immediately from both of the faces in front of me, for if the horn was lost, the magic running through the Jenran Kingdom, and their tunnel back into it, would also likely be lost.

'Then you may have it,' Durna replied quietly at last. 'I know that what you seek to do, you seek to do for the good of all of us.'

The ease of his trust and confidence moved me to step forward and take his arm in a grip of brotherhood, though I could almost have fallen to my knees in gratitude. And I saw the common soldiers of Jenra about us, listening with expressions that bore agreement and belief.

'The Jenrans are ready to see the power of their totem unleashing its vengeance for the suffering of its people. They know it is not just a relic to be hidden away, and that it is time to let its wrath come to their defence,' Aeron commented. 'Who better to wield it than the Raiden of the prophecies, who is destined to bring a storm of change against our enemies?'

Durna nodded seriously. 'I give it to you as a weapon in a show of the great respect we share. I am trusting it to you, when it means everything to us. And it must be returned, which means you must not die.' Durna's face had aged noticeably after leaving Jenra, and it appeared even more sunken with worry now, but he continued with words of hope. 'The horn should work for the Raiden of the Gods' prophecies. And I pray it can help you to show them what it is to fear.'

'I cannot thank you enough,' I told them, and Durna sighed.

'I only hope you do not join the fallen while attempting to do the impossible for us all.'

'Your Highness,' Thorin said softly from behind me, his voice ragged. 'We will take care. We must reach the war we have come so far to fight. And we will be the ones doing the hunting – so we will be ready this time.'

Their faces were haggard, but Thorin and the other Krall men bowed deeply in their appreciation for the foreign King, determination written in each expression.

51

Fifty One

K*iana*

I was waging my own inner war while the storm grew and the wind threatened to suck the Dargons off course.

Battered by the gales and rain, I held one of Scandra's horns while Spud sheltered and clung under my cloak, safely tucked under my elbow.

I focused on Scandra's words – that this was a time for me to learn of another wilder part of myself, and a chance for me to learn to live with that part rather than be overwhelmed by it.

'You're doing well!' I heard Spud yell as his small, strong hand patted my side supportively.

I held him closer, drawing deep breaths while the magic danced through every cell and pore, on the brink of overflowing.

'You just need to stay foc–' Spud's words were cut off by a mighty clash, and Scandra's whole body was thrown backward by a monumental blast of wind.

I felt her muscles tighten and fight even harder to push through the force, before we were stunned by multiple forks of jagged lightning that scarred the roiling clouds.

There were roars of warning from Dargons at our sides, and I felt another sudden building of energy.

The Dargons desperately careened out of the way of more sizzling daggers of light while the thunder roared its wrath in aggressive, booming calls.

The stinging sheets of sleeting rain slashed down as if with targeted intent, and I struggled to keep my grip on Scandra – the water streaming in torrents over her slippery scales.

I could only faintly make out the yowls of the Dwarves and even the Gnomes in their baskets as their buffeted Dargons were heaved about violently.

I winced as Scandra was forced to duck beneath a razor-like scar of lightning that surged in a flash right towards us, and her muscles shuddered at the effort of fighting to change direction. But then one of the other Dargons careened out of control, smashing into us and Scandra roared with the impact, nearly dropping from the sky.

Spud yowled as my hold on Scandra was shaken free by the collision and we slid across her scales, down to the middle of her back.

I kept him pressed tightly in the crook of my arm and caught hold of another horn along the Empress' spine, blinking the water from my eyes as I tried to maintain my one-handed grip.

Scandra somehow righted herself, and flew lower so that she could get under her dazed sister, taking the other Dargon's weight across her own tail.

The other Dargon's neck was smoking from where she had been struck by lightning, and torrents of water poured from the weave holes in her basket. But Scandra allowed her to get her wings back into position, and I heard them both rumble with groans at the sheer effort of pushing away from each other to become untangled again.

Scandra had lost some height, and I felt her muscles bunch and could sense her pain as she fought to rise back to the head of the flock to lead her kin through the storm. But the rage of the tempest was relentless and the moment Scandra pulled herself back into place, a rush of howling air whipped viciously across her back, lifting Spud and I completely away from her and sucking us up into the air.

For an odd, suspended moment I had the chance to register that the Giants below had had to leave the surface to swim so deeply that their lights were no longer visible.

Then Scandra howled with exertion, jolting herself higher to slam us back against her scales and out of the wind's separating force. My face smacked into her hard hide and I was winded, scrabbling numbly but unable to find a hold on any of her spikes.

We were blown forward to slide across Scandra's scales and I caught myself as we dangled over her snout, where I could see the wildness in her deep golden eyes as she fought with the storm. Scandra's panting breath was warm against my frozen skin, before Spud and I were blasted by a fist of wind again – lifted to roll roughly back down Scandra's spine.

Then we slid right to the end of Scandra's tail, and were dragged free of Scandra altogether.

52

Fifty Two

Dalin

We'd marked Tane's grave with stones and the Krall rune for a rebel over his name. Then we'd ridden out, following the scratch-like tracks of the Evexus with grim focus and quiet mourning.

'They've definitely passed this way,' Thorin husked resolutely. Dark shadows stood out under his hard eyes as I knelt with him now, peering at the dust. 'But we'll lose some time trying to discern where they went from here.'

I nodded. Many of the tracks had blown away.

'Wait,' Noal sat up straighter in the saddle, squinting intently just behind me. 'It might not take us so much time to find them,' he said with a frown. 'Seeing as Dalin seems to be glowing in warning.' He pointed over my shoulder, to where I had carefully packed the Unicorn horn in my bag.

I started, finding that the horn was glowing so brightly that it was becoming visible even in the daylight, through its embroidered covering and through my leather bag.

'Its pure magic is reacting to something,' Cadell commented, leaning forward on his Jenran horse as the others did. 'It has to be them.'

'The Evexus must have caught our scent and have circled back to get rid of us,' Thale stated, cracking his knuckles with his brown eyes darkening.

'Well they will find us waiting for them,' Nikon replied.

'Thank the Gods,' I announced, straightening. 'We don't have to search for them anymore. They can come to us.'

Thorin and I remounted, but as the others gripped their blades I drew the horn.

It surged with light for a moment, as if in greeting and reassurance that it would work with me on this. And as the light faded the horn remained warm to touch while its sharp tip made it feel like a fierce weapon.

'I'm getting cold,' Dwyn stated quietly then, and this time the gravity of his words hit all of us.

The archers peered all about at the empty looking desert, arrows at the ready.

'Remember,' I uttered. 'Only *I* will be actually fighting.'

I received curt nods.

'Archers, only loose when the Evexus look set to break free before we're ready. Thale, your group will keep the second Evexus from getting in my way.'

Thale puffed out a grunt of agreement, and dust clouded out from his beard. 'We will be dedicated to keeping you alive.'

The tingle of the horn's ancient magic laced along my arm as I held it steady and, at last, we saw the dust rising as the two Evexus loped with unnatural speed to find us.

'Ready,' I stated calmly, and everyone nudged their horses, spreading out into their groups.

Then the demons were skidding to a panting halt, watching us curiously rather than warily, and seeming entertained by our movements to encircle them.

'Get the ball rolling,' I called to Thale.

I heard his horse's hooves as he began the first charge. Before he had finished, and before his Evexus could react, the next warrior swept in from the other direction.

'Purdor,' I breathed to the soldier at the ready next to me.

He charged without hesitation towards the beast in our own circle. His sabre sliced into its ribs and back out again, and Noal and Ila burst into action across from us – catching the talons that had been rising to hack at Purdor's back. Cadell's sabre caught the lashing that would have been directed at Noal. Then Phobos galloped out.

The Evexus yammered out to each other in what sounded like amusement. Laughter at our cute game.

'Break!' I yelled suddenly, and the others in my group paused while the distance between me and the unprepared Evexus seemed to melt away beneath Amala's hooves.

The horn sank easily into the beast's foul shoulder, and tore its way back out again.

I heard the thrum of Dren's arrow and saw it manifest in the arm that had been aimed at my throat.

But it took a moment before my maimed Evexus truly registered what had happened.

I was already back in my circle and the golden horn was unblemished.

We braced uncertainly, waiting for a reaction, before the Evexus made an abrupt hiss of sucked in air, stooping inward as it seemed to realise that for once the terrible pain wasn't simply healing away.

It screeched then in bewilderment, turning its white eyes to stare stupidly at the gaping, steaming hole.

Its skin was rent open and curling back, shrivelling away from where the pure magic had touched while a fetid stench began issuing from the wound in a yellow vapour.

'Phrixus,' I barked, and we began our attacks again.

Our wounded Evexus whirled, unready, terrified by this unexpected turn of events, and it screamed in panic. It could barely keep up with our sweeps – sabres and the Unicorn horn being aimed often at leg tendons and knees to keep the thing grounded.

One after the other the men also aimed for especially deep, quickly decomposing shoulder wound, and pieces of rotting flesh landed in the dirt while the Evexus' shrieks filled the vast land.

It was scrambling and off balance as it clutched its dangling shoulder.

I could hear the grunts and curses from Thale's group too – the other Evexus also now fighting for real; struggling to break free after having sensed that something unfathomable had gone wrong.

'Hold fast!' I urged. 'One more stroke!'

The beasts were frightened now and it would be hard to keep them, but I wanted to make sure we'd delivered a blow that wouldn't be forgotten.

Amala raced me forward while I brandished my weapon like a knife blessed by the Gods.

I plunged its sharp point all the way into that limp shoulder once more, dragging down with all my might before pulling back. And the entire limb was left dangling by only the manufactured bones that Darziates and Agrudek had given it.

The beast watched its unnatural, ice-white blood drops scorching the ground and I wished I had time for the final hacking strokes that would remove its limb completely. But the other Evexus was frantically trying to bash its way free and I would not risk my men further.

'Halt!' I called at last, and the Evexus both scrabbled away the moment that all resistance stopped.

They retreated like threatened animals, baring fangs but edging backward before turning to flee. They disappeared across the plains; one of them moving with a pronounced limp and hunched torso.

And we all stared at each other – gasping, covered in sweat and painted in dirt – but inexplicably victorious.

'Well done,' I said in satisfaction. 'It's time for a chase.'

53

Fifty Three

K*iana*

My wings shot out to catch Spud and I, and I involuntarily screamed as I was whipped to one side – my wings almost tearing away from my shoulders.

But quicker than seemed possible for such a massive body to be able to achieve, Scandra twisted in the air.

I saw her claws open and I pulled Spud closer before Scandra plucked us from the tumult with her talons.

I pulled us to sit safely in the cramped cave that the padded part of her forepaws made while the wind whipped through the spaces between her digits.

'Frarshk. This is bad,' Spud gasped as we shivered and shuddered in saturated shock, the storm still raging in a frenzy beyond our haven.

Spud crawled up my glowing forearm to put a shaking hand on Scandra's quivering, cushioned palm.

The sound of her dragging gasps were loud as we were held close to her chest, and between crashes of thunder I could hear all of the close by Dargons rasping and struggling onward.

'There's nowhere to land, and there will be no rest for the Dargons when we have fought through this later,' Spud grimaced, his teeth chattering.

Another Dargon must have passed by closely then, as I heard her laboured breaths and could faintly hear the sickening fear of the Gnomes and Dwarves being thrown and half drowned in their basket.

I closed my eyes.

'There is so much power in nature's storm. Wild magic,' I whispered. 'And this fierce power is meant to be part of me.'

'Could you use the energy of the storm to protect us from its harm?' Spud asked me earnestly.

I tried to bring everything together in my mind, and in my soul.

'Let's see,' I told him, frowning as I concentrated now on the feeling I'd had all along – like sparks twirling through my blood.

Reaching consciously towards each spark, willing the energy to ignite into something I could use like a tangible part of my physical body, I opened my eyes again.

Spud was watching me. 'That storm is back in your eyes,' he warned.

'I'm counting on it,' I answered, and I imagined myself flying about outside.

I imagined that I was circling Scandra and the Dargons with a great cloak, draping it over them like a protective shelter. I let the raging magic that was within me spread out, and I felt Scandra jolt in shock.

I knew she was seeing a slowly growing luminous film expanding over them all.

It was agonisingly gradual, and as exhausting as if I was really out their hauling a huge canvas shelter up by myself.

Until I remembered that nature, the Lady, would happily help me to pull everything into place.

I imagined brown hands gripping the invisible cloak alongside my own. Strong arms pulling with me.

And it became easy.

'Gods, Kiana!' Spud gasped in excitement. 'The storm has been muted. You've shielded them!'

Moments later the Dargons nearest us moaned in shock and relief while Scandra released a mighty call of elation.

'You are a wonder,' Spud said adoringly.

'Thank the Gods it worked,' I gasped, finally feeling the tension leaving my body.

54

Fifty Four

D*alin*

We were on their heels – our horses foaming and gasping as we galloped after them.

At one point we had to loop back and circle near the marching Jenrans as we followed the beasts, and while the Jenrans had tensed for battle, when they saw us on the hunt and watched the two Evexus that had once chased the army now fleeing and injured, their heartened war cries spurred us on.

Then at last, when we were lost once more in the wastelands, we found ourselves gaining on the Evexus as our determination grew and the beasts' anxiety increased.

'Groups!' I roared hoarsely, my eyes on the enemy.

Our charge parted and my group relentlessly honed in on the wounded Evexus while Thale's group sped towards the other manic, unscathed beast.

Amala's hooves were kicking up explosions of dirt as if she were willing to give everything to get me closer to my prey. It felt like I was holding onto lightning as I clutched the golden horn, which was sizzling now as though it, too hungered to make that one beast an example of our strength.

'Dismount!' I yelled as we came upon them, and I launched myself at the keening beast before Amala had even skidded to a stop, swinging for a moment on the beast's spiked back as I struck repeatedly at its shoulder before I kicked off and joined my soldiers, who were flinging themselves from the saddle and into formation.

We threw ourselves into our attacks, both of our groups making sure that the two Evexus could not leap away while we hacked and bashed and dragged them down as savagely and brutally as we could.

Blow after blow, I dashed in at each opportune moment while the fiend was reduced to a quivering and panting ball, cowering down in exhaustion and terror with hardly a moment to lash out.

Sweeping and slicing, the horn bit deeper into the creature's shoulder while its companion in the circle behind me fought desperately for a way out.

'There are three other Evexus watching us!' Rai called, and I vaguely registered howls in the distance.

But the sounds were trills of confusion as they watched our attack on their comrades and felt the pure magic of the horn.

'They are too afraid to get close to help their brothers!' Ander crowed.

But I was throwing myself forward with a growl, landing on my enemy's back once more while Dren loosed arrow after arrow at its swiping arm.

I kept my hold, clinging to its neck, swinging as it flailed, and I rained blow after blow over my opponent's upper body, stabbing savagely and always trying to sever the last sinews holding that one nerveless limb.

My head was reeling with the cold, but I had never felt so clear as, with each stroke, I hacked deeper and deeper ... until in a blinding flash of golden light I had cut the arm away from the twisting body.

The Evexus went still beneath me, stunned.

The rotting stench made me gag, but I ducked and rolled away before the venting steam of acidic discharge could touch me.

'Break!' I cried, and my warriors all parted so that our two Evexus could scamper up and leap away towards the other three in the distance.

My whimpering, staggering Evexus left its limb behind, and all five of the reunited Evexus quickly fled from the unknown magic and threat that we wielded – fast disappearing across the desolate plains.

Our cheers were loud for many moments, until we realised that there was a sound of roaring joy in the distance that was even louder.

We turned in surprise as the veil of obscuring dust around us began to settle, and we were finally able to register the huddled mass of an army that had been watching us from far away.

'Are they Awyalknian banners?' Ferron asked raggedly.

A wave of relief, and then sickening nerves made my sense of elation harden.

'Yes,' I answered, my chest heaving. 'It looks like we've found my father's army.'

55

❧

Fifty Five

K*iana*

Spud was sitting comfortably on my shoulder while we both intently watched the team of Dwarves at work. They were showing me how my beautiful dress of silver ore armour had been made – shaping two new suits before my eyes.

Even the Gnomes in the basket had set aside their gambling and chatter to watch, and it was the first time that I had seen a glimmer of happiness on the bearded face of any Dwarf since leaving Eirian.

Their eyes were beginning to fare better in the sunlight after adjusting to the light of the baskets, and they were glad to be busy now with plenty of scales having been donated by many Dargons.

The scales had become silver, but still glowed brilliantly while the powerful hands of the Dwarves melded them into one flowing material, and then melded that into smooth, intricate designs.

'The Dwarves can shape the silver ore material to work in two different ways,' Spud told me, leaning in against my face. 'When it's pulled thin into the shape of war boots the ore becomes both flexible and impenetrable.'

A lady Dwarf peered at me almost coyly, showing me how the boots would bend and flex with the toes.

'Otherwise it is kept thick and becomes completely unyielding,' Spud went on.

Then an obliging Gnome ran headlong into one of the thick plates of armour, rebounding with a chuckle while the silver plate remained unmarked.

'Only Dwarvish fingers could manipulate holes into this type of armour, but even they could never really tear or break it,' Spud elaborated.

I could hardly take my eyes from the dazzling suits of armour that were being forged for my two princes.

I had used my magic to project true to scale memories of Dalin and Noal, and the Dwarves had at once begun developing the perfect models.

'I could never replicate the delicate work of the Dwarves with any tool in a smithy,' I remarked enviously.

'You'll have no need,' one of the grinning Gnomes declared confidently.

He looked like he had giant bug eyes while he played with a pair of the Dwarve's gem spectacles.

'The Three will have the best armour in all the world, and it will last a lifetime.'

'The only problem with this get-up is that it's so glowy,' Spud cushioned an elbow against my cheek. 'If you wish to be unseen you need a cloak.'

'If that's the silver ore's only fault, I would still label the Dwarves' work as perfection,' I answered, and the Dwarves beamed with pride while the Gnomes nodded avidly. 'I think I will unveil mine when the Three are to unite at last against the Sorcerer. The armour will be a symbol of our strength, and of how the shadows cannot contain us.'

'Yes, yes, the beauty can't be stifled,' Spud interjected as he slid from my shoulder, scuttling down my arm to stretch his rotund body. 'But this was our last basket for today, and we've stayed here longer than we stayed in the others. We have to give our time fairly.'

I saw disappointment on the faces of the Gnomes, who were bored of basket life. But I nodded, seeing the blue glow of the designs around my forearm and deciding it was time I visited the Giants.

'I ache to have solid ground to set my feet upon,' a Gnome told me mournfully as I rose as best I could – hunching over in the basket.

'Yes,' I told the little being. 'I would love to rest upon grass instead of the nearest Dargon back or wind pocket or sloshing wave.'

'Stability and the smell of rocks and plants, rather than salt air, would be great,' Spud agreed, coming over to circle his small arms around my ankle.

'But we have passed great distances already, and I am sure the time will soon come for us to reach the mortal lands,' I told the glum Gnomes warmly.

I felt bad for the restless beings as I dragged Spud and myself out of the side door of the basket, quickly closing and securing it again with a knot of rope for the windswept occupants inside. Then, clinging to the woven basket for a moment, I let the rushing air soothe my cramped muscles.

'Oh I know what you would love to do,' Spud called up from my ankle with a daredevil grin. 'Go ahead,' he encouraged, tightening his unbreakable grip.

And with a smile I released my hold on the woven basket so that we were suddenly torn away into the wind, hurtling in a wild freefall.

We dropped erratically, Spud loosing thrilled yowls while I heard passing snatches of conversations between different Dargons, who were completely unruffled as we whizzed past their snouts.

We got closer and closer to the rushing ocean surface while the stinging air made our eyes run and snatched the laughter from our lips.

Then before crushing impact, I reached for the link my earthstone gave me to nature and I let my wings burst out to catch us.

Spud cackled as we hovered ecstatically above the waves for only a moment – before I felt a sucking sensation as a draught of air dragged me upwards.

With a grin, I saw the disapproving golden reflection of Scandra as she swooped down.

'Uh oh,' Spud called. 'We're in trouble.'

'Was that necessary?' Scandra hissed while I beamed up at her horned face.

'I thought you didn't like this little potato shaped ball of annoyance,' I said, and offered her my ankle.

Spud's wiry hair had been sucked straight up into a petrified cone over his head, his arms and legs were wrapped around my boot, his eyes were wide and the biggest grin was plastered across his impish face.

'I don't,' she sniffed haughtily, peeling him off my leg with a talon and nudging him with her other paw to force him to scramble up to her snout.

'She adores me,' Spud stated, spitting into his palm and smoothing his twiggy shoots of hair back.

Scandra snorted a plume of smoke back at him. 'It would be useless to have no regent leading the Dwarvish and Gnomish forces. Your death would be a bother.'

'Well,' he answered, crawling over to latch onto the one un-horned part of her face that he could hold in a tight hug – his arms encircling her nostril. 'I would find it a bother if you carked it, too!'

'Finally,' Scandra snorted more nostril smoke in his face. 'The respect I deserve from the little speck.'

Scandra wheeled herself around in the air then, and I knew that she intentionally created the force of wind that sent me splashing down with a laugh into the waves, where Toru was already waiting with Ahanu and the others to catch me as I dropped into their midst.

56

Fifty Six

D^{alin}

'Can you hear what they're chanting?' Noal asked from where he rode Ila beside me.

'They chant ...' Thale panted. 'For the Raiden.'

We were cantering across the last yards of the hazy wasteland that stretched between us and the army we'd fought so long to get to.

Raiden!

I could feel each one of Amala's tired, deep breaths, along with my own irregular breathing as I rose and fell to accommodate her stride.

Raiden!

The heat beat down across my shoulders and head, making sweat roll down my face and chest while all of the blue, bleeding slice marks I'd received stung and throbbed.

Raiden!

A wave of loud cheering rose to meet us as we drew closer to the Awyalknians. Feet were stamping and dust was swirling around the army, making everything dreamlike.

Noal leaned in closer as we slowed our mares at the first ranks of the Awyalknians. 'You just chased away their fears,' he said seriously.

Then the first lines drew respectfully apart, opening the way so we could ride through their flanks while their voices continued to call out to us in relief.

The crowd closed in behind us as we steered deeper into the army, and with a pang I noticed a ragged procession on horseback that was also progressing towards us.

For the first time in nearly two years, and for the first time since our bitter parting, I glimpsed Glaidin's face – identifying it even beneath the greying beard and the gaunt, dirty features.

At last our two mounted parties were facing each other and the crowds grew quiet to focus on us.

Conall was at my father's side, beaming despite the cracks in his blistered skin. But for a few moments Glaidin simply gazed at the strong Krall warriors and archers at our backs before he searched our faces – Noal's and then mine.

'... Raiden?' he whispered hesitantly at last.

I cleared my throat uneasily while he stared at me as if my presence was a miracle.

'Well met, my King,' I greeted him formally and bowed from the saddle.

I heard the creaking of my archers and warriors bowing too, but Glaidin gaped in incomprehension and I realised he had not understood what I'd said.

'The Fairy tongue!' a nearby soldier husked in awe. 'Praise the questers!'

Surprised at having to think about it, I reformed my words into Awyalknian, but Glaidin shook his head at my repeated greeting.

'My *son*,' he whispered emphatically, almost wistfully. 'My boys.'

He looked again from Noal to me before he suddenly dismounted by half falling from the saddle.

Conall followed and caught him while Noal and I dismounted as well.

Glaidin righted himself, straightening purposefully and leaving Conall's grasp to cross to me while I stood resolutely. Waiting for what he might say about my disobedience and desertion of the palace.

Instead, I was wrapped in a fierce hug and my eyes widened.

I let my arms close around his shaking body, and realised he felt almost frail with emotion and physical depletion. I noticed that my height matched his, and that I was holding him up.

Finally, leaning back to see my face clearly, he spoke hoarsely again. 'Raiden.'

And I heard the crowd echo it behind him.

Before I could be too overwhelmed, there was a flash of red, and Asha abruptly pounded against Noal's chest while he caught her with his good hand.

'Princeling,' the Nymph's muffled voice came warmly from his chest, before she suddenly sniffed as though picking up on a scent.

She pulled back and set her reproachful eyes on him. 'You got a girl didn't you?'

He nodded. 'But I promise you'll like her. She's on her way now.'

I turned back to address Glaidin and Conall more formally again. 'And she is not alone. For while my Krall and Awyalknian comrades are by my side, I have made great friends amongst the Jenrans too.'

'Only Lixrax is unrepresented as the nations of men unite,' Noal confirmed.

And then Conall and a number of soldiers around us gasped in wonder, gazing back towards where we had fought the Evexus.

As if on cue, a massive cloud of dust was filling the horizon, and the glint of weapons could be seen through the haze.

The Jenran army was approaching.

Conall's jaw was hanging while the Awyalknian army began to cheer once more.

'You brought many friends with you,' he husked.

'Yes,' I answered. 'And Kiana is bringing more.'

57

Fifty Seven

K*iana*

With the rising of the sun came our first sighting of mortal lands. The forest spread along the coast, the mountains stood like grand sentinels awaiting our arrival, and Scandra's roar of joy was enough to rouse the entire ocean full of sleeping, swimming Giants – also bringing many Gnome faces to the openings of their baskets.

At last the Dargons beat their great wings and sent us soaring high over the mountains while the Giants put on an extra burst of speed, soon bounding out of the water to leap upon the golden sand below.

'They saw us coming!' Spud crowed as the drums of Jenra began reverberating in greeting.

Scandra loosed another roar in return, making clouds of Griffins that had been hidden throughout the mountains shoot up and flap away in fear while Scandra chortled and Spud and I held on.

The echoing drum beats were accompanied by faint cheers from below as thousands of speck-like Jenrans poured out onto balconies, filled walkways, or spilled from their city gates to gather in the valleys and see the magical ones in the air.

'It is good to hear them cheer with hope,' I said, watching the bobbing crowds gladly.

'Give them something so they remember their hope when we are gone,' Scandra suggested, rolling her shoulder so that I was prompted to lift off.

'Like the time you lit up Eirian,' Spud agreed.

And I nodded, frowning in concentration as I gathered mental images of the beauty of the flying Dargons, images of the Giants glowing as they swam, memories of the Elves brandishing their glowing spears, of the Nymphs surrounded in their fiery light, and of the clever Dwarves and Gnomes shaping solid rock with their fists.

With a breath, I let the images flow outward as a message to the mortals below.

The magical ones have come to join us against the darkness. Have faith in The Army for the World! Let the Sorcerer fear at last!

I noticed the trees of Sylthanryn were throwing their boughs about as if in a dance. Whirlwinds of cool air swept through the mountains, lifting the mist and frost from countless hidden passes while leaves, ice and magic swirled about me.

The Giants on the coast below were gazing at themselves in wonder – their skins consumed by blue fire while my magic entwined with theirs.

The Jenrans also cried out as one with a sound so great that surely the Gods could hear them. And at last Scandra turned in satisfaction as countless hands waved goodbye and the other Dargons and I descended with her, sinking down to finally set our feet on solid ground.

'Mortal lands,' I heard Scandra marvel, elegantly stretching herself out amongst the dripping Giants while waves upon waves of Dwarves and Gnomes began pouring out of her sisters' baskets. Only a handful of Dwarves bothered with their protective gem spectacles, and the Gnomes ran about on the sand, crowing and looking as though the rocks on the beach had come to life.

But I let my own feet instead draw me toward the brink of the Great Forest, stepping under the boughs of the first trees that lined the sand.

Trailing on, the sounds of the lapping waves and the others relishing their rest were replaced by the sounds of dripping water and rustling ferns. There was the smell of soil and growing things, the hushed flutter of an unseen bird borne on fleeting wings, and the tingle of a deep and enigmatic energy that seemed to exist all about me.

And when I happened upon a small glade I found the Lady waiting for me, as beautiful and timeless as I remembered.

Her feet were bare upon the grass and the pale gossamer dress spilling down her lovely form made her smooth brown skin seem warmer still. Her auburn hair was curling in tendrils to her waist and her green eyes regarded me tenderly and calmly.

'Lady,' I whispered, my breath almost taken away. For with my enhanced magic, had come enhanced feeling and sight – and I could now see the faint fracture lines upon her face beneath the impossible sheen to her skin. As if she were made of brittle porcelain.

I could also see, like glimmers out of the corner of my eye, that beyond her physical body her presence stretched out to cover every inch of the forest, and flowed deeply through the earth.

'At last I see you clearly,' I said, and only now truly understood what she had alluded to in our last farewell.

'I am the energy that blankets this place,' she acknowledged gently. 'One day, if the world survives, I will re-join the bodiless personality you felt at sea in that storm, and I will spread my power beyond here. I will help to heal this world.'

I felt stricken as I considered that the body she now animated was only one temporary part of who she was. Really, she was life itself. She was what we were fighting for. She, nature, had to be kept, for all races to survive. But I might never speak to her like this, face to face, again.

'You have grown so much, One,' she told me in her musical voice. 'However, it is now my turn to grow.'

Her time of being able to talk and touch and care for those she knew in a human way was ending.

'I am almost aching to be free of the burden of this body, which has contained me since the beginning of time,' she went on. 'I have spent too long, anchored and watching the world I was destined to guard come to harm, and now I long to be released, and to flow instead everywhere. To live within nature truly and begin its repairs.'

'Yet,' I whispered, 'you cannot do that until all that is unnatural has been ended. You are waiting.'

'Oh no,' she smiled. 'Before I learned of the Three I was waiting – weakened by the corruption of Darziates' line and waiting to perish. Now I am hoping.'

'Then I am glad I am home now. Home to finish our quest,' I answered, though I couldn't keep a touch of sadness from my voice.

I hardly saw her move then, but like a flicker I suddenly found her by my side, arms around me in a motherly embrace, and I knew that this really was the last time I would see her in this form.

Because if we were to win, her magic would be needed and she would have to be free to reach all of the corrupted lands and peoples, to help them to replenish. The Lady would die, but nature would be reborn to live afresh.

'Come,' she said soothingly. 'Let us join the children of magic.'

And with her arm linked in mine we stepped out from our secluded glade and back into the sunlight of the coast. As we did, I felt the many emerging presences of the Elves and Nymphs as they moved through the trees to join their Lady as well.

Tall, dark forms stepped out gracefully, silvery hair shimmering like ice in the sun. And, as if the stars had been hiding in the trees, hundreds of Nymphs rose from the treetops in clouds.

A hush fell over even the most euphoric Gnomes and the island beings came away from the water, the magical races slowly drawing together as if mesmerised.

'Welcome,' the Lady smiled. 'We have missed you.'

Her arm was light about me as if I were already losing her, but wisps of her auburn hair entwined with my own as they danced in the breeze, and her magic, my magic, and the magic of all the gathered races joined in an invisible awe inspiring force.

'Well met Ancient Mother,' Scandra inclined her magnificent head. 'You have fought well to keep life going on the frontlines.'

'Our old friends, we are glad to be back with you again,' Ahanu beamed, stepping forward as the Giant Elders' representative.

Spud, for once, remained enchanted and quiet.

'I feel sadness that I must allow you to be parted from me, to travel on,' the Lady told us all. 'But the Raiden and Noal are uniting the mortals of the world, and they are now in Krall. They will need you for their darkest hour at the Sorcerer's gates, for if the races are not joined then, the prophecy will not be fulfilled, and neither will our pure quest.'

'We are ready,' Frey said, moving forward to stand by Ahanu. 'We will take the same path that Dalin and Noal took. But we shall catch them up when we know that the time to reveal ourselves is right.'

'We accept this strategy,' Scandra acknowledged, 'but must add to it.' Her golden eyes fell to me.

'I plan to take a flock of fifty Dargons with me to Awyalkna City, to give Queen Aglaia help against the Sorcerer's attacks,' I explained.

The Lady considered for a moment, looking into the distance as though she were watching a different scene. 'Yes. Their need for aid is also going to be great. Perhaps you should also take a select few other friends with you to make this a moment of hope for Awyalkna. You could show them exactly what kind of army you've raised, just as you did for Jenra.'

'One representative for each race,' I agreed.

At once Toru stepped out of the crowd to stand beside Scandra, and Spud seemed to have already decided that if Scandra got to come then so did he. Vidar joined us too, tugging on the floating boot of Rebel.

'Yes,' the Lady repeated simply. 'All of us united as it was meant to be.'

Her words were glad, yet her face was nearly pale as she said a final goodbye to her forest dwellers.

'Be safe,' she told me as I came to her last. 'I am sure that, in some way, we will meet again.'

I nodded sorrowfully. 'You're right. You will be the force that I draw my strength from, and will always be my ultimate friend and guide.'

When we parted I looked back for her, and her hair stood out as it twisted and flowed in the ocean breeze, a streak of colour against the pale sand while Scandra flew away.

58

Fifty Eight

D*ren*

The tip of the feather swept like a familiar caress along Dren's cheek as he held the arrow ready, his bow bent.

Dren was glaring up at the sky. where one disappointed Griffin was circling over the recovering united armies. It was getting closer to where Noal and the Raiden were in conference with King Durna in a hurriedly erected tent. Probably creeping in to see if there were truly no more meal opportunities.

'They're watching for a signal,' Ander speculated in a low voice, squinting at a small flock that circled way out in the distance.

The archers had kept up their guard while the Krall men had gone to help the Awyalknians with setting up camp – as most relieved Awyalknians were now losing their last ounces of adrenaline.

'Well we'll watch right back and keep those princes safe,' Dren replied, reflecting again on how much he owed his life to them – transformed from apple thief to Awyalkna's most respected archer because of a moment of mercy that neither prince even remembered they had granted him.

Glyn and Dwyn simultaneously cursed as the Griffin circled lower.

'Just that one Griffin is the size of a horse,' Rai observed.

'Give them the message they're watching for,' a quiet voice sounded from behind the archers. 'A message that they do not want to threaten us even in our weakened state.'

Dren glanced back to see the grave faced Jenran Warlord at his shoulder, and when he turned his eyes from Aeron his bow sprang and the feather whooshed away from his cheek.

'Yeeees!' Rai hissed in admiration, leaning on his longbow to watch.

'FRARSHK!' they heard the surprise of the circling Griffin when the arrow pounded into its chest, embedding into its thick feathers and matted fur. 'EEEEEEEEEEEEEKKK, BLERRRRHHHHHHH, OWWWWWWWWWWWWWW, FRARSHK!!!'

'A fatal shot,' Ander commented.

'But not instant,' Dwyn snorted.

'AHHHHH, FRARSHK!! FRARSHKING FRARSHKER!!!!' the Griffin was flapping crazily as it tried to stay in the air.

'Which means they're all hearing the message,' Aeron nodded in satisfaction. 'Loud and clear.'

There were squawks in the distance and the Awyalknians and Jenrans who were still settling in watched the other distant Griffins turning to hurry away.

'FRRRAAAAAA – ' the Griffin dipped and lost height erratically. 'AARRRRRSHK!'

'Dren,' Dalin had peered up from his discussion with a small smile. 'Our men are trying to rest.'

Dren had an arrow plucked from its quiver and fitted to his bow in a flash. 'Apologies. I'll take care of it.'

'FRRAAARRRSSS –'

An arrow suddenly spitted the Griffin through its open mouth. Pinning its tongue and protruding from the back of its head to cut off life and speech.

The soldiers around them somehow had the energy to cheer once more as the reeking beast flopped down to land heavily in their midst.

'Yes, alright. Message delivered,' Glyn approved.

'I appreciate it,' the Raiden's grin was bright against the dust on his skin.

'You have returned the horn to us and have struck fear into the Evexus,' Durna went on, drawing Dalin's attention again.

'And your people have not just joined ours, but have brought care to our exhausted men,' Noal said just as gratefully, motioning beyond the tent to where Jenran warriors were helping to bind the wounds or set up the tents of Awyalknians who could not yet understand their saviours' words. The gift of *Aolen* would perhaps only spread slowly from man to man because of the sheer size of the mixing groups.

'Your trust and kindness will never be forgotten by us, my great friend,' Dalin said, and he moved to bow before the Jenran King, but Durna stopped him.

Instead, the King bowed to the prince. Low.

'And your bravery will never be forgotten by us,' Durna replied.

Dalin firmly reached forward and clasped his fellow leader's arm in a pointed gesture of equality instead.

'We have been lucky in our rulers, I think,' Dren observed to Aeron, remembering the sweet taste of the apples he'd been granted nearly twelve years ago.

'And soon Krall may have a similar chance,' Thale ventured as he joined them.

He was worn by grief and battle, but he smiled. 'Come friends,' he continued. 'It is time for our archers to join their comrades for water and bread. There is room for all of us.'

Dren's smile matched Thale's as the Krall warrior gestured to where a shelter had been set up for them. It was a sombre but not depressed group of Krall warriors collapsing down and taking off armour under its shelter.

As they turned to follow Thale's lead, Dren noticed his own King, Glaidin, gazing out from a pavilion entrance, his eyes on Dalin as the Jenran King clasped arms with his son.

Dren slung his bow over his shoulder and rubbed at the tight muscles at the back of his neck. He made one last check of the cloudless sky, empty of threats.

For now there were no Griffins. The Evexus had been taught to be more wary and the princes were surrounded in a sea of admiring soldiers.

But still, his eyes would stay sharp.

59

Fifty Nine

Kiana

The great marching line led by Frey, Ace and Ahanu had been long lost to sight. And my assorted companions, all fitting easily on Scandra's back, regarded each other curiously while I swept down to glide over the forest.

Treetops and giant fan-like ferns passed beneath me, and I followed the curving trails of water channels winding through the mangroves below. I could see birds like fluttering butterflies flitting about the canopy, and even from my height I could hear the constant song of insects in the undergrowth.

It was only when our reduced Dargon flock left Sylthanryn behind to begin passing over the rolling lands of Awyalkna that I rose to sit by Toru and Vidar, finding Rebel zipping around Scandra like a backstroke swimmer – with Spud catching a ride on the Nymph's stomach.

Across several days and nights Rebel and Spud challenged Toru to arm wrestling matches, Rebel enjoyed the presence of someone smaller than himself, Vidar lounged over Scandra's snout – avidly listening to anything she said, and the Empress acquired increasing patience towards these attentive, adoring males.

And aside from the delighted squabbling of our two littlest companions, all seemed peaceful as a new night began. We soared beneath the silvery fires of billions of stars – so very like the colour of my Dwarvish armour, left in Ahanu's care. And we sensed nothing until Sandra and the other Dargons suddenly let out unexpected growls, roars and even spurts of outraged flame.

I was jolted forward and Spud and Rebel quickly grabbed hold of Toru as Scandra shuddered in the air.

'What is it Scandra?' I called out, worrying that perhaps the Dargons had been affected by an unnatural magic of some kind.

'We have sensed foulness,' she growled after Vidar had swung himself safely up onto her neck. 'Once beautiful. Once our family. Now corrupted.'

I swallowed in deep horror. 'Dragons?'

'Yes.' Her voice was seething, and in her anger the *Aolen* was blended with a more brutal and reptilian sounding accent.

'SISTERS!' she yelled then, drawing the stricken Dargons to focus. 'You sense that others have travelled here ahead of us, and we will soon come upon those we have lost. They are close. Perhaps they are attacking Awyalkna palace even now.'

Moans and cries came from the Dargons but Scandra rumbled dangerously and they quietened at once.

'Do not hold back!' she growled. 'They will no longer know you. They no longer know themselves by the names we once called them! They hate what they have become – you can feel their torment!'

There were reverberations of assent but pain seemed to emit from the Dargons like invisible steam.

'Ready yourselves,' Scandra now sent her voice back to just us. 'Soon we will find a battleground.'

And as we flew on through the darkness we began to hear mighty booms, roars and screams, and we caught our first glimpse of the beautiful Awyalknian Jewel.

Soaring arches, white pavement and towers, gardens and market squares – alight with fire and a furious attack raging below.

'It appears we've arrived at what was perhaps planned to be the final assault on Queen Aglaia,' Vidar called over the thundering din of the savage grey Dragons crashing around the city.

The massive cracking sound of a roof being clawed off a house drew my eyes and I started as I also registered that there were Griffins swarming the streets too. And riding them, crowing with joy, were Trune raiders.

'How many invaders are there?' Spud asked from where he and Rebel still clung to Toru's ankles.

Scandra counted. 'Fifteen Dragons from the hundred that were stolen. Perhaps a few hundred Griffins.'

Vidar nodded. 'And it is possible that it is all of the Trune raiders, of the two hundred known to exist.'

Many Trunes were being dropped strategically beyond the walls as we watched.

'But the people below do not appear hopeless,' I said. 'And with our help, they won't be.'

At that moment I saw a Griffin far below us snatching a boy from his mother's arms. A boy no more than Tommy's age, and still wrapped up in his blanket for bed.

I dove from Scandra's shoulder, and war cries and deafening roars followed at my back while shouts of wonder rose from the Awyalknians.

I sensed Dragons and other Griffins wheeling away from me, scattering in the air, and heard the tremendous booming of Dargon and Dragon bodies now colliding in battle. But I sliced onward, drawing my sword. My entire focus was honed on that one preoccupied Griffin, which was happily setting down and singing something like: 'dinner, dinner, dinner!' while its captive cried.

The impact as I pelted into the Griffin – over twice my size – sent us both tumbling from the roof. The Griffin was also left with one leg sawn off, the blanket wrapped boy now safely in my grip.

'You frarshker!' the Griffin yelled at me, flapping and hopping on the ground to avoid its stump.

'Fairy?' the child whimpered, and I smiled as I lifted off to quickly blur to a stop beside his mother.

'My deepest thanks!' she moaned as I passed my precious cargo to her.

'Be safe, and make sure to thoroughly clean any scratches,' I called over my shoulder, turning back to the Griffin.

'That was mine!' it hissed, heaving its shuddering, patchy form over the cobbles. 'You frarshking thief,' it cursed, picking up momentum before it threw itself at me.

I caught the full brunt of its matted shoulder and was launched through the air. But I ignored the stench of sweat and rotten meat, and we became locked in a spinning battle.

My sword flicked to every part of its body and its claws and beak scrabbled to lash me in return. We clashed against each other, rising above the city until at last we careened into the impenetrably hard and glittery palace wall.

Rebounding and freefalling down to a courtyard, we landed amid a number of surrounded Awyalknian nobles, fifteen Trune raiders and their smaller Griffin escorts – all blinking at our surprise entrance.

But while I landed heavily, my king-sized opponent hit the pavement lifelessly. So I gruffly pulled my sword from the stinking carcass and turned to regard the disrupted Trunes.

The only movement for a moment was when a frill covered man with a powdered face turned on his heel and fled from where he had been standing with the Trunes. He had been pointing into the crowd of nobles at a woman in her night clothes.

'Well,' I said to the frozen raiders. 'Come on.'

With only a slight pause the two closest Trunes launched at me with their cudgels. The first howling raider flew over my shoulder as I ducked and heaved, and he slid with a hiss across my turning blade. The second Trune caught my boot in his chest, and then my blade in his throat as I swung it out and around from its last opponent.

I heard a swoop of wings and smelt a foul odour from behind, but the Griffin that had suddenly sprung at my back was the first victim of my magic – an instinctive rush of energy catching the springing beast and throwing it away screaming.

Four more Trune raiders and a few other Griffins left the Awyalknian nobles to charge at me now too, and the magic spurred my spins, kicks, lunges and stabs so that my enemies were flying away from me as quickly as they were charging.

I became aware that the Awyalknians, including the woman in her night clothes, had been freed up enough to now be able to turn on their captors to join the fight. But I half flew, half dived to spear tackle the woman when I noticed her clumsily wielding a knife out of one Griffin's reach.

At once a young soldier pounced to the woman's defence when the Griffin made to swoop, and he managed to run the Griffin through as it did.

'Nice work,' I complimented the friendly looking soldier, helping the woman up and dusting myself off while one of the other Awyalknians; an older but still formidable general, was letting the last raider drop from his sword.

'Oh my Gods ...' the woman gasped then. And I followed her wide eyed stare, turning as the wind suddenly seemed to pick up at an astonishing rate.

But it was not the wind. It was the mighty, approaching wing beats of the most swollen Dragon I'd ever seen – taking a nose dive straight for our group.

With an unthinking gesture of my arm all of the Awyalknians in the courtyard were swept up in a bubble to land outside the open Gwentorock gate.

Then I was somersaulting out of the way of a blast of Dragon fire, narrowly missing being scorched.

Bouncing up and lifting off I shot toward the grey Dragon before it could touch down.

It opened terrible jaws again and I desperately used my magic to catch the new, house sized fireball it sent my way. Then, with a massive heave, I sent the fireball back.

The Dragon choked and blinked as its own flame burst back in its face, giving me a chance to thrust myself safely past its snapping teeth to dart higher.

The beast lashed violently around, and the strength of its wing beats was nearly enough to suck me backward. But I gritted my teeth and turned in the air to face it as it chased me down. And I launched an attack of my own.

I had not imagined how overwhelming my magic would be, and was almost taken aback when a blast of silvery blue light, like a thousand lightning bolts that illuminated the whole sky, speared the Dragon's chest – forcing it away from me even as the life left its fierce glare.

The entire world seemed to have stopped as the petrified, limp body of the Dragon hurtled backward away from me, at such a speed that its carcass cleared the outer Gwynrock walls in moments – skidding and creating an earth shattering crater in the fields beyond the city.

I shook myself back to awareness when I heard savage, yowling voices below.

Searching for the source of the noise, I spotted Spud, Rebel, Toru and Vidar down in the city where they seemed to have defeated the last of the Trunes.

My companions were surrounded by masses of Awyalknians – all cheering. Because, as the crowds gazed up in excitement, the skies around me were clearing.

The Griffins and a greatly reduced number of Dragons were retreating hurriedly while a flock of golden Dargons chased them from the city at last.

The chorus of Awyalknian voices only dimmed a little when Scandra joined me in sweeping down to land beside our comrades, forcing the crowds to scuttle backward as the Empress filled the entire square and street beyond.

'Well met,' a gay voice cried over the din, and I recognised the woman in the night gown, flanked by the friendly young soldier and the burly general, as they stepped out of the crowd.

My heart flipped in my chest like a spiralling autumn leaf as I saw now that the woman had honey skin and green eyes. Like the honey skin and green eyes that I loved in somebody else. And as the crowds noticed this woman they lowered themselves with bows and curtsies of deep respect.

But the Queen of Awyalkna, Dalin's mother, hardly paused before she dashed forward, sweeping me into a maternal hug.

'My Queen,' I said.

It took me a few moments to recover from my delighted shock.

'We represent the magical races,' I managed.

I let the *Aolen* wash over everyone surrounding us. I let it sweep outward to seep into every person.

'You are all so very welcome here!' the Queen beamed in response, using her new language.

And I felt my cheeks rise with a smile that matched her own.

60

Sixty

N*oal*

I held a hand over my eyes, willing the shadows of my fingers against my eyelids to blot out the brightness so that my exhausted body could sleep.

I was lying in a portable camping cot, almost like a canvas hammock, safe in the pavilion that had been set up for Dalin and I. And with this short time of reprieve from attack and the savage heat outside I was trying to take the chance for rest, yet sleep would not come.

Giving up, I tried to flex the healing fingers on my other hand, which had stiffened again like purple claws after days on the hunt.

I listened to the sounds of thousands upon thousands of men moving around tiredly outside. Tent pegs were being driven into the ground, wagons were being dragged into place, water and food were being distributed, healings were taking place, and people were grimly working out who had been lost in the chase.

Some voices spoke in Awyalknian, some in *Aolen*. The two groups were trying to interact politely while *Aolen* spread slowly throughout the fatigued Awyalknians. Though I noticed that the assertive and business-like healer voices coming from those working outside sounded incredibly similar no matter what language they spoke.

I smiled, thinking of Maeve, and felt more relaxed at once.

I let my chest rise and fall with a long, grounding breath, and the feel of crisp, clean clothes – kindly pulled out from King Durna's own stores, felt strange against my now washed skin. The material was fresh and not worn out or mended in uncountable places.

I heard the canvas door shift and a high voice drew my attention.

'You're still awake.'

Then when I lifted my bad arm I felt Asha's small body nestle into me.

'I missed you,' she told me before I looked down to find that she had already lapsed into the sudden sleep of the Nymphs.

'I missed you too,' I told her anyway. And her magic seemed to dull the many aches that pulsed within each of my weary muscles so that, finally, I could settle into lasting, deep dreams.

'Perhaps we should let him be,' I heard the rough sound of a Krall accent as Thale spoke so that an Awyalknian could understand. 'He is recovering still from ...' Thale petered off as he realised none of the Awyalknians knew yet what had happened, and because I quickly sat up.

Asha squealed into wakefulness from where she had been curled up against me like a cat, and I caught her before she dropped to the floor.

'I'mawakeI'mawake!' I said quickly, letting Asha float up to perch on my shoulder as she stretched and yawned without any pretence of being awake herself.

An Awyalknian hovered nearby, looking uncertain about having disturbed me, though I could see that dusk was settling over the desert beyond the open canvas door. Fires were being lit to ward off the steep drop in temperature that came with each night.

'It's alright,' I told him, reverting to Awyalknian with an effort, and he relaxed a little and bowed.

'Your Royal Highness has been summoned for the gathering,' he informed me respectfully.

'Thank you, friend,' I replied without formality, but he bowed again reverently before leaving.

Thale chuckled. 'Your Highness.'

'Ugh, I should have made more effort to try the Fairy tongue with them so they were at least close to being ready for you lot,' Asha scowled. 'We'll have to see if Nymph magic might help it along.'

'If us brutish mortals can slowly spread it from one to another, I'd say you amazing beings definitely could,' Thale assured her.

Asha floated from my shoulder to Thale's head, wrapping her arms around his face in a big hug.

'Good answer,' she told him warmly.

Thale patted her gently with a hand the size of her whole back.

'I'm actually here to escort both of you,' Thale announced in a muffled voice. 'All the way over there.' He pointed vaguely across the short distance to where Glaidin's pavilion was.

'An admirable feat,' I commented, but I felt a rush of warmth as I followed the direction of his finger and saw the King and the Raiden of Awyalkna talking outside – looking for all the world like men who were on equal footing as leaders. They still appeared distant and uncertain as father and son, but the dynamic had at least started to shift.

They were standing side by side in the triangle of light at the entrance to the royal marquee, gazing out together at the camp.

'Really I needed to escape all the attention,' Thale admitted through Asha's ongoing bear hug around his face. 'We have been out in the open guarding these two royal pavilions,' he said easily, and I realised that while I had slept, our comrades had remained as watchful over us as ever.

'And I have been asked to attend the meeting to translate for the Jenrans and to represent Krall. But being out there and under scrutiny for another moment before the meeting started was almost too much.'

Asha cackled in understanding as she crawled up to sit on his head like a turban. 'Too impressive for your own good?'

I noticed the Krall men and our archers nearby, where they had established themselves within close proximity to us.

Dren and the archers appeared highly amused while Warlord Conall, followed closely by a group of admiring Awyalknians, eyed the Krall warriors off as excitedly as if they were new toys.

The Krall men, however, were visibly uncomfortable at the open wonder of the Awyalknians, who were naturally wiry and much smaller in stature.

But the Awyalknian Warlord was delightedly marching through their numbers, shaking hands and punching burly shoulders – quite joyous at the thought of the promising amount of new muscle.

Phobos and Vulcan grimaced as Conall sized them up and even squeezed a bicep or two experimentally.

'No Krall warrior has ever been greeted by an Awyalknian army with avid adoration before,' Thale said dryly. 'And it's an intimidating experience.'

I laughed as I made for the door. 'Do not fear, I will protect you.'

And Thale stuck comically close to me as we crossed to meet Dalin and Glaidin, just as Durna and Aeron arrived, and just as Conall caught up to us too.

The hearty slap on Thale's broad shoulder stopped the warrior in his tracks as Conall greeted him.

'Well met!' Conall's deep voice rumbled cheerfully. 'We have much to discuss!'

The Warlord rubbed at his stubbled chin as he looked more ready to take Thale's measurements and list of achievements than for a discussion.

'I'll leave you to it,' I gave my warrior friend up with a grin, though Thale's hand was lightning fast in seizing Asha's ankle as she tried to follow me.

'Hey!' she protested as he held her tightly to his burly chest like a shield. He peered through her hair nervously and he wasn't letting go, so she rolled her eyes and tapped her fingernails on his arm plate impatiently.

'You can both sit by me,' Conall told them winsomely and I smirked and stepped inside the King's pavilion with Dalin, where a large circle of mismatched chairs had been gathered.

Then for the majority of the meeting I simply listened until I was called upon to recount the facts of my experiences with Agrona.

'Gods,' Glaidin breathed at last, sitting back in his chair in weary amazement. 'In the last day we have been rescued from the savagery of the Evexus, have received allies and aid beyond our wildest hopes, and have heard that the Witch of Krall has been weakened to almost uselessness.'

Glaidin turned to Durna and Aeron then, counting on the Krall warriors' translations. 'We are beyond grateful for your aid, as you have found us at our most vulnerable. And perhaps now we can afford to celebrate our new union with a night and day of rest. But in the morning announcements of official thanks can be made to all of our Jenran and Krall kin who have come to help us in our greatest need.'

When the meeting broke the Krall warrior translators appeared extremely gratified as they accompanied Dalin and I back to our pavilion. But they regarded me questioningly when I made to detour away from the group.

'Maeve,' was all I had to say in explanation.

Ferron moved to come with me, but I shook my head.

'Not this time,' I said gently. 'Please.'

Ferron hesitated, and then stopped and I smiled my thanks.

'I will be back soon,' I promised, already retreating towards the centre of the quiet camp and moving quickly in the direction of the healer quarters.

I stepped quietly past each ward-like tent, peering in without disturbing anyone, and moving on when none of the healers was my healer.

Each tent held a glimpse of bandaged, sleeping men and hushed, careful healers tending to them by the moonlight. But when I reached the right tent I was stopped short almost immediately.

In the silvery light her hair shone as if she were an angel of the Gods, and a sense of ease spread through my core at the sight of her.

It was as if a knot of anxiety I carried at all other times would just unravel in the pit of my stomach whenever I spotted her. My chest felt lighter. My mind calmer.

I'd noticed that I hardly had to pinch or make fists or exercise my breathing if she was near. Existing was effortless at her side. She was my calming breath and my soothing thought.

'Maeve,' the word was barely a whisper, but she turned to face the door almost at once.

The faint frown of worry and fatigue that had been upon her brow faded at once and it took every ounce of my strength not to bound into the tent to wrap my arms around her.

I held my hands out in yearning and, after she looked to the other healer in the tent – Amarantha – and received a tired smile of approval, Maeve quickly crossed to meet me.

With a rush of emotion I swept her up as if I could never hold her close enough, and I buried my face against her delicate shoulder.

'You have missed me,' she whispered warmly. Hardly covering the bleak feelings of uncertainty and grief that had darkened those tough days of hunting the Evexus.

I pulled my head back to gaze at her, still holding her up so that her feet no longer touched the ground.

'Maeve ...' I said, stepping away from the healer's tent and carrying her with me. 'It has been so much more than that.'

She sighed contentedly.

'It has been so much more than just missing you,' I tried to explain. 'Because being away from the one you love is like losing half of your soul.'

Her amber eyes searched my face more closely.

'I love you,' I told her.

I saw her hesitate, her face clouding with doubt – for in a normal life we would never have been matched.

But we now lived in a time when petty class norms were insignificant, paling in the face of love amongst the darkness.

My heart was fluttering as my mind began to leap with ways to convince her of this. I had to make her understand that we simply could not go into war, confronting death, without the knowledge that our love was fiercer than any threat either of us would ever face.

It was the last thing Tane had been thinking of.

In fact it was the very thing that was so worth fighting for, the thing we should all be thinking of.

Then Maeve rested her forehead against mine. 'Just as I love you.'

My pent up breath released itself in relief and I gently lowered her to the ground, leaning down to press my lips to hers.

'Then that is all that matters,' I breathed against her lips.

61

Sixty One

K*iana*

An outraged court official burst through the crowds and the bubble of amazed rapture that had descended upon the gathering of Awyalknians was broken.

I felt Aglaia's hands tighten on my forearms for a tense moment before she released me.

'What are you doing, Your Majesty?!' the man blustered in horror.

He was tall and almost skeletal. Like an insect wearing white makeup. His hair was oiled and curled. Lacy frills covered most of him and I recognised him as the one who had retreated from my fight with the Trunes. The one who had been pointing out the Queen.

He glared from me, covered in battle grime and scratches, to Toru, still glowing and as impressive as ever, to

Vidar and his deadly staff, and then with a darkening scowl toward Scandra. He ignored Rebel and Spud altogether.

'Wilmont,' the bulky, older general bristled.

Wilmont covered his nose with a lacy handkerchief.

'Look at all the mess!' he burst out in disgust. Then he jabbed a jewelled finger at Scandra and the rest of us. 'These beasts must go! We cannot trust that they will not be turned against us, too!'

Aglaia's fury was tangible as she drew a heated breath to speak.

'Oh, just shut up!' the young soldier at the Queen's side burst out instead. He seemed surprised at himself, but then continued on. 'You are a traitor and have no right to speak to the Queen!'

Wilmont's eyes boggled, and beneath the white powder on his face crimson colour was rising in his pinched cheeks.

'Insolence,' he hissed. 'Arrest this disrespectful cur!'

He pushed at a nearby soldier, who only glowered at Wilmont instead.

Wilmont whirled in fury. 'Your Majesty,' he began to growl. 'I was clearly trying to tell the Trunes not to hurt you. His claims of betrayal are absurd!'

'Silence,' Queen Aglaia uttered coldly, and she seemed to suddenly grow in power, in command, and in beauty. She was no longer just a woman amongst a crowd, even in her night clothes.

'I have seen you aid our enemies with my own eyes,' she said, and her voice became almost chilling. 'Do you accuse me of lies? Do you order my arrest?' Her face was dangerous.

'You are a coward. And your treachery will no longer go unnoticed.'

Wilmont seemed to shrink.

'This is a misunderstanding, Your Majesty!' he cried, transforming quickly. 'They knew my loyalty to you, our respect and care for each other, and they sought to capture me to find you ... I had no choice.'

'Your life is not more precious than our Queen's!' the young soldier, still standing protectively near Aglaia, protested wrathfully.

'My worth is still great! After all my years of service –' Wilmont began.

'After all these years of trust and favour,' Aglaia agreed fiercely. 'To find you have been serving both sides. I think if we look back, and search carefully, we will find much evidence to condemn you.'

'We should send him to Darziates,' the brawny general commented, and there were a few cheers from the crowd.

'You cannot sentence me without tangible evidence,' Wilmont spluttered. 'The Queen would not be so barbarous.'

'If I may?' Scandra's deep voice issued from between her sharp teeth and drew every eye.

'It speaks?' Wilmont huffed in surprise.

Aglaia and her soldiers turned slowly, their faces now masks of pure shock. They had never heard the Dragons communicate as the noble and intelligent Dargons could.

'I am Scandra, Empress of the Dargons,' my friend spoke evenly, with wisps of smoke being the only sign that she was still distressed by the confrontation with her corrupted kin.

She glittered with the flickering light of torches and the fires still dying out along the streets. 'You have known the Dragons, ruined by the cruelty of the Sorcerer. But we are the Dargons, and we are capable of great things. I think in this instance, I may in fact be of service to a fellow Queen.'

Aglaia was flawless as she graciously addressed the giant reptilian figure that hulked above the gaping crowds.

'Mighty Empress, what else is there that you could possibly do to help me? You have already granted my people their lives when I could not have hoped to save them.'

Scandra lowered her great golden head, her long nose coming closer to Aglaia. I knew it was a strain for all of the soldiers near us not to react defensively.

'Dargons have the gift of true sight,' Scandra replied, and though her focus was not on me, it suddenly seemed that Scandra was impossibly magnetic. 'We can look into the eyes of a being and see their spirit for all it is. I can read this man's essence, and reveal the truth of the darkest and most hidden parts of his soul. If he has betrayed you, looking into my eyes will be punishment enough. If he is pure, then he will find only satisfaction and reward. But none can ignore or remain unchanged by the truth they find in the depths of their own selves.'

Aglaia's eyes widened in amazement. 'How is this justice possible?'

Warmth touched Scandra's burning, golden eyes. 'I can sense that you would find only happiness if you were to look into my eyes,' she told the Queen. 'But others, those who deny even to themselves how rotten their souls are, can never withstand the force of the truth. It is dangerous to share the sight of a Dargon if you are not prepared to accept what you see, and if you do not fully know every crease and corner of who you are. If this man is being honest, he has nothing to fear.'

'You have already done so much for us,' Aglaia told the Dargon Empress. 'And I would be grateful to trust this to you.'

'This is preposterous!' Wilmont screeched, flapping his hands up so that his immaculate frills bounced. 'That beast is just another one of Darziates' tricks! The Sorcerer wishes to hurt me, for I am so loyal to you!'

Like a trapped animal Wilmont cast about himself, but found a solid wall of cold onlookers and no path for escape. Every ash covered, bruised face in the crowd was set with grim condemnation for the spotless official before them.

Sweat stood out across his powdered forehead and he fished in his frills for a red pendant to clutch for comfort, adamantly beginning to mutter his prayers. But no miraculous God of the pendant replied.

Two soldiers stepped forward to seize him, and disbelief and terror made Wilmont's lips tighten over his yellowed teeth so that his face grew skull-like as they each took one of his arms – rumpling the velvet material of his sleeves.

'If you had goodness inside you,' Aglaia told Wilmont slowly, finally shifting her gaze from Scandra. 'You would never doubt or fear these beings. You would feel the goodness that exudes from all of our saviours. It makes my heart warm with joy.'

'No beast will ever break my mind!' Wilmont spat, his feet dragging as he was pulled forward.

And then Scandra turned her eyes to Wilmont and his knees buckled with the weight of her stare.

'If you are innocent then no harm will be done. If you are not, it will be your own self-loathing that will break your mind. Not anything I do.'

'If this man has truly betrayed his country and people, I see your justice to be fair,' Aglaia told Scandra. 'Please, friend, grace this man with your sight.'

The masses around us held their breath and seemed to be just as drawn in by Scandra while Wilmont faced the brunt of her focus.

His mouth widened as his eyes became fixed on the golden, swirling light within the Dargon's gaze. The stream of magic between them seemed tangible, skipping about us all like dazzling butterflies with glinting golden wings.

Wilmont remained absorbed, his manicured nails coming up to tear at his face. A wail of total abhorrence gurgled up from his throat as though demons had been trapped inside him, and were clawing their way free.

Wilmont nearly slumped forward in horror and the soldier nearest to him reached forward to clasp his shoulder again uncertainly. But at the moment of contact, the magic suddenly burst freely from where it had before been contained in a stream between the Dargon and her captive.

It radiated outward and images of Wilmont filled my mind and seemed to slap and bite at me from within.

I heard not only Aglaia gasp, but cries of fear and then scorn as many people were touched by the sweeping magic and found themselves seeing Wilmont, many years younger, speaking reverently to a black bird, leering over the princes, slapping and sneering at servants, glowering murderously out of sight at the King and Queen. Always listening, always searching for more that he could use, and whispering what he had learned to a red pendant that radiated with such evil that it could only come from Darziates himself.

But these images were hardly registered, for far worse was the repulsive feeling that seemed to be seeping out from the man we beheld.

Then as Scandra's search within this wretched man's soul moved deeper, we saw to his core. The image his soul presented was like that of an ugly landscape of dark skies and grey, cold stone – void of life or any redeeming feature.

Wilmont cried out as he saw his true self, and saw that deep inside he was barren of any of the riches he had sought to adorn his physical life with. He saw that he was a wasted shell of a human being, and cracks abruptly appeared in the imposing grey landscape.

I flinched as the cracks widened with reverberating rumbles, as though the place was itself howling with pain, tormented at its grotesque nature being revealed. And as great chasms opened in the shaking stone, it was clear that beneath the surface there was nothing more to see.

The images suddenly disappeared from my mind as Wilmont collapsed into a shrieking ball on the pavement at Scandra's talons.

He quivered, covering his head while I blinked and the people around us stared.

'A Dargon's sight can cause painful revelations,' Scandra broke the stunned silence, and Aglaia stepped across to place a hand on Scandra's warm scales. But when the Awyalknian Queen gazed at the man who had been betraying her country, her mouth set in a firm line.

Wilmont huddled and sobbed, reduced now on the outside as much as he was on the inside.

'Your justice is strong,' Aglaia told the Dargon Empress. 'Much has been lost to Darziates if the others of your kind were once like you, when so much knowledge and understanding is in your nature.'

Scandra's eyes, now back to their normal golden glow, became sad. 'Much has been lost. But fifty of my sisters will be staying here with you. And now that we all stand together much can still be saved.'

62

Sixty Two

D^{alin}

I cupped my hands with water and let it pour down in a stream over my fingers. It splashed in little droplets back into the tub that had graced my exhausted muscles and limbs with blissful weightlessness.

I blinked away a droplet that had escaped from my hair to roll down and sit on my eyelashes, and watched it send shivers over the water's surface. Then I made a bigger disturbance, my watery reflection wobbling erratically as I shifted and rubbed my eyes tiredly.

I was now a member of my father's circle, and the meetings had gone on well into the night with the candles in Glaidin's marquee burning low. But, weary or not, I had to get ready for the Kings' public delivery – speeches to stir hope and perhaps ease the fatigued armies into facing our resumed march again, side by side. So I forced myself to straighten and stand.

The water sloshed noisily and its level dropped as I stepped out and towelled dry, already feeling clammy again in Krall's heat.

I heard someone lift the material of the pavilion door to step in out of the desert sun, but I didn't glance back – expecting Noal, Dren or one of the Krall warriors to have come to fetch me.

'Is it time already?' I asked gruffly, rubbing my face and hair briskly.

'Nearly,' I heard Glaidin's voice instead.

I stopped and turned awkwardly.

'My King,' I said in greeting, feeling literally very exposed to him.

'My son,' he emphasized, handing me the trousers I had tossed carelessly over my cot so I could throw them on.

Though I now carried the heavy and respected title of the Raiden I had always felt tense and inadequate around this man, and it was hard to be at ease when, in the past, expectation had characterised our whole relationship.

'So much has happened,' Glaidin sighed. 'You have changed so greatly.'

He seemed to be echoing my thoughts as he sat on the cot and stretched his long legs out.

'Not that much,' I answered, not sure what to do with myself.

'You're as tall as I am now,' he pointed out with a small smile.

'There's that,' I acquiesced quietly, leaning against the beam that had been buried into the ground to hold the marquee up.

'And you have faced many battles and led the Jenrans to Awyalkna's aid.' He peered openly at me, pleading silently for me to help him to break away the invisible barriers that had always kept us distant and at opposite sides to each other.

'You have become the Raiden of the Gods' foretelling. The man prophesied to lead an army against the Sorcerer in a storm of thunder and lightning.'

'That too,' I admitted. 'Well ... you have lost weight.'

'You've got scars your mother will berate you for,' he returned, the lines on his face seeming less deep when he spoke more easily.

'Each one is proof of survival,' I defended half-heartedly.

'Ahh. So, so,' Glaidin acknowledged. 'Though the things you have had to survive might also cause contention.'

'They have been worth it.'

Glaidin crossed his arms. 'Tell me,' he said gently. Asking as a father rather than as a leader requesting a report, or as a King who had ordered I never do any of this at all.

I considered for a moment. 'Well, if I hadn't got these,' I tilted slightly to show him the lash-like claw marks still visible on my back, and the line along my jaw. 'Noal or myself could have been felled by an Evexus. Without the mark on my thigh, Kiana would have been taken by the Krall warriors she'd saved us from.' Then I traced the jagged, lightning-like scars along my bicep. They still looked angry and stood up from the skin. 'And if I hadn't battled Thale and Nikon for these,' I said thoughtfully, 'we would never have saved my loyal men from Darziates, and they wouldn't have been around to keep me safe from more scars. They have in turn bled and died for me.'

My face grew grim as a momentary image of Tane, the laughing warrior filled my mind.

'Ahh, well. I also know where the most recent bruises and scrapes came from. All worthy marks of honour, then,' Glaidin reflected. 'You can be proud of each. As I am of you.'

I felt my face furrow and I looked down. 'Proud of a runaway who went against your own decree?'

'Proud of a man who did the right thing when no one else believed or listened,' Glaidin's voice was heavy with emotion. 'Proud of my son, who has become a beloved leader and friend to unlikely and invaluable allies. You are a gift to me, and your people, from the Gods. I shouldn't have tried to keep you hidden away safely. It was selfish.'

My eyes were wide as they rose again to meet my father's unwavering gaze.

'Raiden?' Purdor called through the marquee material. 'When the Awyalknian King is found, the able bodied soldiers are all ready and gathered.'

'I have found the King,' I responded after a pause. 'We'll be ready in a moment.'

'Oh!' I heard Purdor exclaim, just as uncertain of how to approach this new royal as I had been. 'Very good, Your Majesty, and um, Raiden.'

My father handed me my shirt and tunic now too, and squeezed my shoulder before he left through the material door to warmly address the Krall warrior.

'A more noble escort I could not find,' I heard Glaidin greet Purdor easily. 'I have heard much of the bravery of the Krall soldiers.'

I hurriedly pulled on my clothes, feeling lighter despite the heaviness of my knotted muscles.

And when I caught up to the others I took my place – between Durna and Glaidin – comfortable at my father's side.

63

Sixty Three

A *glaia*

Aglaia watched the enigmatic Fairy who had burst so gloriously into Awyalkna City. Every one of her generals and Friendly were watching the One too, as Aglaia had convinced the One to stay in the palace for the remaining hours of the night.

The generals who were not still outside directing rescues and clean ups were instead all very obvious in their ogling. They sat transfixed at a long table, laden with hastily arranged food, staring directly across at the unconcerned and very assorted immortals on the other side.

Scandra had remained outside the city walls to join her fifty heartbroken Dargons in burning the bodies of their grey-skinned dead. But the other magical ones ate the food laid out before them hungrily and, in one case, literally with the appetite of a Giant.

The Giant sat next to the vast table, hunching over to reach the food while below him the beings called Spud and Rebel simply stepped around dishes of food – walking over the tabletop to get what they wanted.

The two of them jostled each other and ate with decidedly less decorum than the magnificent figure of the long limbed Elf. He sat politely, and graciously beamed his dazzling smile at each unceremoniously gaping general.

The One herself was seated quietly back from the rest, angular and strong in the wavering torchlight.

Aglaia felt that she could see a slight shimmering that hung in the air around the One, even while the Fairy was calm – focused on cleaning some angry red scratches across her arms.

'Our healers could tend to you?' one of the generals asked her almost breathlessly, as though he had never sustained anything as awful as those gashes.

'I appreciate it, but my mother was a healer and she taught me well,' Kiana replied, steadily dabbing at her bleeding knuckles now as well. 'However, a warning should be sent across the city that all Griffin wounds, even small scratches, must be cleaned to avoid infection. Griffins carry enough filth to turn a tiny cut into a festering wound.'

'It will be done. We will spread the word,' Sumantra assured her, also as captivated as the rest of the burly leaders. For they had all seen the *Larnaeradee* throw a Dragon from the skies after all.

Kiana nodded and leaned back again, seeming unmovable under their open admiration and scrutiny.

Aglaia smiled to herself.

'I can see why Dalin and Noal were meant to find you,' the Queen told Kiana warmly. 'Even if you hadn't been a *Larnaeradee*, they would have needed a woman such as yourself to protect them.'

The One regarded Aglaia now, her lips quirking upward with a half smile. 'I always patched them up,' she promised. 'And every time Noal's stomach emptied, I would hunt something to fill it.'

Aglaia laughed happily. That definitely sounded like her boys.

'But they always rescued me in return,' Kiana added solemnly. 'I could not have done without them. Even if they hadn't turned out to be two princes – prophesied to lead the mortal kingdoms in a war to end all evil.'

'We heard that you were a hunter of Krall beasts before you met the princes and gained your power,' one of the other generals broke in eagerly.

The One nodded, though she did not seem to relish memories of the hunt, and stroked a glittering jewel at her throat while she reflected for a moment.

'I travelled and learned many skills from that lifestyle. But it was a lonely, bitter time.'

'We heard you saved many people!' another general chipped in. 'The Nymph Asha told us that you often stopped the monsters before they even got to us.'

'Awww, Asha!' Rebel somehow mumbled around an impossibly full mouth.

The One grimaced. 'My focus was generally on strategies for slaughter. Grand ideas of helping people were hard to sustain, when by the time I heard of or found a trail, much blood had already been shed. The trails I followed were often gory ones.'

The *Larnaeradee's* face became tired and the Giant seated on the floor beside her reached across to pat her hand with his massive one.

'*I* caught a Dargon once,' Spud stated with a smug grin, taking the focus from the One.

There were exclamations and bursts of questions.

'A baby one,' Rebel, clarified primly. Oil dribbled from his chin.

'I should never have told you that story,' Spud muttered, ripping the final shred of flesh from a turkey bone with stumpy fingers.

'Tell us your stories,' Friendly encouraged keenly.

Aglaia leaned away from the conversation then, settling back in her chair, and musing over how the assorted beings seated at the table had brought about such an incredible turn of events.

But she was caught by surprise when the One quietly, lightly set herself in front of the Queen – having crossed around the table unnoticed.

'I am a little disinterested in more talk of war or competition,' the One explained courteously. 'And hoped you would not mind my intrusion.'

Aglaia regarded the Fairy kindly, patting the open space on her bench seat. 'You have saved my sons and my city. So you are in no way an intrusion. I am indebted to you.'

It was the first time the *Larnaeradee's* face had shown any level of being taken aback. 'My Queen,' she answered in a low voice. 'To you I'm simply the loyal Awyalknian, Kiana. You owe me nothing.'

Aglaia gestured around the vast chamber. Even many of the awe struck attendants lined along the walls were covered in bruises and scrapes, yet none of them appeared miserable. 'This could have been the worst night of all of our lives. In fact it could have been the end of everyone's lives here if your aid had not come. The least I can do is speak with you and offer you a warm tub of water and a bed after this.'

Kiana's expression became soft with gratitude. 'I have been blessed by the Gods,' the Fairy replied. 'For though my mother was taken from me, since her loss I have had the fortune of meeting all of the most influential and empowered females alive. You, my Queen, used Darziates' attacks to embolden your people, and I have gained the friendship of Lady Amarantha, the leading healer of Jenra. I have met Giantesses and Elvish women who are just as fierce as their men. I have grown with the insights given to me by Scandra, the Empress of her kind. And I have been mentored by the Lady of the forest, the Gods' guardian of this world's natural life.'

'The thought of many strong figures all coming together in the world is a heartening one,' Aglaia nodded with lifted brows. 'And one of those strong figures is also yourself – the

One *Larnaeradee*, who seeks to face evil and keep it from taking over.'

Kiana's expression became thoughtful. 'I really only recently began to see traits that are worthy of admiration in my own self,' she revealed candidly. 'But when I found your sons they helped me to properly feel again, and to be part of something meaningful in a bigger way.'

'Sometimes we need to truly be seen by someone else, in order to see ourselves,' Aglaia replied warmly, putting a reassuring hand on Kiana's arm.

But with that simple touch, Aglaia's eyes widened – for she suddenly felt a delicious prickling of warm magic spreading from her point of contact with the Fairy.

Kiana paused, aware of the impact she'd unintentionally had.

'I have been getting better at sharing visions of my memories with others,' she told Aglaia haltingly. 'If you wish it, I could show you what my life was like before I met your boys, and how it changed because of them.'

'Please do!' Aglaia nodded avidly, leaning closer to the One in anticipation.

'My power is not so introspective as Scandra's. You will simply be an observer, objectively seeing images of my past with me,' Kiana reassured the Queen, placing her hand over Aglaia's.

Then Aglaia felt the pricklings of power move further up her arm, soon encompassing her totally. A gradual trickling of images and sounds seeped into her mind as they had for Wilmont not long before. Though now it was visions of Kiana's experiences that she saw.

The raucous voices around the table faded into the background, and Aglaia saw an image of Kiana standing atop a dusty hill in the night.

The One's face was hard and void of emotion, her stance strong and her bow in hand.

Behind her there was a foreign, dilapidated village, with darkened windows that were filled with the peering, sunken faces of frightened villagers. But in front of her there was an approaching pack of strange beasts.

They were massive, with thick, naked torsos, hairless heads and long arms, walking upright, but with their oversized hands dragging.

They lumbered and grunted as they moved toward the village, and it looked as if they already had bundles of animal and human carcasses slung over their shoulders.

They were collecting for a feast.

There were whimpers of terror from the watching villagers. Yet Kiana calmly stood between the creatures and their goal, drawing an arrow.

Her expression showed no feeling at all.

She was focused solely on completing her work ...

Aglaia's breath caught as the scene shifted and she now found herself peering up at her son. A lump of emotion grew in the Queen's throat as she saw Dalin, taller and older than she remembered, seeming to smile fondly down at where she sat, his green eyes crinkled with warmth. But Aglaia turned a little in her chair, and in the vision, to find who he had really been gazing at – and saw Kiana.

Kiana was no longer the hard, fierce figure. She was smiling at Dalin in return, and Aglaia realised that she had rarely seen her son so joyous.

'Gods, I'm starved,' Aglaia heard Noal's voice filtering through the memory from a distance, and Aglaia laughed to herself.

Gladness flooded the Queen before the scene shifted again and this time it suddenly seemed Aglaia was soaring through the air – suspended as though on a cloud beside Kiana and Dalin, who now both had magic in their eyes while Kiana taught Dalin to fly.

The intent on her son's face was clear as he watched Kiana, ignoring a mountain kingdom and every other marvel that surrounded them ...

Then the magic receded, and Aglaia felt her shoulders drop as she had to let the happiness of the moment go.

'My Queen,' Kiana's voice probed softly, before Aglaia found herself blinking about at the gathering around the table again – where everyone else was carrying on as if nothing incredible had just happened.

For a moment everything seemed clearer and brighter than normal, as though a veil had been lifted from her sight, but Aglaia at last felt her mind come back to focus and the Queen gazed at where her tingling fingers still rested on Kiana's arm.

Aglaia now firmly gripped one of Kiana's hands in both of her own.

'Kiana,' Aglaia said softly. 'If you didn't have to fight a Sorcerer, I would insist you stay here. But you must go back out there, take up your cause and reunite with my sons. They need you.'

Kiana's shoulders relaxed, and Aglaia smiled at the thought of the expression on Dalin's face in her memory.

64

Sixty Four

Kiana

I could see Scandra and my other comrades outside the city walls – Rebel's bright orange hair standing out as he flitted around the crowds, probably with Spud in tow, while Vidar and Toru magnanimously allowed both children and excited adults alike to climb up for shoulder rides.

'Fifty Dargons ...' General Sumantra was repeating under his breath, seeming dazed as we stood atop the Gwynrock Wall together. 'We might just stand a chance now,' he went on as he watched a dozen massive Dargons carefully picking their way through the streets inside the wall, helping people to clear rubble and even lift buildings where necessary.

One Dargon was both straightening a pillar with her shoulder, melting a new brace into position for an archway and patiently lifting her tail, stopping it from blocking a pathway three streets away from where she actually stood.

There clearly wasn't room for many more Dargons inside, so the others were either circling above on watch, or were examining the wall outside to see where rocks needed to be shoved bodily back into place.

'I am appreciating the Dargons more and more with each passing moment,' I heard the Queen's voice as she and her soldier Friendly joined us. She wore a plain dress that suggested she was going to be working beside her people in the clean-up, and she wore Dalin's broad smile.

'Kiana,' she addressed me then. 'I can see that there are admiring Awyalknians gathering outside the walls to farewell you, but before you go I desire another favour.'

'Of course,' I replied without hesitation.

She held out a delicate golden ring. 'I want you to wear this.'

It looked like the band was made of two vines of ivy twirling around each other in a circle.

'And,' Aglaia continued as she took my hand and slid it along my finger. 'I want you to look after yourself and find my boys safe and sound again.'

'My Queen,' I responded gratefully. 'I will bring this ring to them as a token from their mother, and we shall all do our best to bring it back to you.'

She beamed. 'Ask Dalin about the ring, I think he will be glad to see it with you.'

I nodded and bowed respectfully.

'Be safe,' I told her seriously. 'And I hope we shall meet again.'

65

Sixty Five

*K*iana

'We will soon find ourselves reunited with the rest of our magical kin,' Scandra called back to where I sat between Toru and Vidar, watching the sun begin to rise over the quickly passing canopy. 'I can feel the magic of our concealed forces,' she told us.

'Oooh, we'd better look the part of returning heroes,' Rebel gushed, fluffing his hair.

'I'm already prettier than all the moss and rocks in the world,' Spud shrugged nonchalantly.

'Even better,' Rebel laughed. 'You look like a potato faced brat.'

'And you look like a pointy toothed baby,' Spud returned affectionately.

'You are both annoying specks,' Scandra growled, and when Spud opened his mouth to protest, two well-aimed balls of ash blew from Scandra's snout – one hurtling back to leave a dirty mark on Rebel's forehead, and the other giving Spud a mouthful.

'We ... are ... the annoying speck champions of Awyalkna,' Spud spluttered. And then he turned to rub at Rebel's sooty forehead while we soared over the last leagues of the forest.

'They are well hidden down there,' I commented, and Vidar nodded as he peered downward.

'Once we're out in the open Darziates will know our exact numbers. But for now Frey planned to stop the march at a safe distance from where Krall begins,' the Elf explained.

'The army's next move will have to be timed carefully,' I mused. 'We cannot be revealed too soon.'

'Well, safely hidden right now or not, my sisters will not be enjoying having their wings kept to their sides,' Scandra remarked with a wisp of smoke. 'And I am not looking forward to it either.'

The trees of the Lady's forest would be tall enough to conceal a standing Giant, but I winced as I envisioned the magnificent Dargons – contorting to fit between the massive tree trunks below.

'And, yet, here I go,' the Dargon Empress drawled sourly.

She angled her body, circling over a clearing that was large enough for a skilled Dargon to land in, and which would be near enough to the hidden camp.

I heard Spud and Rebel cry out in delight as they clung onto her horns, and this time when I peered below I was able to make out a sea of what appeared to be running rocks all clambering over each other and toddling on stout Gnome legs toward the clearing.

Flocks of Nymphs also flew about in excited circles, and Flash zoomed up and past my ear to dart straight at Rebel, hugging him gaily.

Less overzealous, a handful of Giants and Elves had come to greet us as well, stepping gingerly through the hordes of Gnomes.

'Toru! We missed you! It was so quiet without you!' Ahanu yelled, stepping over to us even while Scandra was still managing her tight landing.

'Dearest One!' Ahanu went on with a chuckle. 'You're as puny as ever!'

'Yes. But I did get stronger,' I assured him, floating over to the Giant.

'Oh?' Ahanu asked.

'She learned how to throw Dragons with her magic,' Spud filled him in, launching off Scandra's back, onto Ahanu's head, across to an Elf's shoulder, and then down the Elf's arm to the awaiting mob of Gnomes, all clambering around the big people's ankles.

'Impressive,' Einion congratulated me as he picked his way to his father's side.

'Pretty good,' Ahanu grinned, and glanced over at Scandra as she made two massive trees shake and crack while she squeezed between them. Her growls of annoyance sent a swarm of Gnomes and Nymphs away squealing.

'We best let her testy mood settle before the meetings begin,' Ahanu whispered so obviously that I heard Scandra growl even more loudly.

'See?' he whispered inconspicuously again. 'Testy.'

He stepped out of her way but instead nearly squashed a group of Dwarves, making them scatter.

'Oaf!' one of them cried indignantly, his green beard pointing outward sharply as though it were as angry as the one who wore it.

'You're so cute,' Ahanu sighed, and the angry Dwarf stomped his foot and trod off aggressively. Ahanu shook his head. 'See that? With his little foot? Adorable.'

We followed him as he asked about our trip, with Scandra manoeuvring her way as best she could until she selected a resting place on the edge of the camp.

Then, when Scandra had managed to make herself comfortable and regal enough for all of the other race's leaders to join her, we sat around a bonfire that she had herself lit – Frey, Spud, Ace, Ahanu, Scandra and I together discussing our next moves.

'So it is best if I am accompanied by just a couple of Elves who can speed across Krall,' I stated toward the end. 'Hopefully we will be a quick and small enough group to remain unnoticed until we find the Awyalknian and Jenran armies.'

'When you send word that the moment is right we will move out,' Frey agreed. 'And you can rest assured that when it is time for us to move out into the open, we will cover the distance swiftly.'

'We will arrive to face the darkness and to support the mortals together,' Scandra promised, and I nodded, ready for the morning to come.

66

Sixty Six

D*alin*

I rubbed tiredly at the dusty stubble on my rough jaw, and Noal yawned next to me – his hair brunette now with dirt.

'Last campfire visit. Over there,' I said, jutting my head toward a group of weary soldiers near the edge of the camp.

'Last one,' Noal agreed, squinting across to where Dren and Rai were also circulating the camp with Thorin. They were taking a turn at helping us in what had become our nightly effort to meet as many weary, careworn people in the camp as possible.

The group of Awyalknian soldiers we approached now hailed us respectfully and appreciatively, but they still had the haunted, gaunt look of those who had been chased to the edge of death, and who had seen too many others left to lay in the dust during the chase of the Evexus.

They made to rise as Noal and I drew close, but I held my hands out. 'Please, friends. Rest!'

And the soldiers nodded and smiled gratefully, despite their flaking, sore lips and chafed cheeks.

'How goes the journey with you all?' I asked, trying not to stare at where one of them had managed to get his boots off his swollen feet, which were covered in peeling sores and blisters. Tomorrow those feet would face another whole day's march.

'The Jenrans have taken over most of the duties that require extra toil at the end of each day,' one of the soldiers rasped stoutly. 'They turn away Awyalknians who rise to help with setting up the healer quarters and night watches. So we are fortunate and able to rest.'

The soldier closest to me reached out to shake my hand, and his grip was firm.

'We thank you for bringing our allies.'

I took heart in his appreciative smile and when we left their group to cross to Thorin and the archers they were receiving similar proclamations of gratitude.

Rai was smiling as one soldier shook his hand vigorously, saying: 'we were looking shaky before you came along!'

'Did you see that man's feet?' Noal winced at me, speaking quietly as we walked around others who were settling down to rest. 'Maeve says that each night the healers bathe and bind many Awyalknian soldiers' feet, but they can only use up their bandages on the ones who have the worst swelling, blisters and burns from running the hot plains in tattered boots.'

Noal smiled and nodded as a couple of haggard soldiers greeted us while we passed.

'Maeve also says,' he went on. 'That many soldiers are coping so well because their feet have simply become numb.'

I was grimacing as Thorin, Dren and Rai fell into step with us, and we hauled our own exhausted bodies over to our pavilions.

'Don't be so glum,' Thorin told me soberly, guessing at my concerns. 'A march can be rough. Depleting resources, and lives, almost as effectively as the actual fighting. But your soldiers are fortunate.'

'They are falling apart,' I frowned.

'I admit,' Thorin said, 'the condition of the Awyalknians when we first arrived was poor. But now they have united with a stronger force, they have had the chance to re-bolster and have found motivation. As well as that, with such fair hours and provisions, their morale is holding up. Even physically, things could be worse for them. Except that you and your fellow leaders don't think twice about giving time for recuperation whenever we're not being harried by the Sorcerer.'

I raised my eyebrows, glancing around the camp with new eyes. People were tired. Sore. But they were not beyond hope. Some were still standing about the camp discussing where nets could be placed, or where ropes and traps could be set in case of attack.

I could see Jenrans offering Awyalknians help with setting up tents, and Awyalknians offering Jenrans rations that they had cooked. Roth, Lydon, Gideon and Rendor were taking water around the camp, and nobody watched these men of Krall with suspicion.

'This march is like no expedition any of us Krall warriors have ever experienced,' Thorin went on. 'I never knew such a happy army could exist.'

I gave him a grateful smile, but knew that he was not truly happy himself, for after the loss of Tane he had begun to appear increasingly gaunt, too.

'On that note, have something to eat,' I told Thorin as I stopped at the doorway to my pavilion. 'You need your strength.'

'My prince,' he made a slight bow.

I smiled as Dren put a brotherly arm around Thorin's shoulders, steering him off to find dinner.

Then, sighing when Noal and Rai left to visit the healer quarters, I splashed my face in the basin of water at the door of my tent and sagged onto the cot to unlace my own boots.

'Gods, Kiana,' I said softly to myself. 'Please come to us soon. If anyone could bring real relief in such a hopeless place – it would be you.'

67

Sixty Seven

K*iana*

Colour was only just beginning to cross the velvety blue morning sky when Scandra gently touched the tip of her vast nose to the top of my head.

'Wake, Kiana,' she breathed warmly with a musky scent of ash. I had fallen asleep between her fore-paws.

'Is it already time to go?' I asked, certain that most of the camp still slept.

I could hear only faint movement as a few beings stirred, rising to farewell myself and the volunteer Elves who would be coming with me – Vidar and the elder Elf, Bard.

Scandra softly nuzzled at me and I sat up, putting my arms around her snout as far as I could in a hug.

'It is time,' she agreed through my arms. 'But before you set out, there is news.'

I leaned back to gaze at her great face more clearly.

'When I read the traitor Wilmont's soul so deeply, a kind of trace of him was left in my mind,' she explained, her golden eyes burning like embers in the dark. 'So in the early hours of this morning I felt it when the Sorcerer's servant was suddenly burned to death in his cell by unnatural magic. The magic came from his globe necklace, which nobody had thought to take during the rush when he was imprisoned.'

I felt my face grow grim. 'So Darziates used his magic to kill his captured spy. This will be another piece of news for Dalin and Noal,' I sighed, pulling my tunic on over my shirt. 'Though I suspect even they wouldn't have wished for their childhood tormentor to have been ended in such a way.'

'No news will overshadow the joy of your reunion,' Scandra told me, and I nodded, turning to place my palm on her golden nose until we both saw Toru emerging from the trees with Ahanu in tow, bleary eyed and yawning.

Ahanu grinned more wakefully when he saw me, and stooped to pick me up.

'Good morning little One, make sure to fry any evil beasties of the desert. But don't fry in the heat yourself. You really are quite pale.'

'You just make sure to wait and stay under cover yourself, water-being. The desert won't agree with you if you leave too early.'

He jostled me as he put a hand to his heart. 'I swear that, as agreed, we will wait until you personally return to tell us it's time to go. And I'll also keep your pretty silver armour safe until then.'

I patted him on the arm and he pressed me quickly in a light hug before he lifted me higher and threw me to Toru.

'I will miss you friend,' I whispered to Toru. 'And will come back to you as soon as ever I can.'

He nodded glumly as he set me down.

'One,' I felt the remarkable presence of Bard as he stepped toward us with Vidar at his side. 'We are ready.' The midnight Elf's deep voice rolled like waves. 'It will be an honour to run with the *Larnaeradee*.'

I nodded with a smile and stooped to scoop up and shoulder my pack – which seemed heavier than I remembered as I crossed to join the Elves.

'Well met, Kiana,' Scandra hummed quietly behind me.

'Well met, Empress, and farewell my friend. It will be a good day when we meet again.'

Then Vidar, Bard and I stepped out into the Krall desert, away from the sweet atmosphere of the forest.

'Do you wish to run or fly, One?' Vidar asked. 'To reach the armies in two days, we will need to go at quite the jog.'

'I've been carried for long enough. It's time to fly,' I said. 'I'll go slowly for you.'

Despite the foulness of the Krall environment Vidar laughed and launched himself into a blurring run, disappearing before my eyes.

Bard shook his noble head, and in a few lopes he blurred into an even greater speed, his massive power leaving ripples that stirred the desert air.

Shrugging my strangely heavy pack into a more comfortable position for my wings, I at once shot through the air to propel my way between the sprinting Elves.

'Hurry up,' I called, and sped away.

68

Sixty Eight

D^{alin}

A fierce shriek wrenched me into wakefulness.

'What the frarshk!' Noal scrambled up from his cot as I did, already stiffly feeling for his sword with his healing hand.

There were sounds of running feet and the night grew bright as bonfires were lit beyond our tent.

'That was a Nymph's voice,' I said, pulling a shirt on. 'They're raising a warning.'

'What is it Dren?' Noal asked, crossing to where the archer stood beyond our door.

Dren's bow was ready. 'Griffins are approaching, but I'm not sure that's what the warning was about.'

The yowls and threats of the Griffins grew louder and closer as Noal and I left the tent to join our Krall soldiers and archers. Cadell and Ferron rushed Ila and Amala over, already saddled.

'It's the Rucksha,' the Nymph Adahy gasped then, even as he abruptly materialised in front of our group. He was gone again in an instant.

Noal's eyes met mine, both of us thinking back to the descriptions we'd heard of these rock beings.

'Second rank, lads,' I said.

The Griffins had begun to circle over the nervously forming lines like a gathering storm.

'You're gonna get it you little frarshkers!' one called.

'Gizzards for dinner!' another sang.

'Eyeballs and man feet!'

'Waaaatch out!'

The noise of their excitement was almost deafening, and their reeking bodies roiled over us like feathered, odorous clouds as the diseased flock blotted out the night sky.

Asha was at the frontline, and I glanced back across the distance to see Aeron and Durna organising the archers. Further back a ring of foot soldiers was arranging the last of the healer and supply carts into a protected circle – a final front. And in the lines of massed men behind our own second rank, I knew Glaidin and Conall were preparing their cavalry for charges against Rucksha that might get by us.

In my own line most of the soldiers carried ropes in pairs – perfect for tripping big feet. And others wielded axes, torches, knockers and other clobbering weapons. Mostly tradesmen of the greatest bulk, they had been picked for this job because of their skill in wielding tools with strength.

'I can't hear myself think,' Phobos yelled over the jostling, spitting, swearing and flapping Griffins.

'I'mmmmmmmm gonnnnnna geeeeeettttttchaaaaa!!' one Griffin teased as it soared over our heads.

'READY!' Asha shrieked.

And then suddenly it seemed as if the world had sucked its breath in and had begun to tremble.

Amala and I were jolted to the side and cracks formed in the dirt as the ground groaned and surged.

'The desert's tearing itself apart,' Thale cried out.

'Over there!' Dwyn shouted, before accidentally knocking into Glyn.

'Gods,' Rai gaped.

The Griffins laughed manically as a huge, heaving mountain began quickly forming in the dirt near the frontline. Something was pushing to get out.

'They're not of the Gods,' Purdor disagreed, wobbling as a shaft of earth lifted beneath him from the pressure.

'There are six others,' Ander croaked. 'They've spanned themselves across the whole frontline.'

'Didn't Conall say there were four last time?' Nikon grunted.

'He did,' Noal answered, watching while, like mountains bursting out of the cascading dirt, giant men were being born of rocks before our eyes.

'They could have materialised anywhere in the camp,' Thale groaned. 'I think they *want* to bash their way through us.'

And then in another moment they were shaking themselves free, testing their massive limbs.

The colossal being closest to us shook its mighty head and released a cry that echoed across our army.

'Hold steady!' I yelled across my rank, before the world shook again as the bouldermen took big, stomping steps toward us.

I raised my sword and sensed the men all around me mirroring my action.

And we stood; an unwavering barrier, as the Rucksha lurched forward to meet us.

69

Sixty Nine

*K*iana

We had blurred through the hours and across leagues of the desert without pause.

Until I felt a sharp internal pang, and froze mid-air.

Vidar and Bard skidded to a stop while I hung still, halted by the strange and confusing feeling that continued to pull on my senses.

'What is it, One?' Bard rumbled, his hand on the silver cylinder that concealed his double ended spear.

I squinted through the settling dust. I could see the distant sun; just a faraway globe suffocating in the sky. It was half concealed by pre-cycle change clouds that were scudding across its burning shape like smoke.

'I'm not sure,' I admitted with a frown. 'I felt as though something was calling for my attention, but I can see nothing around us.'

Then I gasped in shock as my heavy pack began to wriggle against my back.

'It was probably me!' my pack groaned.

'Frarshk! You are a rogue, Spud!' I cried in exasperation as Vidar reached into my moaning bag and withdrew a very crumpled Gnome.

'Hi all,' he managed to grin widely, climbing up Vidar's arm and into the sling across the Elf's chest – making the strap of Vidar's pack into a Gnomish hammock.

'It's much better up here.' Spud put his hands behind his head. 'There's air.'

'Spud,' I lectured. 'You were not invited to this party.'

He blew a raspberry at me.

'We could make you walk all the way back,' I told him with narrowing eyes.

But he held up his hands in a placating gesture. 'Don't worry. Scandra says I'm but an insignificant speck. I'll be completely unnoticed. A subtle being.'

I sighed. 'If you do not act like an insignificant speck, Darziates may guess at the presence of the others. So far he only knows a few Nymphs and Elves have surfaced, and perhaps that fifty Dargons have come to avenge the enslavement of their kind.'

Spud winked. 'Just a speck. A speck with rock-like fists should that Sorcerer send any Rucksha through the desert to squash you all.'

I groaned.

'Was it Spud's presence that stopped you?' Bard asked, his beautiful face lined with beads of sweat from Krall's unnatural heat.

'No,' I answered slowly, and I forgot my admonishment of Spud as I realised that he had not been the cause. 'It was a strange sensation that stopped me. A sudden feeling of needing to go back to something that had been left behind.'

I peered around the wasteland and took a few steps back the way we had come.

'I can't see anything out of the ordinary. The only marker out here is that rock pile way back over there,' Vidar suggested, pointing past a number of small mounds in the dust.

The Elves followed me cautiously when I moved toward the rocky pile, stopping to stand before it and realising with a sinking feeling that each rock had been arranged with purpose.

I lowered myself slowly down to the dirt.

'A marked grave ...' Vidar commented quietly.

'This is the Krall warrior Tane's resting place,' I answered, my eyes on the Krall runes spelling out his name, and above it the sign for a rebel.

I gazed around myself once more, feeling as if my chest had been weighted with lead. There was uneven ground in many places around this marker, and I realised we had been crossing bumpy terrain for quite some time.

'Now that I look more carefully, I believe many may have lost their lives in the journey through the desert,' Bard said unhappily.

I shuddered as I threw my mind about with greater concentration, and as though I had stretched invisible hands out, I touched upon traces of cold presences and rotten residue.

'Both Griffins and Evexus have been here, and have left many dead,' I said, swallowing the lump in my throat and placing a hand over the runes scrawled over the stone tribute.

Closing my eyes, I imagined a quill was held in my hand, and that as I moved the quill over the stone, it wrote in shimmering silver letters – tracing the runes that were already there so that the script glowed. A net of silver curled around all of the stones over the grave, weighting them down as securely as possible.

'No Griffin will rob this site now,' Spud stated certainly, for once being respectful. 'It glows like a beacon, and must be the purest site in all of Krall.'

I nodded, standing sadly.

Bard placed his hand on my shoulder, and I felt his energy wrap around me like a comforting embrace. 'Your magic on this gravesite will serve as a ward against evil in this whole area. The others will not be disturbed any further in their rest.'

I sighed. 'This makes me wish to reach our surviving forces with even greater speed.'

'We will move faster than any Elf has moved since the beginning of our seclusion in the forest,' Vidar promised.

Spud licked his hand and slicked his wiry hair back, getting a good grip on Vidar's bag strap. 'I'm ready.'

I resolutely settled my now lighter pack back into position and let my wings raise me from the earth.

'Then let us find our friends,' I said grimly.

70

Seventy

D*alin*

There was a resounding bellow when our Rucksha felt a rope circle its ankles, before the straining men on each end of the rope heaved.

Our group teetered and the ground lurched as the boulderman hit the earth. But the men didn't wait, scrabbling forward to try to bludgeon the rock being back to nothingness.

Noal handed me the other end to the rope he had wrapped around his good hand and elbow. 'You and me,' he said.

I kicked Amala into action and as Ila carried Noal out to our side we lengthened the rope between us.

I felt an arrow whiz over my head, catching a Griffin that had swooped toward me with open talons. I dipped in the saddle and did not falter.

'Duck!' I yelled, and the swarm of men still battering the creature paused their hacking to stoop down as Noal and I thundered forward, and the brute was unable to regain its balance before our stretched out rope caught its thick neck.

I steered Amala around so that Noal and I passed each other and our rope tightened into a loop.

The taut noose drew streams of dirt from the Rucksha's neck, giving our soldiers on the ground a chance to pummel the pinned beast in earnest.

'Get those archer frarshkers!' I heard a shrill voice cry when another Griffin was hit before it could claw Noal.

Our archers were encircled by six of the Krall men, and the archers themselves were focused entirely on protecting us from Griffins while we were busy.

'We'll catch you off guard one day,' a Griffin promised the archers from a safe distance. 'You can't protect your pretty princelings forever!'

'And you can't grow your feet back!' Ferron yelled in return, lopping off a pair of outstretched, cruelly clawed feet that had been aimed at Rai.

'Frarshk!!!!!!!!!!!!!!!!!!' another Griffin careened past me, an arrow lodged in its eye socket as I struggled to keep hold of my rope with burning hands.

Noal grimly wrapped his rope ending around Ila's saddle pommel.

The other Krall men had joined the soldiers with bludgeons and hammers now, bashing at the Rucksha so that the beast became covered in dents and puncture marks.

'Drag it backward while the ropes hold!' I yelled as I saw its thrashing movements begin to weaken ever so slightly. 'Asha! Ready!'

With groans of exertion, the men surrounding the boulderman heaved, thrusting their feet into the dust and pulling at the beast and its binds.

Noal and I joined their effort, backing the mares up so that the beast's head had to follow our path until, inch by inch, the creature was dragged toward Asha and her bonfire.

With a final burst we dragged the beast all the way into the fire, and it howled but did not yet break apart.

'Clear!' Asha yowled, and everyone backed away while Nymph fire began to build around her fists.

It became almost too bright to look at when it burst along her arms, travelled over her chest, engulfed her legs, and cascaded from her little feet. Then, with an inhuman screech, Asha blasted her plume of flame into the chest of the Rucksha so that it was completely drilled down.

The Rucksha's limbs beat into the earth, but from within the extreme heat there were the sounds of its torso cracking and at last it began to disintegrate.

'We did it!' one jubilant pikeman crowed, but instead of rejoicing with him, my focus was unexpectedly caught by the sound of a familiar voice crying out from the ranks behind me.

Somehow, across a battlefield, I had heard my King – my father's cry.

I turned Amala in an instant, galloping through the chaos toward Glaidin's shouts, and toward what I had just spotted to be the most colossal of all bouldermen.

The soldiers fighting the immense rock creature were in a losing battle – countless ropes hung uselessly from its towering back and limbs, and while chunks of rock had been dug out of its vast torso, countless abandoned weapons remained wedged uselessly in its notched body.

Many men, including Glaidin and Conall, were diving out of its way and rolling out from its feet, desperately trying to get clear of its rampaging while Amala and I rode fiercely closer.

Springing over the dead, darting around fighting figures, skirting debris, and ducking the Griffins that were too slow to catch us, I hardly knew that I had leapt from the saddle even while Amala still galloped. But her strength and speed added to my own inertia and I found myself soaring through the air as though Kiana had launched me off with my own wings.

My arms were stretched wide and my shout was enough to make the rock creature's head swivel before, with terrible force, I caught myself around the creature's throat, swinging my weight around and dragging its head backward with a jerk that shocked the both of us.

A foot that could have squashed four wagons in a row, and that had been looming over my father, Conall and a number of other soldiers, was suddenly wrenched backward as the beast reeled for balance.

'Save your King!' I roared down at the now uncurling and miraculously saved soldiers, who were blinking in surprise to find that the giant rocky foot had been withdrawn from over their heads.

With new life the soldiers scattered clear, pulling the King and Warlord to safety – and I grimaced as the mighty boulderman turned its attention to me, raising an immense arm to clobber me out of existence.

But even while I gaped in dread the Rucksha and I were both suddenly jolted by a new staggering blow as something rammed into the boulderman.

I clung on desperately and blinked down to see Amala backing up from where she had obviously just delivered the most satisfying bucking kick ever performed by any horse, while an avalanche of rock now poured away from the hoof holes that had been left in the Rucksha's leg.

'Target the legs!' Conall yelled, and I saw the Warlord desperately trying to keep up with the blind charge my father had just led.

Their attacks made the boulderman lurch as it tried to keep its footing and I was nearly shaken free while it teetered.

With a grunt I shifted my grip, pulling myself toward its shoulder so I could stand.

'Well,' I gasped, letting go with one hand and drawing my sword. 'This worked on the Evexus.'

I aimed for the swivelling joint line where the boulderman's arm connected with its torso.

And, steeling myself and getting my balance, I let my other hand go – lifting my sword with two hands before thrusting my blade down into that line with as much force as I could.

The blade slid in surprisingly cleanly, and it seemed that something inside the Rucksha's arm went loose. The men below had to again scatter while the creature reeled, and I toppled as my sword slid free of its anchor.

I slipped down the beast's rocky front, but before my feet could touch down on solid ground the Rucksha let itself begin to disintegrate.

What had been firm earth suddenly felt like a dusty whirlpool, and I felt myself slip down as if into deep, grainy water.

'Dalin!' I could hear Glaidin's hoarse voice, but I could only see darkness as soil and stones from the Rucksha poured over me and I sank beneath them. Crushing, suffocating, they were dragging me under.

Dirt filled my nostrils and mouth as I fought to breathe and my fingers went numb as I tore and scrabbled, trying to pull free.

But then through the blind fear of being buried alive I heard another familiar voice.

'Raiden! Fight your way to me!' someone with nimble footing had climbed the collapsing mound.

I heard a dagger digging and loosening packed dirt so that I could push my hand free. The air on my fingers made me yearn to breathe. To escape the constricting, rushing, dry drowning.

I could feel the Rucksha sinking and that it meant to take me with it.

'Oh no you don't!' I heard the voice shout, and the dagger dug around where my hand had sprouted out to the surface. More dirt broke away and my arm was exposed up to the elbow.

'To me! Free the Raiden!' the dagger was digging frantically now.

Then I felt a strong grip take my hand, and I did my best to hold that grip too.

'I've got him!' I heard Thorin's muffled voice.

'Raiden!' the cries of my Krall men became audible as they must have rushed to join the digging.

I felt myself sink lower and the dirt around me got tighter. My chest and skull felt as though they would cave in on themselves, and my cheeks were being pushed inward so much that it felt as though my eyes would pop out of their sockets.

But finally I felt the tightly packed dirt ease just enough, and then that firm grip on my hand was wrenching me through a waterfall of dust.

Someone grabbed me around the chest and hauled me away, and everyone that had climbed the Rucksha's remains had to leap free as it sank into a swirling whirlpool of earth, dragging nearby bodies and debris with it.

Helping hands heaved us out of the massive, sinking crater that had formed, laying us down to get our breath at the top.

I gasped loudly, rubbing earth from my eyes and coughing it out of my lungs.

'Raiden?' Dren's arm was still around my chest from where he had hauled me out.

I looked at the dagger in his hand and the dust covering him from head to toe.

'That's not your weapon of choice,' I managed to choke out, and he smiled, laying back tiredly.

'Arrows weren't going to free you. I had to come up with something else.'

'I thank you ... friend,' I puffed through irregular gasps. 'For the arrows that did save all of us from being Griffin dinner. And for saving me from being carried down into an earthen tomb.'

He shook his head. 'My friend, I feel that at least a part of my debt to you has been paid, and I am glad to have you back alive.'

'Yes,' I sighed, though I wasn't sure of what debt he meant. 'I am glad to be breathing. Even if I might be having nightmares about rocks for the rest of my life.'

'That brute was the last of them. But the tents got wrecked. So perhaps we can just sleep here now,' Noal groaned as he and Thorin climbed to where we sprawled in exhaustion.

'In the dirt?' Thorin questioned with distaste.

'Actually,' Noal considered. 'After seeing what dirt can do, I'd be happy to never see another speck of it.' He frowned at the pit we perched over with distrust. 'We nearly lost the whole army in one dirt swirl.'

'Yes,' Thorin remarked. 'But at least this wasn't lost.'

I chuckled with wonder as he placed my sword beside me.

'And there is still a King of Awyalkna because of Dalin's rashness too,' Noal added. 'Glaidin's sprawled out as inelegantly as you are on the other side of this crater.'

'Thank the Gods,' I replied, but then sat up at last when the whirring sound of an approaching Nymph caught our attention.

'Noal!' Asha yelled excitedly. 'Guess what!'

'I sent you to the healers. You were so drained,' Noal reprimanded her.

'I did go,' she said. 'And guess what happened while I was there to recharge me quick-smart!'

'I don't know,' he answered tiredly. 'Darziates surrendered after seeing how well we survived?'

'Noooo,' Asha bounced in the air. 'Your ... Maeve ... has ... been ... promoted!'

Noal froze.

'Amarantha was knocked out and even the noble, experienced healers fell to panic without her direction. Maeve told them all off and gave them their orders and ran the whole operation. She's still running it now, bossing about Jenrans and Awyalknians alike,' Asha gushed. 'And when Amarantha woke, she made Maeve her second in command. She presented her with the necklace that has a leading healer's insignia on it. One day she could be a head healer or ambassador of Jenra if she chooses – and she will now carry the title of a Lady.'

Noal looked as though the Gods had given him a new breath of life.

'Then ... a bond between us could be legitimate!'

He made to scramble to his feet but Thorin caught his shoulder and pulled him back.

'Didn't you hear the Nymph? Maeve's busy saving people. Our job is done for now, hers is just starting.'

Noal became crestfallen.

'But,' Thorin said reassuringly, 'if we survive more attacks, and the actual war, and if the world doesn't end, you will have plenty of time to be together.'

'Right,' Noal groaned. 'But really, if we do survive, I'm going to ask that Lady to be my wife.'

I shook my dusty head in wonder. So much violence and death and dread stretched before us, and here was something to be glad of.

71

Seventy One

The Sorcerer

He had felt it the moment she had stepped within the bounds of Krall.

Just as one struck by lightning feels every bolt and sizzle that wracks each of their cells – he'd felt her.

He had stopped mid swing of his practice sword, holding his chest and dropping to one knee in stunned agony as the purity of her had dashed across his lands in a surge.

Darziates had blinked in amazement, to have at last felt the extent of her wild magic for himself, with no buffering through a scryer or by the dulling power of distance.

She tasted of nature, of life, of sheer bounding energy, and she was like no other magical being to have ever existed.

He'd hardly given any heed to the faint taste of other, foreign magical beings entering the lands of men, for they were far away and would be of no matter anyway. Instead what mattered was that she was within reach, and that in Krall he would always feel her.

Perhaps, even feel *for* her.

In fact, as she moved closer he would hardly be able to forget her presence. It would haunt him like an ache of yearning usually felt by lesser men – not by the Sorcerer.

He'd broken from his reverie only with great effort; slowly standing like a man reborn, forgetting his practice sword and thinking only of her.

She was coming to him now, and would be within his reach when it was time for his quest to be fulfilled.

Together they would subdue and cleanse the world, and then unite what was left by controlling every molecule of life.

Together they would face the enormity of the threats to the world and at every turn they would be victorious.

For none could stand against such a match, and any who did not conform would easily be washed away by the purging of their new order.

72

Seventy Two

Noal

I held Maeve close despite the heat, and could almost forget that we were on a cot in a moving wagon on the way to war.

It was only when our wagon stopped for the evening that I stroked her golden hair away from the creamy, smooth skin of her forehead and kissed her brow.

'Wake darling,' I whispered. 'It's time to get up.'

And I saw a faint smile make her rosebud lips turn upward.

'Just who are you to wake this tired healer?' she asked, but nuzzled against me more tightly.

'The one who loves you,' I returned.

Then I lightly traced a finger over the thin, glittering chain of her necklace to where a tiny, delicate hand of gold hung from the chain. A healing hand.

'The one who is my prince,' she added.

'Yes, yours,' I agreed – before our peace was shattered by the sound of the Nymphs' call to arms, and we both stiffened.

'Another battle is upon us just as another night is upon us,' Maeve breathed as she reluctantly crawled out of my arms.

I quickly helped her to tie her pinafore on over her smock and then buckled my sword at my waist.

Then I took her chin in my hand and tilted her head back, leaning down to steal a kiss that was filled with warmth and worry, knowing that we had to spring away and into action far from each other's posts.

'Be careful, my Lady,' I told her solemnly.

'And you, my prince,' she kissed me quickly again.

And then we were sweeping out of the cart – ducking under a sky that was refilling with coarsely yelling Griffins, and hurrying away in opposite directions while soldiers filled the space between us.

I wove through the forming ranks until I found Dalin, already mounted, and holding the golden Unicorn horn.

I raised my eyebrows, having also noticed that Warlord Conall was in the second line this time – assuming command in Dalin's previous position.

'Two Evexus have been spotted in the distance,' Phrixus filled me in as I mounted up.

'And Durna agreed with the Raiden that we should make sure the beasts focus on us instead of running wild through the army,' Vulcan added, handing Ila's reins up to me.

The ground started to shake again then, the earth groaning. But the quaking was lesser this time.

'Look!' Ander cried. 'The bouldermen are so much smaller! And only three have come back!'

'I wouldn't say 'so much smaller,'' I screwed my face up.

'Here they come,' Dren warned, though he wasn't talking about the Rucksha.

His eyes were fixed on two lean shadows stalking forward, and I heard some nervous mutterings as Awyalknians and Jenrans alike spotted the Evexus.

The very slightly diminished Rucksha shook their feet free and stomped forward like charging bulls to meet the frontlines again. But we kept our own focus on the Evexus.

Dalin turned to me then.

'Let's get their attention.'

I nodded, spurring Ila to follow Dalin and Amala in a charge towards the beasts.

73

Seventy Three

N*oal*

'We won't be able to keep this one much longer!' Thale yelled out from the other circle.

'Hold on!' Dalin cried. 'I'm going to widen that gash.' He gripped the Unicorn horn intently while our trapped Evexus snarled and clutched its side.

'Beware!' Dren called urgently, felling a Griffin before its outreached claws touched down on Roth's shoulders.

Dalin circled Amala around, relentlessly returning to the attack and wedging the horn under our beast's armpit for a moment – hoping to leave lasting internal damage that might reach the creature's heart.

Thorin quickly leapt to catch the blow that was aimed at my brother in return as Dalin galloped free, but Thorin cried out as a drop of the beast's sizzling blood dripped onto his arm.

His skin immediately turned blue and bubbled around the scorch mark, and Phobos scrambled to yank Thorin out of the way while our Evexus gurgled and teetered.

'Watch out!' Thale wailed, and the second Evexus broke free, pouncing across to land in front of Dalin.

'Raidensgra,' it hissed, slashing a hand toward him.

'That's right,' he barked, and there was a miraculous flash of light, the Evexus' burning eyes widened, and its taloned hand fell away from its wrist – landing in the dust.

Thale charged like a battering ram straight into the maimed Evexus' chest, plunging his sabre into its sternum with such force that it staggered backward in confusion, nearly trampling its wheezing comrade.

Ila and I rushed in, leaning down to hack at the tendons behind the creature's legs, and then Thale threw a heavy boot into its knees so that the Evexus fell to land beside the other.

Nikon rammed his sabre into the skull of the first beast, pinning it, while Purdor clambered quickly onto the second beast's heaving chest – stabbing his blade into its throat. He put all of his weight onto its neck so that its head couldn't snap up at us.

The others rushed in, taking hold of any free part of the two creatures while Dalin quickly dismounted.

He leapt onto the nearest thing's stomach now, slamming the horn into its chest wound like a stake.

'It's no good!' Dalin grunted as he fought not to be bucked off the spasming beast's body. 'Dark magic keeps this thing alive when all others would perish!'

'Need help?'

The Evexus both shrilled in terror while everyone of our group spluttered and gasped at the sound of that voice.

'Oh thank the Gods!' I cried out as Kiana alit on the nearest Evexus' chest beside Dalin.

'Kiana,' he uttered in wonder. And then he smiled and motioned toward the horn. 'Tru *Larnaeradee*, only the purest of magic can compete with the darkest.'

Her eyes were sharp and flashing brightly as she placed her own hands on the Unicorn horn.

'Graaaaaax ...' the Evexus hissed with loathing at Kiana's touch and as the horn at once crackled into true wakefulness – its golden light bursting into visions of fire and magic while the skin around the Evexus' wound smoked evilly.

'Get clear,' she warned, and we obediently drew back.

The light around Kiana grew and the Evexus' skin became silver – the whites of its Other Realm eyes turning crimson with inner heat while it yowled.

And then it erupted with a force so great that red steam burst outward in a rush that made me flinch. But the explosion seemed to billow around us, rolling over what appeared to be a big, translucent bubble shield that had popped up around our untouched group. The torrent carried on around us to knock nearby soldiers down and throw Griffins off course above until the red spirit finally dissipated into nothingness.

The other Evexus was squealing hysterically – beyond terrified – and it somehow managed to tear free from where it had been staked. The near maniacal creature bounded up, despite its injuries, and made to flee, ploughing through Dalin as he tried to stop it.

Dalin was sent flying as if he'd been hit with a battering ram, arcing through the air.

'No!' Dren cried.

'Raiden!' I heard others yell as our bewildered, winded prince sailed over the lines.

But a graceful figure suddenly soared into the air to catch Dalin mid-arc, bringing him safely back down.

'Was that ...?' I squinted.

'Bard,' Kiana informed me with a smile. 'And Vidar is here. Along with another friend.'

She lifted into the air – scorching a clear path through the Griffins and drawing cheers from below.

'Look at that!' Purdor crowed as we hurried toward Dalin's landing site.

Bard and Vidar were now working with the galvanised soldiers, methodically breaking down the boulderman that had been assailing Glaidin and his lines. Beating the creature into dust.

As we reached Dalin, Kiana's magic once again rumbled and lit the sky in the distance – suggesting that the next Evexus' soul had fled into the desert atmosphere. Vidar and Bard also now dusted their hands of their work, and the sudden reprieve left us all standing like gaping children.

Bard bowed deeply and respectfully.

'Well met. Once again I have had the fortune of catching you, great Raiden.'

Dalin bowed in deep honour in return. 'Bard ... my thanks.'

'Just as you saved my life, I would give mine for yours,' the Elf answered.

'But for now, let's see if we can catch any low flying Griffins,' Vidar told the elder Elf, and they disappeared in such a quick blur that everyone around us was left stunned.

'My sons,' Glaidin uttered at last. 'I am continually impressed by your selection of friends.'

'Well,' Dalin replied. 'Wait until you meet Kiana.'

74

Seventy Four

K*iana*

I found Dalin helping a wounded soldier to limp over to the healers, and I easily slotted in under the other shoulder of the man that Dalin had been supporting.

The man groaned in relief as my magic at once began to soothe and strengthen him, making Dalin grin.

'I wish I could have a healing effect on people,' he said.

'You always make me feel better,' I replied honestly.

Then as we approached the healer quarters I caught sight of the healer in charge, calling out orders in a no-nonsense tone.

It was not Amarantha, who was in the distance performing as confidently as this one. It was little, timid Maeve.

'She followed Noal,' Dalin informed me, watching the small woman taking charge so easily. 'She has done much to help us, and has been promoted to Second Healer in Command. She now has the title of Lady because of her talent.'

I raised my eyebrows, impressed that she had achieved the fast promotion ahead of other senior, high ranking healers.

'That means,' Dalin went on. 'If we all live, Noal and Maeve can be a match. Uniting Jenra and Awyalkna by legitimate marital bond as well as by political allegiance.'

'Over there, please!' Maeve called to us as we searched for a space for our soldier.

We lowered him down where she had pointed, and her face cleared for a moment as she recognised me.

'One,' she called in warm greeting.

'Lady Maeve!' I answered, and she smiled in acknowledgement before turning back to the many men needing her attention. She did not hesitate to begin packing a nasty Griffin bite in one man's arm with wads of material covered in a poultice.

'Tane could not be saved?' I asked softly as Dalin and I stepped our way through numerous patients.

Dalin sighed and rubbed at his dirt smeared forehead. 'He saved us from an Evexus attack, and was too badly wounded in the process.'

I placed my hand in his.

'We lost Aiolos too,' he said tiredly, before he glanced down at my hand with a frown.

'Is that ...?' he gasped, staring at Aglaia's ring.

'Yes,' I told him. 'There will be much for us all to discuss. But, I did happen to meet your mother. And she gave me this token to bring to you.'

I moved to slip the delicate golden ring from around my finger, but Dalin stopped me from taking the intricate band off.

'Keep it,' he said, with warmth in his tone. 'She meant it for you.'

'Raiden!' a young messenger hailed Dalin then, catching up to us breathlessly. Then he paused. 'One ...' he addressed me with wide eyes.

'What is it, soldier?' Dalin asked in a friendly way.

'The King ...' the young boy petered off, overwhelmed. 'King Glaidin said that the leaders are gathering and you're needed.'

'Well one cannot keep a *Larnaeradee* to themselves for long I guess,' Dalin lamented, following the young messenger but keeping my hand in his.

'And one should always obey his father,' the boy agreed companionably, suddenly much more eager and at ease. 'Or his King,' he added.

'Smart lad,' Dalin answered. 'I'm guessing you have already been sent after Noal, seeing as he wasn't within vicinity of Lady Maeve?'

'I caught him on his way over, Raiden,' the boy answered proudly. 'Though he didn't like it. And I collected the Krall warriors too.'

'You have been busy,' Dalin commented.

'Not as busy as you,' the boy exclaimed with bursting admiration that made my heart grow warm. 'And not as busy as the One,' he added shyly, glancing at me again as we drew near a hastily pitched pavilion.

'Finally!' Thale's voice growled, and in a moment I was being yanked from Dalin and squeezed into a massive bear hug.

'Thale cried every night you were gone,' Thorin confided, though I could see his spirits were not as light as his comment was.

I reached out to squeeze his arm in greeting, thinking of how terribly Tane's loss would be hurting him. But I felt a different kind of hurt about him, and peered more closely at a blue tinged burn in his skin – full of ice and darkness.

'It's a wonder you're not in tears right now yourself,' I told him as I examined the wound. 'This must hurt. I wonder if ...' I thoughtfully pulled his sleeve up. 'Though I can't heal mortal wounds with my power – I might be able to help magical ones.'

I let my palm fill with light and pressed it to his skin. At once the small wound seemed to seal with a new silvery, skin-like covering that had an imperceptible shine to it.

'How we all missed you,' Thorin remarked with genuine relief.

Noal poked his head out from the pavilion. 'Please hurry up! The sooner everyone is impressed by Kiana, the sooner we can rest.'

'With Kiana here we won't need to translate anymore,' Thale commented, and the messenger boy gasped as he realised he'd been unconsciously speaking in *Aolen*.

'Thank you,' Dalin told him kindly. 'Your duty is done.'

The messenger bowed low to Dalin and I as we passed into the pavilion, where we found a large soldier beaming up at Vidar and Bard, pumping them on the arms in boisterous welcome.

'That's Warlord Conall,' Dalin told me with quiet mirth.

'I can see that you are warriors of great strength,' Conall was saying happily. 'Are the rest of your kind built so well?'

'Each Elf's existence revolves around keeping our bodies and minds fit, so that we may be attuned to nature,' Bard replied in his low voice.

'Oh,' Conall stated dreamily. 'How nice.'

There was a rustling at the door then, and the material was thrown to the side.

'Alright, I'm here. We can get started.'

I saw the confusion of the gathered leaders, and of the Krall soldiers on guard outside, as everyone's eyes moved downward and the owner of the voice sauntered into view.

Spud, only just higher than most people's ankles, strutted in as if he were the biggest presence in the room.

Still standing between Vidar and Bard, Conall's mouth moved without making any sound. He obviously wasn't sure how useful such a little Gnome could be.

'He's *gorgeous*,' Asha announced from where she was lovingly squeezing Vidar's left shin.

'Thanks sweetheart.' Spud sauntered over to an empty gap between Noal and Aeron's chairs.

He punched his little fist into the earth between their seats, easily breaking it. Then his strong hands quickly melded the crunching dirt and crackling rocks into a strong chair. It was as high as everyone else's and he effortlessly bounced up to get comfortable.

'Well met,' Noal said politely.

'Chyeah, you too buddy,' Spud lounged back.

'I think it could be fun to have you along if the Rucksha turn up again,' Conall breathed, practically alight with enthusiasm again.

Spud smirked. 'It would be crossing an item off my bucket list to get into a Rucksha head and scratch out a rock brain,' he shrugged and wiped at his bulbous nose with a stumpy finger. 'Did a Rucksha sit on your hand?' he questioned Noal then, and I grimaced as I noticed Noal's damaged fingers for the first time.

'Don't you worry,' Spud went on reassuringly. 'When Kiana goes back for the magical races, thousands upon thousands of others like me will be here to help.'

'Darziates will outmatch our numbers no longer,' Glaidin commented, taking his own seat now. 'It seems that nature and the Gods are on our side.'

Asha yawned and flew across to Spud. 'But for now I'm sure the Gods wouldn't mind if we just shared news and then had some sleep.'

Spud didn't argue as she picked him up. Instead he lifted his arms obediently and let her cradle him above his rock chair.

'I'll start,' I said, taking a chair beside Dalin.

And I began to recount my journey, and every step I had taken to get back to them.

75

Seventy Five

Kiana

'Come and tell us more about Aglaia,' Noal said as we at last broke from the meeting. 'And give us your whole attention. It's annoying having to share you with the absolute whole wide world now.'

'I should give you time to wash,' I responded, running a finger along the dust on Noal's cheek and showing him the grubbiness on my fingertip.

'Alright, but come straight to see us after you've cleaned up as well!' Noal acquiesced.

'Anything for the one who kept Agrona from coming for me,' I told him seriously. 'Your bravery allowed me to unite the magical races.'

'Kiana,' he answered just as emphatically. 'I could not have betrayed the quest. And, by the Gods, I would never have let that fiend come for you.'

He pulled the three of us together for a moment, before we exited the pavilion and I had to let them go again for at least a short while.

I was grateful to find that Wolf and Phobos were waiting to show me to a shelter they'd made to be my own. And I splashed myself clean in a washbasin of water that had kindly been brought in, slipped into fresh clothes, and pulled my hair free of its braid.

But then I hurried across to where Dalin and Noal's marquee was and slipped inside, wanting nothing more than to be reunited with my princes.

At once I felt my lips twitch in a small smile, finding that Noal – who had been so insistent, was flopped over on his cot asleep.

But further back in the long marquee Dalin was straightening from washing his face and neck. He wore clean trousers, but droplets of water still ran over his shirtless back.

With silent footsteps, I approached and caught a water drop in its track along his spine.

He became completely still with my touch, and I circled his body without removing my hand from his skin.

I smiled up at him, remembering the memory I'd shown Aglaia, of how he had been one of the first people to have made me really smile again at all.

He took my hand and moved it up to his heart, holding it there under his own.

'When your hand was here last,' he said quietly, his green eyes blazing. 'You were saying goodbye.'

I reached up to trace the scar along his jawline with my other hand.

He looked at the blue design around my forearm, and then the ring on my finger. He used his other hand to claim my free fingers now too.

'Explain the ring to me?' he asked, and I leant my head upon his chest, making him shiver a little as greater contact spread more of my magic into his own body.

'I had thought she meant me to bring it to you as a token,' I said.

I felt his chest rise as he spoke again. 'I know that ring. It definitely wasn't meant for mine or Noal's fingers.'

I smiled. 'I guess not.'

'Come,' he said quietly, and led me over to his cot without disturbing Noal. We laid facing each other, our noses close.

'What led my mother to give it to you?' he whispered then, his breath light on my cheeks.

I frowned. 'I suppose it was because I had just saved her city and her own life.'

'That *is* incredible, but I know that wouldn't have been it,' Dalin persisted.

'Then perhaps,' I speculated, 'it was because we came to really understand each other.'

'How do you mean?' he asked.

'Your mother wanted to know more of me, and to be shown her sons,' I explained quietly. 'You see, I have learnt to project thoughts, images or memories to other people, and I chose to be very open. I showed her how hard and cold I had been during my hunting days, until you and Noal came to change everything.'

Dalin brought my chin up with a touch.

'Kiana, my mother always said she would have passed that ring on if she had a daughter of her own. It was given to her by Glaidin's mother, who also only had a son.'

My breath caught.

'Aghhh,' he grimaced then. 'So my mother knows more of you than I do now?'

'Possibly,' I smiled. 'The way people have been looking at me does suggest I've changed again since I saw you last.'

'Otherworldly and intimidating. You're still my Kiana,' he reassured me with a small smile. Tracing my cheekbones, and then tracing the curve of my lips. 'Being around you is just the same as usual,' he added more seriously. 'It still makes me feel twenty times greater than I am.'

I sighed. 'How I missed you.'

'And I you,' he said in earnest.

76

Seventy Six

D*alin*

Kiana had been met with awe by the Awyalknians as she'd joined Noal and I on our campsite visits. But she had put them all at ease, even joining different groups in games of runes.

Now, though the sun was only freshly setting over the camp, she had already beaten three circles of delighted challengers.

'At least she isn't targeting *our* purses,' Thale burped into his beard before taking another gulp of the putrid, experimental ale that Ferron had concocted.

'She knows there's nothing left to take from mine and yours,' Wolf lazily blew a smoke ring; pleased to have won a pouch of pipe leaves himself.

'Well she knows the same about mine now too,' Noal groaned.

Vulcan rose from the game in defeat now and crossed to us, shaking his head. 'She takes no pity, even if you're her friend.'

'You know you're her friend when she stops being polite about your feelings,' Noal told him.

'She was never polite of my feelings,' I disagreed.

'Join us in loss then, comrade!' Ferron crowed from where he'd sprawled shamelessly on the dirt. The questionable brew was blurring his words.

Cadell tsked from where he was cooking a broth with bits of meat from a mean, almost child-sized desert lizard he'd caught. 'If you don't sit up Ferron, you'll go to sleep and we'll eat your share.'

'You sounded like Roth just then. He never talks except to give sage advice,' Ferron chuckled. 'Or perhaps it's Rendor, I'm not sure. They're both very similar aren't they?'

'Gideon can tell them apart,' Vulcan shrugged as he sat beside his intoxicated friend.

'But *he's* an awful lot like Lydon,' Ferron went on.

'Aren't they brothers?' Thale asked.

'Which of the four are brothers?' Ferron hiccupped.

'They don't look alike,' Cadell disagreed, tasting his broth. 'But we could ask them.'

'Who are you talking about?' Purdor asked as he left Kiana's game in defeat too.

'The brothers,' Ferron confided.

'Oh, Glyn and Dwyn? The archers?' Purdor questioned, wanting to be filled in.

'Are Rai and Ander brothers too, do you think?' Thale mused. 'I know Dren's not related to them.'

'Did you all lose your senses as well as your money?' Wolf groaned. 'You're giving me a headache.'

'Thorin looks set to beat Nikon, Phrixus and Phobos, so he hasn't lost his senses,' Purdor informed him. 'But Kiana looks set to beat Thorin and about five other soldiers, so they'll have definitely lost at least their coin purses, if not their wits.'

'I think,' Ferron hiccupped again. 'That we've been through enough together that we're *all* basically brothers now, ey? That's niiice.'

'Lovely sentiment,' Vulcan agreed, clapping Ferron on the shoulder so that the lolling warrior flopped over sideways.

'Gods,' Wolf rolled his eyes in supplication.

'Hello lads,' Dren approached.

'Brother!' Ferron giggled as Dren stepped carefully over him.

Dren took a seat beside me, but shook his head when I offered him a drink.

'I've actually come to fetch you,' he said regretfully.

I sat up and took more notice of his serious expression now. 'What is it?'

The archer frowned uncomfortably. 'The Krall inventor wants an audience.'

'WHAT?' Thale exploded.

'The double traitor still has a right to squeak! Speal ... speak!?' Ferron spluttered as he lifted his head.

Thorin and Kiana were watching us now.

I waved them over, and I heard moans of disappointment as Kiana and the remaining Krall warriors stood.

'What's going on?' Thorin asked as they approached.

'Oh, it's just that the man who nearly killed Noal twice, and who betrayed the quest, wants a word,' Vulcan rumbled.

'Agrudek?' Nikon growled in shock.

'Gods, in all honesty I'd clean forgotten him,' Phobos admitted.

'Kings Glaidin and Durna feel that if Agrudek has information, it may be of value,' Dren explained.

'I agree,' Noal grimaced. 'If he can achieve some good to redeem his miserable life before the eyes of the Gods, we should at least listen.'

There was silence as the men all scowled. Agrudek had been saved, just as they had been. And he had sullied the goodness of the act by turning back. On top of that, he had twice hurt Noal, who they had sworn to protect.

'Well, if Noal says it,' Thorin said grimly, 'then that's it.'

I stood and pulled Noal up beside me and Kiana took his other arm in hers.

'Who out of you lot is sober enough to join us then?' Thorin asked, kicking Ferron's boot. Ferron had begun to dribble.

'I'll mind the baby,' Cadell replied dryly as Ferron turned in his sleep and whispered something about brothers.

Thale nodded at Wolf, Phobos, Nikon and Vulcan, who rose to join Thorin and Dren – as if they expected the little inventor spy was going to bring Darziates himself upon us.

'You're a better man than I,' Thorin informed Noal. 'I would have killed him in the forest. And I would certainly not be listening to a dead man's words right now.'

'Perhaps you are the smarter man,' Noal sighed. 'I was happier having forgotten about him while he was locked away.'

When two soldiers brought the little, snivelling figure into Glaidin's pavilion, Agrudek found himself faced with a room full of hard stares. He cowered in the middle of the floor, encircled by the chairs of our leaders.

'Your ... Your Majesties ...' he stuttered.

Durna's expression was cold.

Agrudek closed his bloodshot eyes and swallowed. 'I ... I h—a-ave a m-m-message ...'

'How is this possible?' Aeron growled. 'You were stripped of your communication jewel.'

'Y-yes ...' Agrudek whispered in agony. 'But if the S-s-s-orcerer wants you, he will h-have you. If he wants you to listen ... you w-w-will hear. If he wants you to talk ...'

Sweat matted his orange hair, as he held up a new scryer globe. 'He sent this to me the night that th-the One arrived ...'

'He sent it to you?' Conall questioned.

'It appeared, b-b-b-burning in my hand,' Agrudek shivered. 'Fortunately, I did not know e-e-e-nough for him to wrack my mind ... But all he w-wanted to find out was ...'

'What?' Glaidin growled.

'All he wanted to find out was if ... the *Larnaeradee* was a-a-among us,' Agrudek glanced at Kiana, but her face was as impassive as ever. 'At once he saw the memories in my m-m-mind of her magic across the skies from that night ... I had seen it from the window in my c-c-cart.'

'Why do you choose to report this now?' Aeron glowered.

'Because ... I have l-l-learned ...' Agrudek let out a choking cry. His eyes were so red rimmed it was as if sand had been rubbed into them. 'I am n-n-ot needed now that he knows of the One's w-w-whereabouts.'

'So you are free?' Conall frowned at how distraught the inventor was.

'Oh y-yes ...' Agrudek shuddered. 'And when I asked i-i-if my family could be free now t-too ... He said they had died not l-long after I was c-c-c-cast out from Krall.'

'So you come to us now, as you have nothing to lose,' Conall sighed, obviously trying not to pity the wretch who had caused others such harm.

'I come n-now ... to warn the k-kind woman who first helped me in the f-forest ...' Agrudek's red rimmed eyes went to Kiana again. 'He wants you ... Gods h-how he wants you ...' he turned to the others, and then to us. 'He means to t-t-take her from you, and to k-keep her for his own. He has found his match ... he wishes to bend her m-m-magic and mind so that they can rule ... together.'

'Does he not know that his darkness would stifle and kill all of the goodness that is the life force of Kiana?' Asha demanded.

Agrudek sobbed. 'He believes he can f-fill her with a new k-kind of life ... It is as if, in his own w-way, he loves her. And if he s-s-succeeds ...'

'We will not let this happen,' Thorin snarled from behind my chair.

But everyone else appeared as sickened as I felt.

My heart was beating hard within my chest, and my stomach felt as if it was falling from a great height.

Only Kiana remained outwardly impassive.

'I do not know that he can be stopped,' she said. 'If Darziates wishes to take me, he might find a way. Just as he managed to snatch the Dragons.'

There were moans and promises of protection for the last *Larnaeradee*, but she waved it all aside.

'Yet I swear, I will die before I let him use me against you.' Her eyes were dark and narrow with the seriousness of her pledge.

And we all knew the truth of it – that either way, if Darziates got her, we seemed sure to lose her.

'I ... I wish to l-l-leave ...' Agrudek said then.

Nobody answered. Hardly anyone acknowledged that he still existed.

'I wish to g-g-go into the desert alone ...' he tried again. 'You will never be b-b-bothered by me again.'

In his physical condition, it was suicide.

But none of us stopped him. Our eyes were empty as they followed him to the door, and at a glance from Glaidin, the soldiers barring the way let him pass.

He disappeared from our minds and vision very quickly, as Kiana stood.

'I am tired,' she announced steadily.

'It has been a long day,' Vidar cleared his throat and tried to appear unworried, but the midnight colour of his skin seemed a couple of shades lighter than usual as he regarded her.

Beside him Bard was staring down at his bunched fists and Asha was hugging Spud to herself tightly.

Noal stood beside Kiana, and I tried to get feeling back into my legs, managing to stand resolutely as well.

She didn't wait for anyone else to rise, but gave us her small half smile, and swept out the door.

And out of all of us she was the only one who was able to really conceal a feeling of awful tension from then on, as our Krall warriors and archers kept close each day and night that followed.

By day she rode Amala, sang songs to us and laughed. She spoke to the soldiers, who loved to find ways to strike up conversations with her at every turn. But as we were now just two weeks' march from the walls of Krall's Kingdom, and as we all knew Kiana would have to leave us to summon the magical races soon, we only grew more nervous.

'One?' Yet another soldier found an excuse to approach her as she sat amongst Noal, Thorin, Phrixus, Thale and I one evening. 'Do you think you could soothe Morris' burns again, like last time?'

She smiled at him. 'Of course,' she said. 'Just lead the way.' She rose and dusted her pants and each of us made to get up.

'Don't even think about it,' Kiana's tone stopped us in our tracks. 'I will not be tailed by an entire squad.'

But as she turned her back on us, I waved madly at Dren, who had been walking the other way.

He nodded and inconspicuously changed direction to walk at a safe distance after Kiana and the soldier.

'You'll pay for that later,' Thorin grimaced on my behalf.

But all the same, we stayed up long after we usually would, until she came back with Dren now in tow like a thief who had been caught and scolded.

'You took an age!' Noal exclaimed.

Kiana raised an eyebrow at him. 'I realised I could use magic to soothe, if not cure, a lot of hurts. So I cast a magical blanket over the healers' section.'

She pointed over her shoulder, and in the distance we could see a faint shimmering light, as if a bubble had formed around the healer area.

'It will fade, because I don't want the healers themselves to become too soothed to work. But their patients will feel no pain tonight.'

Noal's eyes were wide. 'Very good,' he managed.

Dren nodded vigorously. It had obviously been quite the sight.

'And unlike the rest of you, Maeve was very happy to let me be of use,' Kiana reproached.

She placed her fingers together then, and as she drew them apart, a nexus of magic spread outwardly between them. Like a piece of cloth, she leant over and draped it over Thale's head, and at once his frown cleared.

'There, that's better for that headache, isn't it?' she asked.

He sighed, and patted her hand. 'You are always useful, and always go beyond what everyone expects. We just care for you.'

Kiana softened. 'I know. Just as I care for all of you.'

But I could not put my fears aside and could not relax despite her beseeching. And when she later came to find me on my cot, I opened the light blanket and was not even relieved when she slipped in to curl up against me.

I squeezed my eyes shut as I stroked her hair, trying to force down the feeling of growing dread and panic inside of me.

Because even with her held so close, I felt as though I had already lost something that I desperately needed.

77

Seventy Seven

Kiana

'Even the extensive piping matrix beneath Krall appears impenetrable.' Durna was examining another map. 'We definitely need our magical friends to help us breach this fortress.'

'Kiana will have to leave in the next day,' Aeron commented with a touch of despondency.

I stared past them toward the door. There were overcast clouds scudding across the sky outside, and I felt strange and restless.

Asha had visited earlier, complaining of the same feeling. And the Elves and Spud hadn't been themselves either.

I rose, and Noal made to follow while Dalin just watched me. His eyes had been on me all morning.

'Stay,' I said. 'I need to move. Put my mind at ease.' I belted my sword around my hips and put a hand on Noal's shoulder as I passed, pushing him into his chair. 'I'll return,' I promised, feeling them all staring after me.

Dren was directly outside the door, and I saw him motion to the Krall men coincidentally moping about while everyone else purposefully broke camp.

I tried not to feel smothered as Thorin and the others caught up, casually trailing me while I searched out the forlorn forest dwellers.

They were sitting in a tense circle and Spud glanced up, but the Nymphs all looked like wild creatures with pained scowls on their faces.

'Are you all well?' I asked, though I had a sense of sick foreboding in my own chest. As if I were on borrowed time.

'There is evil in the air,' Bard answered. His spine perfectly straight and stiff, identical to Vidar's.

'Darziates bends his energy toward us,' Asha agreed, and my skin prickled. 'Or toward *you*.'

'I know,' I admitted. 'And I feel like nowhere in the world can hide me.'

The clouds above were darkening though the morning had begun, and ripples of power were rolling around us. An awful kind of power.

Thorin grimaced. 'Let's return to the Raiden.'

I shook my head. 'The princes are safer where they are and you would be safer with them.'

Dren held his bow ready and it was clear that they all unconsciously sensed the building menace too.

'Please go ba –' I began. But then suddenly felt something pull at me from within, making me gasp.

Like an anchor, it nearly dragged me down.

Come to me ... a dreadful voice whispered, and Asha cried out, putting her hands over her ears.

Larnaeradee.

I whirled, scanning the skyline while my head pounded with the pressure of the presence that had just crossed it. I put a hand to my forehead as if I had been dealt a blow.

'Did you hear that?' Spud shuddered.

'He calls for her,' Asha whispered.

The Elves stood tensely, their midnight faces grim. The ends of their weapons ignited.

'Ready,' Thale ordered, his sabre in hand.

K i a n a...

It was as though a breath was being drawn beside my ear. But the whole army seemed to have paused. The word had scorched everyone's mind, it had been so strong. So close.

The Nymphs rose like angry wasps.

I drew my sword, becoming numb and focused.

The Nymphs released their fierce call to arms and the army burst into action, soldiers diving for weapons.

And then he appeared.

The Sorcerer was just ten steps away – as perfect and cold as he had been in the Jenran Cave painting.

He stood perfectly still as the Nymphs surged toward him, only to ricochet as if they'd hit some kind of force-field. The Elves were also sent arcing backward.

He took a step forward, sending a ripple of power outward that made me stagger back with nausea.

The Krall warriors lunged toward their past oppressor. But they were instantly frozen – lifted to hang as though trussed up with nooses. Their eyes boggled, and they could not speak or move.

Darziates stepped toward Thorin, the nearest warrior – releasing me from his focus for a moment, and I found myself only then able to draw breath.

'I can tell what you are thinking,' the Sorcerer told Thorin in a hypnotic, layered voice. He raised his hand to Thorin's temple, sparks at his fingertips.

Shaking, and rocked to my soul by his gutting wrongness, I managed to draw my sword and pull my senses together enough to launch at the Sorcerer.

He was distracted from Thorin, blocking me with a blade that had materialised in his grip and appearing to relish the gap closing between us.

I felt as if I were fading in and out of reality while he drove forward, pressing so close that we almost touched.

My pulse pounded and I felt burnt, but he grew more enlivened, sweeping in again.

There was nothing for me to do but match each blow and try to pull my mind back from getting lost.

I could hear the beat of our footfalls. Could feel the breaths we each gasped in as we wrangled blades.

We are evenly matched. Fighting is useless. His words were cut into my brain. *Come with me.*

With a surge of fear, as if tearing myself from a dream, my wings appeared and carried me to a safe distance.

I hovered above my friends while Darziates allowed himself to be drawn away, his awful magic lifting his body into flight so that he faced me again.

Below I noticed vaguely that all of the hundreds of soldiers who had been near to the Krall warriors were also frozen and hanging like suspended puppets. The rest were dashing about in chaotic panic.

Darziates halted, his eyes on mine as he very obviously raised his hand, palm upward, and the clouds surrounding him grew darker. The air sizzled, and with a roar the sky gave up a dazzling bolt of lightning to him, which he caught with ease.

You cannot protect them all.

He let the burning, twisting bolt drop down into the army.

Time is precious. They are not. Come with me.

Tents, dirt, cots, armour, people all exploded where the strike landed while he calmly swooped to touch down amidst the devastation.

I saw him call more electrical strikes into his raised hands, the bolts blazing down from the sky – and he used them to lash at the men while the earth cracked and flew about in chunks.

Either way they will be mine, or they will die. But you can work with me. You can be with me.

I focused on the lightning blazing in his grip – counting on the fact that lightning was of nature, and should match my magic better than his. I held my free hand out and beckoned to the bolts.

At once they leapt out of his control, the free ends shooting up to where I still hovered, landing on my own palm, and wrapping around my hand.

I yanked on the bolt ends and forced the Sorcerer forward on his feet, but then he yanked back and I was twirled in the air – dragged downward while he compelled the bolts to wrap around me like belts. I spun all the way down to his arms, and he caught me as if in an embrace.

Every drop of blood in my body seemed to ice over as I recoiled, yanking myself free and staggering away in a fog of disgust.

I heard the approach of a charge of soldiers as I let the lightning dissolve and somehow kept my footing. But my heart sank as I caught sight of Dalin and Noal at the forefront of the charge.

The Sorcerer set his cold gaze on them, and suddenly the hundreds of soldiers in that area too – along with my two princes – were stopped in their tracks.

Stopped in nearly every way. Barely even breathing. Not even blinking.

But before the Sorcerer had returned his focus to me, there was the sound of a scraping boot. Somehow one foot was being dragged forward from amongst the suspended, paralysed masses.

My heart sank as Darziates cocked his head with a faint show of surprise and as we both saw Dalin – his teeth gritted and his face savage as he dragged another step toward us.

Dalin continued fighting his epic battle against the Sorcerer's invisible bonds, until Darziates crossed to my prince and put a hand to Dalin's chest to physically stop him.

Blood pooled around Darziates' fingers as they sank into Dalin's chest – burning a hand shaped hole into Dalin's skin through his shirt.

I forced my limbs and mind to reanimate and I lunged across the distance toward the Sorcerer's back.

Darziates turned, but I raked him away from Dalin and threw myself into my attacks so that I would not be overcome by the fog of his power.

Sparks flew from our blades, silver flickering around my sword, and the light poured from me as the effort of the battle consumed the last of my control.

Darziates was forced to let darkness cover his own blade, and it dripped like ash with each strike.

The atmosphere was vibrating, adding to the heat that already addled my brain, but the mark of Toru around my wrist had become nearly blinding and I was sure that I also felt the strength of the Giant behind each of my blows. The strength of the Lady. Perhaps even the strength of my lost kin, stirring within me.

As we fought on – a blur of frenzied action rising into the sky, Darziates' face showed the effort that he was drawing on to match me.

Choking grey smoke writhed and curled along his arms and I threw myself into every motion, lashing out until at last my sword tip drove toward his stomach and his sword tip drove toward my chest.

I snarled, ready to fill him with my blade, and ready to join everyone who had gone before me into golden peace. Ready to end the threat.

But suddenly Darziates' mind bled into mine again.

S t o p.

As the thought seared into me and echoed all around us, thousands of soldiers groaned and found themselves being lifted upward.

And with that thought it was infinitely clear to myself and to all of his captives that he could corrupt every single one of them just as he had consumed all of Krall. Or kill all of them with a thought, and conquer the world with a gesture.

The soldiers below meant nothing to him. For in the face of his power and at the mercy of his whims, they *were* nothing. Just pawns of his game and just heartbeats away from being forgotten.

'I am not here for their eradication. In fact I am not here to deal with your mortals yet at all,' he said then. 'I came for you. Just for you. And we can both see that I cannot defeat you without losing you,' he uttered. 'However I can easily hurt all of them to convince you to come with me.'

Dalin was brought careening up toward us then, to jerk to a painful stop just a yard away.

Blood was saturating the front of his shirt.

So much blood.

It is your choice if they survive this day.

Out of the corner of my eye I saw Dalin's feet begin to twitch before rasping, bubbling noises began to come from thousands of throats.

They were truly suffocating. The last mortal armies for the world were choking to death.

Feeling a knife of ice in my chest, I blinked at Dalin. His nose was bleeding and his green eyes were bloodshot.

'I will let them live if you come with me.' Darziates held a strong hand out. 'I just want you.'

I let myself sink downward, and Darziates sank with me – Dalin dropping with us. I saw Noal's face turning purple as my boots touched the ground. Both of my princes' eyes were bulging.

And I dropped my sword.

My sword had never known what it was to be discarded in surrender until then, but I moved to catch Dalin as he and thousands of others slumped down; released as had been Darziates' word.

I lowered Dalin gently to join the countless others who were heaving for breath. But Dalin had fared worst. He had been the focus.

Men stared up at me and clawed at the air as I straightened grimly, lifting my face to the sky.

I let a nexus of protective, shimmering magic spread above them all. Sparkling and sending down a cool mist of comfort as I forced it to flourish.

Then I lowered my arms and looked at the Sorcerer.

He had allowed me the dignity of one last free act, and now Darziates stepped over the gasping men, placing his hands on my shoulders.

I cried out despite myself, for the pain of his light touch was intolerable. But beyond his own power this time I also caught sight of something appalling pressing in along with him.

Red ghouls and terrors from another realm began materialising around us, swooping in, and as I sank with the pressure of it all he stooped to lift me.

Carrying me into oblivion.

78

Seventy Eight

N^{oal}

Maeve had told me that the wound in Dalin's chest had not melted deeply enough to kill him. She would be able to keep it from infection if the unnatural, hand shaped crater healed naturally and gradually refilled with new layers of skin.

I found him bandaged, staring at the tent roof from his cot.

'She's gone?'

Dalin's voice was rough and he did not look at me.

'She is gone.' I felt as though my jaw would set with the heavy, grim mask that would not lift from my face.

'She felt him coming for her,' he said.

'And she put distance between herself and us,' I agreed.

'She would have hated you and I for coming in the end anyway,' he said.

'She would have hated that we loved her so much to come into harm,' I corrected him.

'The Kings?' he asked mechanically.

'Safe.'

'Aeron and Conall?'

'Waiting for your recovery.'

'The warriors?' his eyes came to me at last.

The Krall soldiers had suffered greatly in the few moments that Darziates' notice had come to them.

'They have revived,' I answered. 'Waking to the same nightmare as you.' They had not been able to help Kiana, and she had been stolen.

'We must send the Elves to tell the magical races that they need to set out to join us,' Dalin stated.

I glanced away myself then.

'The magical beings were found with eyes open and hearts beating, but no other signs of life. They have been starved in a way, of what it is that allows them to survive. Maeve thinks that, because they are fuelled by nature, and were attacked by the Sorcerer's unnatural magic, they have been crippled.'

'Then ...' Dalin's voice had become a whisper.

I swallowed. The rest of the army were already coming to terms with this realisation. We had lost Kiana, and we had lost our link to our magical allies.

'The magical races cannot be reached in time,' I told him. 'We will face the darkness without them.'

Dalin's face contorted, as he pulled himself to sit up.

I could see blood beginning to seep through his bandages. Slowly filling in the shape of a crimson hand.

'So we have no aid. And he has taken her from us.'

'The army was secondary. We were all meaningless,' I confirmed.

'There's nothing I can do to get her back, is there?' he asked in an empty voice.

'Nothing.'

His head fell into his hands.

I felt sick.

We both knew, everyone who had felt that power now knew, that though we would march on and try to our last – there was probably nothing that we could do or could have ever done to help the quest or the world against the threat of the Sorcerer.

'We know he doesn't want to simply kill all beings, though he will do a lot of that anyway,' Dalin rasped flatly through his hands. 'He wants to conquer us. To subdue all peoples into unifying under him. But now there is also no denying that he wants to do it with Kiana as his Queen.'

I knew I could say empty things. I could say that if we won, we could breach the walls and get her back. But she probably didn't have that long, and it was foolish to hope.

'Yes,' I said instead.

His expression was hard, but his shoulders straightened with resolution instead of despair.

'Yet we cannot be weak. I must play the part of the Raiden. I must bring some form of purpose to the last days of freedom for our mortal armies.'

He lifted his head and then, with an effort, he stood.

The bleeding hand was like an emblazoned badge of courage burning across his chest as he walked toward the door, eyes locked straight ahead.

I hurried to keep up, and Maeve and the other healers did not argue as the Raiden passed them, upright and unbroken, leaving the healers' section.

'Where are you going?' I asked, watching crowds of care-worn soldiers straightening and respectfully making way for him.

'I go to pay my respects to the fallen Nymphs and Elves,' he said. 'I go to soothe my men, as they suffer for joining my cause.' His stride was as strong as ever, and he carried himself proudly. 'And I go to war.'

79

Seventy Nine

K*iana*

I became aware of satin draped beneath me, cool and silky at my fingertips.

I felt the chill of a fine glass being pressed to my lips before the gentle flow of water revived me a little.

And I noticed how terribly I ached. As if I was being pressed by a great weight.

I registered that a magnetic voice of rolling velvet had been speaking to me soothingly, hypnotically, and that it had been drawing me out from where I had been lost. And when my eyes opened I found a beautiful face watching mine.

The man's face was calm, and his arms were the support beneath my body, holding me as we rested on a lounge of gold and black satin.

I tilted my head, captivated by how his eyes were like ice under a grey sky. Why had I expected green eyes?

The sun was streaming down through the towering doors of a grand, open balcony. It was casting light into the vast stone bedroom, lighting all the way up to the impossibly lofty roof. Yet I realised that I could feel no warmth.

I frowned as I registered the cold, and the fact that my chest was tight with the effort to breathe.

Gods I was hurting. And my mind was so very fogged.

'Has the world slipped from its axis, to be dragged the other way?' I whispered. 'Because every single thing feels wrong. Yet I cannot decipher why.'

Now the beautiful man stroked his free hand along my cheek and his touch was soft. However the line he had traced across my skin was searing.

It was a sensation that gradually went further, throbbing within my bones. And a seed of fear started to grow within me as it began to feel as though my lungs had been stitched closed.

Desperately I struggled to even blink, and for a moment my eyes flickered back to the open balcony. But there was no comfort there, as I caught a brief glimpse of swirling, red figures hovering outside. They seemed to dance and tease at the edges of my sight. Red like wavering flames. Red like ...

And then for an instant I thought I remembered a bleeding red handprint that had been burnt into a chest.

Green, pained eyes ...

Gasping, I shot away from him to land in a crouch across the expansive chamber.

The glass that had earlier been pressed so tenderly to my lips tinkled like music as it was knocked, shattering into a thousand crystal sparkles across the stone floor.

I stared at my soothing healer, the cause of my pain, as Darziates stood now himself.

With a burst of warmth from my earthstone my wings appeared and I threw myself forward to collide with him savagely, driving him all the way back to the wall. Then I smashed my fist into his face so that his head cracked and bounced against the rocks.

Spring-boarding myself away, I hurtled to where the veil of his magic stretched across the great balcony.

I careened into the forcefield, and I felt a surge of hope as I sensed the invisible barrier tearing a little.

But then the awful magic pressed in more intensely, as if I were being sucked into thick fluid instead of breaking my way through it.

I struggled against the dense power, sickly willing the pure magic of my earthstone to form a shield around me. When I had enough of my own magic gathered I started to melt the darkness and to pull my way forward, though I had not got far enough when I heard a soft chime of laughter from nearby.

I cried out when his arms circled my waist, moving through my shield just as slowly as I was pushing my way through his own enchantment.

He gradually pressed in enough to take a firm hold on me and to pull me back against himself, like a comforting part-ner hugging his muddled beloved.

'You are so much stronger than the others were. Even while so young.' He spoke against my ear softly, fondly, and I couldn't move.

I felt him drift us down toward the expansive balcony, and I was beginning to feel numb and heavy and hardly like myself.

Our feet touched the stone together, and he turned me gently to face him.

In some small place I heard Kiana's voice yelling at me to push away, but Darziates' voice seemed so much more important.

He reached for my throat with one hand, keeping me pressed to him with the other as he lifted my earthstone away from my skin and pulled it free, making another piece of me fade away.

'I will mind this until you can be trusted with your wings,' he said, and though I felt faint – as if a key part of my spirit was sputtering out, it sounded reasonable.

'How good does it feel when there is no longer that controlling conductor keeping your magic chained within you?' he asked reverently, his eyes flickering about us while our conflicting energies whirled and surged so crazily against each other that I was at risk of drowning in it.

Such energy swirled through and about me that I noticed my forearm had lit up with a beautiful blue pattern. But I could not remember where I'd got that marking from.

'Perhaps it will help if I show you why you should accept the life I have brought you to. It is hard for one such as you to see the benefits of my ways.'

He let his magic barrier fall from the balcony like a dropping curtain and kept his hand pressed into the small of my back as he led me to its edge. Together we stepped up onto the ledge and then stepped over it, drifting down to the barren farmlands where peasants laboured, stooping and coughing while they raked at the baked dirt.

We landed in the middle of one of the bare fields and I blinked at the foulness of the noxious vapours seeping out of the overwhelmed soil. The pasture had been pumped so full of magic that it now overflowed, spewing back out in fumes.

'In my world there will be no starvation,' Darziates told me as he took my hand in his easy, strong grip.

I felt the press of a ring on my finger, but I was sure he had not been the one to give it to me.

'I can produce crops to sustain my people, and they will in turn have purposeful work.'

I felt the overwhelming waves of dead magic building inside of him before, as he simply gazed out at the open plains, his will was done.

The earth shuddered and groaned. There were screams and the peasants scattered to get out of the way even as fluffy heads of wheat, bigger than my two hands put together, forced their way up through the cracking dirt.

Long stems as wide as sapling trees began to follow, tearing their way skyward.

'Wheat,' Darziates announced magnanimously. 'Or sugarcane.'

His eyes flickered toward more land beyond.

Instantly swollen shoots of sugarcane broke from the earth and began bulging in size until all of the empty plains had been filled with a sea of thick crops.

The darkness curled around me but I felt the throbbing in the grey tinged earth as it was engorged and poisoned, and like a slash across my awareness it brought me back to myself again.

I gasped as a sleeper does when startling forth from frightful dreams, and suddenly I felt as though it were really me standing there in my boots and not some dazed imposter. I could not fly free, but with a burst of fury I whirled to face Darziates, ripped my hand from his grasp and hurled an unharnessed and uncontrolled bolt of pure magic into his chest.

The surge was so formidable that I worried I might be swallowed up in it and disappear myself, but he was sent flying backward through the wheat stalks and I did not pause, sprinting into the cover of the wheat.

I plunged through endless walls of reed-like leaves that pressed in, and the shoots were too thick to see through or over. But I let my feet do the flying for me now as I fought to put distance between myself and the numbness he was drowning me in.

I nearly ran into a wild eyed peasant as he wandered lost in the forest of wheat too, and he cried out in fear, dropped his scythe, and vanished into the stalks.

I scooped up the scythe and ran on, trying to hack a clear path through the rustling, swaying green walls.

Kiana, I heard a whisper as if from beside me then, and my heart shuddered and raced.

I am going to find you. And I am going to keep you.

His presence raked like heavy fingers over my brain, dazing me as I leapt on through the never ending field.

Until there he was – materialising out of what looked to be nothingness, but what I felt to be a rip between the Other Realm and our own world.

My throat burned with sickness as the waves of corruption washed over me from that icy place, and I wildly swung the scythe and carved the air where he had been standing. But he vanished and then his strong hand somehow came from behind me and caught the farmer's tool to stop me from whirling to wield it again.

He held the scythe close at both ends so that it trapped me against him while the stalks of wheat that had faced my scythe in his place toppled in halves and dropped to the ground.

Then the scythe was loosed from my fingers and was discarded, and I was already feeling my mind fading again as I slumped back against his chest and he held me tenderly.

'So clever and strong,' Darziates whispered. 'You will eventually see the rationality in my way of life.'

He pressed down and kissed my neck while my eyes stared vacantly and my internal screams faded.

'I can show you that there is also finery and beauty in my ways. Not just fields of wheat. I have an eye for creation too.'

I had the odd sensation that all of the seams holding me together were being frayed away. The person I had been before was a disintegrating memory.

He lifted us out of the seas of rustling wheat and we soared toward his own royal courtyards around the castle. He effortlessly set us down in a large, walled in garden of rock, where a grand fountain was featured in the middle of the stone pavement. The quiet song of the falling water drops filled the otherwise empty, hard area and, in a cold way, just like its master, the place was striking.

'Let me show you how growth and life can begin anew when we seize this world and start it all again.'

He guided me to a clear spot beside the fountain.

'Watch,' he said. 'From nothing but stone I can make something grow.'

My eyes widened as red condensation began to soak its way upward, rising out of the cracks between the cobbles. It became a trickle of thick red liquid that ran all in one central direction, pooling and rising quickly. And I wondered if this was nature's life blood, being eked out from the earth and forced to surface.

The liquid was rushing now, like little rivers springing up between the cracks and trickling quickly to puddle in front of us, getting deeper but growing upward rather than seeping outward.

It became a whirlpool of spinning fluid, as though an invisible sculptor was moulding liquid instead of clay on a turning pedestal. But the shape that was forming was that of a thick, growing tree trunk, steadily solidifying before my eyes.

Behind us, where snaking trickles of liquid still ran, the shapes of tree roots formed as if they were digging down into the stone. The quickly thickening tree trunk itself grew taller than the stone walls of the courtyard and its boughs began to stretch out and form leafy fingers with tips of blossoming flowers.

Finally the rushing fluid slowed, thickening and setting, and I found myself staring up at a magnificent tree.

But my breath was taken away by its filth rather than by its magnificence. For it was only the mockery of something natural, and not the true thing.

Its crimson leaves rustled in the wind, and a few loosened and began to fall like rose petals, or blood drops. They floated through the air, scattered on the ground and landed on the fountain's rippling surface.

Darziates must have seen the frown forming on my brow, for he softly placed his hand upon my cheek and angled my face towards his while I groaned at the touch.

The agony he gave me was the kind of agony that one gets when they are fevered and hot, and feel the scorching touch of a cold compress as it both stings and cools their flesh.

His face appeared youthful and strong. Almost like a mask. And yet when I looked so closely, there were lines there that suggested the mask hid great cares and deep thought.

Those lines showed the sacrifice of grim action, not the lines of laughter and compassion that should also be worn by those who truly know life.

My heart softened toward this strange, hard being.

Had he not known happiness? Comfort? Warmth?

Then my own hand began to lift, to reach for his smooth cheek in return.

80

Eighty

A *hanu*

Ahanu and the wise ones were all gathered around a fire that Scandra had created.

He could see Toru watching them forlornly from beyond the trees, holding the designs on his forearm as though the magic there pained him.

The One had still not returned, though they had expected her summons and now there was instead only concern in her place.

'She isn't one to be late, especially when the meeting of the mortal and immortal kinds is depending on her timing,' Scandra was saying.

'Perhaps she has been delayed,' Ace rumbled.

'We must give her more time,' Frey stated. 'If the magical armies are revealed at an inopportune moment, and we do not trust in Kiana's promise to return when it is most suitable, all could be lost.'

'Yet if she has been kept from returning to us, and we are needed,' Scandra countered, 'we will have the world collapse in around us while we hide beneath these trees.'

'We could give her two more days before we set out then,' Ace suggested. 'And we'll just have to hope that we are not too early or too late.'

Ahanu felt so disquieted by the situation that he decided to find peaceful sleep in the stream beside the camp that night.

He clapped Einion on the shoulder, and clasped Toru's forearm before he made his way into the water. And while the patterns on Toru's wrist gave Ahanu the most disconcerting feeling, Ahanu shook his hand and shrugged the sensation away; too preoccupied by the day's disappointments.

As he laid down to let the sweet water rush over his body, lulling him to sleep, Ahanu saw Toru sitting tensely by the bank, as if waiting for a sign from Kiana. But when Ahanu woke to the refracted rays of sun glimmering over the water's surface, and sat up to breathe the air above, he found that Toru was no longer there.

With water cascading from his clothes and hair, Ahanu stepped out of the stream to find Einion. Leaning over his son – his water droplets falling and making the patterns on Einion's skin glow, Ahanu asked if he had seen where Toru had gone.

They searched, but when some of the Dwarves pointed out that the three silver ore armour sets were missing Ahanu went to the Dargon Empress.

'He would not have gone without the clear idea that Kiana needed help,' Ahanu explained.

'Then, Gods, let him be able to help,' Scandra replied, standing slowly to stretch out her golden limbs and claws. 'And while he goes to his Fairy, we will go to the aid of the mortals.'

Eighty One

K*iana*

As my hand lifted toward his cheek I saw a dim light begin to grow there in his hard eyes.

Yet at the edges of my awareness I felt there was something else that I longed for. More than the hollow, aching wonder and sadness that I felt for this man.

A brief flash of memory dazzled me suddenly, of standing in a similar way with another.

I remembered green eyes again, gazing down upon me, from another young, strong face.

This face had known pain and seriousness. But it had also been quick to show mirth, and passion and care.

My own eyes widened and my fingers stopped to hover inches from Darziates' skin.

Instead of a gentle touch, I slashed my hand down and broke out of the Sorcerer's hold. He shuddered as I turned to flee and I saw the faintest trace of hurt in that normally un-touchable face. But he did not pursue me and I fled through a stone archway that led back into the castle and along cold pillared halls.

My breath was coming fast, as though I were a swimmer resurfacing from a near fatal tidal wave.

Panting, I passed a couple of arches that opened up into long walkways, each leading in different directions. I skid-ded into one and found myself right in the middle of two guards.

They stared at me as I gasped, a cornered escapee.

My arms had immediately risen and my feet had auto-matically placed themselves in a defensive stance, and yet those two big soldiers did not move.

Their eyes were wide, as if they'd seen an apparition – and I remembered how my Krall warriors had reacted when first exposed to pure magic.

Now I had accepted my magic, and without my earth-stone's guidance, it whipped about me chaotically, cutting brutally through all they'd ever known.

Why don't you seize her? She belongs to your King.

The stabbing voice almost drove me to my knees, and yet it sounded merely contemplative. The Sorcerer was in-trigued by the conflict of his soldiers.

One of the soldiers took a small, uncertain step forward and then stopped to clutch his head, stooping over. The other did not move.

Stopping me seemed the last thing that they wanted to do, and after a lifetime of mindless following, this was an agony of disorientation.

I turned from those wretched men, and ran to the next hallway without being accosted.

You are fast, my chosen one. But you are not free of me. You belong with me.

I covered my ears, careening down the stone hall while his footsteps echoed in my mind.

Do not fear.

I am here.

I plunged desperately on, my heart in my throat.

Don't fear. I'm here.

For the world.

For you.

I could hardly breathe through the awful panic.

I heaved against the first sign of a wooden break in the hall, and slammed the thick door closed with a resounding echo.

But my anxiety only grew as I stared at where my hand rested on the door, and saw that the wood was covered in a layer of ice. Though the heat of my skin on the wood had left a spreading imprint of melting frost, dread bunched in my stomach as my breaths billowed from my lips in clouds.

'The quest you believed in is no longer the course to follow,' his audible voice whispered so softly, so tenderly beside my ear. I could feel his lips brushing against my hair, his warm breath against my neck.

'Turn, and see that your original path is hopeless.'

In this room, leeched of all warmth and humanity, I felt that I should weep with hopelessness. Instead, I obediently turned.

And I found that I was in a chamber full of line after line of hulking, fully formed Evexus.

Countless beasts, illuminated here and there by the light filtering in from boarded, high up windows.

The slight rising and falling of slouched, spiked shoulders showed they were breathing, if not aware.

'When I awaken them properly they will become the guardians of the races I will control,' Darziates spoke at my side. 'They will keep order and inspire obedience and assimilation so that our reign will be a true one over a united world.'

My eyes moved from the endless lines of Evexus to his composed form.

'We will be strong in the face of any threat, and as you and I share the gift of eternal life we could devote ourselves to this cause, and to each other, forever.'

I had forgotten the crippling cold. He consumed my whole attention.

'We could move through life together in our work, sharing each stretching, immortal moment.'

His hand sought mine, and I was hardly aware of the sting of his touch or how smothered I felt.

'We would never waste a moment. Never allow harm to come to the world at any age in time.'

His hand was cool as he drew me closer and the room around us began to fade. Crimson clouds of smoke started to close in on us, spreading and curling around us like a closing flower that seared my skin.

Nightmarish voices in fleeting shadows came from the smoke and rushed past my ears, uttering incomprehensible, ancient, hateful words.

'Your presence hurts them just as much as theirs hurts you,' Darziates explained, and I knew vaguely that the atmosphere of the realm he was bringing me into would be poison without him shielding me.

'But together we can lead them so that the Other Realm can be united under our rule too. We can prevent even other-worldly threats.'

I felt as if my soul was twisting while Darziates stepped us out of our world, and completely into the chaotic realm of demons.

My legs buckled, as though the tendons had been sliced from the backs of my knees, but I felt Darziates pulling me closer by the waist and I pressed my face into his chest.

The demons whispered and cursed in their strange words, the voices increasing ten-fold until they vibrated within my skull. But while I was under his protection they dared not touch me.

'Look, my Fairy,' he instructed, lifting my chin with one of his cool fingers.

I let my eyes climb up along his pale collarbone, over the curve of his throat and strong jaw to his angled face. They lingered there for a moment, and then moved beyond him finally, to the Other Realm.

It seemed to be made of shifting, vaporous mists where half visible things cast spiked shadows and threw enlarged and misshapen shapes against smoky pillars. They watched us from the edges, glowering with malice while crimson dust particles floated upward in protest at our disturbance.

'We can rule here, and everywhere,' he said. 'If you will be my Queen.'

My head was spinning and I sickly blinked downward to escape the terrible visions. Then I saw that I was somehow now clad in a magnificent gown of black and gold, fit for a Queen.

'You are the only one, in all my time, that I've really wanted. Really felt anything for.'

I stroked at the glorious folds of material in fascination, only pausing when I noticed something glittering upon my finger.

The golden band again triggered a dim memory – of another Queen, who'd had the same green eyes as ...

I heard myself suddenly cry out, stricken. Realising once again that I was losing myself.

I felt crushed by the weight of his presence, the stupid dress, and my own fear while the red smoke pressed in again, covering everything as I swooned sickly and the Sorcerer King lifted me.

He held me in a strong grip and his lips found my shoulder, my throat, and then my own mouth while my body shut down.

And when he began to carry me easily in his arms, like a possession to be kept close, it was ghastly torment and seductive pleasure all at once.

82

Eighty Two

*D*alin

Apart from our other terrible losses, we had woken in the night to the shock of rain.

Now we slouched forward under clouds that were heavy and dark. The temperature had plummeted, and the skies sporadically opened to cry their tears over the wastelands that were Krall.

Every step became a momentous effort. The dirt quickly turned to thick mud that clung to flesh and tore at clothes. It dragged at our calves so that our soggy boots sank down and our swollen, cracked feet became too wet and heavy to use with any grace.

By the darkening expressions of the Krall warriors, back constantly at my side in a show of strength, it was clear that this was how the unnatural season change began. So the cold cycle had descended in time for our arrival on Darziates' doorstep, and we all marched on in the face of this new challenge, feeling, if possible, even heavier than before.

Amidst it all the armies were watching anxiously to see that Darziates' mark was not going to kill me. But as lightning forked across the sky to the drum beat of the resounding thunder, I forced myself to appear as the unshakeable Raiden and strove for the armies to see only strength in me.

When passing men sought to clasp my hand with grim, respectful acknowledgment, I always made sure to hold their arm with enough power to be reassuring in return.

I could not let them see that, instead of healing, my wound was slowly spreading as Darziates' magic continued to burn into my flesh, blooming outward and eating down into layer after layer of skin.

The handprint had now swollen to cover much of my upper chest – the finger marks had become long as they reached for my collar bone, and the palm print stretched below my sternum.

The wound wept and bled sluggishly, scorching and hurting further with every sloppy, wet, muddy movement. And Maeve had warned that infection was beginning to set in.

Thinking on it now, I pulled at my dripping clothes, making sure my bloodied bandages were not visible under my sagging shirt as I trudged onward. Because, while fever might kill me, or the slowly deepening wound might bear down into my lungs and my shattered heart – it was more likely that we would all die in battle first. And the prophecies had made it clear that I would be leading the armies to

their doom or victory, trying to inspire them rather than ailing among them in the face of this threat.

With this purpose driving me onward I continued to grip
my life with both hands, gritting my teeth and hauling my
stuck legs forward as I tried to guide Amala safely through
the swamp-like muck.

In turn, Amala pressed her warm, velvety shoulder
against me, a comforting support.

'Good girl,' I muttered as she steered us around a boulder
that protruded from the mud. But then I miss-stepped myself, sliding a little instead of sinking.

The unexpected movement made me suck my breath in
while I lost my hold on reality for a moment – everything
before my eyes seeming to flicker and tilt, and Amala whin-
nied worriedly.

'Frarshk, Dalin!' I heard Thale hiss while I blinked until
my eyes managed to fix on him.

He had somehow manifested to be holding me up against
Amala.

'Raiden?' Dren fought his way through the mud to slide
my arm over his shoulders.

'Look at his shirt,' Nikon rumbled.

I ran a shaking hand over my eyes, letting Thale and Dren
keep me up while it felt like pinpricks were covering my
whole shivering body.

'Get him to Maeve,' Noal grimaced, pushing his way towards me. 'The dressings need to be changed. He's bled
through and the wet is getting into the wound.'

'His skin is on fire,' I heard Dren say, and though my men had dutifully positioned themselves so that I was cut off from everyone's view, I was overly aware of the passing footsteps and voices of soldiers around us.

'Don't make a fuss,' I said. 'I am recovered.'

I was met with the hollow eyed, down cast expressions of the archers and warriors in return as they gazed at me like they were losing me now too. And then Glaidin and Conall struggled their way through the mud and the barrier of my men.

The last thing Glaidin needed was to see his son being eaten alive by dark magic. The last thing any of my men needed to see was their supposed prophesied leader weakening before their eyes.

'I'm alert again,' I told them gruffly, forcing my legs to support themselves, and consciously not wincing as I withdrew my arm from Dren's shoulders. I forced a smile that felt more like a contortion.

'You need to be seen to,' Thorin told me, looking ghastly himself with the pressure of mourning three of his closest friends already. Tane; buried before his time, Kiana; taken, and me; death walking before his eyes.

'I will. But I will walk myself and cause no outward sign of alarm. All will be fine.'

'Thale, Nikon,' Thorin grunted. 'Go with the Raiden so that it looks like you are in counsel together. We will stay close.'

Cadell moved sluggishly forward to take Amala's reins and I nodded my gratitude, straightened, and scrunched my shirt so that the blood would not show.

But just as lightning continuously split the sky, I felt that I too was being torn open in a way that would never be healed.

83

Eighty Three

K*iana*

He carried me through a blend of dreams and night-mares.

I could hear my silken gown rustling as he stepped easily, as if I were no more than a paper cut-out that might float away in the wind.

The high ceilings, stone hallways and arches passed dimly by as my eyes opened and closed, but I could see that we were often half in the demon realm.

The red whirling mists curled stealthily around the edges of the blurred walls and paved floors, and they made the ta-pestries and sculptures seem as if they were alive. Moving and leering.

Hurting deep inside, I often turned to press my face into the now familiar sting of contact with Darziates' shoulder. And I listened to the cadences of his voice, his words washing over me until at last I felt cool, untainted air touching my skin.

It brought comfort to my lungs – which were tight, as if I had been breathing in ash and embers, and I roused a little to find that he was looking out from his balcony again.

But, where fields of wheat and sugar cane had towered before, there were now cleared paddocks as the farmers removed the last wagons of the harvest.

The scorching sun had also hidden away behind clouds that had spread to choke the whole sky in a dense, grey and purple blanket.

'We are a pair, you and I,' he was saying softly. 'We will outlast them all. We will be joined by a common, crucial cause. To save all life.'

'We each have a cause ... But we are each too different,' I managed the words through a fog.

'In some ways different. In some ways similar,' he answered gently. 'Deimos cut away his humanity, and I inherited the inhuman ability to draw my life force from the impenetrable strength that is left when all of the other things are taken from a man.'

I shuddered.

'And it is similar for you,' he went on. 'But to an opposite extreme, my *Larnaeradee*. For you draw from nature's vitality and life. You draw from all who came before so that your ancestors are practically reborn in you.'

'I am life. You are ... death?'

'I use death,' he clarified. 'To secure life. I will kill as many as I need to so that we can start again efficiently.'

I was beginning to awaken slightly, and I could feel that time had limped on without us. But instead of fear, I felt both revulsion and a strange pang of sympathy for the Sorcerer.

'How easily you turn to destruction,' I said as my voice became a little stronger.

'How easily the races turn from each other. It is why there is a threat at all,' Darziates uttered. 'Even now your mortal armies march here alone and unsupported. And such divisions have been the reason that I have been required to rise, to devote my life to a cause, and to be rid of any who would aim to stop me.'

I felt him hold me a little closer, giving me a fond hug while he referred to his genocide of my ancestors, and the movement made the horrible wrenching inside me amplify.

I had never felt so attuned to another, and so estranged. As if we two were filled with magnetic repulsion.

I wanted to be close to him, to his addictive power. I wanted to escape him, to think and feel clearly once more.

Though I was beginning to surface now, and could feel how unalike we were – the wrongness of him – it was still hard to remember much beyond the fact that I was a *Larnaeradee* and he was a Sorcerer.

'Yet I am not brutal in my use of death. I do not often prolong the suffering of those I must be rid of,' he continued. 'For instance, it will be a simple matter to quickly end the unaltered, non-conforming Dragons when I turn my energies to across the seas. Just stealing the oxygen and fire that they need to survive would do it.'

I had a flash of memory as he spoke. An image of a powerful, golden body, and eyes that burned with wisdom, love and ferocity. But somehow, in the back of my mind, I knew I had to be careful with my thoughts. He could not be allowed to see the shadows of crowds that I dimly remembered.

'On the other hand, I could dry the water out of the Giants to make them into dust spirits like the Rucksha.'

His voice was calm and practical, but I tried very hard not to dwell on the vague memories of those friendly, towering creatures, swimming within my addled mind.

'I could starve the Nymphs and Elves of nature.'

More memories of forgotten friends tried to surface before my eyes, which began to feel like two hot coals. My throat was tightening.

'The Dwarves and Gnomes could be stripped of their mineral life source,' he mused, his voice as hypnotic as before. 'Though they could be useful in helping us to reshape landscapes as we like.'

He paused. 'And the mortals ...'

My stomach lurched as I helplessly envisioned the green eyed prince. The image blazed across my mind too starkly to suppress, and at once Darziates' breath drew in as if he had been winded.

'Your heart has been given to one who would die and leave you?' he asked slowly.

Dalin, his name was whispered through my thoughts. And as Darziates stiffened I knew that he had heard. I felt for a moment, strangely, a hollow sense of pain from the Sorcerer.

'Watch how easy it is to lose a mortal,' he said quietly, before his magic crept into my mind.

He was gentle but the pain was horrible as my head filled with red and grey, and I screamed as he took control of my vision.

Then it seemed that we were swooping over drenched, yet barren lands, plunging through the darkening clouds, until I saw and remembered at last – the Army for the World. The quest that I had been a part of. I was Kiana.

The moment of complete awareness felt like being jolted through shattering glass, though I still could not step out from behind the frame that had held me trapped.

'It takes no trouble to triumph over mortals,' I heard Darziates say from where he still held me out on the balcony I could no longer see. 'I could choose any method at all and it would work. Quick, slow, big, small – anything could end such fragile beings.'

I watched as the mud beneath the army began to buckle and tilt while people were thrown forward.

It shifted and sloped on an angle as if it were the rolling sea and I heard thousands of cries as the world seemed to drop away from under the soldiers.

I heard horses scream, wagons splinter and bones break. But then, when everyone had lost their footing, the sludge began to change.

Red moisture started to seep upward to colour the already saturated dirt, the same that had risen from the cracks in the courtyard to create the tree.

The mud became like thick, bloody liquid, with men sinking and struggling, trying to haul friends free while their own limbs sank. The muck had taken on a life of its own, bobbing sluggishly in waves and dragging everyone down into its thickness.

I felt tears on my cheeks, but then, cutting across the desperate cries of the armies – there was the sudden roar of a familiar warrior's voice.

Immediately my enhanced, controlled sight searched for the source of the cry, and like the crowds of struggling soldiers, I found myself looking to Dalin.

The Raiden, my green eyed prince, had pulled himself up to stand high upon a jutting rock; fury like a storm across his brow and blood spattering through his clinging shirt.

'Be STILL!' he roared in command, his voice carrying over their fear.

The men cried and reached out to him – hundreds of red, mud coated hands clawing desperately while they sank further in their violent thrashing.

'BE STILL!' the ferocity of Dalin's voice tore across the mud filled desert again.

A crash of thunder rumbled in a growl beneath his words, and, like startled sheep, it stilled the sinking men.

The Raiden glared upward then and the power of his glare seemed to focus itself on me – on where Darziates' presence held us.

'Sorcerer!' he roared in challenge. 'You use trickery and cowardice to meet our defiance? You do not understand what you face. You are not made of the stuff of Kings!'

I felt a flicker of contempt from Darziates while Dalin spread his arms out, his palms facing the sky.

'Come! Face me as leaders in a war should! Kill me with your own two hands!'

I felt nervous hope from the mortals watching the Raiden.

But I myself felt a terrible wave of dread. Because I could sense the sinister intent that emanated from the Sorcerer who held me.

He was building a shocking surge of malicious energy. Ready to be unleashed on Dalin alone.

84

Eighty Four

D^{alin}

I had paused to rest gratefully against a rock that jutted up from the mire. Maeve had spotted us and was saving me the steps, coming to meet us.

But before she had closed the distance between us, the whole world was suddenly turned to chaos.

I heard her scream, I heard my men cry out, and I heard the whole army's terror as the ground surged abruptly ... and appeared to turn to blood.

The roiling ceiling of clouds seemed full of malice and I felt that Darziates was somehow there.

I gasped as my feet slipped from underneath me, but I quickly pulled myself up onto the high rock at my back, teetering with the burning pain that lanced across my chest.

Yet I found my voice when I saw that the flailing army was sinking faster with each frenzied movement. My call of warning echoed across the churning ocean of red mud, so that I felt as if my chest might burst as I forced the words out. And when I turned my challenge skyward, I was grimly satisfied to have the crushing sensation of the terrible malevolence above our heads honing in on me alone.

The challenge, a mere distraction to gain my forces a moment of reprieve, had scarcely left my lips to ring across the plains – before suddenly the large rock beneath my feet shuddered, and then shot violently upward.

A sharp shard of stone that surged skyward like a knife of earth – it would have impaled me if I had not side stepped and caught myself, holding onto the rising peak.

When the tearing, towering growth of rock jolted to a stop I drove my fist into the crumbling peak and broke it off. Then I hauled myself back up onto the top and, looking at my precarious position, laughed.

Darziates had given me a platform and all of my men could see me, mostly unscathed.

'Raiden!'

'Raiden!' their voices rose.

'Do not panic!' I bellowed. 'Do not move rashly. Free yourselves carefully. Help each other and use the survival instincts that only mortals can feel! He does not understand the perseverance or comradery that we have been born with!'

They were stuck fast, swallowed deeply by the red pit. But one by one they took each other's hands.

I saw one soldier selflessly thrust a young healer toward a half sunken wagon. His own body slipped further down with the effort, but she pulled herself free and turned to help him manoeuvre himself.

I saw Thale drag Nikon closer to the base of my soaring, jutting rock. They scrabbled to find a grip so that the other men could use them to climb over and find purchase on my platform too.

Ander pulled Rai so that the young, mud covered archer was holding onto his shoulders like a child. Chains of men were hauling each other toward any safe kind of purchase or anchor that could be found, and a faint smile flitted across my face.

But then I felt the invisible being above pool his magic again. Before my eyes the sloppy red mud dried almost instantly, as if I were watching ice spreading across a lake in fastened motion. And at once anyone still half submerged began to cry out in pain as their limbs were encased in crushing rock.

Then, worse still, my eyes widened as a wall of impenetrable earth began to rise up in the distance.

The ground rumbled and wailed and the men trapped below gaped in horror as the wall began to roll towards us in a landslide wave that would obliterate the entire army.

But I could call out no comfort, as my chest suddenly felt exactly as if Darziates' physical hand was burning into it again.

85

Eighty Five

K*iana*

I gaped at Darziates' catastrophic tidal wave of earth.

This hadn't been the Sorcerer's plan, or he would have wiped the mortals out with disasters long ago. But something about Dalin, and the thoughts my captor had felt from me, had driven Darziates over the edge.

And even now I felt the Sorcerer's magic pressing down on my Raiden in particular.

Dalin was fighting to keep his balance, his face agonised while the shirt across his chest smoked and smouldered – the material falling away as the swelling burn mark of Darziates' hand glowed red.

At last I truly, fully shook myself awake, my own unbridled magic ripping through the bonds of confusion that Darziates' power had laced around my soul. And, far from

442

the scene playing out before my eyes, I felt my physical body break free from his iron grip.

I felt my feet touch the ground and carry me away from him. And while I felt the starkness of being separate from him – the isolation and sadness that my liberation cost me, his focus slipped for just a moment too.

With my eyes still trained on the vision of the faraway wasteland, I drew my wild magic about myself, letting it build into a swirling tornado.

And when I flung it outward, the uncontrollable force hit him where he stood on the grand balcony, and also shook his presence over the armies.

The sky over the trapped armies was rent with storming clashes of light and colour as the force of my energy collided with his, and with an ear splitting boom my magic drove onward to cut through his landslide – turning the surging wall of bleeding earth and rock into a disintegrating cascade of silver dust that fell gently over those trapped below.

Then, like a cooling balm, I spread my mist-like power over the earth so that it softened and freed those who were caught.

From where we stood on the balcony I felt Darziates take a faltering step backward. We both saw soldiers laughing in relief, re-surfacing from sparkling cascades of silvery dust.

And then there was only one battle, one person who Darziates had not forfeit – as Dalin's body was now held up mainly by the electrifying currents of dark magic flaming from his chest.

The Krall soldiers were struggling to pull themselves up to Dalin on the strange wedge of rock. But they could not help.

I blocked out everything other than the sheer will to heal Dalin – intent on driving out the magical horrors being forced into his body.

This time I felt Darziates physically stumble as his will met mine, and my healing energy washed his best efforts to damage away.

For every particle of anger and heat being driven into Dalin, I created a soothing salve of nature, of growth, and health.

And I was successful because Dalin had been right. Darziates could not understand or counter the kind of mortal persistence, selflessness and care that dwelt within me, and within Dalin.

The admirable traits that Darziates saw as weaknesses to be driven out of the soul, were my greatest power. And I could feel it all in Dalin, and use it. Spreading the goodness through him and casting out all else.

I could almost see the silver light growing in my prince, created by the purity within him and everything I was giving him of my own. Until at last I saw Dalin shudder, and lift his chin.

A hush descended as the army gazed up to the Raiden, staring at a glowing silver hand print that now lit up his chest. My magic had bound itself to him, sealing his unnatural wounds with a sheen of new, luminescent skin. It was if the God of Beauty had dipped into a fountain of starlight, and placed her painted hand upon the Raiden in blessing.

'The One is still fighting for us!' a soldier rejoiced. 'She lives!'

And then the scene dissolved and I was standing opposite Darziates.

He stood still.

'Only the ones you love can truly have the power to hurt you,' he stated at last, slowly and with surprise. As if this was the first, and most damaging, unexpected blow that had ever been dealt to him.

'You are not really hurt,' I answered through the haze of our magic, which hung between us like an electrified wall. 'Because of Deimos you were not born with the ability to love.'

It sounded as if my voice was tinkling with the music of the magic. It resounded with each word, and I felt as though I might cause the whole balcony to shatter if I were to take a single step.

In turn, I could feel the desolation pouring from him.

Lightning forked behind his tall frame, and the cold hardness of him was illuminated against the purpling horizon.

'I know all there is to know of you,' he said. 'I have never been so fully aware of, or caring of another being. Who else in the world could understand you as well as I? We breathe magic like no others can.'

Again, I did not let myself think of the others who had truly understood and cared for me.

Carefully I stepped back from him and the air rippled around my ridiculous sweeping skirts, as if the atmosphere was uncertain of how to react to my movements.

I was acutely aware of his own power, his body and will, and the intensifying energy around us.

'You are not what I need,' I told him. 'You have meant only pain to me and to those that I have loved. It hurts me to be in your presence and you know nothing of me or the flow of nature that fuels me.'

His posture did not alter. He appeared as unmoved as ever. Yet it was as if I were raining blow after blow over him, and I could feel the damage causing ripples inside this being – who had never had reason to question himself before.

The impact was reverberating around us, as if each word was slicing away parts of his essence to fill the space between us with magic.

'We are opposites,' I went on. 'You suffocate me. And if I were to become what you want, I would die.'

The Sorcerer's gaze was penetrating. 'Our souls are made of different shades of the same powers and yearnings. I would never let you die.'

I stepped further away, and my own uncontrolled magic shuddered through the stone balcony as the thunder rumbled around us.

'You might be able to keep my body alive, but the dark shadows of your soul cripple the colours of mine. There is no love or harmony that can exist between us.'

Then I threw out a blast of silver fire, catching him in the stomach and sending him reeling. And when the next flash of lightning scarred the sky I held my hand out to call the bolt to me, catching the writhing, crackling flash and working it so that it widened and spread into a growing circle.

I filled it with my power, and before he had recovered his footing I sent the circle of hissing sparks and light hurtling toward him – a round blanket of lightning that swallowed him like a net. And I both felt his radiating pain and heard him roar as the prison of pure magic trapped him within.

I forced the sheet of natural magic to harden and expand into a dome so that he could not throw it off, and the air howled and swirled around the electrified prison, creating a vortex of wind across the balcony.

I sensed groups of the Sorcerer's soldiers running towards his chamber. But I was calm as I held my palm out towards the sparking dome, mentally calling for what I knew he kept hidden from me.

My mind found what I sought, buried within his secret realms, and while his magic was briefly stifled, I pulled my earthstone free from him with a tug.

Immediately, a sense of completion swept over me as the cool tourmaline stone touched my fingers and I secured its chain about my neck. And as I called my wings I felt them find me again.

A muted explosion sounded as the dome was shaken from the inside, and blasts of devastated fury shuddered outward from the sizzling prison.

There were slight fractures forming in the electrified dome walls, and I turned as a troop crashed out from the Sorcerer's quarters and onto the balcony.

They made it in time to see me step to the ledge and dive off with my wings outspread.

86

Eighty Six

N*oal*

My friends were emerging from cascades of silver and I caught Maeve as she sprinted toward me like an angel surrounded in shimmering star dust.

I heard Dalin laugh then, and squinted back up as he opened his arms in delight, revealing the radiantly glowing handprint before he caught a red haired Nymph against his chest.

'We're awake, we're awake, we're awake!' Spud yelled, bursting out of a muddy healer wagon and sending clouds of silver into the air as the other Nymphs careened out of the wagon behind him, hooting with energy and laughter. They threw light about themselves in colourful explosions of celebration while Bard and Vidar pulled themselves lithely out of their toppled wagon – both of them appearing thoroughly rejuvenated as they effortlessly bent to turn the wagon the right way up.

Despite many bruises, everyone was jubilant as they set about righting wagons and dusting off friends.

'Your chest bares evidence of the purity and strength within you, great Raiden,' Thale called up as Dalin released Asha to dash about with her comrades. 'But how do you intend to get down?'

'No fear,' Dalin called back from his great height. 'I suddenly feel up for any challenge.'

With that, unfazed by the drop, Dalin stepped confidently from the soaring plateau to land with inhuman balance amongst us – alighting in a burst of silver, and smiling at us broadly.

'You won't be needing my aid now,' Maeve cried in awe while I spluttered.

'Your eyes are different,' Conall leaned in to inspect Dalin. 'Sharper.'

'Like Kiana's,' agreed Thorin.

'Anybody notice the chest?' Wolf interjected, holding an egg sized lump on his forehead.

'Now, now,' Dalin grinned, almost illuminated with energy. 'Compliments can come later. We need to set this army to rights.'

'Oh aye, you just glow prettily and we'll do some dirty work,' Nikon grumbled, cracking his knuckles.

But our warriors were happy as they followed Dalin, and I laughed as I saw him effortlessly help Vidar and Bard lift a wagon to refasten its wheel.

'This life never ceases to amaze me,' Maeve declared, raising her eyebrows while Dalin moved on to begin almost singlehandedly breathing vigour back into our campaign. 'And although I'm not ready to lift any wagons, I feel quite able to patch a number of wounds before the sun goes down.'

I smiled, but as she turned to leave me, I found myself unable to release her hand.

She turned back with a quizzical expression, and I pulled her across to stand against a righted wagon.

'What is it Noal?' she asked.

I winced at the sudden niggling feeling that had clouded the relief of this moment.

For though Kiana had given us a sign of hope, though Dalin was saved, and though a crisis had been averted – it was with regret that I realised this scene was not actually yet perfect.

Something seemed to be pulling at my mind, as if a part to the slowly finishing puzzle still remained beyond our reach and there was something that I was personally meant to be doing about it.

'Maeve,' I replied at last, drawing the word out with feeling. 'I think I need to leave you for a little while.'

My tongue felt as if it were not my own, and perhaps it was not. Perhaps it was being guided by the prophecy, just as it had been when I had told Dalin that we should bring Kiana on our quest.

Perhaps my role had not ended then, by forcing the Three to come together. Perhaps I had been being unintentionally used as a tool to create links between the nations through-out the whole quest.

My poisoning had forced Dalin to come to an under-standing with the men of Krall. I had forged a new, unbreak-able connection between Jenra and Awyalkna – my heart belonged to Maeve and together we would be ambassadors of each country. But still, one link had been left without completion.

I saw Maeve's shoulders dip. '... Lixrax.'

I nodded, taking both of her hands in mine.

She managed to maintain a hushed tone. 'I will go with you. Or at least the others will go.'

I gazed down at her hands in mine, an unbreakable knot. 'Just me. You're needed, and this is my role to play. If I fail, one person missing will be easily covered. It must be secret.'

Glancing up I saw misery etched into her face, and I leaned down to press my forehead against hers, willing her to understand. For now I felt strangely resolved, as though my path had already been set, whether things would be well for me or not.

'You and Ila will be easily spotted though, and even if you manage to reach the Lixrax troops, you will never make it back to us in time,' she whispered after a moment in a thick voice.

'We'll do our best,' I told her gently.

But before she could reply, a light scuff of a boot made us both glance up.

Towering above us a little sheepishly, was Vidar.

'Forgive me for overhearing. But I came in search of you, and perhaps the Gods made it so. Placing me in just the right spot.'

Vidar regarded us both earnestly as we stood, suspended in surprise. 'I pledged my strength to the Three, and to the quest. It seems now that one of the Three is in need and could use my help to complete their task in the prophecy.'

'Vidar,' I said. 'It would put you at extreme risk. I at least can blend in amongst millions of mortals around Krall, but Darziates might sense you.'

Vidar nodded, acknowledging the danger, but seeing hope beyond it. 'I believe Darziates is busy at the moment, battling with Kiana's will. He thinks he has incapacitated Bard, the Nymphs and I. This may be the one clear chance to speed around his kingdom, to the wastelands and hopefully back again without being noticed by one who is normally all knowing of the magic within his lands.'

He shrugged his shoulders then. 'And you know, I really am very fast. The army will hardly notice a missing prince and Elf for just a day.'

'You are a Gods-send.' Maeve laughed, tears dropping onto her cheeks. 'Yet,' she said thoughtfully, letting me wipe them away. 'While I know you must complete your task, and go in secrecy – for the army would fear losing another member of the Three ... perhaps you could seek the support of just one other person.'

I frowned.

'You will need more than just two beings and good faith to convince an Emperor to put his people at risk,' Maeve went on. 'And I think Warlord Aeron might be able to keep your secret and give you a token that can show what kind of power exists in our unity. The kind of power that could be a match for the darkness of the Sorcerer.'

I let out a pent up breath. 'The Unicorn horn?'

She nodded.

'Would that not put us at greater risk of being sensed and exposed?' Vidar asked curiously.

'I think that horn can look after itself, and may even serve as a shield to the both of you,' Maeve replied, her voice strengthening.

'Just like Kiana's magic kept the Three shielded when she entered Sylthanryn ...' Vidar reasoned. 'This is a good idea! I will seek him out, and give you time for your farewells.' Vidar withdrew with a smile, purposefully speeding away almost instantly.

'Yes. Our farewells,' Maeve said less brightly. 'The Gods are guiding your footsteps away from mine.'

I drew her close. 'And I will do everything within my power to secure the quest, and to return to you.'

She reached up to kiss me slowly, and when she drew back sadly, I kept her close and whispered in her ear.

'This is not forever. Just for now.'

'Of course,' she whispered back. 'Just for now. But,' she drew a breath. '... Be safe.'

'And we shall meet again,' I completed the formality with warmth in my heart.

When Vidar returned in a rush of air, holding the cloth wrapped Unicorn horn and a bag already stocked with supplies, she let her arms fall to her sides, and I let our cheeks lose touch, stepping back to take Vidar's outreached hand.

Immediately I felt the magic taking me over, and knew how Dalin must feel with the strange new energy Kiana had infused him with.

But my enhanced focus was stolen by Maeve, and I could see every tear's track on her face.

Then she nodded her head, golden wisps of her hair seeming to shine, and Vidar and I swept out across the empty wastelands, gone in moments.

87

Eighty Seven

Kiana

I was buffeted by gales of wind, holding my arms up as a shield against the building storm while I hurtled towards Darziates' net of magic around the castle.

Not pausing, I flung myself at the barely visible barrier and was at once winded by the impact. As if I had been thrown into a wall of ice, my vision was overwhelmed with red-grey mist and my skin burned with the extreme cold.

But worse still, I was dragged short ... and I could hear them. Things from the Other Realm, jeering. And though they weren't truly manifested in my realm I could feel the invisible owners of those voices jostling in close.

I pushed with all my might to fly forward but only found myself becoming so embedded in the malicious web of freezing magic that I was at last stuck fast.

I felt one of the wraiths pull itself closer. And then I felt it touch me.

Invisible claws dug into my forearms, wrapping themselves around in a tight grip, and I saw the frostbitten indents of pressure on my skin as those unseen fingers pressed harder.

Slashes of evil coloured my mind, but with a cry of pain and anger I gathered my strength and managed to throw my magic outward, gasping as the wraith's grip loosened enough for me to claw my way back out to the balcony, close to the shuddering dome once more.

'Frarshk,' I gasped raggedly, accepting at last that the Sorcerer's trap was literally alive, and that I could not break through it to the open skies.

I winced at the lines of blue welts blistering across my forearms, but shook myself and desperately moved on to fly closer to the castle and its surrounds, rushing over courtyards and walkways – afraid that at any moment I would feel the Sorcerer breaking free of his prison.

My heart raced as I saw only further walls of magic or carpets of stone and no weaknesses, cracks or hope for escape. But if I lost this opportunity it was certain that he would never allow me to think or breathe freely again. I would spend eternity in a cloud, miserable and addicted to it with no idea as to why.

My eyes darted backward and forward as I sped one way and then the other, indecisive and helpless while I could see ordinary people rushing about, fleeing the storm.

Soldiers were beginning to run through the streets as well, taking notice of me – unlike the terrified townspeople. However they appeared unable or perhaps unwilling to shoot their Sorcerer's prize down, and they simply chased uselessly backward and forward as I flitted about. All they could do was wait for my choice of landing spot so that there they could converge.

And, just as my panic was convincing me that there would never be a spot, I saw the fountain in the courtyard with the terrible crimson blossom tree. Despite the wrongness of the tree, the sight of the silver water dancing in the middle of that courtyard gave me a pang of hope. For if I could not escape by land or air, thanks to Toru's water gift, perhaps I could go beneath.

I remembered Durna once commenting on how hard it would be to break through the fortress that this castle was, as even Krall's extensive underground piping system seemed too perfect. It stretched beneath the entire city, and beyond that, it connected to stores of groundwater outside the walls …

Immediately I angled my body to shoot like an arrow for the lonely courtyard, and before my feet had even touched the cobble-stoned ground I had thrown up magical barricades to block the arched entryways; cordoning off the space.

The soldiers who had sprinted to catch me at my landing ran at full pelt into the glimmering barriers and were thrown backward into their comrades. I heard their swords clanging uselessly against my magic, but I turned away and focused on the courtyard.

The blood red blossoms were rustling, and there was the tinkling music of the water.

My hands were shaking as I took hold of my regal gown, ripping the skirts so that the material fell away and left my legs free.

I crossed the cobbles to the circular fountain and leaned to look over the paved ledge and into the pool. The fountain itself was quite old, but was still a large and lavish feature of cold, striking beauty.

I could just make out the giant pipe that had been fashioned to force out the water, and I prayed that pipe was big enough to carry me out to the canal waterways before I drowned or Darziates' magic could stop me.

Then suddenly I cringed as if I'd been hit, an abrupt shattering sensation telling me that the Sorcerer was at last smashing his way free of my magical trap.

I hurriedly sprang up to land in the fountain's cold water, which splashed around my waist, and I waded across to the shooting jets spouting out at the centre.

I held my hands out and visualised each particle of my power spreading across the fountain surface, and then beneath. I pictured my magic taking hold of every drop and sinking to mingle with the water flowing under the city through the canal system.

Forcing my mind to go further, I found that in my mind's eye I could truly see the actual journey of the water, along with sparks of my power spreading through the ducts beneath Krall. I also saw that the source of this fountain, and of many wells from this area of the city, was one ultimate lake outside of the kingdom's walls.

There were not many sources of water in such a wasteland, but Darziates had strengthened ones such as this to nourish his people.

Taking a deep breath and keeping my eyes closed, I sought to change the direction of just this one inconsequential duct. Frowning with the sheer internal effort, I willed the bonded magic particles and every drop of fountain related water to begin to turn from their normal path.

Soon I felt the rush of the fountain starting to slow from where it had been arcing above me and I opened my eyes to find that my magic had brought the water to life, illuminating it with bright blue lights that were sparking beneath the surface.

The sparks were following the changed direction of the water, sucking downward as the force of the fountain ebbed away – going back into the pipe that had before been shooting it out and upward.

The water began to gurgle, spinning within the pool as it drained.

'Hurry,' I begged the water, feeling a sense of growing dread that told me he was coming.

I pushed to make the magic stronger. I aimed to widen the pipe. And I heard the fountain crack.

The water began to surge downward in a rush, the concrete shuddered, buckling beneath me with the force of the downward pulling, and all the while I could feel Darziates, hurtling toward me.

Praying for success, I knelt and circled my hands around my feet and all the way up to above my crown, creating a miniature bubble of air around my body, much like the bubbles I had learned to create in the city of the Giants.

Terror struck me as I saw him almost crash land beside the blood tree, touching down with such force that the stones split beneath him.

His eyes stormed just like the skies did while the rubble and dust settled around him. But then the surging of the swirling water pulled the fountain completely in on itself and, imploding, the pool's floor gave way.

I was dragged down into tunnels of darkness, leaving the Sorcerer's surprise and grief behind on the surface.

The tight water tunnels grazed me even through my film of protective magic, which eventually began to flicker and wear away. The water rushed in to press against my face. It blocked my nostrils and filled my ears.

Despite Toru's gift, the darkness and lack of air were never ending.

The roar of water was my world.

88

Eighty Eight

R^{ai}

'Frarshk.'

The Raiden's sharpened eyes flashed with emerald fury as Warlord Aeron calmly informed the council of Prince Noal's departure with Vidar.

Rai looked to Dren for his reaction and saw that the lead archer had closed his eyes to compose himself.

The Raiden paced agitatedly while King Glaidin simply became increasingly pale.

The colour had withdrawn from the Awyalknian King's face first, and then from his neck, all the way to his hands.

Thorin, meanwhile, was driving his fists into his eye sockets, and the other warrior present, Thale, was pulling at his beard in distress.

Only Bard and the Nymphs remained contained, if pensive. They each would have done the same thing if a quester had needed help to perform their role.

'He was right to do it,' King Durna stated. 'The prophecy is clear. And so is his role within it.'

'Nobody is denying the bravery and the need for it,' the Raiden sighed finally. Though, just as it had around Kiana, the air seemed to shift about him as if a subtle torrent of his mood was manifesting.

'I do not like being parted from him in this,' the Raiden went on. 'But whether or not his efforts are successful, by the end of this day we will see Krall's walls and the army must not hear even a whisper of Noal's absence. No seed of doubt can spread.'

'Gods, if word did get out, that we've lost another one of the Three, *and* the horn to defend against the Evexus ...' Warlord Conall grimaced.

'The worry over Noal will be ours alone. But we are not defenceless,' the Raiden answered. The luminescent fingertips of the silvery brand showed above the laces of his shirt. 'We will find a way.'

Rai felt the stress of the leaders as they parted, ready to step out into the dark morning to begin their final march for the Sorcerer's gates.

'What's going on?' Ander asked Rai as the young archer followed Dren and the Raiden from the tent.

Glyn and Dwyn fell into step with them too.

'A war,' Rai raised his eyebrows.

Ander groaned, and Dren glanced back over his shoulder.

'One on each side,' he instructed quietly, and the archers broke away from each other to surround the warriors and the Raiden.

As the march began again Rai kept his eyes on the heavy skies, where the surly clouds hung low enough to touch. He swallowed the lump of apprehension growing in his throat, and only the smoothed wood of his bow was reassuring in his palm as they toiled on through infinite mud.

Despite the struggle, every now and then someone would hail the Raiden as he passed by, elevated in the saddle.

'Looking well, Raiden!'

'Strength to you, Raiden!'

And he would reply with encouragement as if nothing were amiss.

Sometimes they would ask where Noal had got to, but the Raiden would just point out that Lady Maeve was not on duty at that moment, and there would be nods of understanding in response.

Rai envied those easily convinced soldiers as they smiled and moved off. Instead his own nerves only increased when dusk set in and Dren gave a whistle to his archers for eyes skyward.

Rai could just make out some tiny, dark flecks circling, dipping and diving amongst the clouds.

'Guardians of Krall's gates,' Ander grunted.

'Griffins,' Glyn spread the word to the Krall soldiers, and Purdor left to give word to the leaders.

'Griffins only appear when a meal seems to be on offer,' Vulcan glowered darkly upward.

Rai's stomach tightened.

'Something exciting is obviously waiting at those gates,' Wolf muttered with little enthusiasm.

The sky grew darker as they trudged on, and more Griffins gathered overhead.

Asha came to perch on the pommel of the Raiden's saddle. 'What orders do you wish to spread?' she asked.

'We need to start fortifying our position now while we move, so that we're nearly as soon as we arrive,' he told her. 'Something is sure to happen when we get in sight of the castle. We won't have much time to make ourselves comfortable.'

'You want healers and supplies surrounded and protected?' Asha asked, walking up Amala's neck.

The Raiden nodded. 'Archers with Aeron and Durna, to the sides. Foot soldiers to the front, and cavalry ready to charge.'

'The usual,' Asha agreed.

Rai could hear the distant laughter and curses coming from the Griffins, and he shivered as a light rain began to fall, shrouding them in drizzly mist.

'Kid, you look frozen,' Ander teased, slapping him wetly on the back. Rai forced a smile.

But soon the sound of dark whisperings began filtering back from the ranks ahead of them, and then they pulled themselves up the sloping mud banks and followed the rest of the army onto even ground to see what was ahead.

There they beheld the sprawling outline of the imposing castle, and the great walls of Darziates' stronghold. The walls spanned the landscape like an immovable shadow, and a dark mass was gathered at the base.

The millions of Krall soldiers that had been camped and waiting now started to converge into one strong formation. Their cries of challenge began to stretch across what would become the battlefield.

Rai gripped his bow tightly, his heart already beating faster while the Awyalknians and Jenrans continued to trail their way up the muddy banks, rank after rank climbing to level ground and then immediately arranging themselves.

'That's a lot of enemies,' Ander husked.

Thale grunted.

'We would have more than matched those numbers if the magical races had reached us in time,' the Raiden commented.

Then the soldiers of Krall's army began clashing their weapons against their spiked armour and shields; a barrier of strength and noise ahead.

'I think I see my brother,' Ferron jibed wryly, squinting through the rain.

The Griffins swooped lower, shouting with hunger and hate.

'This is not a nice welcome home,' Phrixus grimaced, pulling his foot free of the mud.

And then the situation suddenly worsened.

Rai's heart stuttered as the Nymphs cried out a Rucksha warning, and the Griffins from high above all abruptly tucked their wings in, dropping into dives so that it looked like the sky was falling.

'Frarshk!' Rai heard Glyn hiss, aiming upward at the Griffins while at the same time the sloppy earth ahead of the front lines began to ooze and bubble into the shapes of melted nightmares.

Amala reared as the Raiden raised his sword to the men flocking around him.

He was urging them forward.

Rai's breath was coming fast, but he mirrored Dwyn and Glynn as they raised their bows nearby.

Rai released arrow after arrow to ward off the Griffins as the Raiden charged the nearest Rucksha – delivering blows with inhuman strength.

With a resounding cry, the Raiden lopped off the front of the beast's great face, its gurgling features sloshing away while mucky, dripping arms blindly fumbled at nothing. With one final charge Thale and Nikon sent the beast tumbling backward to burst into a pouring mudslide of wet earth.

Glyn released a whoop of joy at the beast's defeat, but the whoop was cut short and Rai started as he saw Glyn suddenly disappearing – plucked from the ground.

Dwyn shouted in horror and aimed an arrow after the Griffin that had snatched his brother, but another swooping Griffin cackled and darted in so quickly that it managed to make a mighty rip in Dwyn's middle. Dwyn crumpled just as Glyn's scratched body was dropped back down to land in their midst.

Rai yelled sickly, aghast at the speed of the ruin of his friends, before he felt an awful grip of claws as they now fastened around his own middle.

Then he felt the vicious sharpness of a beak slicing into his neck and collarbone.

His mouth was an 'o' of surprise and the stink of wet feathers enveloped him as the bite separated his shoulder from his body.

When the Griffin released him Rai was left blinking at the empty faces of Glyn and Dwyn on the ground beside him.

Rai felt Dren's arms lifting him from the wet, but he stayed cold and his arm swung in a nerveless arc.

Dren was howling and Rai found himself wishing that it hadn't all happened so fast.

His death was feeling as quick as his life had been.

'Look … It's Noal,' Rai murmured to Dren, and he smiled at the sight of the prince and Vidar rushing into view.

The Krall soldiers and reunited princes were lashing at the Griffins with sabres and swords that seemed to glow silver with their speed.

'Look,' Rai tried to say again. 'Noal made it back.'

But Dren's cries were shaking Rai up and down.

The icy water and thick mud were seeping in at Rai's back and he tried not to think that he would have to be buried in that mud. Mud on his face, filling his nostrils and ears.

Rai saw Ander stabbing a fallen Griffin in fury as it shrieked and scrabbled to get away. He cried and swore and beat it over and over until it collapsed.

'This is war,' Rai tried to say. 'We knew.' But not a sound came out.

Rai's eyes fell onto the last bright thing in the mud and rain.

The silver magic across the Raiden's chest glared like a warning in the night.

'Don't worry.'

In war, in death, they would be reunited again soon.

89

Eighty Nine

R *azek*

Razek could not believe his eyes when a mud covered young man and a towering immortal stepped into his pavilion during his morning meal and meeting.

Not one member of the Lixrax army had seen them cross the boundaries, before the two strangers had become visible – blurring to a stop outside the doorway to Razek's pavilion, respectfully waiting to be invited to enter.

Just as Darziates' arrival had always stunned them, so too did this apparition. But Razek and the heavily robed leaders who had been dining with him did not feel dread. Only wonder.

Razek marvelled at the newcomers, his eyes sparkling. The bizarrely tall but enchantingly dark-skinned being released his hold on the young man and both of the visitors bowed low from the doorway.

'Hail, Emperor Razek,' the young man said, and Razek found that he could somehow understand the words of the strange tongue, and he leaned forward on his cushions.

'Guests, I feel no harm about you,' he said carefully. 'You are not of Krall. Why do you come?'

The two strangers straightened, and the young man's expression was earnest as he replied. 'We have come with offers of aid and friendship.'

Razek smiled thoughtfully through his oiled and twisted moustache. 'You are welcome then, to talk with us. Though it is at your peril, for Darziates knows all of our doings.'

Razek's attendants rose at their Emperor's invitation to the newcomers. They quickly fetched silken pillows for the two guests so that they could join the leaders already seated around the luxurious pavilion's rug.

'We believe the Sorcerer is focused elsewhere,' the tall being stated politely.

The Emperor inclined his head as the two newcomers entered to take their places. 'In many ways you have arrived at the right time then,' Razek told them. 'You find me with my most trusted leaders, all gathered to break our fast.' He beckoned for the attendants to bring two more cups of the sweet wine his party shared.

The young man shared a smile of relief with his tall companion, whose presence seemed to fill the small room with incredible energy. Then he focused his foreign, lightly coloured eyes upon the Emperor.

'I am grateful that you are willing to receive us,' the young man said sincerely. 'I am Prince Noal of Awyalkna, and one of the Three chosen by the Gods to unite the peoples of the world against the threat of the ninth age.'

The officials seated around the newcomers could not keep from staring, but Razek settled on his cushion, rustling the many robes he wore to ward off the pervasive cold.

'We have run all through the night to reach you, so that we can return to our forces as they reach the castle later today,' Prince Noal continued. 'Fortunately we have so far been unscathed and unnoticed.'

'I am Vidar, a forest dweller of great Sylthanryn,' the second being spoke then. 'I have dwelt within the Lady's protected realm for centuries. But my kind has stepped out into the world now, to face this threat with the mortals. It was with my magic and my speed that we have arrived so swiftly.'

In the tanned faces of his children, lined and solemn after months of enforced camp in hated lands, Razek began to see new light.

'Elves like Vidar are able to connect with nature on such a level, that their bodies flow through it and become one with it,' Noal explained.

'Though your goodness is clear, and you have risked much to meet us, it pains me to remind you that we have been made enemies in this lifetime,' Razek said in return. 'I should have ordered your execution from the moment you appeared, lest my children face punishment for my betrayal of the Sorcerer in letting you live. For his power is great and terrible, and can crush both my people and all magical peoples very easily, just as he has wiped out different divided races before.'

'If I may?' Prince Noal withdrew a relic of some kind, wrapped safely in protective cloths. As he unwrapped it, Razek's eyes grew wide.

There were gasps around the gathering as the pointed horn glowed with brilliance, casting golden light about them.

The warrior nearest the door quickly loosed the material flap, and the shelter became closed in and private.

'The horn of a Unicorn!' Razek gasped in wonder.

'Yes,' agreed Prince Noal. 'It contains the kind of pure magic that Darziates would only dream about. Another weapon that we have though, is knowledge. The Lady of the forest and the people of Jenra have shared knowledge of a prophecy that Darziates has never been aware of.'

'He believes the world faces a great threat at the end of the ninth age,' Razek interjected.

'But he has never heard the rest,' Vidar replied.

Prince Noal leaned across to Razek, offering him the ancient horn. Marvelling at the beauty of it, Razek took the horn in his hands, and at once felt nature's great magic there.

Then the prince went on to describe the Lady's second prophecy of the Three questers, and their mission to unite the world against the threat. Darziates had described a similar goal, but this prince spoke of forming lasting alliances rather than conquering all nations as the Sorcerer intended.

'Though they have not arrived yet to be with us, we are supported in full by each of the magical races,' Noal said. 'They are real, and they are loyal to us.'

With the horn in his hands, and such purity filling the whole pavilion, Razek could somehow feel that the prince spoke the truth.

'We have the allegiance of Jenra,' the prince went on. 'And our greatest friends are the first freed men of Krall. So the only nation in the entire world not in some way united against the threat that looms before us, is Lixrax. Instead, Lixrax has been forced to join with the one thing causing the world's peril. The man who is the threat of this age.'

'The Sorcerer is the threat,' Razek blinked.

Prince Noal nodded solemnly.

The jewels upon the Emperor's fingers glittered as he rubbed at his tattooed brow. 'We have no choice but to be joined with the Sorcerer. He has threatened to enslave my children and I have seen the ease in which he invades minds. His entire reign in Krall is made possible because of it.'

Vidar leaned forward to wrap the horn back up in its coverings. 'So for now, while the Sorcerer's mind is distracted, we keep it secret that you no longer serve him. Your generals will only spread the order to turn allegiances at the final moment.'

The leaders sitting with open mouths glanced at each other with growing eagerness. It would mean turning the Desert Storm against the Krall forces at the last, so that danger came from behind as well as from the front lines.

Prince Noal gave a small smile. 'Perhaps your people can avoid being corrupted if Darziates only realises you are not allied to him when it is too late. But if he does somehow get control of you, the pure beings of this world will do every-thing within their power to reverse it.'

'In fact, we also hope to liberate all of Krall's people and to restore the lands if we are victorious against the Sorcerer,' the Elf added seriously.

Razek considered the boggling idea, which was almost too amazing to absorb.

'Will you join us and the rest of the world?' Prince Noal asked, watching as the Emperor reflected.

'Gods smile on you!' Razek answered, clapping his jewelled hands together. 'We join your path!'

He took from his smallest finger a golden ring with a strange stone.

'This is a black opal, with harlequin patterns,' he told Prince Noal. 'It is found in our region, and is most rare and most brilliant. However, look upon the band and find a symbol of our binding oath in the pattern of interwoven vines.'

The Emperor pressed the treasure into Prince Noal's hand, and the prince wondered at the dazzling patterns of the stone, and traced the intricate vines and delicate leaves lining the band.

'The design will represent growth, eternal friendship and binding trust, a bond that cannot be broken,' Razek told the fair prince. 'A gift to you for bringing hope back to my people. And a token of evidence to take back with you to the Raiden – evidence that he must honour his word, as we will honour ours.

90

Ninety

*T*oru

Toru had been running for two days, weak from thirst and sending up clouds of dust until the rains had begun – bringing moisture and light back to his skin.

At one point Toru had felt foulness in the air and the ground had seemed to moan and lurch beneath his feet. He had kept his balance and squinted against the storm, certain that he could also hear mortal cries of distress from far away.

Saddened, he had continued on, though he'd known that he was passing the mortal regiments of the Army for the World, and that they were in trouble.

He had lowered his head and moved faster so that soon his long strides had carried him away from the sounds and the ground had stopped lurching.

And though it had been bad to leave the allies to their fight, it had given him the opportunity to approach the lands to the side of Krall's walls unnoticed.

He had stopped intuitively by the edge of a great reservoir, a distance away from the foreboding rock kingdom. Somehow the still water there had seemed to call to him, so he had dropped his bag to wait in silence, patiently gazing into the rain choked lake.

The water surface was unchanging for some time, simply reflecting the low, surly clouds like a mirror for the sky God.

Then, gift of all gifts, Toru had begun to sense Kiana, and that she was on her way to him, coming to this very spot.

She had to be traveling beneath the ground, weaving through the water systems. But he became anxious, becoming aware that it was now only his connection to her and his close proximity keeping her alive.

Toru's heart quickened when the light across his forearm began to fade and she had not emerged.

He watched the water intently but realised he could no longer sense her magic and now the design on his forearm was barely visible.

It seemed an age until the water of the lake began to bubble in its centre.

Toru desperately ploughed into the reservoir, wading towards the churning spot before, very suddenly, a jet of water exploded up from the bubbling point.

It spouted in a forceful shower, shooting up into the air at high speed ... but she did not appear.

Toru dove into the reservoir and sped to the bottom, fighting to get close to where the water was bursting free. He could see a pipe that had exploded wide open but he was buffeted by the magic that had forced the water to change its course. He was thrown backward, forced to surface again beneath the gushing flood of spurting water.

Yet just as Toru was ready to despair he saw a small form shooting up amongst the jets of water, hurtling high into the air.

With a gasp, Toru leapt to catch the water logged body of the last *Larnaeradee*, cradling her as he crashed back to the bank of the lake to lay her down.

He found that no breath rose in her chest, and there were no beats from her heart.

Her skin was deathly pale, covered in abrasions and with already blossoming bruises. Her lips were purple and her black gown was ruined.

Unable to believe that a friend of the water people could be allowed to drown, Toru hurriedly took Kiana's limp arm in his hand and he joined their two linking water patterns together.

No sparks rose at first, but he pushed. He focused his whole being on willing his magic to find connection with hers again.

A growing blue mist, like sea spray, formed about their hands and it settled upon her skin.

It danced around her wrist to spread about her forearm.

Until finally, her marking lit up.

He pushed further, urging the magic to grow with each of his own heartbeats, and slowly the veins inside her arm filled with light.

The light travelled along her shoulder and sank far beneath the surface of her skin while Toru began to rub her arms in his hands.

With fierce concentration he visualised the light sinking into her lungs and spreading there. He visualised his power flowing through her airways to clear the water and to return room for air to her lungs.

Soon a spurt of water did burst from Kiana's mouth, as the magic forced it out of her body, but her eyes did not open. She did not gasp for more air.

Toru focused on keeping the air moving within her, and with his help her blood began to send colour back into her skin.

He also focused on her life force, now placing one mighty palm over her chest.

There was still no beating. And Toru looked at the tiny, fragile being with only slight hesitation.

If an inexperienced cub ever got too water logged back at Margate Isle, nobody thought twice about pounding life back into them, and perhaps taking such a risk on the tiny One was her only chance.

So, hoping he would not crush her beyond repair anyway, he placed one hand over her chest and his other hand over his own heart, and found the rhythm.

Then he pushed on hers.

It was but a light force to him, but it moved her whole form.

He pushed again, and she sank into the muddy bank.

He begged the Gods and he begged the water spirits as he pushed again and again while a purple fist mark spread across her sternum.

But it did not seem to be the Gods or the water spirits who answered his prayers – because when he next released the pressure, a sparkle of silvery light crackled beneath his fingers.

He pulled his hand away in surprise, but did not feel any burn. Only clean magic. And the sparkle grew above her chest. It swirled over her core, glimmering and growing in brightness.

It radiated with such good power that Toru's whole body became spectacularly alight and he was engulfed and dazzled.

He raised a hand and squinted through the growing light, from which he realised he could hear whispers. He could feel faint touches of warmth and friendship against his cheeks. He could sense the presence of those he had not felt in a long time.

Not since before Kiana; the last of her kind.

Tears ran unbidden down his sloping cheeks and he felt his muscles radiating with the strength of his cubhood.

He saw the bruises fading from the One, and the mud dropping from her skin. Her bones aligned themselves back into place and her chest began to rise and fall.

He saw her eyes open, reflecting the light from the ancient energy of her ancestors. Ancestors who were reaching across normally impossible boundaries between realms to aid the last One of their kind.

She smiled, filled with understanding and connection to those who had gone before her, and who still powered her steps in life.

Only when the intense brightness began to fade, and the whispers and gentle greetings grew too soft to hear, did Kiana turn to Toru.

'Gods I am glad to see you, friend.'

Toru sat back on his haunches in relief.

'You look well,' she smiled wider. 'Very well indeed. And I feel ... reborn.'

Then she sat up as if she had only been lightly asleep. 'We must go to find the magical races, and lead them to the rest of the Army for the World.'

Toru leaned over to lift a bag that was much too small for him.

'Ahh,' she nodded. 'You're right. Not in this.'

The One *Larnaeradee* looked as if she had been clothed in starlight as she at last adorned herself in the silver ore armour of the Dwarves and Dargons.

She let her wings glimmer into visibility and lifted to hover beside Toru.

His strength had been restored, the lines on his face had been smoothed, and youth had returned to his veins as he leapt back into his loping run while she flew easily beside him – a twinkle of light in the dark.

91

Ninety One

The Sorcerer

Lightning illuminated the dark room and then faded.

Darziates' shadow was elongated and stooped as it was thrown against the stone wall from where he gripped the steel armrests of his throne.

The occupants of the castle beyond his room huddled with dread as his devastated fury had now permeated each chamber in an almost tangible way. He had never felt raw emotion before, and it seeped out from him to dominate every space.

The two guards outside had earlier sunk down beneath the pressure of their King's deep depression. One had suffocated on the darkness while the other had fallen on his sword to escape the horror, and nobody else who was sane would now dare to come close. Only Angra Mainyu lurked outside the room loyally.

At first the Sorcerer had tried to search for her with all of his being. Yet he had not once been able to sense her. Instead he had seemed able to sense touches of pure magic all throughout underground Krall, almost as if she were everywhere – her magic seeping into the earth itself after her impossible journey through the waterways.

And for the first time in his existence, with every fibre, Darziates yearned to forget his quest. He wished to be freed of the duty of his bloodline so that he could find her. Could find life.

Yet now, fast approaching, was the moment he had been carefully planning for hundreds of years.

He rubbed at his aching chest. Then, like a grimacing gargoyle brought to life, Darziates rose from his chair to sweep towards the doors, pushing them open with his magic.

Angra Mainyu stood unashamedly from where he had been rifling through the pockets of the soldiers' corpses in the hall, and he grinned manically at the Sorcerer.

'My King.'

'Come,' Darziates ordered. 'It is time to put the final touches on my army.'

'This is the time you've been keeping me for,' Angra husked with excitement, obediently following his master through the halls.

Each torch snuffed out as Darziates passed, but it only added to Angra's delight, and he was keening like an animal when Darziates opened the door to the massive chamber that radiated with cold.

Angra's teeth began to chatter as his eyes darted around the hall of hulking Evexus. Unlike Kiana's earlier disgust, the Warlord exulted at the sight.

Their spiked shadows stretched freakishly across the walls as the lightning flashed once more. Their chins sloped down to their chests and their shoulders rose and fell, but there were no real signs of intelligent life.

'It's time they wake up,' Darziates glowered. 'Time for my allies to experience their new life in this realm.'

Angra just nodded frenziedly.

Darziates focused on the Evexus shells and the magic heated his fingertips and eyes to throbbing points.

At his beckoning the red mists began to appear, circulating around the dark, spiked figures in the room so that the air became thick and oddly frigid with rancid smoke.

The Other Realm spirits within the smoke stretched and spread themselves out to fill every corner, and Darziates could hear their voices and feel their spite.

He sent shocks out to force them into formation and, hissing, they obeyed his will; hovering in more distinct shapes over each Evexus shell.

Then Darziates reached out with his mind to take hold of each ghoul's essence.

Angra whimpered a little as Darziates turned to his Warlord next, sending out invisible hands of magic to reach into Angra's corrupted and cracked spirit. The impact lines where his soul had been shattered and damaged in different places were clear, but the Sorcerer went deeper.

For the Sorcerer had learned that to make the best Evexus, who were still rational spirits inside their earthly shells, they needed to be given some kind of internal, earthly anchor – a piece of spirit from someone of this realm that their own Other Realm spirit could hold onto.

Only someone with a soul as fragmented as Angra's could share enough pieces of an earthly anchor around, and Darziates would need a lot of material to use for the hundreds of Evexus waiting to be truly born.

Like last time, when five pieces had been withdrawn for the Evexus that had served Agrona, Angra howled and cried. Invisible incisions were made within his spirit, and pieces were carved out and taken away. But as each piece was pulled free to float to an Evexus, Angra became less agitated.

There was even less to care about with less humanity inside of him.

The Other Realm spirits in turn shrieked with the revulsion of accepting a piece of mortality into their beings, yet with each anchor absorbed, each spirit was able to take hold and sink into the Evexus shell they had chosen to attach to.

Finally the Warlord stood with barely any awareness at all within his eyes and the Evexus shells had been filled.

The Evexus began to shuffle uncertainly around the room, bumping into each other as they became used to their new bodies.

When one Evexus fumbled against Angra, Darziates watched the empty Warlord reflexively step out of the way of the blundering beast, putting his hand on his sabre. After a moment's consideration Darziates again reached with his mind into the Other Realm and used his magic to catch a particularly high ranking ghoul by the scruff of its neck.

The other ghoul leaders shrank back from the Sorcerer's presence as he dragged their screaming comrade away, and the red smoke surrounding the writhing spirit now became visible beside Angra.

Angra shook as his body was filled by the alien presence, but he also laughed.

He laughed as he flexed his fists and laughed as his eyes truly glinted red with the light of a possessing spirit.

Darziates left the stumbling mass of Evexus to the whims of their new master and Angra rolled his shoulders in anticipation.

Darziates let the doors close behind him as Angra began barking orders.

He walked down the halls, knowing that he had just achieved a great feat for his quest. And yet, his hand gripped at his chest once more. And his mind had returned to her.

92

Ninety Two

Noal

Dwyn and Glyn first. Rai. Then Lydon and Gideon; picked off by Griffins without the archers to protect us.

Vidar and I had made it back, only to join a battle to keep the men at our sides on the ground.

Most of us had suffered various scratches, and they burned like fire as Aeron ordered the healers to vigorously scrub out any bacteria that could be in the wounds.

But all the same we lost two more men in the night when Roth bled out from a thigh wound and Rendor sickened from a gash across his stomach. They'd been hurt trying to save Lydon and Gideon.

Ander was soon to follow – rattling for breath and feverish from deep, poisoned gouges he'd suffered while lashing out at the Griffins in his devastation.

Dren was hollow at the loss of his team, each member stripped from him in one night, and he had been silent while we had buried our dead as best we could in trenches of mud.

The mortal soldiers of Krall had not had to move an inch to contribute to our losses, and now they sang songs of blood lust and victory across the distance.

I could not even spread word of hope to the battered soldiers of our own army, as my success with Razek had to remain secret from all but our leaders.

Instead the Jenran and Awyalknian soldiers only knew that we had suffered many losses on the first night of reaching Darziates' doorstep, that survivors had a bleak fate looming ahead, and that it seemed there would be no other aid to come.

'I fear that seeing Maeve will be the only comfort I shall find this morning,' I muttered to Thorin as he walked beside me, his hand resting on his hilt.

Phrixus, my second escort, nodded on my other side. 'You are fortunate in some ways that she is here to comfort you at the last. In other ways, unfortunate.'

Maeve would be readying to sleep now as the sun rose behind the stormy ceiling of clouds. And, as Phrixus had hinted, I could not predict if this would be our last time together. But because of this, my mind was focused on something that I had to do.

Phrixus and Thorin stopped outside Maeve's wagon, and I swallowed nervously.

'Why so hesitant?' Thorin asked. 'You are the great, prophesied link. You do not balk at the sight of wagons.'

'Oh yes. You are a brave soul,' Phrixus agreed, and then he lowered his voice. 'Lixrax's friendship is now glittering on your little finger as evidence.'

'For now it is,' Thorin raised his eyebrows with dawning understanding. Then he held his arm out to me. 'No fear.'

I took a breath and clasped his arm warmly, before I turned to Maeve's door.

I knocked quietly, and at once the door opened and she pulled me inside into a relieved hug.

The door closed on the hellscape outside; she gazed up at me with gladness in her eyes, and I leaned in close to press my lips to hers.

Then I held both her hands in mine and kissed her fingers.

'I love you, my Lady,' I told her quietly, watching as the warmth of that sentence lit up her face.

'And I you, my prince. With all my heart.'

I tightened my hands around hers. 'Then, Lady Maeve, I am asking you to be my life partner. Because I love you so greatly that, whether we are promised in betrothal for a day or a year, I want what time we have left to be brightened by the pledge that we are together.'

Maeve's eyes had widened.

'Yes,' she breathed. 'No matter how long or short our lives together may be, they are entwined.'

I slipped Razek's ring onto her thumb.

'This ring is the ultimate symbol of the unity between races, and is one of Lixrax's prized jewels,' I told her earnestly. 'I want it to be yours, in promise that we will be joined with the blessing of all of the nations when peace is won.'

It seemed the sun was within her, lighting up her being.

'I have never been happier than right now,' she whispered. 'In the middle of this nightmarish world, with you.'

'You will have sweet dreams now then,' I scooped her up and carried her to the cot to set her down to rest, hugging her to me with a full heart. 'And I will find courage in my memory of what has just passed when I need it later.'

She nestled into me blissfully, beholding the ring.

'The only thing is,' she said after a moment. 'This isn't really the best place for me to wear a ring bestowed by an Emperor and a prince in promise of unity.'

I peered at the glittering jewel, which was too big even on her thumb. 'Wrong finger?'

She laughed. 'Wrong profession. It would be embarrassing if it were to get lost when I use my hands so much.'

I shuddered at the thought of just how it could get lost. 'You're right. Keep it somewhere else.'

Maeve lifted the delicate gold necklace that Lady Amarantha had given her. The little healing hand trinket glittered as she unclasped the necklace and threaded the sparkling ring onto the chain where it clinked against the hand as she put it back on.

'There,' she said in satisfaction. 'Now, my Awyalknian betrothed, this gift of Lixrax is over my Jenran heart, but always upon my healing hand as well.'

'Clever, clever,' I agreed, putting my hand proudly over her creamy skin and the two jewels.

We settled against each other, trying to ignore the sounds of growing rumbles of thunder from outside. We had to pretend that the screeches starting to pierce the air were just a faint imagining. And we both stayed cuddled together even as we felt the world outside pressing in and an uncertain future creeping closer.

93

Ninety Three

N*oal*

We were startled awake by growing noises of alarm out-side and a shattering, cracking sound as something crashed into the wagon wall.

The whole wagon lifted onto an angle for a moment and Maeve and I gripped each other as the wagon groaned and crashed back down. Then we heard a polite knock at the door, followed by Vulcan's voice.

'Ahh, hello you two. That was just a Griffin. One of the Jenran archers took care of it, but there's quite a few more now and ...'

'Time to get up?' I called back.

'Yes. It might be best,' I heard Phobos call through the door. It sounded like he had been running.

It was hard to leave that cot, knowing it may be the last moment we would have. But we parted as another shuddering crash came from the wagon's roof and we both unconsciously ducked and protected our heads.

Then Maeve and I opened the wagon door together. We stepped out into an afternoon that had been painted with dark grey, wincing as the noise intensified while Griffins careened past like wraiths. Some were even landing to fight on the ground.

'Noal!' Vulcan said cheerfully over the chaotic scene. 'You did it!'

A Griffin's swearing was cut off from behind him as Wolf mercilessly stood on its throat and hacked its head off while Cadell and Ferron pinned its deadly talon lined paws.

'I'm guessing she said yes? Or perhaps she just overpowered you and stole that ring for her necklace?' Phobos asked with a grin, wiping a smear of mud from his armour.

'Did he do it?' Wolf bellowed.

'Yes!' Vulcan roared back.

'And did she accept?' Ferron yelled.

'Yes!' Maeve called.

They crowed in the distance.

I squeezed Maeve's hand, and her fingers tightened around mine.

'Be well, my love,' I told her.

'Be well,' she said after taking a deep breath. And I carefully etched every golden detail of her face and every intonation of her voice into my memory.

'I know we shall meet again,' she finished firmly.

And then we had to let each other go.

Phobos went with her, and I left with Vulcan, feeling steadily colder as the distance between us grew.

The generals, Warlords and Kings also gave me their congratulations. They clasped my arm and promised that we would all unite to celebrate at a better time. And when we all hurried off to our posts I prayed to the Gods to let it be so.

But it was hard to imagine it being possible when the rain began again. As if the sky was dropping all of its burdens over us, we were soon drenched to our souls while we stared out at the looming enemy lines and waited for some kind of sign that the battle should begin.

My heart jumped when the sign was delivered – a fork of lightning splitting the sky and illuminating three dark shapes lined atop the walls of Krall.

The hulking Evexus waited one more moment before they unleashed such fierce battle cries that the sounds carried across the noise of the Griffins and the storm, all the way to us.

Ila shifted warily beneath me as the Krall army came properly to life in answer to the calls. Their own wild voices carried to us, filled with almost animal abandon, and I frowned at how mindlessly they yowled at us. Baying hungrily, as if suddenly delirious with adrenalin. Or something else that was much less natural.

'Rucksha are coming!' Asha yelled then.

'We're coming tooooooooooo!' the low flying Griffins cackled.

Then the Evexus screeched from the walls again, and Krall's army began to advance.

94

Ninety Four

D*alin*

The Griffins battered and harried us with chaotic purpose, making it impossible to maintain an organised advance.

The thick bellows of the Rucksha, and their belligerent stomping also scattered our lines, as the beasts were swelling up into existence amongst us, and were somehow growing taller and stronger instead of absorbing back into the mud when we pushed them down.

And all the while the unassailed army of Krall was advancing steadily while we haphazardly battled our way forward.

'This is not a good start,' I grunted as I clasped Thorin's arm, hauling him up onto the saddle behind me.

'Thanks,' Thorin gasped as a Rucksha's foot stomped down on the place where he'd stood. Its foot narrowly missed Amala's passing tail and her nostrils flared as she tore free.

Dren's arrows squelched into the beast's eye cavity and it jolted backward, throwing drops of mud from its mighty hands as Nikon and Thale also frantically led charges through the mud, trying to tear the beast down.

'Gods!' Ferron cried as a Griffin dragged him backward through the muck, but Phobos lunged at Ferron's lashing legs and tore his comrade free.

'Look at the wall!' I heard Noal yell urgently.

His golden hair clung to his face and his eyes were wide.

'Frarshk,' I heard Thorin hiss from behind me. 'Oh frarshk.'

There were no longer just three Evexus on the walls. A smaller human figure had stepped up to stand with them ... and hundreds of other Evexus had joined them too.

I squinted through the rain as Amala pranced underneath me and the world seemed to rage from every direction.

The human in the middle of the Evexus raised his arms. And at the shadowy figure's signal, one Evexus after another began to drop lithely from the tops of the walls, landing easily and loping forward through the marching Krall army.

'Ohhhhhh that's not allllllllll,' a circling Griffin sang gaily. 'There's more to come!'

Then jets of flame seared the sky, exploding through the rain and somehow projecting terrible heat despite the piercing cold.

Great, grey monsters rose up from behind the castle that were bigger than the towers themselves, and as they released more plumes of fire the Griffins chittered and gushed in deference, scattering to clear the air.

'Raiden, King Durna said you're going to need this!' I heard Vidar's urgent voice then as he and Bard flashed to a stop at Amala's side.

Vidar held the golden Unicorn horn out to me.

It glistened in the wet, radiating with golden light as I sheathed my normal blade and took it in my grasp. At once I felt a sudden burst of energy as the silver handprint over my heart prickled, seeming to cast its own light as well.

I lifted the bright Unicorn horn into the darkness, and yelled to those around me: 'My brothers! Together! MOVE FORWARD!'

'MOVE FORWARD!' the men of the Army for the World roared my command down through the lines.

'Dismount and be less of a target,' I told Thorin. 'And guard Noal's back.'

Now the stirrings of *Larnaeradee* magic that had been sweeping through my soul since Kiana's healing were truly igniting to a new, boggling extreme. My skin felt as if it could hardly contain me.

I clutched the Unicorn horn and thrust myself out of the saddle, arcing lightly away from Amala and Thorin to land beside the Elves.

Bard placed a hand on my shoulder, and together we blurred through the rain and darkness, not hampered by the mud as we flew across the distance to be the first to meet the enemy in battle.

Bard launched me through the air so that I landed on the closest Evexus easily.

My feet landed on its chest and I used it as a springboard.

I slashed its throat deeply, finding my mark more easily with my new strength, and I leapt away before its acid blood could burn me.

But the charging, enslaved men of Krall who were nearest to its falling corpse screamed in agony as strange smoke emitted poisonously from its body. The mist choked those around the dead beast before dissipating.

I landed beside Vidar and ducked as the Evexus he was fighting swiped at our heads.

I launched myself up to land on its shoulders, slicing through its dark casing with the piercing tip of the horn. I heard the tear of the Evexus' skin, and of the unnatural spirit trapped within. Then I dropped down to Vidar and away from the Evexus' spreading smoke poison.

Another Evexus leapt toward me and I felt the energy build in my calves and thighs. My knees bent, and then my feet had launched my body away from the ground so that I shot upward to meet the snarling beast mid-air.

The pure magic burned brightly from my chest and from the Unicorn horn as I lifted my weapon and plunged it into my enemy.

And I heard the Army for the World calling out. Following me into war.

95

Ninety Five

Noal

We were carried forward together, a tidal wave of brothers.

Then there was the first clash of the frontlines, and our blades met their sabres with resounding clangs that rang louder than the moaning thunder in the purpling sky.

Our opponents were intimidating – loosing loud war cries; the demonic spikes of their armour glinting. However my first rival quickly lost his sabre and an ear to me, and I saw that he was nothing like the Krall warriors that were my comrades.

Our adversaries instead appeared to no longer have any connection to being human, except, in the end, the cost of mortality itself. They appeared to be mindless; driven solely by a burning hatred instilled by another into their minds.

And, worse, all of our charging mortal foes truly looked possessed.

The pupils of their eyes had swollen as though Darziates' dark enchantment over them had been upped, and had been delivered through an inky injection into each eyeball. But when they were dying the grey darkness spilled free, running over their cheeks like oily tears that were diluted by the rain.

It was unnerving as my next opponent charged me like a witless animal, even coming at me with his bare hands after I had disarmed him. He continued his fight as I dealt deadly blows, and he did not seem aware of his condition until he had begun to sink into the watery sludge. Then he lost his energy, blinking up nauseously in his final moments.

Sickened, I had to turn to my next opponent, whose powerful, stocky legs drove me backward in a wet slide. But I sank my dripping blade into the unprotected skin under his arm – something that not even an unfeeling puppet could come back from.

Leaking inky tears, he slipped away from me, and I could hear Thorin swearing with almost rhythmical curses as he dispatched possessed warrior after possessed warrior nearby.

My own Krall comrades fought stoically around me, miserably cutting down their mindless kin. But despite our advantage of awareness and quick thinking, we grew tired and stumbled more regularly while their violent energy never diminished. Slice by slice we were drained, and I could feel trickles of my blood mingling with the rain as I was sapped from more minor cuts than could be counted.

The more lives I took, the more marked and exhausted I became. And as we hauled ourselves through the mud even our muscles started to feel like intolerable weights to carry.

'Their numbers are too great!' Purdor yelled eventually; echoing all of our thoughts, and what we had known all along.

'Press on!' I hollered back hoarsely. 'We mustn't be overwhelmed!'

'For the quest!' Thale agreed, pulling Nikon up from where he had been thrown before swinging his sabre at the next yammering warrior.

So we toiled forward, driving face after face backward. Felling each witless opponent. And grimly stepping over the dying – our boots pressing their bodies into the mud while wave after wave of bewitched men kept coming.

96

Ninety Six

N*oal*

The night and our battle stretched on.

I stepped over desperately reaching hands as my enemies cried oily tears at my heels.

Explosions of fire rained down over our forces from above, the stunning light leaving frozen images of harsh faces and contorted bodies imprinted on my mind.

'AHH FRARRRRSHK!' a Griffin squealed as it swooped by crazily, trying to put out the Dragon fire that had singed its wings. Ash and burning feathers showered down as it careened away.

'Gods!' I heard Purdor cry out as a sudden ground tremor threw us all off balance.

'What the frarshk was *that*?!' Phrixus roared as he and Phobos beheaded a struggling Griffin.

'Darziates?' Thale yelled through the rain, remembering back to when the Sorcerer had made the whole desert come to life.

The earth buckled again, and this time the quake was accompanied by an explosion of fire so great that it lit up the night and many men had to shield their eyes.

'I think ... the Dragons are touching down!' Cadell called, before felling his startled enemy.

'They're landing?' Ferron groaned.

The Griffins began to cackle and swoop in low again; braver now that the skies weren't so dangerous.

'Watch out!' Wolf hollered, lunging forward to lop the head off a fallen soldier who had reached up with a final effort to stab Ferron from the ground. 'They may be landing, but you need to concentrate on what's right here!' he growled.

And we all grimly forced ourselves to continue to push through the onrushing wall of bodies, trying to ignore the way the ground shook and the air cracked.

'Woah!' I yelled out as I turned to face a new opponent, but instead found myself in a suddenly rising, corpse littered mud hill.

'Rucksha!' I shouted as I became stuck fast.

Thorin roared as he saw me being dragged upward in the growing mound. He leapt forward to push me free and we both landed together in a thick puddle at the legs of the growing boulderman.

The brute gurgled densely through a mud thickened throat. Its feet sluggishly pulled free from the mire, throwing sludge all over us.

'Together!' Thale yelled in his mighty voice, and the others immediately began to back toward us – some turning to the Rucksha, some facing the mindless soldiers, and one trying to desperately fire on any Griffins that got too close.

'This ... is ... hopeless,' I heard Nikon growl while three puppets of Krall hammered at his armour and he fought to fend them off.

'You're right,' Phobos grunted beside him. 'But keep going.'

And it was clear. We were losing.

Our force of tens of thousands of pure willed men would never be able to withstand a force of enslaved and magical millions.

With honour.

With bravery.

We were losing.

97

Ninety Seven

*K*iana

We had left the sounds of war behind and the time for dawn had come and gone, yet the sky remained unnaturally dark. The thick, surly clouds roiled with a red and purple hue as Toru and I raced through the rain and across the muddy wastelands.

'Do you feel that?' I whispered, and Toru and I managed to move even faster when we sensed the approaching force of magical beings, fighting just as hard to race to us too.

Then we could see the glowing outline of the marching Giants, all lit up by the rain. Scandra broke away from the throng with great thrusts of her wings, crossing the vast distance that remained between us in barely moments.

Somehow she managed to catch me mid-air in an embrace of her enfolded wings.

'My One!' she hummed when she released me at last. 'I had thought you were lost to us.'

The sound of the rain hitting her scales was like music. Her eyes glowed warmly and I hugged her snout with cold, wet arms.

'I am glad you did not wait, my wise friend.'

'It was this Giant who started the trend,' Scandra announced as her wing shot out to drag Toru against her powerful, golden torso. 'A worthy male.'

'One!' Ahanu cried as he and Frey sprinted towards us, but then the Giant stopped short. 'And ... Gods, Toru ... you look positively youthful.'

'A new light and energy seems to be upon you both,' Frey observed with a smile, and it truly did feel as though the divine energy of all of the past *Larnaeradee* still surged in my blood.

'We are both well, and both ready to join you in a race to get back to the castle,' I agreed keenly while the sound of the rest of the approaching army resounded across the bleak land like the beats to a war drum.

Come! I let the word ripple across the thousands of mixed beings in the distance. *The world awaits us!*

98

Ninety Eight

D*alin*

I felt a searing chill as my feet springboarded off the forehead of a snarling and dissipating Evexus, and I held my breath against the toxic fumes that poured from the slit in the Evexus' throat.

Tiny freezing slices covered every inch of my body, seeping sluggishly. But as I arced upward into the storming sky I drew energy from the horn burning against one palm. And with my other hand I reached out to catch hold of the matted neck of a Griffin that had been soaring high above.

The Griffin screeched indignantly, shocked as I swung from soaked fistfuls of hair and feathers.

'What the frarshk are you doing?!' it hissed down at me. 'Get the frarshk off!'

It tried to twist to nip at my legs with a sharp, clicking beak, careening us through a pack of other biting, attacking

Griffins, but I simply held the horn out so that I left a trail of dropping, burning Griffin bodies in my wake – as well as the smell of singed feathers.

Hordes of swearing Griffins began to pull away from us while my hostage Griffin became even more frantic, its anger vibrating in its throat, and it managed to curl its talons up high enough to tear at the skin of my chest.

I gasped and inhaled rotten odours, but then quickly noticed the pain, surprisingly, starting to change. As if cool sparks were dancing across my skin to draw the torn edges of the wound back together. At last I grinned, releasing the Griffin as the silver hand print on my chest completely healed itself.

Meanwhile the blood from my chest, brimming with the purity of Kiana's magic, had ignited like fire that burned the Griffin's claws. The Griffin shrieked as it butted into its comrades, setting them alight as the pure flames began to catch spread to the others and I fell away from them, the air rushing in my ears.

Vidar plucked me from the air as he and Bard sped by, and we sliced our way back to our forces like three arrows.

'Our side will never make the walls at this rate,' Bard said as we pushed through the throngs.

'There has been no chance for our ranks to regroup,' Vidar agreed, angling himself carefully as the ground shook with another Dragon landing.

'Will you throw me that way?' I asked as I picked Noal and the others out through the sheets of rain, and Vidar didn't hesitate.

I twisted mid-air and reached out in readiness, sinking the horn into the muddy wrist of a Rucksha that held Thale and Phobos.

I ripped the horn free and swung myself up onto its dripping arm, hacking at the sloppy wrist again to free my mud covered brothers.

Dren somehow managed to scale his way up onto the beast's shoulder to join me, driving an arrow into the boulderman's eye cavity to keep the beast preoccupied.

And though my boots were sinking into the ooze, I raised the horn repeatedly until the wrist gave way – dislodging and dropping in a giant mud ball so that Thale and Phobos splattered free in cursing heaps.

'Ha!' I crowed, before I heard the men shout in warning below, and I became aware of the thudding sound of massive wings beating close behind me.

'That one! Get *that* one!' the Griffins cried nearby, leading a Dragon to us.

'The one with the silver handprint!'

'The frarshker with the burning horn!'

The pressure of the wind as the Dragon's wings pulled inward and outward sent the rain billowing all about haphazardly. The Rucksha even began to step uncertainly backward as loose mud was blown away from its body in waves.

'Get him!' the Griffins screamed.

I grabbed Dren's wrist and dragged him down to cling to the protesting Rucksha's neck, but suddenly our legs and then our bodies were being dragged up by the suction of the air.

My ears popped with the pressure, my eyes felt they would be pulled from their sockets, and before I could think, Dren had shoved me so that I went sliding around to the Rucksha's other shoulder.

'Dren!' I cried in horror, even as the Rucksha howled and – with one mighty lop, half of the Rucksha's head, its arm, shoulder and the archer opposite me were torn off in the Dragon's curled claws.

The Dragon dragged itself skyward again while I cried out raggedly, pushing off from the sinking Rucksha and catching hold of the Dragon's free leg.

In a slash of exploding silver the leg ripped free and I thrust myself away to catch a spike at the Dragon's chest.

The Dragon bellowed, but I already had the tip of the burning horn at work again ... this time sizzling away the hard scales over its heart.

I kept my grip on the Unicorn horn and let the magic melt through the scales and then down into the soft flesh beneath.

In panic the Dragon tried to scrabble away from its strange, small attacker, but I did not allow myself to be shaken until its heart had been pierced and hot, dark blood painted my body, mingling with the slanting rain.

As the beast careened downwards I tore the horn free and launched myself across to catch hold of the taloned forepaw impaling my archer.

I grimly tucked the horn into my belt and took hold of Dren's shoulders.

'I am sorry my friend,' I told him before, with a sickening lurch, I levered his body free.

His screams mixed with those of the falling Dragon as I wrapped my arms around him and dove away from the creature.

Dren's body hung limply in my grip, his head lolling against my shoulder while we rocketed to the ground.

Following in the Dragon's wake, the speed of its collision was so great that a tunnel was torn through the mud and the force of the impact made my teeth clatter together.

Mud banked up in walls all around us and I wheezed in agony as we squelched to a stop, with Dren still clutched to me like a ragdoll.

'You better not have done yourself damage,' I heard Dren's laboured voice, and I blinked my vision clear, quickly looking down at him. 'The point was to not have you joining me in where I'm going.'

'Gods, Dren ...' I sat up and saw that I had barely moments before I lost another friend.

'But thank you for this,' the archer managed. 'I did not want to face the end alone.'

'I could never allow that,' I told him, just as my Krall warriors slid down into the trench-like crater to find what was left of us.

'Oh for frarshk's sake, Dalin!' I heard Noal sob in disbelief, but there was anguish on everyone's faces as they saw that Dren was leaving us quickly.

'He has given his life to save mine,' I told my comrades, and I felt the words scrape in my throat.

'They need you. It is a debt well paid,' Dren answered softly, before he was gone.

99

Ninety Nine

D^{alin}

Flashing white then orange; forks of lightning and then bursts of flame.

The rain sliced down like falling arrows, stinging any exposed flesh and sending splatters of ricocheting, bloodied mud exploding upward.

Each breath was like a sharp battle of its own and each little slip was an age of uncertainty.

Exhausted and outnumbered, I caught the weight of an opponent on the point of my sword. His breath warmed my cheek as he slumped against me and the sky was slashed with white.

White then orange.

His grey teardrops fell and then he was sinking backward to join the other bodies in the all-consuming mud at our feet.

Another blast of fire imprinted my vision with tens of thousands of churning limbs and weapons, and I saw my despair mirrored on the faces of all of those who were dying, and those who were slaying.

It was endless. It was hopeless. And then suddenly the earth was moving with a new shuddering, resounding boom.

The ground began to rumble as if a hundred Rucksha were surfacing and a hundred Dragons were landing at once.

I heard the fear and despondence all around me.

'Is it the Sorcerer King?'

'He has come for us at last!'

'STAY ALERT!' I bellowed darkly. 'LIFT YOUR WEAPONS!'

'Gods,' I heard Noal breathe.

From behind the Jenran and Awyalknian base there emerged hulking, impossibly colossal shadows, distorted by the rain.

Some were glowing blue.

Others glimmered gold.

Hundreds upon hundreds of them marching closer while the ground jolted beneath their weight.

I winced then as another fork of lightning, brighter than the rest, split the sky. And it did not fade.

Thale grunted in surprise beside me as the light made his opponent pause. I frowned in consternation too, finding myself without a new challenger.

'What is this?' Purdor panted, waving a hand in front of his foe – who was staring at the swelling silvery-white illumination.

'Why would Darziates halt his own soldiers?' Vulcan shoved at his nearest stunned opponent, but received no reaction.

Phobos shook his throbbing arms, relieved by the sudden, shocking reprieve. And now I heard many cries of confusion and gladness as the men around us found their unfocused enemies stood frozen too.

'They've all stopped!' Wolf called out. 'They're hypnotised by the light.'

'What the frarshk is that?' I heard one Griffin hiss, and I realised that though the Sorcerer's beasts hadn't been stilled, the Dragons and Rucksha seemed confused as well.

'It's hurting me,' another Griffin whined uneasily.

'Can you feel that?' Thorin asked, his own opponent shielding his blank eyes and cowering from the growing light. 'The air feels ...'

'Like energy,' Cadell supplied. But he frowned as he watched the soldiers nearest him now whimpering in confusion. 'Good energy.'

'The *Larnaeradee*,' voices began to cry out. Some in fear, some in wonder.

All at once the defined shape of my One emerged from the light and Krall's soldiers started to reanimate. Enemy bodies now moved to converge under the light that was Kiana – conflicted by the desire to churn away from her magic, and by the need to get closer to it.

Thousands of Jenran and Awyalknian voices lifted with renewed hope and ferocity.

'For our world! And for us all!' Kiana roared, and the magical races behind her surged forward to join our mortal ranks in a glorious wave.

100

One Hundred

Kiana

Angra Mainyu bellowed from atop the wall and the Evexus screeched and stalked through Krall's confused soldiers, trying to scare them back into a frenzy. Galvanised, the Sorcerer's men fought on, but their crazed, spellbound bloodlust had been broken.

Gold Dargons were colliding with grey Dragons across the purpling sky. Like glowing flames the Nymphs were dancing through the rain and making skyward pathways of fire through the Griffins. Elves engaged with hissing Evexus while Giants and Dwarves set about pounding the Rucksha out of existence. And hordes of Gnomes ran gleefully through them all, tripping soldiers, covering Evexus and overrunning the Rucksha in cackling swarms.

Griffins dropped like snow as I passed through the air myself, their mottled brown feathers turning silvery grey as they fell away, leaving a clear view of Razek's men fanned out behind Krall's lines, cutting off retreat.

I wiped rivers of rain from my eyes, turning in the air until my spirit leapt at the feel of the Unicorn horn, and the sight of my own magic over the heart of my prince.

Then the rest of the world blurred as I fought my way to where he moved with enhanced grace and balance, each gesture filled with speed and precision.

He felt me coming, and he whirled to face me while the soldiers who had been battling my princes and Krall warriors stared and shrank back – pawing at their faces as oily magic drained from their eyes.

I threw up a magical shield to keep them away as Dalin held his arms out and I threw myself into his embrace in the middle of the battle ground.

Pulling back and seeing past the mud spatters and rain that dripped from his hair, down his cheeks, from the tip of his nose and away from his chin, I saw those green eyes searching mine with just as much feeling.

Those green eyes were even sharper now, seeming to flash and burn, and I placed my fingers over the illuminated handprint that showed through the material clinging to his chest.

'I must thank the Gods that Darziates maimed you with his magic rather than with his sword,' I managed to say. 'Or I would not have been able to heal you.'

Dalin let a flicker of a smile touch his chilled lips. 'Now is the first time I feel truly healed,' he uttered in response.

'Even in the middle of a war you are spectacular,' Noal laughed from behind me, before I felt his own sopping arms surround both Dalin and myself.

'You'll be just as grand and hope inspiring in the Dwarvish armour I've brought for you,' I told him.

'Kiana! Great to see you!' I heard Thale exclaim. 'But your shield is putting off the enemies, and we must appear rather exuberant to everyone else doing battle outside this bubble.'

'Hush Thale, the reprieve is nice! We're definitely not complaining,' Ferron assured me, allowing Phobos and Cadell to help him wrench his sunken legs out of the sloppy mud.

'Still, perhaps we should resume our contributions,' Thorin sighed, right as a decapitated Rucksha head splattered against the surface of the bubble.

'No, you're all needed elsewhere now,' I informed them, just as I sensed the pounding of a Giant's footsteps.

'Sorry we're late!' Ahanu boomed as he skidded to a stop through my dome's wall, showering Ferron in mud again. Phobos avoided the shower, stepping backward out of the bubble in shock so that his boot sank into the boulderman's head.

'We got caught up with a Rucksha!' Einion added excitedly as he squelched in to join his father.

'Ah,' Ahanu exclaimed cheerfully. 'I see you've found its head,' he congratulated Phobos with a mighty pat on the back. 'You're actually standing right in its nostril.'

Toru was more dignified as he caught up, stepping on enemies and sweeping them out of his path before he entered the bubble. He merely nodded politely before stooping to pick up a handful of my stunned Krall warriors.

'Right you are my friend,' Ahanu agreed. 'Rucksha hunting must wait. We are to be the transport.'

Thale gaped as he and five others were scooped up next.

Einion rounded up the stragglers while I took Dalin's free hand – lifting us into the air and following the Giants as my bubble disintegrated.

Ahanu walked over ten startled enemies in a single step, heading off and crossing the chaos easily while my comrades warbled. The three Giants only stopped to set their Krall warriors down when they reached a crowd of similarly stunned mortal leaders who had already been collected – plucked unceremoniously from their battles and placed in a protective circle of magical beings with Ace and Frey.

Asha soon carried Spud along, and Vidar and Bard also appeared, depositing a delighted looking Conall beside an already delivered King Glaidin.

Then Scandra touched down regally, and the circle expanded in a rush.

'We are united,' I said, and raised a new protective bubble to block out the sounds of the battle and the storm. 'Now it's time to take control before the Sorcerer reacts.'

'The magical races have already allowed us to regroup,' Aeron rumbled, appearing relieved even as he held a bloodied rag to his head.

'The mortal lines will now be able to advance,' I agreed. 'And each of the magical races have different skills they can use to support that advance.'

'So we now have every means for progressing to the walls,' Dalin frowned, beginning to realise why I had gathered everyone. 'But what then?'

'The gates are shut,' Noal grimaced. 'And behind them ...'

'Darziates,' Asha glowered.

'We will be fortunate if he does stay behind his walls,' Frey commented. 'He could tear his way through us all in moments.'

'Then how can we triumph over the Sorcerer, and the threat against our world?' King Durna asked.

'I need to go back,' I answered. 'I need to face him again. On my terms.'

As I spoke I felt Dalin's hand tighten around mine and there was a pause in our muted dome.

'Tell us what you need,' Frey said at last.

'We'll need more men to bolster the thinned out lines of Lixrax. They must form a solid barrier against the wall,' I began.

'And someone will need to take care of *him*,' Conall glared across the battlefield at the distant figure of Angra Mainyu stalking up and down the wall. 'My Warlord counterpart seems somehow to be controlling the Evexus' movements.'

'We also need to transplant a large number of men to breach the walls,' Glaidin added. 'Infiltrating the city.'

'Well, it turns out Giants make great people movers,' Ahanu suggested. 'I could take a handful of fifteen men easily.'

'I could take more than fifty,' Scandra announced dryly, the embers dancing between her teeth in the dark. 'If they hold on.'

'So a few Giants here and there and a Dargon or two, and we have the wall covered,' Vidar reasoned.

'To defend our position at the wall ...' Durna shared a glance with Aeron, who nodded.

'We men of Jenra are excellent archers. And very good climbers,' Aeron told the gathering.

'We're great climbers too,' Spud added, sizing the Jenran up. 'If a few Gnomes scale the wall before you, we can break hand holds into the rock to make the process faster. But, even better,' Spud grinned impishly then. 'While your archers distract everyone, the Dwarves can get started on tunnelling under the walls and breaking through the concrete on the other side. We'll have an easy ground entry for our mortal army in no time.'

'Kiana, while all of that's happening, we could go with you,' Thorin suggested, but I shook my head.

'I am the One who can get to the Sorcerer, and the One who must,' I answered. 'And I ask only that Scandra come with me in this. For I will need more than force to defeat the Sorcerer.' I looked to her. 'I will need truth.'

'Of course, dear One,' Scandra agreed, her eyes narrowing in understanding. 'You will not be alone.'

101

One Hundred and One

A *grudek*

Something had kept him alive across the wastelands.

Something had forced his soul to stay tethered to his withering physical body.

Then something had helped him to move unnoticed, and to find a small drain in the castle walls.

He had been able to burrow through the slime like a worm, passing into Krall's capital, right into a courtyard within the gates. And there, in the shadow of the narrow drain, something had kept him. Urging him to wait.

He waited there still. His red raw eyes staring. His breath whistling between cracked teeth – broken from constant falls. And his Sorcery-torn mind, baked and clouded in the dusty heat, then addled in the terrible wet, couldn't remember much now. Other than the fact that he was going to find the evil one.

He paid little heed to the echoes of the war on the other side of his drain. And he watched only blankly even when there was sudden action right on the wall to the courtyard in front of him.

He felt only slight recognition as the *Larnaeradee* passed over and dropped the Raiden onto the wall and out of sight.

He watched, unmoved when there was next a boom of fire before an incredible golden beast landed in the courtyard, carrying a mass of soldiers on her back.

But then something hurtled down from the wall and into the courtyard. A sharp thing that clattered against the stones with a shower of golden sparks. A bright thing that felt inexplicably pure as it skidded to a stop just near where he huddled.

And something told him to slither out into the rain and to take it. To tuck it into his ruined robes. To carry it with him as he limped on, unnoticed, toward the castle.

Armoured men of the Sorcerer rushed about to begin closing the city sector's internal gates, ushering him in without a second glance. For he looked like nothing more than a frightened urchin leaving the commotion.

102

One Hundred and Two

D*alin*

The mighty Empress Scandra flew ahead of us and a warm hand held tightly to mine.

Our bodies, clad in shimmering, lightweight armour, rose and dipped through the tumultuous wind, the scars of lightning, the din of the thunder, and the clouds of churning Griffins.

And I could almost feel Kiana's silvery magic pulsating in my chest like a new heart beat, humming through my veins permanently now.

'Many of Darziates' soldiers are waking up,' I heard Kiana say. 'I see so many of them, standing still in the middle of the chaos. Crying away his magic.'

We jolted upwards, riding over the turbulence left in Scandra's wake. I heard the soldiers on her wet back groaning as they grimly held on.

'If Darziates stays away his soldiers could be healed just by the magic in the atmosphere,' I agreed.

I sighted Noal below in his shining armour, like a guiding star amongst crowds of glowing Giants. He was directing large numbers of our soldiers to be collected for transportation through Krall's ranks, and while the Giants lifted fifteen or so men each, they also allowed countless others to cling to their backs or arms before they began to run.

Immediately I noticed the energy of Lixrax burning anew as Giant after Giant bounded into their midst with reinforcements. Beyond that I could see the Gnomes crunching their way up the wall while at its base a group of Dwarves held small hands out over the mud. It was hardening and shifting; clearing and dropping away in a circular shape that would become a large tunnel in no time.

'Those Dwarves have talent,' I observed.

'You think the wall is impressive? Look back to our base,' Kiana told me, and I squinted back to our previously battered healer section in the distance.

I gaped as I saw that the land beneath the besieged wagons and tents had been raised and solidified so that they were stable.

I felt a surge of energy from Kiana as well, and a shimmering roof of pure magic suddenly spread over that area, forcing the Griffins that had been trying to make easy meals of the wounded to suddenly disperse.

'So if we win this?' I asked.

'We can heal this landscape, I am sure of it,' Kiana answered. 'Natural life will be possible here with the Lady and magical races' aid.'

We heard cries from ahead then as a swarm of Griffins made to pick off the soldiers clinging precariously to Scandra's spikes.

Kiana rotated quickly, sending me flying to land on the Empress' back. I quickly raised the Unicorn horn and ran my way along the Dargon's spine, ducking and slicing at the feathered beasts within reach while Kiana attacked them from the air.

I ran and slashed until there was no more Dargon left, and plunged off the tip of Scandra's snout to land with a choke hold on another Griffin that had been darting at her eyes.

'Frarshk you!' it howled before I stabbed it with the horn tip and then hurtled down to land on another.

'GETOFFFF,' the next Griffin squealed, and it shot upwards at breakneck speed, whirling crazily through the flock.

I was consumed by a flurry of feathers, curses and a foul, burning stench until a nice blaze was going and I dropped back down to be caught by Kiana again.

'One, we are close!' I heard the strange, exotic sound of the Dargon Queen's voice. 'It's time we play our part!'

'You're right, my friend,' Kiana called back, and I felt a tug of her magic as we soared with a final burst of speed to be high over the wall.

Scandra angled herself downwards to drop her men off below, clearing the way with a plume of fire.

'Ready?' Kiana asked me.

'For that I am,' I motioned down at the fuming Warlord of Krall. 'But not to let go of this,' I squeezed her hand.

'Never fear. I won't really leave you,' she replied, glancing at my chest. 'I now forever have a hold over your heart.'

'You already did,' I answered honestly, and I pulled her hand to my lips before letting it go.

Losing contact with her felt like a physical blow as I free-fell down to the wet stone ramparts.

She paused a moment, before she and the silver light surrounding her moved on across the sky toward the castle.

'What have we got here?' I heard from behind me then. And I turned to face Angra Mainyu.

His body, exuding an arctic chill, seemed oddly swollen; his skin grey and puckered. He was like a bruised, dented fruit that had gone rotten inside.

There were cracks around his glowing eyes as his gaze was drawn from me, to where Conall was sliding along a slippery golden tail to land beside me on the stone ledge. Then a moment later another powerful figure was pulling up onto the ledge from the outside of the wall. Aeron.

The Unicorn horn burned like a bright warning in my hand as the Warlords of Jenra and Awyalkna joined me against what was left of the Warlord of Krall.

'You've got a challenge. That's what you've got here,' Conall told Angra Mainyu.

And Angra snarled in contempt. Charging forward.

103

One Hundred and Three

The Lady

She stood at the edge of the forest, looking out, knowing it was nearly time to let go and move forward. To start her next task in guiding and healing the world beyond.

She pressed her hands against the cool bark of the trees before at last turning back. Crossing lush carpets of grass and brushing her fingertips over bobbing flowers – taking her time to get to the clearing she had chosen.

When she reached the circular clearing she stepped forward to peer into the round pool at the heart of the dell, gazing at her rippling reflection.

Beneath the surface image of auburn hair and glowing brown skin she could see her true self – her spirit dancing and surging, waiting to be free. To be allowed to grow.

Feeling ready, the Lady dipped her fingers into the glittering pool, and sent her thoughts towards the oceans, the rivers, and all hydrating springs and wells. She willed her magic to go toward nourishing every channel of water in the world and, as she focused, tiny pinpricks of blue light twirled daintily around her body and away from her, skipping their way into the water and beyond while in turn her reflection grew hazy.

She leaned back a little, closer to the final resting place of her long passed friends, Sylranaeryn and Kinrilowyn. And she was serene.

Now she held her hands out to catch the warmth of the sunlight, and this time she let some of her spirit dance into the air. With the beautiful sensation of release, her delicate arms became surrounded in more twirling pinpricks of light, bright white stars that circled her fingers and rose into the sky, floating free into the atmosphere.

She slowly laid back into the grass and saw that the shapes of her outstretched arms were harder to define, as if she were fading or becoming translucent. But even as she was growing increasingly faint, she let her hands rest upon the grass, allowing bursts of green light to dash away from her and into the earth.

Finally, as she seemed to shimmer where she laid, looking like only the last remnants of a heavenly dream, the Lady thought of the world's races in their time of need, and of Kiana.

The Lady smiled and turned her eyes up to the circular opening in the trees above the clearing. She put her hands to her heart and a glowing rainbow light swelled there.

And as she faded, the light grew.

Burning brighter and brighter, until her hair, her eyes, her smile, her dress, her body were no longer there.

The rainbow flame finally shone so magnificently that it burst, exploding forth into a shimmering flock of a hundred coloured, singing birds.

In a rush of liberated energy and joy, the rainbow flock swirled in a cloud up and out of the clearing. Bursting out into the world.

104

One Hundred and Four

The Witch

The wet rolled off the tip of her bent, burnt beak and pooled under tattered feathers that were no longer water proof.

Her clawed, scarred feet scrabbled to find a hold as she landed heavily on the saturated castle wall.

Her shoulders bunched as she panted and drew her wings in, and she squawked at the demented being who had been pacing the wall, somehow directing the Evexus. Somehow part of them.

What was left of Angra Mainyu laughed when he saw her. Laughter, despite the fact that the battle behind them was becoming frenzied, and their possessed mortals would likely soon be overcome, by death or by awakening to purity.

'Not going to shape shift for me this time, Witch?' the Warlord asked in a loud, multilayered voice.

He was in some way half the man he'd been, and yet seemed doubled in presence. At another time she could have liked him with this twisted new sickness, but she hissed at him, and glowered.

'You want my help again, don't you, vermin?' he cackled.

The fool actually seemed pleased with how his war was progressing. Glad that the enemy was getting closer. Glad even that Lixrax had turned.

She glanced up, straining her bulging neck, to direct his gaze to the silvery light approaching in the sky. The 'One'.

'Still jealous at our King's infatuation with that *Larnaeradee*?' Angra Mainyu's grin widened, and his ashen skin pulled tight. 'So she's going back to him. He's won her over. He's won. He'll plant his seeds, spawn greatness, and we'll watch the new world grow. This battle is nothing.'

Agrona made a gurgling sound, enraged.

'Who cares about all this? He doesn't. This is just one part of a major play, bringing all the pieces of the game together.' Angra swept his meaty hand beyond them. It seemed to be pulsing and swelling – ready to burst. His fingers were increasing in size to look like overfilled sausage skins.

'I can control this scuffle,' Angra smirked through fattened lips. 'Let them all dash themselves apart at our walls. And then once the herd has been culled the King can come out with his Queen and sweep through the rest of the world, converting what's left.'

Agrona bristled. Angra was useless and her maker, her sire, had let his focus slip. He was letting it all slip. The purity was breaking their army ... and it was breaking Darzi-ates too.

He truly could have appeared right then, and ended all the mess in a moment. But instead, though time was precious, he waited. For a *Larnaeradee*.

Agrona watched as the silvery light passed over them with a revolting wave of goodness, heading toward the castle while a princeling was dropped onto the ramparts.

She realised that the princeling too had somehow become more, before a golden Dragon landed inside Krall's walls, depositing warriors while a tunnel was also opening magically into the courtyard below.

Angra again stretched his bulging lips into a smile, even when he noticed that the wall was swarming now with agile climbers, mortal and immortal. who were scaling their way up.

Angra turned from her, unintentionally hiding her from view, and she dropped down to take cover in the shadows of the ledge.

'What do we have here?' Angra asked the Raiden, as if a breached kingdom was only worth his piqued curiosity.

The Witch was unsurprised as Angra stupidly ran at the enhanced Raiden and his Warlords instead of calling back some Evexus helpers. And she watched darkly as the Raiden launched into combat.

They were both skilled swordsmen, but Angra's body was weighed down – bloated, rotting and dense.

The agonisingly pure weapon in the Raiden's hands lopped off more and more of Angra's anatomy, and with each sweep Angra's new Demon spirit dissipated little by little and his strength waned.

Angra, or the spirit inside him, seemed infuriated as each bit of his inadequate casing degraded and dropped away. He fought even harder, but used no caution while the Raiden ducked, leaned and retaliated much too quickly.

At last Agrona heard Angra howl in rage, spiked through the middle by the Raiden's weapon – which burned right through Angra's spiked armour.

Angra struggled, widening the hole until his thrashing weakened and finally a rush of steaming hot air burst free from his gut.

The storm seemed to be abating even as the Raiden pushed the dead Warlord off his weapon. The purple sky was starting to lighten and an awful feeling of hope seemed to saturate the very cobblestones beneath her.

In a fit of rage Agrona painfully spread her wings and launched herself at the Raiden, swooping towards his heart with her vicious talons outstretched, building her seething, erratic red magic.

With a harsh cry she thudded heavily into his chest, clawing and snapping, but she did not expect the sudden explosion of pure magic that clashed with hers and Agrona was pelted up into the sky, where she fought to stay airborne.

The Raiden was thrown back and the magical weapon was sent flying from his hands, down into the courtyard where it seemed to disappear as the prince and Warlords rushed to peer down after it, disregarding her as a threat entirely.

'Do not worry Raiden,' the Jenran Warlord said as he straightened. 'The horn will find its way back into the right hands, and it will be useless for most others.'

Reeling in indignant fury, the raven screeched loudly. But even her outrage was cut off by the sounds of new cries beyond the wall.

'What is that?' the Awyalknian Warlord asked, his eyes wide as what appeared to be a massive, multi coloured cloud surged into view over the battlefield.

It swarmed in a mass, forming shapes and rising and falling quickly, but Agrona realised that it wasn't a cloud. It was a flock of birds of all colours, shapes and sizes, and they seemed to be bringing the sunlight with them.

Those multi-coloured birds held magic. An ancient magic that promised life and natural growth.

And it was the final insult.

Agrona turned raggedly in the air, knowing beyond doubt now that she had to be the one. The one to put a stop to all of this flourishing rejuvenation.

It was up to her. And it was time for her to take over. Or they would lose.

105

One Hundred and Five

*K*iana

I felt nauseated as I returned willingly to the Sorcerer, forcing myself to continue through the thick waves of anger, grief and desire roiling from his balcony.

My wet skin prickled as if the Demon of fevers was running his fingernails over my arms, but I braced myself and landed carefully and conspicuously on the open balcony where Darziates was observing me from the high ceilinged chamber inside.

Warily, I took paced steps into the lofty entrance and out of the rain – his eyes following each move.

'You have come back to me,' he said at last, and his granite eyes almost took my breath away.

'I have come back to destroy you,' I answered, though I was very aware of how easy it would be to lose myself again in his delusions.

'Then ... you have come to destroy yourself,' he stated quietly, his gaze burning on my face.

'Perhaps,' I agreed. 'I am not afraid of that.'

He shook his head almost imperceptibly, taking a cautious step toward me. 'But why would you choose it? I offer my love, and would share the greatest responsibility of all time with you.'

I subdued a shudder. 'Even your love is used in a hateful way. To meet your goals,' I replied, feeling as if he was pulling me towards himself, though he was not physically reaching out.

'I love in my own way. With total devotion, and with appreciation for the advantages that a union between those such as us could have.' He stepped closer again and I felt I might lose my balance. 'I want a union of strength, and so should you. Unlike the past *Larnaeradee*, who allowed their dependency on the Unicorns to become their undoing.'

I squared my shoulders. 'Well then, let us test how well we would match,' I said, trying not to let my voice shake. 'Let's see if we could really make each other stronger.'

'You are willing to try?' he asked slowly, and though he surely felt a growing, golden power approaching behind me, my words held his attention.

He stepped closer to where I was framed in the vast doorway.

'You are willing to try to unite with me, and to join in my quest for this world?'

He moved to within reaching distance, and his arms lifted toward me slightly. I felt nearly overwhelmed by the force surrounding him.

'I am willing to show you that you're wrong in your desires for the two of us, and wrong in your quest,' I answered.

He slowly closed the short distance between us and placed his hands on my arms, focusing on me intently even while the sounds of beating Dargon wings drew closer to the balcony.

'I mean to secure this world,' he told me gently. 'I am saving life.'

It felt as if he was setting me on fire, his touch burning me all over.

'You are subduing and stifling the world,' I told him. 'You cannot nourish life, or me, in such a way.'

He came closer to help me stay upright – and at the same time made me weaker in his support.

'I am welcoming the tenth age with war and blood, so that there can be rebirth.'

'You are creating a world of death.'

His hands pressed my back as I lost my balance, but there was only more pain in his touch.

'How can you keep this world alive, or a union between us alive,' I asked imploringly, 'when your touch is killing the nature inside me?'

'I will sustain you,' he promised, leaning forward as if to place his lips on mine. 'I will sustain it all.'

I flinched, but then the expansive balcony behind us shuddered as Scandra at last burst through sheets of rain, setting down and flooding the darkened room around us with the feel of her golden magic.

Her eyes were already blazing with internal fire, swirling so much that I quickly glanced away before I was drawn into her gaze. But the Sorcerer frowned in transfixed fascination, his eyes held by hers – for she had caught him off guard for perhaps the first time in his entire existence.

'I am here to show you the truth, Sorcerer,' Scandra told Darziates. 'For you think that you have sacrificed your soul to save the world. But the path you have chosen – of unyielding hate and a willingness to destroy, means you can never be the one to heal it. Instead, you are the one to threaten it.'

Blinking up at him I found that he was frozen, his granite eyes now swirling with gold fire instead of stone and ice as he saw whatever she was forcing him to see.

'You are the threat,' I told him in a whisper, and each word caused a ripple in the spinning magic that permeated the room. 'You are the one monstrous thing that we all must defeat. In trying to mistakenly conquer the world, you will be its destroyer.'

His grip had tightened around me, but Scandra's magic was strengthening me and I could hear sounds of battle around the city sectors now. The walls had been breached.

'There are gardens and farms covering all of Awyalkna,' I went on. 'The people of Jenra flourish within a mountain by the ocean. In Lixrax, the desert is their home. The island nations survive by air, rock and sea. And the forest dwellers draw life from the very trees. But here in Krall there is nothing natural. Health is damaged, youth is taken, and the land chokes. You create only an imitation of life and nature. Here, where your quest has left you dead inside, you threaten to spread that death. Here, you threaten to become the world's greatest peril.'

'You are twisting the words of the prophecy,' Darziates almost winced, managing to speak even as his fire filled gaze was held by Scandra's. 'My ancestors had to do something. I am the one who has been needed.'

'You are not fully informed,' I answered softly, straightening. 'It was never up to you or your line to take charge, instead your rule is what we have had to unite and defend against.'

With each heaving breath, rivers ran down Scandra's scales, however the sky behind her was beginning to change and to lighten. 'Sorcerer,' her voice simmered, and the velvety word coiled elegantly from her poised, sharp tongue as she lowered her mighty head into the room and out of the weather. 'You just have to keep looking into my eyes, and you will see the truth.'

Possibly by choice, I felt him succumb to his curiosity. He became rigid, completely ensnared, and I remembered the feeling of slipping away from everything else.

Knowing that nothing could now break Scandra's hold, I was just beginning to carefully pull myself away from the entranced Sorcerer when suddenly a cold, wet grip clamped on my wrist and I was abruptly dragged from his arms to fall to the floor.

'So he would hold you in an affectionate embrace? Trust you with his mind? And ... his heart?'

It took me a moment to register the identity of the woman now snarling down at me, and then my eyes widened as I took in the ghastly remains of Agrona.

Even as my wings flashed into action, propelling me rapidly away, I could not tear my gaze from the few straggles of black hair that clung to her blistered face and to her bubbled, humped back.

She gurgled in fury and drew her gnarled hands up as high as they could go, letting red lightning build erratically between them.

'I may be ruined,' she rasped. 'But everything I have left is reserved for destroying you.'

Then her stooped body stretched back fast as she sent the explosive red blast at me. And though I raised a sheen of magic as my shield, the blast threw me backward to smash into the far wall, my head clattering against the stone.

My wings caught me as I tumbled downward, but when I righted myself I saw Agrona again poised as if readying to crack a whip of magic, this time towards Sandra.

I rushed to catch and block the blast, which exploded around us and brought a shower of debris down from the ceiling and walls. But before I could recover I was winded by a sizzling sphere of red magic, which crackled into my armour with such volatile force that my stomach burned with the heat and I was thrown backward against Darziates.

I winced at the painful contact with the Sorcerer, yet even worse, as I held my hands up in defence I realised that the red sphere of energy pinning me in place was not fading. It was instead swelling as Agrona forced a continuous stream of magic into it that arced from her own hands and across the chamber like a bridge of evil light.

The jet of power was starting to scorch my palms and I was surprised by the effort it took just to let my own magic form into protective gloves.

I had to push until my head pounded before at last a few inches of my magical torrent could push hers back.

She was throwing every ounce of her life force into trying to burn me out of existence and her fingers seemed to be curving backward with the strain. Her face was distorting and sagging further, dropping in on itself. But she hardly seemed to notice.

My muscles were straining and my breaths were heaving as I fought to push her power back, but the red light hardly receded while I was driven harder against Darziates, and his energy was enough to put spots in my vision.

I realised I could hear faint catches of what Darziates was hearing, and it was the familiar voice of the Lady, her words replaying as they had when I'd shared the memory with Scandra.

If the world does not unite before the beginning of the tenth age, and the threat is able to succeed, the world will be destroyed in a storm of ice and fire.

I heard Agrona cursing as she kept driving her magic towards me and the air smelled singed and sour.

Darziates grunted in consternation, and images of what he was seeing flashed fleetingly and disconcertingly before my eyes.

Images of the creation of the Lady's and the Gods' world – green, lush, vibrant, and thriving with life and abundancy. Then images of a dry, lifeless, dark landscape. Krall?

No. His internal landscape. Worse – much worse than Wilmont's had been.

I shook my head to try to clear it, getting dizzier with the buffeting of Agrona's magic.

My own magic had stretched forward a yard or two across the chamber, but hers was billowing out and around mine, getting close to Scandra's nose, and I shook as I tried to hold it back.

'Please,' I moaned to the Sorcerer and Scandra. 'Wake up!'

But they both kept dreaming, interlocked in their visions, and I had no idea if things would in fact be worse, or what Darziates might choose to do even if he did wake up.

I refocused properly on Agrona when I heard her cry out sharply, and through the spots in my vision I started when I saw that a small, wretched figure had staggered through the chamber doors to throw itself at the Witch.

I gasped as I squinted toward the urchin who was viciously clawing at Agrona, for the creature was Agrudek, who had shrunken in on himself – his scrawny body being swallowed by soiled robes.

The spindly inventor's jerky stabbings elicited another scream from Agrona, her magic sparking at the disturbance, and I realised with a jolt that Agrudek's weapon was the golden Unicorn horn.

Agrona screeched when Agrudek managed to drive the horn right into the solid hump deforming her back, making her lurch forward so that her stream of magic slammed me harder into Darziates.

I cried out with the agony and also heard a burst of the Lady's words again, her voice now recounting the end of the second prophecy.

Live in joy and love. Create life and goodness.

Guide the Three to bring the world to the steps to freedom.

There was another flickering glimpse of the disturbingly dark landscape that Darziates' consciousness seemed to be exploring, but then his mind appeared to notice my agonised presence and I felt his body moving. He was turning, and then an arm was coming around my waist – drawing me into a supporting embrace that stung and clouded my world even more.

I fought to refocus, and to straighten against Darziates' bracing arms while I heard Scandra roar with anger at the sight before her waking eyes.

I had managed to keep my hands out, floundering to keep my magic flowing to protect Scandra, Darziates and I from the red force of the Witch's power. But now Darziates – appearing almost taken aback by Agrona's incredible abandon, inexplicably chose to add his own magic to mine instead of hers.

Scandra also released an almighty plume of fire toward Agrona, managing to keep her steady burst of fire going, but Darziates' magic seemed to twist around mine and rebound away from it at the same time.

'You would choose them?' Agrona screamed in a breaking voice. '*Them?*'

Darziates appeared truly floored as he glanced at me then.

'Yes.'

But though it had become clear that he was trying to defend me; the only remaining daughter of an entire race he'd massacred – his power was counteracting mine and Scandra's. And when Agrona took a determined step away from Agrudek, kicking him and the horn free of her twisted body, we were all pushed backward by her power so that even Scandra's claws scraped and sparked alarmingly on the stone.

Darziates grunted in further surprise while Agrona laughed with manic effort and stepped forward again.

I heard a groan escape my lips, feeling suffocated by the unnatural powers surrounding me, even as one was directed, bizarrely, toward helping me.

At last I cried out: 'we can't work together,' and I felt him flinch. He knew it too.

'Your magic is adding to hers, even if you don't intend it to,' I gasped helplessly.

'Yet something incredible has been unlocked in Agrona. And if I let go ...'

Scandra's fire stopped as she heaved a mighty breath. 'We won't survive without your help either,' the Empress panted. 'But if this standoff goes on, it will destroy everything,' she warned. 'The clashing forces of magic will disturb the atmosphere and surely ruin it.'

'Could it be that Agrona ... my creation ... has become the threat?' Darziates' face creased with uncharacteristic signs of exertion, but also wonder.

Then unexpectedly a bony, grimy hand shot out from beside Darziates and I as Agrudek thrust the horn into our stream of lashing magic.

At once parts of his one good hand started to disintegrate, but the magic we had been directing haphazardly became one focused beam.

Relieved, Darziates and I lowered our hands to the horn to join Agrudek's. Silver poured from me, and grey shadows from Darziates, all mixing together while Scandra aimed her fire back into the stream to add to the force.

Agrona cursed, stepping forward more quickly now while losing what appeared to be a mix of draggled hair and ... feathers. But we were not forced backward this time.

'The h-horn,' I heard Agrudek rattle with effort, and I squinted through the flames toward Agrudek's withering hand, gasping as I saw that the horn was turning a grey, bruised colour from the side that Darziates' power was being channelled through.

His magic was polluting the horn with splotches like disease spots, but where my magic and Scandra's fire were focused the horn glowed as vibrantly as ever.

As Agrona prowled closer again the tip of the horn started to burn red and at her next step across the chamber the red colour began to spread.

'M-my touch is as r-rotten as y-yours now,' Agrudek hissed to Darziates, his voice only just audible over the sound of the colliding forces of magic. The foul colours on the horn were spreading rapidly under his raw, bloodied grip. 'My s-soul is as corrupted.'

I cried out as one of the blossoming bruises of colour touched where my magic was channelling through the horn, but my voice was plucked away by the vacuum of air.

Darziates appeared oddly torn as his eyes shifted from the horn, to me, and around the stormy chamber. Even as he watched, his swords along the walls, his bedding, drinking glasses, even the great curtains all tore free to whip around the room.

'Well, I've made ... my choice!' Agrudek growled, and his wrist, forearm and all the way up to his sharp cheek bones seemed to be breaking down into dust – whirling away into the swirling atmosphere. 'I will be with my family ... So I must choose to be rotten no longer!'

He lifted his face as if to the heavens before releasing his hold on the horn and taking a step into the surging beam of magic.

Being consumed by the magic, a dazzling yellow glow burst outward from him – his soul alight with his pure choice, and the bruises that had been growing around his part of the horn faded as Darziates and I clutched at it.

The magic stream burst more brightly with gold and silver, and Agrona was pushed a step backward while the radiating red glow at the tip of the horn receded an inch.

Darziates was watching the fast disappearing, though sublimely smiling Agrudek as, at last, the tortured little inventor faded entirely.

The brilliance of Agrudek's spirit flared within our channel of magic, but once it was gone the horn started shaking under the pressure again.

I sobbed as Scandra's flame died then while she inhaled great gulps of air.

'Kiana ...' I felt Darziates' arm tighten around me and I again felt both better and so much worse.

My breath was coming in rasps as I struggled to breathe through the dense air, feeling as if someone was holding a thick, hot, wet gag over my nose and mouth. The room was full of spinning gales that sparked and whirled, too thick for my lungs to accept.

'She can't breathe!' Scandra gasped. 'You're both stifling her!'

The Sorcerer said nothing, but Scandra urged him on. 'You saw your truth! You need to make your own choice now!'

Agrona shrieked then, ducking at some new attack from the balcony, and I could hardly believe it when a cloud of vibrant colours and wings – a swarm of tiny, delicate birds, suddenly rushed into the chaos of the room.

Even as I rasped, a light smile played across my lips as I felt the comforting power of those rainbow birds. Their gossamer wings were spreading the cooling relief of the Lady's magic.

Darziates watched me, almost looking hurt at the obvious need I had of nature's healing.

He moved his face closer to mine to peer into my eyes, but when I gasped in pain as he jostled me his mouth hardened.

Then he pushed me away.

106

One Hundred and Six

N^{oal}

We had found ourselves blocking rather than fighting our mortal opponents while we defended the Dwarf tunnel and our men poured into Krall's capital.

But all defending, all tunnelling and all invading stopped when there was a sudden explosion from far behind the wall. The blast of swirling silver, grey and red magic burst outward from the distant castle like a growing whirlpool and we all froze, wondering if this was when the end – or new beginning – was meant to be decided.

We didn't have a chance to even shout in fear before the ground beneath us abruptly tilted up under our feet and then dropped away. Nymphs and Griffins alike suddenly lurched in their flight and Dargons and Dragons collided by mistake rather than in battle. Even the Elves, Giants, Rucksha and Evexus lost their footing and toppled.

Then there was a horrific ripping sound from all around and above us, and at once, as though the world had been punctured, we were all sucked upward.

Horses, corpses, wagons, kicking and screaming soldiers, all started to lift into the air.

Fighting to sheathe my sword I grabbed hold of my neighbour, Wolf's wrist and gripped onto a stone in the wall as my legs lifted up from underneath me.

Like backwards rainfall I saw droplets of mud move upward before my eyes, and a Gnome went spiralling and swearing past my face as he tried to kick himself to a stop – instead pin-wheeling faster upwards.

'There's a light growing over the castle!' Phrixus called in warning. He was now high enough above where Wolf and I floated to see over the wall. 'Oh Gods! It's going to –'

Before another explosion rapidly rippled outward, a swell of rushing noise, gales and light.

Everyone was knocked out of the air again, thrown hard into the muddy ground as the boiling rushes of energy blasted our hair back and ripped at our skin.

And all we could do was curl up in the mud to helplessly wait – eyes squeezed closed, hands over bursting ears, knees up to protect our chests while the roaring of the magic sucked our screams away.

107

One Hundred and Seven

*K*iana

I was launched outside, skidding across the balcony before I dizzily rolled to look back toward the roiling chamber.

The horn was shaking in Darziates' grip and Scandra was sagging. The colourful birds were struggling to pierce the turbulent winds to dart at Agrona in the eye of the storm, but the Witch was undeterred.

Her haggard hands maintained relentless streams of magic despite how her arms curved backward and her skin charred and flaked away.

The stone floors of the chamber were rippling and cracking under the pressure. Furniture, glass and loose stones were being dragged in circles, banging against the groaning, shaking walls. The air beyond the balcony was sparking, being sucked inward toward that building tornado inside the castle.

After the moment's reprieve I stood, lifting my own hands and sending a new arc of silver light toward Agrona so that she had to disrupt her blast to deflect my attack with one almost backward curling hand.

The terrible atmospheric shredding sound receded a little as Agrona's focus was split now, her gaze fixing on me instead of returning to the single minded onslaught she had been building inside.

'You ...' her hateful lips snarled through the tumult.

'You,' I returned. 'The one who took so much from me.' I let my eyes flick to her Sorcerer. 'And now here I am. Taking everything from you.'

Furiously screeching, her radiating red power curled up over her melting arms – rolling up her shoulders and ebbing against her smoking core.

'I have found my true power, I have proven myself,' she shrieked at me. 'I have lost nothing to you!'

With hate filled eyes Agrona gestured at one of the sparks burning in the air and the spark flared up before a terrifying splitting noise seemed to bring time to a stop.

A tear became visible in the air, a widening wound in the atmosphere, and Agrona's ruined lips curled. She jerked her hand, and suddenly a shadow had pulled itself free of the mid-air rip.

Behind that shadow a red and grey misted skyline was almost blotted out by masses of more writhing shadows jostling to be free.

I heard the Sorcerer shout in warning and then saw the first deliriously happy, vicious Other Realm spirit careening straight for me. I quickly formed a translucent shield as the Demon vapour, shaped like an intangible Evexus, manifested and drove me backward, boring into my chest and pushing me roughly into the ground. My shoulder blades and wings were mashed against cold stone as the spectre lashed against my shield, before it had to turn and disappear back to the rent open slash in the air.

Agrona was laughing, alight with energy despite how her physical body was dropping away.

'I am reborn on the eve of the new age! An invincible Queen of the Evexus. Of the world!'

She sent two fresh Other Realm Demons steaming my way while Darziates kept hold of the Unicorn horn – now splintering and emanating with darkness.

'At last, my Witch has been able to summon great magic,' the Sorcerer managed, his words inside our minds as much as spoken aloud, and I shuddered as I remembered him for who he truly was. 'You are willing to sacrifice all you've got for the cause.'

'Now you can choose me,' the Witch cried, and I noticed that all of the openings in her flesh were radiating red – as if she would shed her skin and become a whole new threatening creature.

'You can still be my companion in greatness!' she yelled at her Sorcerer wildly.

And for a moment he was silent.

Then he carefully enunciated each word of his response.

'Even now, you are not enough.'

Agrona slumped and pawed at her burning chest. 'I am EVERYTHING!' she screamed.

But her voice was coloured with awful desolation.

'No. You're nothing that I want.'

Then, like Agrudek had, Darziates stepped forward, into the surrounding magic that had been created by the horn.

Inexplicably, incredibly, the Sorcerer of Krall made a choice to embrace a power that was opposite to everything his entire being was made of. Willing to sacrifice himself for a cause.

The beam of light flared brightly – purely radiant at his single selfless choice, and Agrona wailed in shock, her red magic slowing and the crack in the atmosphere shrinking fast.

My demon attackers squealed and dissipated as her attention slipped, and it was the chance I needed to be able to take my turn in giving my all now as well.

In abandon I built my own magic. Everything I had inherited for this particular moment.

Silvery light grew around me and I struggled to keep my eyes on the Witch as the sky seemed to inhale, sucking me upward with a pulling force – everything natural about the atmosphere reversing and breaking. My stomach muscles tightened and my teeth gritted with the effort of staying grounded and the magic became a glowing sphere around me, a spinning world of its own.

I put everything I had into the building power – the memory and love for all those who had been lost, and whose power I was part of.

It grew with each heartbeat, the light pulsing with my life, and it crackled as it cut through the corruptive red force surrounding the nightmare scene.

Then I launched it all towards Agrona, letting it all go.

At once I fell, gasping and clutching my chest as my energy faded. Darziates smiled grimly and the Witch yelped as the silvery light detonated over her and clashed with her power. And there was an instantaneous, blinding explosion that flung me back towards the damaged edges of the balcony once more. My fingers scrabbled to find purchase and I cried out as the rushing air plucked at me roughly.

I heard Scandra roar. There were clattering sounds and cracking sounds as the uncontrollably hurtling debris abruptly dropped. There was screaming from the Other Realm spirits as the tear totally sealed over.

I grunted then as my own body weight abruptly seemed to increase, flattening against the rubble as the sky stopped sucking upward. I blinked and gaped, my blinded eyes only catching the flashing impressions of the final vision I'd registered – an image of two battling figures, a Sorcerer and his Witch, being blown apart from each other.

Then everything was quiet.

Stillness descended.

And the world did not end.

Stars burst in my stunned eyes, my chest was heaving, and I laid still for a moment while the foundations of the castle went on creaking.

At last I shook my head, scrabbling forward as my vision returned between the flashes and dots.

Squinting, I noticed that somehow the sun had burst free of the unnatural clouds. Its rays were falling into the half destroyed chamber doorway.

'Scandra?' I called unsteadily, pulling myself over the wreckage at the entrance.

'Alive,' she coughed back and I slid over a dropped section of the roof to touch down in the hazy chamber, trying to wave the clouds of dust away.

I took a step forward, but froze when I felt a crackle under my boot.

I pressed my hands to my mouth.

I had stepped on the burnt bone of an arm.

The stained bone fingers at the end of that arm flickered with movement while Agrona, now nothing but a deformed skeleton lying on her side, suffered with the last of the magical life that still clung to her charred remains.

Oily liquid drops slithered from her empty eye sockets and I lifted my boot, staring in horror at the woman of my nightmares as her bare skull quivered and her jaw twitched as if to make a sound.

I was suspended in an agony of shock until the jaw slackened and the skull slowly stopped shaking and gradually tilted toward the floor.

Then the Witch's bones started to collapse in on themselves, disintegrating into powder before my eyes.

'Kiana?' Scandra's voice came again, sounding from behind mountains of rubble and sheets of dust.

I retreated from the Witch's remains sickly, only pausing briefly to pick up the fallen Unicorn horn, tucking it into my belt and rushing on.

Half scaling and half flying over another pile of rubble I sobbed with relief as I saw Scandra's shape through the clouds and staggered my way toward her.

'One,' she crooned gently as I leapt for her snout, hugging her as best I could.

But then I heard a wheezing sound and pulled back to look at her in apprehension.

Her eyes met mine, and then she gestured slightly – nodding her head down towards her forepaws.

Swallowing with unease I slowly lowered myself to the ground, touching down to find Darziates slumped between her great forelegs. And I was not entirely surprised to see all of the little birds huddled comfortingly close to him, as if mourning his tragedy. His fate.

His gaze rose as I carefully crouched down at his side.

When he reached for my hand I hesitantly took it, but I felt no magic there. No goodness, no darkness. No real life force at all.

He nodded faintly. 'I have been enlightened,' he said softly. 'I have been wiped clean.'

'But now you have nothing left ...'

'Yes,' he agreed. 'Because I had nothing to begin with. No soul. Only the dark.'

'Why did you step into the horn's magic?' I asked. 'When embracing the pure power was poisonous to every element of your being?'

His eyes moved away from mine.

'I saw the truth,' Darziates answered flatly. 'My truth.' He drew in a shaky breath. 'I saw everything I had ever known about myself, and I saw that I was the greatest misunderstanding and most terrible joke in creation.' Darziates looked at my hand passively. 'Then I made a choice to overcome that.'

'The new age has started with your good choice,' I said. 'Not with your threat. You can be glad of your actions in the end.'

He shook his head, gasping and letting himself sink further backward. 'I am not made to be glad of anything that is to come. Even now I wish I had succeeded. I relished everything I did for my great purpose. Every gruesome choice was what gave me meaning. I even wish I had been able to corrupt you ... though then you would be in the situation I am in now.' He drew a shuddering breath. 'I want it all still. It is who I am. Was. But instead I must let go. I must rest and desire and be driven no more.'

Scandra and the delicate little birds watched on in silence and I sat down properly beside him, swallowing carefully.

'Then I'll be right here.'

He closed his eyes. 'That is something I can be glad of. And the strangest thing of all.'

And as the sun's light crept across the room and finally fell over us in full, the Sorcerer's breaths grew weaker.

Until finally, he breathed no more.

108

One Hundred and Eight

Noal

Enemies and allies alike laid gasping in the mud, blinking blankly. Our bodies had been forced down and half buried by the pressure.

I pushed myself up, and yanked on Wolf's arm.

'Up, up, up!' I roared at the floundering Army for the World, not knowing what new evil to expect as an outcome of that magical onslaught.

Our stunned soldiers struggled to reanimate, pulling limbs free from the sludge.

Then I heard a partially submerged Dwarf nearby exclaim in surprise: 'The Evexus!'

The Dwarf pointed excitedly behind me, and I whirled to see the Elves and Giants leaning back from their foes in fascination.

The spiked nightmares that had haunted our entire quest were now fumbling around sickly. pawing at the ground in panic. And, one by one, their case-like bodies were beginning to smoke with poisonous vapour, collapsing like empty shells.

I gasped when there was a ginormous thud and one of the remaining Rucksha fell backward in the distance. It sat aimlessly on its behind as its features started to slide and melt into nothingness, and another two faraway Rucksha fell on their faces while bits of their bodies slopped off and lost shape.

'It must have been the One!' I heard someone yell.

'The Sorcerer must be dead!' a Nymph celebrated above. 'Without him, they can't survive!'

Sporadic cheers broke out but I did not smile.

'Keep focus!' I yelled. 'The Griffins and Dragons are returning to the fight, and we do not know what to expect from the people inside Krall. So keep moving!'

I saw those around me darting nervous gazes skyward and I urged the streams of men who had earlier been tumbling and slurping toward the tunnel to get going again.

'Your Highness?' an uncertain voice asked, and my attention turned to a confused Jenran as he struggled towards me. 'What do we do about the soldiers of Krall?'

I followed his uncomfortable gaze, and only then registered the sight of thousands of soldiers from the Army for the World standing over their opponents in indecision.

'We can't attack them like this,' the Jenran winced.

It appeared that, while the Army for the World had recovered from the tremendous magical detonation, not one of Darziates' mortal soldiers had risen.

A couple of nearby Awyalknians tried to pull a Krall soldier to sit up in consternation, unsure of what had stricken their foe so completely, but the soldier crumpled back down with a groan.

'See how they cry?' Wolf observed grimly, and Phrixus grunted, nauseated as he joined us and gazed at the strange battlefield of prone enemies, all crying oily tears.

'They're not our enemies any longer,' I told the waiting Jenran firmly. 'They need to be watched, not harmed.'

'Do we call in the healers?' the man asked, scratching his head.

I sighed. 'They have our wounded, and all of Krall to care for. And these men need more than the help of any healer. Spread the word that our opponents are simply to be collected and kept under guard.'

The soldier bowed, relieved after having spent the night slaying undeserving and belatedly awakening opponents as we had.

'Will they even heal?' Phrixus asked nauseously.

'Kiana was able to help you before she even had her earthstone,' I replied. 'I think there is hope.'

He nodded and straightened as we noticed a new, muddy, royal group approaching.

'You have done well, princeling!' Razek's glad voice called as he trundled through the mire beside the taller figures of Glaidin and Durna.

A brightly coloured bird was perched on the Emperor's shoulder, and another was pecking at Glaidin's hair. I noticed now that there were many more beautiful birds alighting on the inert Krall troops.

'I am glad to see you again Emperor Razek,' I smiled wearily. 'And this time I am not the only one garbed in mud.'

'Tunnels are clear! Your turn Noal!' I heard Dalin yell down from the wall above.

Glaidin waved me off to join his son. 'I can keep directing traffic here,' the King said firmly, strong despite the filth and bloodied cuts.

'Better hurry or you're going to miss the whole take over,' a new little voice warned me from the Dwarf tunnel, and I glanced down to see Spud crawling out.

'What do you mean?' Durna asked, gingerly nursing a badly burnt arm.

Spud roughly swiped at his dirty button nose. 'Our hordes of tunnel invaders had managed to split up and make it all the way to the gates of three city sectors before the magic blast of the century happened,' he explained, sitting himself back in the mouth of the tunnel and looking for all the world like an unwashed potato. 'I was there when Warlord Aeron led a force to South Krall Domain, ready to have a whole new battle on his hands. Instead, after the world stopped for those few moments, he found the civilians throwing the gates open to surrender.'

'You moved quickly to bring us this news,' I grinned, peering behind him expectantly.

'He had my help. In fact we've been all over together.' There was a rush of air then as Asha appeared at Spud's side. She stroked Spud's sprout-like hair.

'We caught up with Conall, who had marched on North Krall Province. And he found the citizens waiting for him, crying out for healers and aid. His soldiers have quickly become nurse-maids for the people there.'

'And,' Spud went on, 'Thorin and Thale are now the heroes of the Western Sector. So if you don't hurry up, you really will miss it all.'

I wondered if Thorin would already be searching for Tane's family.

'Let's go then,' I told the little beings, and slid down into the tunnel with them, hurrying to climb out on the other side while more soldiers followed on my heels.

'Finally brother!' Dalin stepped off his high-up ledge to land effortlessly at my side. 'Good to see you,' he told me seriously. 'I thought that was the end for a moment there.'

I nodded and clasped his shoulder tightly before we led our group toward the Eastern Region of Krall.

As we marched we turned our faces up toward a faintly falling sun-shower, its rainbow misting moisture washing the grime from our arms and hands and tinkling on our armour. It was cleansing Krall.

'Look there!' Phrixus cried out, and before we had reached the end of the road we saw the gates to the city sector ahead being thrown open by its civilians.

They ran toward us, calling out in surrender and relief, and in turn our forces rushed forward to meet them – with comfort instead of with a clash of violence.

'Oh thank the Gods,' I heard Dalin utter from beside me, and there were cries of joy as others gazed skyward too.

One elderly man collapsed in my arms, crying and shaking as he felt something in the air that he had never felt before. And I held him tightly, beaming up at the sky with him.

Happiness poured from the crowds and hands were reaching upward with hope and need.

Reaching up toward where Kiana was flying.

109

One Hundred and Nine

D*alin*

Rows of bony shoulders were hunched wearily in front of me, and the smell of sweat and toil permeated from the immense crowd.

The gathering was of both magical and mortal beings, all gazing out together at the final resting place of our many dead.

Sorrow hung over us, but also a sense of harmony after we had joined to create the mass grave in the wastelands, and now paid our respects and shared our grief together.

Our light, rasping whispers and lamentations were offered to the Gods, the hoarse voices of our unified peoples joining as we said our goodbyes to those who had been lost.

I thought of those I was farewelling as I held Kiana, and I was comforted to see Maeve and Noal together ahead of us.

As I watched them, their neighbour – a withered farmer of Krall, swayed under the warm sun and Noal took hold of the overcome man's sinewy arm to steady him. The man in turn placed a leathery hand over Noal's, as if enmity between Awyalkna and Krall had never existed.

Kiana gave me a squeeze then as the endless rows of mourners at last began to step back from the endless pit, leaving only the Dargons on the grave's edges.

With the shifting crowd watching on in silence, the Dargons released streams of rolling fire that filled the expansive grave like a blanket of lava.

I closed my eyes to the blinding orange light as the heat radiated over my cheeks and forehead.

I heard sobs and felt the waves of sadness as strongly as I felt the waves of heat.

It was fitting that each of the dead would rest together in unity.

And in unity, those who remained mourned them.

110

One Hundred and Ten

*K*iana

'Close your eyes and rest,' I told the child lying in my arms. 'I've got you.'

I kissed fingers that were finer than twigs, attached to brittle arms reaching up wonderingly towards my face.

He was a smaller size to what my Tommy had been, but it was impossible to tell this child's age. The little one was so malnourished that only his swollen belly showed any sign of growth. However this sight was not a new one to me, as I had gone with the healers to treat many children like this in the poorer parts of the sectors, as well as meeting too many tired adults who were numb and careful – hard faced even while polite and thankful. And the story was an even worse one as the Elves journeyed out again and brought back the neediest villagers from the border lands.

It was becoming clear to all of the 'invaders' or liberators of Krall, members of the Army for the World, that whether these people had been prosperous under Darziates or not – they had been starved of health in many ways and their recovery would take a great deal of time.

'There,' I whispered to the child as he blinked his large eyes heavily. 'You're safe.'

I settled the little one back on his cot, tucking in those small hands, and was gratified when I received a big, sleepy smile before his eyes closed.

'And you will one day learn to smile all of the time,' I promised.

I heard quiet footsteps and turned to find Maeve, drying her hands as she crossed the ward.

'Half of these patients don't understand why they've been brought here, when they're not wounded like our soldier patients,' Maeve grimaced.

I nodded in grim understanding. 'Darziates gave them a thread of life to cling to. They do not realise that one needs more than survival to be healthy. It's all they know.'

'So they're alive, but they're unwell.' Maeve let her focus shift across the room full of mortal and Elven healers. 'And now we'll fix it.'

'I have every faith that you could do it almost single-handedly,' I told her with a slight smile. 'You and your betrothed are fast becoming the champions of Krall – bestowing aid and compassion.'

Maeve's expression softened. 'The people here have stolen our hearts.'

She moved to check on the next patient, who was peaceful in his sleep as a little coloured bird perched like a tiny guardian on his pillow, bringing sweet dreams and comfort to the man.

I stood with one final look at the child on the cot, gladdened when another colourful bird flitted over to perch nearby.

'Now I shall get back to playing my part too,' I said, stretching my tired muscles.

'Have a care for your own health,' Maeve shot me a stern warning over her shoulder. 'Your magic hangs over our quarters full time as it is, and you have not paused in offering healing and care to those who have needed it. You don't want to wind up confined to a cot yourself.'

'No fear,' I lifted and dropped my shoulders. 'I don't seem to get sick or to stay tired or sore for very long anymore. I have a lot of energy I can give. Though I could pass you the same warning.'

'Noal keeps me in check,' Maeve waved away my response.

'Yes,' I answered warmly. 'Because Noal adores you.'

'And I him,' she brightened. 'In my heart, the wedding has already taken place.'

'Well, you'll have to relive it,' I said. 'Or you'll have a line of Kings, a group of Warlords, four mortal nations and all of the magical races to answer to.'

'Also,' Amarantha's voice cut in, 'one very unhappy friend.' The healer crossed her arms from the doorway. 'I have spent too much time in search of the finest dressmakers here.'

'Queen Aglaia is also being flown in by Dargon especially,' Maeve added in awe.

As I passed Amarantha I put my hand on her shoulder in farewell, sending a stream of energising magic into her before I stepped back out onto the street and into the sunlight.

'It's the One,' I heard, being echoed along the lane, and I tried not to hunch under the overwhelming attention I was not ever going to get used to.

Soldiers of Krall who were starting to think and feel for themselves had begun stopping me to just hold my hand, and everywhere I turned I was constantly being thanked by citizens of the sectors.

'Kiana!' I turned to find Ahanu and, as I lowered my eyes, Wolf waving to me in the distance. At once I lifted up to fly gratefully towards them.

Wolf ducked under Ahanu's big legs to meet me as the Giant steadied someone's roof.

'It's still crooked,' I told the Giant.

'Careful,' Ahanu replied. 'I could drop it on you.'

'She'd catch it,' Wolf protested confidently.

'Feel like some non-roof related house visits?' I asked Wolf, and he grinned.

'I haven't been too valuable here,' he admitted, glancing up as Ahanu easily straightened the chimney of the now fixed roof too. 'These magical folk have repairs well in hand. They'll be ready to start healing the rest of Krall soon.'

Even as he spoke a group of green bearded Dwarves began completely remodelling a half obliterated house down the lane. The house owners were watching in wonder as the mineral materials in the remains of their dwelling were manipulated and re-shaped like water.

Further on again a Gnome was busily demolishing the remnants of a collapsed wall by single-handedly smashing his way through the stone. Another Gnome briskly scooped up the rubble, ready to rebuild.

'How many houses do you have to check?' Wolf asked, and I peered along the street.

'Twenty or so on this lane.'

Wolf sagged. 'Right. How many more lanes do you need to cover in this sector?'

I rounded it down. 'Thirty.'

'Ahhhhh,' he dragged his boots. 'Let's do it then.'

We passed another Giant digging out a well with one brightly lit fist. Then we saw some Elves and Nymphs pressing their hands to the ground and lifting them again to reveal new sprouts of grass. Further along we noticed a group of Dwarves dawdling down the lane, calling what seemed to be liquefied rock to its surface, and as they stepped on the rising liquid the once muddy road became smooth – the rock hardening over it like icing on a cake.

'My desolate home is starting to look beautiful and new,' Wolf said gladly after a while.

'Yes,' I answered warmly. 'Krall is going to be just fine.'

111

One Hundred and Eleven

D^{alin}

'I'll be calling slip before you know it,' Ferron muttered, bleary eyed beneath his bruises.

Cadell yawned beside him, unenthused.

Though most of our limping, battle scarred comrades had returned joyously to family homes or barracks when it came to sleeping arrangements, they always worked with us by day, and then came to find us as night set in and our tent was lit with Nymph lights.

'You in, Raiden?' Thorin asked me, setting out the runes for a new round.

His battered face was tired after a day of toil, though he had still made sure to come after he had checked in on Tane's family, as all of us seemed quietly determined to spend what time we could together, before life changed too much.

I shook my head. 'I'm content where I am,' I answered quietly, gazing at Kiana – who had fallen into an exhausted sleep while she'd been leaning against me on my cot.

I lightly brushed a strand of her hair from her cheek, thanking the Gods for allowing us to somehow both still be alive.

'Maeve's busy again,' Noal was glum as he made his way into the large tent and held the material door open for Phrixus, Vulcan and Phobos to follow him in.

'My helmet is cracked,' Nikon said, pausing from picking at his teeth with a knife. 'But my head is not, and Krall is liberated.' He cleaned the knife. 'We can't have everything.'

'Perhaps if our honoured Awyalknians chose better accommodation she'd make time for her prince,' Cadell shrugged and then winced at the pain from a wound in his side.

'She's just busy, she doesn't care about the tent,' Thale burped reassuringly into his beard, lifting an arm that was bound tightly. 'She kept Purdor's innards from becoming outtards when we brought him in after the battle. Sleeping in a tent wouldn't scare her off.'

'The accommodation here is just fine,' I added wearily. 'From first light until dark we're out helping to get things running again anyway, and Krall's castle servants don't need us to worry over.'

'I'm glad every leader has declined accommodation in the castle,' Thorin said. 'Until a council has been held after the clean-up, nobody wants to make it appear that anyone is trying to impose their rule.'

'The people aren't thinking so politically when they offer nice rooms,' Phobos grunted as he lowered his injury riddled body to the ground. 'Everybody just wants the best lodging for the kingdom's new darlings. Lady Maeve and Noal's love story is the first nice thing to have been heard here in living memory,' he went on, picking up the dozing Ferron's runes and joining the game. 'The approaching wedding is giving the whole nation something to look forward to.'

'I do feel abnormally beloved,' Noal rubbed at his face drowsily, sitting on the end of his cot and giving the notion little further consideration.

But the thought of what the kingdom's adoration meant gave me a small pang of sadness, for he and Maeve had become like celebrities throughout the city sectors, their marriage seeming to symbolise the fresh beginnings and unity of the new age. And Glaidin had warned me of what to expect at the morning's council.

I hugged Kiana to myself and, as fatigued as I felt, I was glad that everyone stayed for a while longer.

I listened to Noal lazily offering suggestions to the players from his cot, and watched as Nikon pocketed the winnings after ignoring those suggestions.

I appreciated every laugh and every grumble from this group that had become my family.

112

One Hundred and Twelve

N^{oal}

I gaped as Thorin and I climbed the expansive steps to the much changed castle. It had transformed into something elegant and striking, with every façade polished to gleaming – dazzling us while we took our seats amongst the crowd of leaders.

'Those Dwarves are gifted,' I gasped in awe, struggling to remember the dark stone and rubble filled halls I had seen when we'd first taken the city.

The whole place was now filled with natural light from open balconies, and the Dwarves had remodelled every hall and every room to be their work of art – with intricate details and decorative floral carvings on each pillar.

Perhaps the Giants had helped too, as fountains rose outside each wide window.

'Never thought I'd say the Sorcerer's castle was a marvel,' Thale rumbled as he sidled in to take his seat.

'It's not the Sorcerer's castle anymore,' Phrixus told him, eyeing the sweeping ceiling – which had somehow been engraved with hundreds of different scenes of each race's way of life.

Humungous mosaics of coloured stones and tiles had been put together for the walls as well, depicting mountains, the Great Forest, green lands, desert temples, and islands of paradise.

'I no longer fear every shadow in here,' Kiana agreed quietly, slipping into a seat beside Dalin. 'It feels like a new place.'

'I could love a place like this, even as much as the Awyalknian Jewel,' I said with surprise.

But Dalin just took Kiana's hand and sat back as the leaders each began to speak on behalf of their people.

'The Lady has ensured that *Aolen* has been recorded into magic laced texts for every city so that the language cannot fade,' Frey promised at one point. 'Though each race must actively seek to avoid developing completely separate lives once more.'

'We must all pledge to commit to living together in this new age. We must find more permanent and tangible ties,' Glaidin agreed.

'The forest dwellers will open our city to any who wish to access its histories and the peace that the Lady's final refuge will always hold,' Ace announced.

'We also pledge to rediscover this world,' Frey added. 'The forest will be our home. But so shall all of the lands.'

Scandra spoke from her place then, where she glittered magnificently in the sunlit grand entrance. 'A number of my flock will stay here while Krall is rejuvenated. We will continue to help to repair Awyalkna's palace, and we will set up posts throughout the Jenran mountains to team up with the Jenran Griffin hunters.' She looked toward where Ahanu and Spud were. 'The Dargons will also resume an ancient practice of our kind. For those who wish to take part, there will be an annual migration from the Isle. The Giants, Dwarves and Gnomes may join us. The seas will never be a barricade to our peoples again.'

Ahanu scraped his massive hall-table-turned-chair back loudly. 'Well, we've thoroughly explored Margate's island. So I'm betting we'll be visiting here often for some new fun. Also,' he beamed down at us. 'I've talked it over with the One, and she says that she will work on creating more underwater Cities for us,' he rubbed his hands together happily while I leaned forward to peer at Kiana with raised eyebrows.

'So we'll have some lovely holiday destinations opening up,' Ahanu went on. 'And we'll make them nearer to Jenra. Then we can carry anyone from the main land who feels like a visit in one of Kiana's transport bubbles.' The table creaked alarmingly as he grinned and sat back, pleased with that positive final note.

Spud puffed up his chest to project his voice in his own turn. 'We'll stay to restore buildings. We'll catch rides on the Dargons too. Now the Dwarves have a taste for fresh air, they've come to like it, and us Gnomes love a good challenge and adventure.'

I could only imagine what life was going to be like as various leaders offered trade agreements or skills to other nations in friendship and I listened comfortably until Glaidin rose to speak, with Durna and Razek flanking him.

'There is just one final nation to be spoken for,' Glaidin announced then. 'And the mortal Kings have discussed at great length who may have the training, the kindness and the strength to be the new voice for Krall,' he paused for a moment. 'I have the honour and duty of announcing the decision, as it means I must be losing one of my own.'

My stomach dropped suddenly then, and I frowned at Dalin, who was already heir to Awyalkna. And his eyes met mine.

No. They did not mean Dalin.

'When Prince Noal and Lady Maeve wed, they will also be attending their coronation,' Glaidin declared proudly, and it took me a moment, as the applause rang across the hall, before I could get up.

I cleared my throat and tried to stand straight on hollow legs.

'We will care for Krall,' I croaked numbly across the echoing space. 'And we will treasure all of the aid that has been offered from the magical races. With friendship from Lixrax, my Awyalknian blood, and my Jenran bride, Krall will also become the symbol of all mortals united.'

My tone did not convey how extremely stupefied I was, but as my gaze fell on Aeron and Conall I felt a seed of resolve forming at the pit of my stomach.

'And as every King and Queen needs a loyal Warlord, generals and advisors,' I continued. 'I can already announce that mine are sitting behind me, and represent the heart of Krall.' I gestured to the Krall soldiers who had become my brothers. 'I name both Thale and Thorin as my Warlords. Though in this new age my Warlords will work to prevent war and for the good of all people.'

The stiff posture of Thorin and rigid stance of Thale, both as off guard as I had been, eased as the applause broke out again and I took my seat with my own face still frozen in a stunned mask.

Dalin reached across and took my hand in his grip. 'You were the one to bring the Three together in their quest, and you are the one to keep the partnership of mortals strong.'

I sat back in a daze as the wording of the prophecy circled in my mind and washed over me.

Maeve was hardly going to believe this.

113

One Hundred and Thirteen

D^{alin}

I closed my eyes as the dropping flower petals danced gently down my cheeks.

They fell like snow from the hands of the Nymphs as they let soft buds rain down over all of us. They covered our table and had blurred the last image I'd caught of Noal and Maeve as they had waved and disappeared into the colourful shower.

I opened my eyes again when I felt someone sit lightly in the chair beside mine.

'Alright?' Kiana asked, and I nodded, leaning forward to brush the soft petals from where they had landed in her hair. I took her hand, stroking the golden, ivy-like ring on her finger; so similar to the one that now bound Maeve and Noal in marriage.

'He's going to be great,' I said honestly. 'And he's going to be happy.'

Kiana inclined her head. 'The Gods have made it so that Krall will actually become the hub of all life under Noal's reign.'

'Yes. Only Lixrax will not have an actual representative living here,' I traced the velvety surface of a pink petal with a fingertip, and gazing out toward the dancing crowd.

Beautifully bronzed, dark eyed and dark haired women were swaying to the music that the Emperor of Lixrax had provided. Their dresses shone and tinkled with gold as they danced. But Kiana's eyes were on my parents, the King and Queen of Awyalkna, as they held each other and swayed.

Thorin was nearer to us, holding a young child in one arm and twirling a young woman with his free hand. Mil and Locke.

As I watched Thorin accidentally knocked into one of the exotic women of Lixrax, and he stopped at once. 'Excuse my clumsiness,' he said politely. 'I fight better than I dance.'

Her dark eyes glittered with mirth, and the many earrings lining her ears twinkled as she tilted her head to regard him. 'Me too. But I thought your dance was a fine one, with your wife and babe.'

Mil scrunched her nose up in a way that Tane would have adored.

'Oh no, he's more like a brother ... or a servant,' Mil teased, taking the child into her arms warmly. 'Thorin just watches over us.'

And the woman from Lixrax regarded Thorin more carefully then, her face softening.

'Perhaps I could teach you to be more confident in your skills then,' she offered Thorin.

'More confident in my dancing skills or fighting skills?' he asked with curiosity.

'Perhaps both,' she said, and took his hand in her own tattooed one to draw him back to dance with her. He in turn looked completely enthralled.

I laughed softly and Kiana smiled, nodding towards where a few of our other Krall soldiers were coyly asking the Lixrax warrior women to dance.

'So Lixrax may be represented too,' Kiana speculated.

Our remaining comrades were otherwise spread out at numerous tables in various states of euphoria with raucously laughing Nymphs and Gnomes.

Further back from the noise the Dwarves seemed to be getting along well with the more peaceful Elves, while Kiana's quiet friend Toru was leaning in through a window, offering Vidar, Frey and Bard his attention. As the Giant silently listened to their conversation a hoard of Gnomes and Nymphs used him as a slippery slide, dropping from his head and whirling down his neck and arm to land out the window.

I leaned over with a grin as three tufts of bright hair wandered past our table then, and I peered down to find Rebel and Flash with their arms slung over Spud's shoulders in comradery.

They were chatting about Asha and I saw that Spud's wiry, sprout-like hair had somehow been fluffed up into a wisp of green that looked like new moss, and it floated upward from his lumpy little head.

'Asha's gonna love it!' Flash cackled as they went in search of her.

A heavier beat was added to the music then, so much so that the ground thumped and the glasses on the table jangled, and Kiana and I swivelled in our seats to face the large window behind us, peering out at the courtyard beyond.

The sun was setting in the courtyard, where a broken fountain had been revived by the Dwarves, and where a startlingly pure, silver tree blossomed in full life.

Ahanu had started the Giants dancing in the courtyard and they thumped their way around the amused Dargons – with Ahanu having wrapped his arms around Scandra's foreleg like a partner.

'Thank the Gods I've been blessed with wings,' Kiana said quietly then. 'So I'll never have to really say goodbye. And neither will you.'

'Thank the Gods,' I agreed, missing Noal and this life already.

114

One Hundred and Fourteen

*K*iana

The Bwintam cottage was empty and quiet as I leaned in the kitchen doorway.

Sun beams streamed warmly in through the windows and it all felt so safe, peaceful and contained after so long being out in the wide, wild world.

But as I moved to the centre of the room and lightly ran my fingers over the wooden table, I felt that this was not my place anymore. And it was hard to think of a single physical place that really was home now.

I heard light footsteps creaking the floorboards of the hallway then, and a warm hand reached from behind me to rest on mine on the table.

I looked at that hand. And knew.

There was home.

'You look like a Queen crowned in sunlight.'

'I have not one royal drop of blood,' I replied, glad just to be near him.

'What greater Queen could there ever be?' he asked. 'Than one who represents unity and hope? Royal blood is not royalty making.'

I leaned a little so that my back was against his chest. 'What greater King could there be, than one who could lead all people against the darkness?'

'King one day,' he agreed, putting his arm around me. 'But not yet.'

'No, not yet.' I granted, and I tipped my head back so that my cheek was against his.

'Glaidin was right all that time ago,' he mused, his rough cheek moving against mine. 'I'm not ready to settle down and be King.'

'And I am not ready to lose you to a throne,' I answered.

'You will be beside me in a throne of your own. Keeping me from being lost.' His voice was serious this time. He turned me to face him, and interlaced his fingers with mine. 'But for now, we have an entirely liberated world. And I have years to spend exploring it with you.'

And with his hand held tightly in mine, I led him to where the sun streamed in from the door.

'I do have so much to show you,' I said warmly, stepping outside and leading him across the wide open fields.

'So much beauty to see,' he agreed, his green eyes on me.

I smiled as he followed me lightly, our steps becoming weightless as our feet lifted from the ground.

And, together, we took to the sky.

Other Books By Shelley Cass

The Raze Warfare Series

'A Fairy's Tale' Epic Fantasy Series:
Book One – 'Huntress'
Book Two – 'Raiden'
Book Three – 'Krall'

Dystopian Future:
'Awaken Dreamer'

Contemporary/Action/Fantasy/Erotica:
'Darkling'

The Sleep Sweet Series for children:
Book One – 'Little Pixie's Christmas'
Book Two – 'The case of the bored baby Ace'
Book Three – 'Mum and Me'
Book Four – 'The Cloud and the Flower'
Book Five – 'Hush'

Access bonus Raze Warfare stories at shelleycass.com as a thank you for being one of my appreciated readers.

About the Author

I was an awkward, reserved year 8 student – totally in love with the escape and comfort offered by novels I read. I could hear the voices of the authors' characters, I could tune out my stresses and uncertainties as I journeyed with each protagonist through their own troubles. And then one day I could hear the voices of characters who hadn't been written yet, in places that hadn't been created, and I decided to write my own world.

It took a quest of over fifteen years to get that world perfected in three novels – because of course the real world kept getting in the way.

In the real world I became a high school teacher, and faced the epic battle of staying afloat in all the papers that must always be assessed. And in the real world the magic was also sometimes hard to find. Stress and disunity surface like cancer – making the nightly news too hard to watch on most days.

But in the real world there was also inspiration – incredible students, loved ones, golden memories, growing up, warm hugs, big laughs and good people.

So I wrote of the things that threaten the world, and of the things that save it.

I wish for a real world where the air is clean, the trees can grow without concrete borders, the darkness can be cured with the switch of a light, and the people can all have long days and happy lives.

Acknowledgments

Thank you so much to the friends who have encouraged me with my writing of this series, a process that has taken over fifteen years.

Thank you to those who put such time into helping me, by reading this novel and offering advice, even when the manuscript was triple the length it is now. Wendy Glover (the most helpful neighbour to have ever lived), June Laurie (the first author I ever befriended, and creator of the 'Blake Collider' series), my uncle, Lee, and my mum, Linda.

Thank you so much mum, dad (Robert), Melissa, Andrew and Leigh, for being the warmth in my world.

Thank you Jack, Elyssia and Sophie, for making the future world worthwhile.

Thank you to my extended family, for being everything I needed.

Thank you to Jarryd and baby Myla, for being the magic and loves of my life.

And thank you to the hesitant little Junior High School version of myself, for picking up that pen to write.

www.ingramcontent.com/pod-product-compliance
Lightning Source LLC
Chambersburg PA
CBHW050559170726
48283CB00001B/25